I0737971

SINNER'S GROVE

Sinner's Grove Suspense Book One

A.B. MICHAELS

SINNER'S GROVE

Sinner's Grove Suspense - *Book One*

Copyright © 2014 by A.B. Michaels

All rights reserved.

ISBN 978-0-9915089-3-8

No part of this publication may be reproduced, distributed, or transmitted in any form or by any means, including photocopying, recording, or other electronic or mechanical methods, without the prior written permission of the publisher, except in the case of brief quotations embodied in critical reviews and certain other noncommercial uses permitted by copyright law.

For permission requests, please write to:

Red Trumpet Press

P. O. Box 171162

Boise, ID 83716

Cover Design by Tara Mayberry

www.TeaberryCreative.com

Also By A.B. Michaels

In the **"Sinner's Grove Suspense"** contemporary series:

The Lair

The Jade Hunters

"The Golden City" historical series:

The Art of Love

The Depth of Beauty

The Promise

The Price of Compassion

Josephine's Daughter

For Susan
It took a while, but we saw it through.

Acknowledgments

This story took a long time to put on paper—so long, in fact, that sometimes it's hard to believe Sinner's Grove *doesn't* exist, at least for me. Thanks to Maggy and Donna and Susan and Rachel for helping me weave the many plot strands together; to Paul and Dominick for their professional expertise; and to Mike and Adam for applying logic to situations when mine couldn't be found.

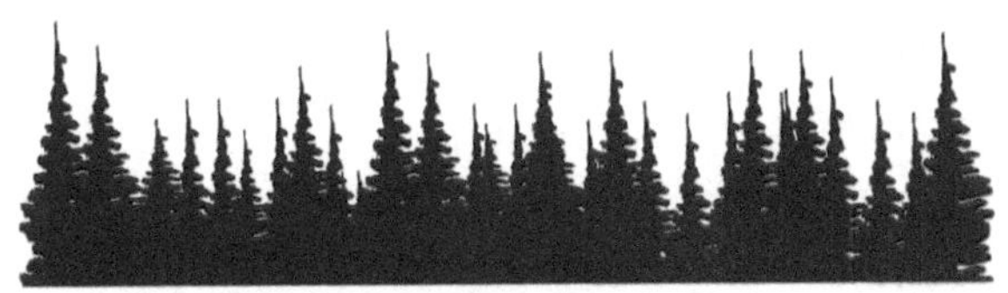

THE ORIGINAL GROVE RETREAT

August (Gus) Wolff—*founder*
Amelia (Lia) Starling Wolff—*founder*
Giselle—Gus and Lia's daughter
Mandy Culpepper—*artist's model*
Peter Raines—photographer and Lia's assistant
Sander DeKalb—artist and family friend
William (Will) Firestone—friend and business partner

THE NEW GROVE CENTER FOR AMERICAN ART

Ethan Wolff—*founder*
Britland (Brit) Maguire—*architect and partner*
Jenna Bergstrom—artist and Ethan's granddaughter
Jason Bergstrom—*Ethan's grandson*
Victoria (Tori) Winston—*interior designer*
Don Rodriguez—*foreman*
Sherrie Phelps—*office manager*
Parker Bishop—*crew member*
Kyle Summers—*crew member*

Lester Small—*crew member*

TOWN OF LITTLE EDEN

Ralph Dorman—city councilman and architectural draftsman

Myra Dorman—*Ralph's wife*

Boyce Wheeler—leader of SPEAR, the no-growth opposition to the Center

Daniela (Dani) Dunn—innkeeper, computer expert, and friend

OTHER

Robert Perris—Grove Historic Trust attorney

Declan O'Connor—KTRN reporter and Jenna's friend

Reggie Firestone—*jewelry designer*

Walker Banks—*photographer*

Gabriele (Gabe) de la Torre—*detective*

Chapter One

So what if she comes back? Brit Maguire stretched his neck and rolled his shoulders at the same time, throwing himself off-balance as he stood on the high scaffolding. He grabbed the nearby roof truss just in time to stop his fall. "Shit," he muttered.

"You okay over there?" Brit heard Josh, one of the wing men stationed at each side of the huge wooden structure, ask through his Bluetooth.

"No worries," Brit said. *Come on, no woman's worth breaking your neck over—especially not Jenna. Focus on the job.*

Problem was, the job wasn't going so hot, either. Renovating The Grove was the biggest commission of Brit's career. He'd risked nearly all of his capital on it, not to mention his company's reputation. But hell if it hadn't been a nightmare from the beginning. Not the design work or the construction—he loved all that— but the road blocks they'd been dealing with from day one. Hoop after bureaucratic hoop, not to mention the sneaky acts of sabotage that had plagued them once they started moving dirt. Somebody didn't want The Grove to re-open and Brit had a pretty good idea who it was. Too bad he couldn't prove it. Still, it was putting him and the rest of the crew on edge, and that wasn't good. And to add Jenna to the mix? That was just about the last thing he needed right now.

Despite the chilled morning air, Brit pulled a bandana from his back pocket and wiped the sweat from his face and neck. Since daybreak he and his crew had been installing sixty-foot-wide roof trusses for the last new building, an amphitheater he'd designed for performances and lectures at the new center. Three more to go and they could send the crane operator to his next job, earning a badly needed discount for finishing—for once—ahead of schedule.

Brit tapped his Bluetooth. "Ready for the next one, guys?" Josh and Andy didn't bother answering, merely giving the thumbs-up signal. They were set to help Brit center up, stabilize, and attach the enormous wooden brace. "Okay, Larry," he relayed to the crane operator. "Bring her over."

The crane's raucous engine made even loud conversation impossible, but while the sound didn't fit the wooded setting, somehow the crane's movement did. Brit watched the dance of the boom as it gently lifted the mammoth triangle and began to swing it slowly toward the structure, like a prehistoric bird in flight. After so many years in the construction field, it still amazed him how mankind found such clever ways to do the work of giants.

Watching the truss, he didn't notice the movement down below until the frame was almost overhead. He saw his project partner, Ethan Wolff, standing on the ground next to the building, gesturing to him. *What the —?* He didn't even have a hard hat on! "Wait a minute!" he yelled down. "Better step out of the way!" He waved his arm to emphasize his point, then turned to help stabilize the frame.

The men on either end had already caught the guidelines and released them when a gust of wind came up and caused the swaying truss to twist and slap against its already-installed counterparts. Suddenly a loud crack filled the air and the massive structure split apart, raining two-by-fours forty feet down to the ground floor. Brit and the wing men ducked to avoid getting hit, and when Brit looked down again he saw his partner stumble and fall backward.

"Jesus, Ethan! Somebody help him!" Brit climbed down the scaffolding as fast as he could, jumping the last six feet and racing over to where Ethan had fallen. Josh got there at the same time, with Andy not far behind. "Ethan, are you all right?" Brit took off his shirt, rolled it up, and put it behind his partner's head. "Josh, call 911."

Ethan, struggling to sit up, stuck his hand out. "Don't you dare, young man. No ambulance for me. I mean it."

Brit ran his hand through his hair in frustration. Ethan looked all right, but the old guy was already in lousy health. A fall like that couldn't be good, no matter what. "Damn it, Ethan, this is a construction zone—

you're not strong enough to be out here. What the hell were you thinking?"

"I was thinking that at the age of eighty-seven, if I want to check on how things are going, then I'll damn well check on things." He rubbed the back of his head. "And nothing hit me, if you must know. I just stumbled as I moved to get out of harm's way." He looked mulishly at the much younger, stronger men. "And that could happen to anybody—even young bucks like you."

Brit sighed and helped Ethan up. He tapped his Bluetooth again. "Fifteen minute break, Larry." He gestured to the broken lumber littering the half-built structure. "Guys, see what the problem was on that frame, would you? That shouldn't have happened, even with the wind gust."

Josh and Andy moved to clean up the debris while Brit helped Ethan over to a couple of folding chairs the crew had set up near the site. "You wanted to tell me something?"

"Ah, testing my short-term memory, are you?" Ethan smiled. "I assure you it's intact. I just wanted to remind you I'd be leaving shortly to go into the city with Don."

Brit scowled. "I know. Jason's graduation ceremony is tonight."

"You don't sound happy about that." Ethan looked at Brit intently.

"You shouldn't be going anywhere after hitting your head the way you did."

Ethan shook his head slightly. "That's not why you're displeased."

"Oh yeah? Then why?"

"It's because you know I'll be with Jenna…and you know I'm going to ask her again to come and work with me."

Jenna. Just hearing her name set his teeth on edge. Brit took a deep breath. "Why should I care about that?"

"That's what I keep asking myself," Ethan said. "I think, why would Britland care about me bringing my granddaughter here to The Grove if he didn't care anything about her?"

"Because you don't need her, that's why." Brit could hear the whiny quality in his own voice and it ticked him off. "You've got Dani to help with the computer research. You're going to have your grandson and his buddies here for the summer. I'll assign all three of them to you if you like. You'll have all the help you need."

"But not the kind of expertise Jenna brings to the project," Ethan countered. "She's the most qualified to help me, Brit, and you know it." He paused. "And she needs to come back, for her sake, if nothing else."

Brit snorted. "Don't you get it, Ethan? She doesn't give a damn about the family. About your legacy. About any of it. She's all about Jenna."

Ethan got up wearily from the chair and brushed off his pants. "You couldn't be more wrong, dear boy. But you're going to have to figure that out on your own. In the meantime, I suggest you 'gird your loins,' as the Good Book says. Because, Brit?" He paused to make sure Brit was looking at him. "I am going to do everything in my power to get her here."

Brit had mixed emotions as he watched Ethan walk back toward the construction office. The old man was feeling Father Time breathing down his neck and he wanted all his family back in the fold. But hell, why did it have to include a selfish user like Jenna?

At that moment Josh walked up, two pieces of lumber in his hand. "Bad news, boss," he said.

"What have you got?"

"Somebody sawed both the webbing and the bottom cord just about halfway through, then glued it to cover up. If we'd put it up without knowing, sooner or later the load would have collapsed it. We're lucky we caught it. Larry's got two extra trusses if we need them."

"Assuming they're intact." Brit examined the wood, working hard not to howl out loud. When was this bullshit going to end? When was Boyce Wheeler going to call off his goons? In as calm a voice as he could muster, he said, "Hold these tampered pieces separate from the rest. Maybe we can get the police to take us seriously for once. Then you and Andy better go back up and check all the installed trusses. While you're at it, tell the guys to break for an early lunch. And let Larry know we're going to need the crane for the rest of the day after all."

After straightening up his tools, Brit headed back to the Great House, determination and frustration churning inside his gut. Best to keep Ethan out of the loop on this one, but Brit had had it up to his eyebrows with problems like this. Maybe he couldn't pin the sabotage on Wheeler's boys, but he could sure as hell put The Grove's attorney on a war footing. Ethan could have been seriously hurt, for Chrissakes!

On the way, he stopped by the construction trailer to pick up his messages. In addition to letters and invoices, Don Rodriguez, his foreman, had left him a note, apparently before heading over to San Francisco with Ethan:

Surprise: Electrical inspection failed this morning. Some cabrón cut the conduit leading from the substation to the pool house. Third time the inspector's had to write us up for noncompliance. Even he can tell we're getting the shaft. Lemme know if you want me to file another vandalism report—as if that'll do any good.

Brit cursed and crumpled the note, then opened the letter with a City of Little Eden return address. He scanned the contents. The building department wanted to know why Vintage Maguire Restorations and The Grove Center Historic Trust kept screwing up. If changes weren't made, they were going to have to reconsider permits already issued. "Like hell," Brit said.

He reached the Great House and jogged up to his third-floor private office. For once he didn't stop to enjoy the incredible views from the master suite but headed straight for his desk.

"I'd like to speak to Robert Perris," he said to the receptionist after dialing his attorney's number. "Brit Maguire calling. Tell him it's urgent."

Thirty minutes later, sandwich and ice tea in hand, Brit headed out to the front porch for a quick bite before returning to the roofing site. He pulled up one of the Adirondack chairs and stretched out his legs on the front porch railing. Tomorrow he'd see Perris and plan a legal strategy. *You'll get through this,* he told himself. *It'll be worth it.*

And it would be, because everything about the estate and long-time artists' retreat spoke to him. As an architecture student, one of Brit's favorite periods had been the Arts and Crafts movement, and the Great House was a stunning example of it. August Wolff and his wife must have given their architects, the Greene Brothers, a blank check, because it looked like no expense had been spared. From the beautifully designed cabinets, bookshelves, and stained glass windows to the rock-solid wood and stone exterior, the house was magnificent. The 1906 earthquake had rattled the place, of course, but it had obviously been repaired shortly after that event and since then had withstood the test of time remarkably well. Brit and his crew had enjoyed every minute of restoring it because they knew it for the gem it was.

But the Great House was only part of it. The mansion stood on a small plateau overlooking the ocean on one side and a gorgeous redwood grove on the other. And within that grove, along with the original refurbished artists' bungalows, there were now several new buildings—including the almost-roofed amphitheater—that Brit had designed in the same architectural style. When it opened in the fall—and it would open by then, or he was going to have somebody's head—the new Grove Center for American Art would not only bring artists and patrons together again after nearly seventy years, but attract regular folks who wanted to learn about this amazing slice of history.

The beauty was that from the Great House itself you couldn't see any of it. The founders obviously enjoyed their privacy and now Brit was reaping the benefits. If only the cloud that had hung over this project from the beginning would just go away.

He was about to head back to the construction site when he heard a car drive up and a door close.

"Hey, Brit, Josh said you might be up here. Thought I'd take a chance. I need to ask you something."

Brit looked over the railing to see Victoria Winston, or Tori as she liked to be called, approaching the steps to the porch. The interior designer for The Grove restoration was a living, breathing example of *feng shui* with her skin tight jeans and soft green sweater that fit her near-perfect body to a T. Normally Brit didn't go for petite redheads, but Tori was put together supremely well. "Sure," he said. "What do you need?"

Tori sauntered up the steps and stopped to pose against one of the pillars. "I, um, I've got an appointment to drop my car off at Anthony's Garage in Little Eden this afternoon, but he's got to keep it 'til he gets the part he needs. Tommy—you remember, he's the lighting contractor—said he'd give me a ride back here tomorrow morning, but I need a lift home tonight." She put one of her red lacquered fingernails on her lips. "So…any chance you're heading to the city after work?"

"Actually, I am. I've got an early meeting with the attorney tomorrow and was heading into town tonight, so I can give you a ride. Pacific Heights, right?"

Tori graced him with a very sexy smile. "Hey, I really appreciate it. Shall I meet you at the garage at, say, five o'clock?" At Brit's nod she walked halfway down the steps and turned around, knowing damn well he was watching her butt. "Oh, and Brit?"

"Yeah?"

"I've got a whole passel of fabrics and color schemes to show you for the last group of bungalows and I hate to bring them all the way here, so would you mind coming in for a bit when you drop me off? It'll only take a little while, and I'll even feed you. I promise."

She sent him another sultry smile. The head between Brit's shoulders thought, *Uh oh, you really should plan on staying elsewhere,* while the head in his jeans said, *Hmmm.* Brit smiled back at her. "Sounds like a plan." He watched Tori drive off in her little Alfa Romeo and comparisons between her and Jenna popped into his mind. Jenna with her long, long legs. Jenna with her golden hair—

Redirect. Redirect. Brit had used that mantra a thousand times over the years to keep from getting riled about Ethan's granddaughter. Most of the time it worked.

Today, however, the painful memories wouldn't stay in the mental box he'd constructed for them. Worse yet, they were likely to stick around for a while, because whether he liked it or not, Jenna Bergstrom was part of this place, and sooner or later Ethan was going to succeed in bringing her back. No doubt she'd show up to complicate matters right when things got nasty with Wheeler or whoever had it in for The Grove. Brit let out a frustrated sigh. Events weren't shaping up quite as easily as he'd hoped they would. Not by a long shot. But he was used to moving forward, and the work still had to get done, so he resolutely headed back down the hill.

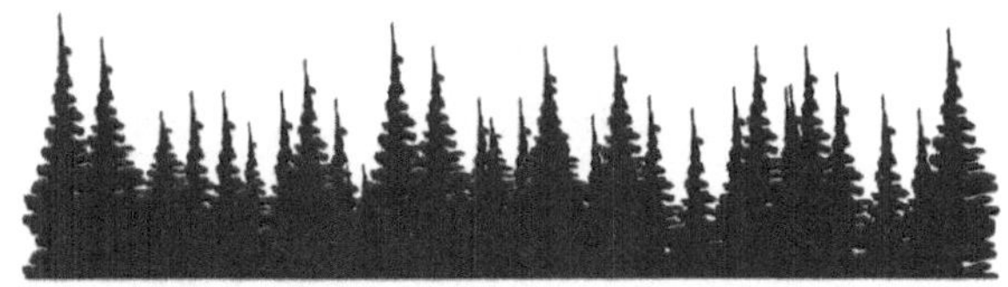

Chapter Two

Jenna Bergstrom tamped down her emotions as she watched students file into her final "Introduction to Art" lecture. It was her last day as an instructor at the Saylor Academy and the beginning of a new phase of her life. Conflicting feelings tumbled through her: sadness, excitement, anticipation, worry. Her grandfather, Professor Ethan Wolff, wanted her help to re-open The Grove, but that was his dream, not hers. Besides, working with him meant seeing Brit Maguire again, and that came with a whole other set of problems. She could resume her art career, but in what medium? And where would she go? Back to New York? Maybe she should travel to Europe. Expand her portfolio. Take some classes. Like a flight of swallows, the possibilities kept swirling around her head but never settling on anything, and she was left with the persistent and unnerving sensation of *now what?*

She paused to put it all into perspective. Her troubles were nothing compared to what many of her students had been through, including her own brother, Jason. The Saylor Academy was an "alternative educational experience," according to the marketing materials, designed for troubled teens who couldn't make it in public school, who acted out in ways society deemed unacceptable. Some of them attended Saylor courtesy of the juvenile justice system or were put there by parents who just didn't know what else to do.

Jenna looked around the room. Which of her students might be stressing because the structured school year was over? Camilla? She'd been fighting her latest bout of depression for the past month. Rocky? He looked happy, but his wounds ran deep.

She glanced over at Parker Bishop, slouched in the far right second row. A long, lean, and scruffy seventeen-year-old with puppy-dog eyes, he was one of those poor little rich kids whose parents tossed him around like a hot potato. Him, maybe?

After the class settled, Jenna turned to the white board behind her and wrote in big letters:

ART IS MEANT TO DISTURB

She faced the class again. "It's good to see you all today for our last class together. Over the past several months I've enjoyed sharing with you my love for art in all its forms. We've talked a lot about the mechanics of creating art this semester, but in the end, what is art all about?" She pointed to the quote. "The French painter Georges Braque, for instance, believed this. What do you think he meant?"

A few students raised their hands.

"Miss Lorimer?"

With spiky pink hair, wearing the school's required polo shirt but in a size much too small for her round figure, Hilary Lorimer sat up straight. "I...I think it means, like, art is supposed to make you, like, uncomfortable."

"Uncomfortable how?"

"I don't know, like, maybe make you feel stuff you'd rather not feel or something."

Kyle Summers, a beefy gingertop who might have made the football team had he been another kind of person at another kind of school, sat with his chino-clad thigh bouncing spasmodically up and down. He was staring at Jenna with agitated eyes.

Ah. He's the one.

He raised his hand.

Against her better judgment, Jenna called on him. "Yes, Mr. Summers?"

He stood up, raising one leg and putting it on his chair. Like Hilary, his polo shirt was also too small; the muscles of his arms and chest strained the material. "If what Hill the Pill says is true, then you qualify as a work of art."

Here we go. Jenna kept her tone neutral. "And why is that?"

"Because your bodalicious body has been disturbing me all friggin' semester, and my hard on is making me damn uncomfortable." He grabbed his crotch and sniggered, looked around to get some response.

Parker obliged. "You asshole!" He rose out of his chair like an avenging angel and plunged toward Kyle, grabbing him by his too-tight shirt.

"What the fuck?" Kyle yelled as the two toppled to the floor. Despite his smaller weight, Parker fought viciously, getting in several punches to the face. Kyle quickly turned his size to advantage, slugging Parker's midsection and chest with his meaty fists.

Jenna shook her head as she pressed a button on the wall. The teens were still grappling with each other when two older men wearing jackets labeled Security came in and pulled them apart.

"You were so close, Mr. Summers," Jenna said. "That little outburst cost you a level."

"I can't help it," he whined. "I just want you so bad. I just wanna—" He grunted while making pumping motions with his lower body.

"That's enough, Mr. Summers," one of the guards said. "Time to go now." He reached for Kyle's arm.

"Fuck you," Kyle spat, wrenching his arm away.

"Keep that up, son, and you'll be busted all the way down to zero," the other security guard said. Both men stepped in and used their combined strength to slip restraining cuffs on the teen.

"Yeah, well, I'll just talk to my dad about that. Oww! You're bending my wrist!" Kyle looked over at Jenna to plead his case. "Come on, you know I was only joking. You know."

The first guard asked her opinion with his

eyebrows. Jenna shook her head again. He led Kyle out the door and Jenna could hear him wailing indignantly all the way down the hall.

She turned to Parker. "And Mr. Bishop? I appreciate your gallantry, but that reaction wasn't necessary. I'm afraid you'll lose points as well."

Back on his feet, Parker nodded as he wiped his nose. "Sorry. He just pissed me off, is all. Dip shit."

The second guard began to put a set of cuffs on Parker, but Jenna touched the guard's hand. "He's all right, aren't you, Mr. Bishop?"

"Yes, ma'am." He went willingly with the other guard.

Jenna calmly turned back to the class. The tittering died down and eventually stopped.

"Now I believe we were discussing the merits of Georges Braque's assertion that art is meant to disturb. Mr. Whittaker?" She singled out a student dozing in the back. "What say you?"

"Sorry I missed your farewell faculty luncheon. I heard it was a delight." Declan O'Connor, a local television reporter who taught a journalism class at Saylor, stopped by Jenna's classroom after the students had left. She'd already stripped the walls and was packing up her art supplies.

"Yep, you missed the cake topped with a velvet painting done in black and red butter cream frosting. I think the matador's head is left. Want a piece?" she pointed to the leftover cake box on her desk.

Declan smiled slightly and shook his head. "I also heard what happened in class. Not a grand way to end your tenure."

Jenna shrugged. "Actually, I feel bad for Kyle. He's sweet most of the time. He just has too many hormones and too few filters."

Declan stepped into the room and shut the door halfway. He wasn't a big man, but he was a heart-breaker with his wavy black hair, indigo-blue eyes, and slight Irish lilt. Gorgeous, so he should have been a jerk, but he wasn't. He was a good reporter, always tried to show both sides of a story, and taught that level of integrity to the kids. Jenna liked that he was willing to work nights and weekends at KTRN so he could teach the class at Saylor. And he was smart—smart enough never to be caught alone with any of Saylor's students, male or female, without another adult nearby. She followed that policy most of the time, too. No point in taking chances.

"You really like these kids," he said.

Jenna paused; she'd never thought in those terms before. "I suppose I like them, but more than that, I understand them."

"Why, because your brother's one of them?"

"Something like that. Or he used to be, anyway."

Declan picked up an apple-shaped piece of onyx that one of the students had given Jenna as a farewell gift. He held it in his hand, rubbing his thumb across its smooth surface. "You know, I covered the accident and the aftermath involving your family," he said slowly. "Since I've known you, you've never talked about it."

Jenna felt herself closing off. "It's a long story."

He put down the carving and looked at her. "I'd love to hear it...over dinner some time." When she started to protest, he raised his hand. "Now, I remember the last time I asked you out, you told me you never date co-workers." He made a point of looking at his watch. "As of, oh, a wee bit more than an hour ago, I believe we're no longer coworkers." Then he smiled.

For God's sake, even the man's dimples had dimples! Declan O'Connor could have any female he wanted. Why on earth was he pursuing her? She couldn't help but smile back. "I bet you don't get turned down very often."

"Not very," he admitted. "But I have a feeling you're going to make me work for it."

"I don't mean to," Jenna said. "Really. But...it's complicated."

Declan leaned in closer and tipped her chin up so that she'd look at him. "I'd love to have you explain it... really." He smiled again. "As they say, you've got to eat anyway, so—"

"Uh, Jenna?" Parker stuck his head around the door. "Sorry, I didn't know you had somebody in here. Hello, Mr. O'Connor."

"Hello, Parker. Are you supposed to be here after school hours?" Declan's tone sounded authoritative.

"Oh, it's all right. Parker often meets my brother here after class." She turned to the teen. "Jason's at the chapel for graduation rehearsal, remember?"

"Oh, that's right. Thanks. I'll see you later, then…at the ceremony?"

"Sure thing," Jenna said. "Jason's grandfather and I will be there."

Declan watched Parker leave. "That lad plays it close to the vest, aside from the short fuse."

Jenna nodded. "Only child, parents are divorced. He's an outlier, and I wonder if maybe they blame each other for that instead of focusing on him. I know he doesn't think he has much of a family. That can weigh you down."

Declan looked as if he were trying to gaze into her soul; she wondered what he would find there. "You probably know a little bit about that," he finally said.

"A little…" She took a breath and let it out, reached out to touch his arm. "Declan, I'd be a liar if I said you weren't attractive. But I'm just finishing up a big chapter in my life here, and I have no idea what direction I'm going to take next. Jason's headed for college in the fall and, well, I might move Back East and work in a gallery, or travel to work on my portfolio, or—"

"Look, you're a beautiful woman and I like talking to you. And those two qualities don't always coincide. So, what do you say we take it one steak at a time?" He paused, waiting for her response.

"No expectations?"

"None. Scout's honor." Declan held up two fingers in a mock salute.

"Were you really a Boy Scout?"

"Sad to say, I didn't make it past Beavers. I was too

rambunctious. Kept running around trying to get the inside scoop on every group leader."

Jenna chuckled, wrote her cell phone number on a slip of paper, and handed it to him. She added the left-over cake to the banker's box she'd almost filled. "Since you're here, mind helping me carry my stuff to the car?"

"I am yours to command," he said, flashing that grin again. "Onward."

Loaded with the last remnants of her time at Saylor, Jenna and Declan walked out to the parking lot. Jenna noticed that Kyle was talking earnestly with Parker. Good. Maybe they were working things out. Both boys turned and looked at her.

Declan put the box in her car and waited while she got behind the wheel. "I'm working tonight, so I'll miss seeing you at graduation. Until that steak, then," he said.

"Until then," she agreed. As she drove out of the parking lot she noticed in her rear view mirror that Parker was watching Declan, and Kyle was still watching her.

Later that evening, Jenna and her grandfather watched as Jason, along with fifty-six other teens, graduated from the Saylor Academy. Tall and thin with rangy muscles and tousled brown hair, her brother looked both comical and endearing in his baggy academic robe and tennis shoes. She caught his eye and smiled.

He beamed back, glowing with the youthful energy and promise of an all-American kid. Four years ago he'd been a completely different person. Now, he could be a poster boy for Saylor Academy's mission.

"It's been a long road, but we made it," Ethan said, patting her hand.

Jenna glanced at her grandfather. "Long road" didn't begin to cover it. It seemed a lifetime ago that she'd been a rebellious art school graduate, bound and determined to go her own way by creating a life for herself in New York. She'd had very little use for her parents, who seemed to have it all, anyway—until they lost it on a moonless night at a curve in the road. Jenna learned the hard way that it's a lot easier to reject a family when you actually have one. Who can you rail against when they're gone? After the accident and its aftermath, she couldn't imagine what she would have done without the kind old gentleman sitting next to her.

"It means a lot to Jason that you're here," she said, reaching over and squeezing her grandfather's arm.

"The boy's got a lot to be proud of…as do you."

"Me? Jason's the one who turned himself around."

"With your help, Jenna. You were there for him… like family ought to be."

Those last words were meant to hit home, and they did. Jenna looked away, her eyes misting. How often the guilt washed over her. When her father died she'd gone into denial, pure and simple. She'd been a selfish, self-centered fool, feeling isolated and preferring to lick her wounds alone clear across the country rather than think about what her mother and brother might be going through. Jason's alcohol-clouded grief and attempted suicide shortly after his mother's death changed all that, and Jenna had finally realized what she had to do.

She'd come home.

Chapter Three

"Hey, pretty sweet, huh?" Jason bounded up after the ceremony, proudly handing his diploma to his grandfather and draping his arm over Jenna's shoulder in an affectionate hug. "I did it!" He pulled off his mortarboard and plopped it on Jenna's head. "Hey, we need a selfie." He stuck his cell phone out at arm's length and leaned into the shot. "Say, 'Free at last!'"

Jason looked over Jenna's shoulder and waved at someone. She turned around, saw that it was Parker, and returned his wave.

"Parker's dropping me off at the all-night party at Ty's, so I gotta run. Oh, and Da?" he said, turning to their grandfather. "Thanks for getting Kyle and Parker on at The Grove this summer. You're the best!"

"What's this about Kyle and Parker working at The

Grove?" Jenna had invited her grandfather to spend the night and they were relaxing on her living room couch, indulging in jumbo garlic shrimp and cashew chicken from Jenna's favorite Chinatown haunt.

"Ah, I wondered if he'd applied to you first, but it appears he wasn't risking your refusal. Smart boy."

"I just wish he would have talked to me about it."

"What would you have said?"

"I don't know. There's some animosity between those two—Kyle and Parker, I mean."

"It's my understanding he mentored both boys this past year as part of some kind of leadership training. I'm sure he'll help them work out their issues…" Ethan paused. "Just as I'm sure you and Brit can resolve yours."

The shrimp, which had tasted so delicious a second before, now formed a heavy weight in Jenna's stomach. "What do you mean, 'resolve our issues'? We're never going to—"

"Oh yes you are," Ethan said firmly. "And you're going to do it as soon as possible. Tomorrow, in fact."

Jenna tried to calm her racing heart. She'd known this was coming. Felt it for some time. But tomorrow? How could she face Brit after she'd left him in the most despicable way possible? She gazed at her grandfather. "I don't think I can do it."

"You must," he said quietly. "I need you to help me with the restoration of The Grove." Jenna started to interrupt. "No," he said, his voice gruff with emotion, "please let me finish. I know you think that just because you don't share your mother's

DNA you aren't part of this family, but that's simply not true."

"We aren't related, Ethan. Not a drop of your blood flows in my veins."

"And that has never made a goddamn bit of difference to me."

Surprised, Jenna stared at her grandfather; she couldn't remember ever hearing him curse. "What do you want from me?" she asked.

"I want you to remember who you are. Not who makes up your gene pool. You. When you were young and spent summers with Gramma Nancy and me at The Grove, you were mesmerized by the history of the place. I used to tell you all about your great-great-grandmother Lia Wolff and how she came to The Grove, and all the wonderful people who lived there. You knew, even then, that someday you'd be the one to carry on the legacy of that magical time and place."

"That was before I found out the truth."

"I'll tell you what the truth is. The truth is you used to say to me, over and over again, 'Da, tell me about how Gramma Lia and Granpa Gus fell in love.' You'd ask me all about the paintings because you loved to draw and paint just like she did. I would tell you stories and oh, Jenna, how your eyes would light up. Do you remember? I said the world would learn more about Gus and Lia when the time was right. Well, the time is right, my dear. In fact, I'm afraid it's running out."

Jenna stared at her grandfather, tears welling up before she could stop them. "Don't say that, please, Ethan. I don't think I could bear it if you—"

"You're going to have to bear it. Just like you bore the loss of your father, and yes, your mother. Because she was your mother, in every way that mattered."

Jenna stared at her lap for several moments before answering. Everything he'd said was true. Growing up, she'd always assumed she'd take over her grandfather's role as "keeper of the flame." She finally spoke her thoughts aloud. "I wish my…mother…had been interested in The Grove. She could have helped you years ago."

Ethan smiled sadly. "One of life's little ironies," he said. "Miriam's gift was in getting others excited about the arts, but she never felt the soul-stirring passion, the true connection that you do." He took Jenna's hand in his. "Of all the members of our family, you are the one best suited to carry on the legacy. I knew it from the time you were small. And look at you now. You've grown up to become an artist in your own right. It's in your DNA. Yours, not hers."

Jenna nodded. She *had* felt the connection, until she'd accidentally stumbled upon the family's dirty little secret. From that point on, she'd felt different. Like an outcast. And some dark part in her had reveled in it. Embraced the outrageousness of it. Defined her new self by it.

By fifteen she'd begun leading a different kind of life. Gone were summers at The Grove. "Da" became "Ethan." Soccer, her favorite sport, took a back seat to edgier artistic activities. She explored mixed media, using photos and fabric, newspaper and paint, to comment on the self-created soap opera her life had become. She could have easily gotten into Stanford, but chose instead the small but prestigious Steinmann Art Institute in Manhattan. She and her mother clashed; her father avoided the unpleasantness.

To keep her in the fold, her parents tried withholding financial support. It backfired; she simply got scholarships and grants. By the time she'd graduated from college, the ties were almost completely severed. Only once did she fly back, to attend her grandfather's retirement party—a party she would never, ever forget, because that's where she'd met Brit Maguire. He was distantly related to Ethan, a descendant of the child Amelia Starling had had before she met August Wolff, whereas Ethan's lineage was through Amelia's union with August. But even Brit's tenuous link was more connection than Jenna could lay claim to, and that truth had seared itself onto her soul.

"You, my dear, are just what this family tree needs," Ethan said.

Jenna shook her head. "Can't you see I'm not a good bet? I'm a coward. I ran from my troubles. I ran from all of you."

Ethan disagreed. "I would never use the term 'cowardly' to describe you, Jenna. You came back when Jason needed you. And now, The Grove needs you." He took a deep but labored breath and continued. "The new center's going to house the collected works of the original retreat. That's hundreds of works, Jenna, in storage or on loan, each of which has to be identified, analyzed, and put in historical context for both the museum and the catalog. It's work best done by an artist, like you. Beyond that," he added wistfully, "there may be another family secret to uncover. You aren't the only one who has questions about the family tree."

Ethan's words brought Jenna up short. "What do you mean?"

"It's a long story with many gaps. Suffice it to say you and I may have more in common than you think. The more pressing matter is how you are going to mend fences with Brit, before it's too late."

Jenna froze. The idea of something happening to Brit flashed through her, taking her breath away. "Too late for what?" she finally asked.

He sighed. "For the whole shebang. Something is happening at The Grove and it's not good. Brit's doing all he can to keep the opening on track, but he can't help me with what I need. Only you can do that."

Inwardly Jenna breathed a sigh of relief. She started to clear away the take-out cartons and paper plates—anything to avoid the feelings that were bubbling to the surface. "If I could live my entire life without crossing paths with Brit Maguire ever again, it'd be fine with me."

Ethan looked at her with unsettling clarity, laced with a dash of pity. "Ah, but it wouldn't be fine with him—no matter what type of front he puts up. The two of you must face up to your past, put it to rest, and move on. You've got to. There's too much work to be done. Too much work." Looking more frail than he had in a long time, Ethan headed slowly toward Jason's room for the night.

It's going to be a long summer, Jenna thought as she sipped green tea in the bay window alcove of her living room. Twilight had settled over the city, bathing the skyline in dusky hues of pink and gray. The last of the kite flying diehards on the Marina Green were packing it in for the day. One lone dragon danced between the updrafts, defying the growing darkness. At the nearby St. Francis Yacht Club, sailboats festooned in twinkling lights bobbed at their moorings.

Normally she took delight in the fanciful display, but not tonight. With Ethan safely tucked in bed, she finally had a chance to sort through the events of the day. After four years, Jason no longer attended the Saylor Academy, and she no longer taught there. She would miss it, she had to admit. So many of the kids were lost souls. Rudderless, like she had been at their age. Like she still felt, no matter how many times Ethan tried to reassure her.

She gingerly rolled her head from side to side, trying to relieve the headache building at the base of her skull. Perhaps she'd been too harsh with him. He'd been a rock, helping her and Jason through their nightmare, all the while grieving his own losses. She and her brother certainly owed him a debt of gratitude.

Still, she did have a career to get back to and it rankled that Ethan believed his goals to be worthier than her own. Why couldn't he accept the fact that she needed to make her own mark in the world?

Jenna focused on the teacup clenched between her

hands. *How petty I am.* Ethan had never begrudged or belittled her aspirations; he'd only asked for her help. When she cleared away all the excuses, it really did boil down to one thing: Jenna was afraid. Afraid she'd care too much and want too much. Wanting to belong with all her heart, and not feeling like she did, almost seemed worse than death, because every day she was reminded of how she didn't quite fill the bill...how she wasn't quite good enough.

With a frustrated sigh she put her cup in the dishwasher and headed to her bedroom. Tomorrow she had to face one of the biggest mistakes she'd ever made —all six feet two inches of him.

Several hours later Jenna awoke, groggy and disoriented. She'd heard a groan coming from her brother's room. "Jason?" she mumbled, knowing something wasn't right. When the sound came again, she sat upright. It was her grandfather, not Jason. He was awake and in obvious distress.

"Ethan, what's wrong?" she said, hastily wrapping the ties of her bathrobe together as she ran into the room.

"Can't...breathe too well," he gasped. "Better call..."

"Yes, yes I'll call right away! Da, you stay with me. Da!" Jenna ran to the living room and dialed 911 before rushing back to see how she could make him more comfortable. He was still breathing, thank God, but they were short gasps and he seemed to be getting weaker by the minute.

"It's gonna be okay, Da. They'll be here any second," she crooned, loosening his pajama shirt and holding his head in her lap. "You just hang in there. Please, for Jason and me. Please!"

"You called me 'Da,'" he said weakly, reaching his hand toward her face. "From the time you could talk, you called me that." He labored again to breathe. "Always liked it."

Jenna swallowed to keep from bursting into tears. "Da it is, then," she whispered.

At two in the morning, Jenna sat on a cold plastic chair in the waiting area of the emergency room of San Francisco General, hoping someone would come and give her a status report. She'd left a message for Don Rodriguez, the foreman at The Grove's construction office. Don would know whether Ethan took his medication when they'd stopped for lunch on the way into the city. Her grandfather was diabetic, but he hated having to deal with it. For the umpteenth time she closed her eyes, silently berating herself for pushing him too hard.

"Please don't die, Da..." she murmured, her hands clasped tightly. "Please, God, don't let him die. I'll make the time to help him—I promise. Please, just don't let him die." As she repeated the prayer, an icy sensation washed over her and she knew, she just knew, who was standing over her. The voice was deeper and infinitely colder, but she would have recognized it anywhere.

"What the hell have you done to him?" Brit Maguire growled. She looked up into the same gray eyes she remembered from seven years before—only this time they were hard, angry, and piercing her with blame.

Chapter Four

He regretted the words the minute he said them. She looked so vulnerable sitting there. So vulnerable, and so…beautiful.

"I don't know," Jenna said, a tinge of desperation in her voice. "He seemed very tired and went to bed early. Around one o'clock he woke up and had trouble breathing." She didn't even bother sounding defensive; she merely stood, wrapping her arms around herself as if for protection. "He may have had a heart attack, but they've got him stabilized now. I'm just waiting to get an update. It's been awhile."

Brit felt guilt settle on his shoulders. She probably didn't know Ethan had fallen the day before, and he didn't have the guts to tell her because then *he'd* look like the bad guy. Instead he stood there watching her bear the weight of her own guilt. After a minute he couldn't stand it.

"Look, I'm sorry I blamed you. Ethan…Ethan took a fall yesterday morning and refused to go to the ER and get checked out. He didn't want to miss your brother's graduation. So maybe that had something to do with it."

Instead of getting mad, Jenna merely looked up at Brit with a sad smile. "That sounds like Ethan. Of course he wouldn't mention something like that. He wouldn't want the fuss."

Brit caught himself staring at her. Her eyes were larger than he remembered, and an even richer shade of brown. She wasn't wearing any makeup and her hair, no longer the short, spiky cut of seven years ago, fell to below her shoulders in honey-colored strands. The striking college co-ed he remembered had matured into an all-natural, downright gorgeous woman. Brit's heart kicked heavily in his chest. He glowered down at his work boots, angry at his visceral response to her. When he glanced up again, she was looking at someone else.

"Brit! There you are, honey. I step into the ladies' room and you disappear on me. I swear. Men." Tori's four-inch stilettos tapped rhythmically along the tired linoleum as she hurried up and wrapped her nails around Brit's bicep. She leaned into Brit possessively while extending her right hand. Her overly bright smile was more a question than a greeting. "I don't believe we've met. I'm Tori."

He saw Jenna glance at him before extending her own hand.

"Jenna Bergstrom. My grandfather—"

"Of course! You poor thing, you must be so worried." Her brows puckered as she glanced around the empty waiting room. "My goodness, are you here all by yourself?" Tori snuggled closer to Brit's side. "Well, never mind. We're here now, and Brit's just wonderful when it comes to dealing with emergencies."

"Tori, I'm sure Jenna is perfectly capable of—"

"Good Lord, the professor." Tori cut in. "How's the old darling doing? We were so glad to hear you were there when it happened, weren't we, Brit?"

Brit tamped down the urge to throttle the woman glued to his side. "No question." Bowing to the inevitable, he made the formal introductions. "Jenna, this is Victoria Winston, the interior designer for the new Grove Center."

Jenna's eyes betrayed nothing as she nodded and said, "Thank you for coming."

"Oh it was no trouble. No trouble at all. It's obvious you're a wreck, and we're here to help in any way we can, aren't we, honey?"

He was going to kill the woman, he really was. "Well, one way you could help would be to get us something to drink from the cafeteria. You still prefer tea, Jenna?" *Damn, where had that memory come from?*

"Uh, yes please. That would be great." She stared at him, apparently just as surprised that he'd remembered such a detail.

Brit gave Tori a look that signaled he wouldn't take no for an answer. She frowned. "Oh. Well. All right then. I'll be back in a jiff."

Brit watched Jenna as her eyes followed Tori's departure. "Don't pay any attention to Tori. She's not usually this obnoxious. She hasn't had much sleep tonight and—" Brit ground to a halt as he took in the pained expression on Jenna's face and realized what he'd just implied. *Christ*.

She turned away, staring down the vacant hallway. The cold, lifeless cast of fluorescent lights magnified the air-conditioned chill permeating the building. Jenna began to shiver.

Without thinking, Brit took off his jacket and draped it around her shoulders. Despite her trembling, she put out her hand as if to hold him at bay.

"For God's sake, take it," he hissed. Their eyes locked for an instant before she acquiesced. A flutter of white in the doorway broke the tension as a slightly built middle-aged Asian woman in a lab coat approached them.

"Jenna, it's good to see you," the woman said, offering her hand. She acknowledged Brit. "I'm Dr. Lu, Professor Wolff's internist. And you are?"

"Brit Maguire. We're business partners. And very distant cousins."

They shook hands and the physician turned back to Jenna. "You'll be happy to know your grandfather's awake. You'll be able to see him shortly."

Jenna glanced at Brit before replying. "He's going to be all right, isn't he? We had a very busy day yesterday, what with my brother graduating, and I'm not sure if he took all his medications. Plus, he apparently fell yesterday morning."

"Yes, we noticed a bump on the back of his head, but we're fairly certain the arrhythmia was caused by a missed insulin injection coupled with some dehydration. We'll run some more tests to be sure, but it looks like he was lucky this time—in part because you were able to call for help so quickly."

"What do you mean, 'this time'?" Brit asked.

Dr. Lu looked from Brit to Jenna, as if weighing her words. "You no doubt know that Professor Wolff has been struggling with diabetes and its stress on the heart for several years now, and frankly, he is beginning to lose some ground. That doesn't mean he's in any immediate danger. He's actually doing quite well for a patient his age. We've stabilized his blood chemistry, and his heart doesn't seem to have suffered any notable damage—all good signs. We'll watch him for another day or so, and assuming everything checks out, he'll be ready to go home."

Brit watched Jenna's eyes fill again with tears. She seemed to sag, as if, now that the crisis had passed, her body's adrenalin had taken a hike.

"Thanks. Thank you, doctor," Jenna said. "Excuse me. I've got to call my brother." She turned away and pulled a phone from her purse.

Tori, who'd apparently hovered nearby rather than get the drinks, stepped forward and slipped her arm once again through his. "Well, that's good news," she said brightly to no one in particular.

The doctor promised to check back in a few hours and continued down the hall. There was an awkward silence as Brit watched Jenna talking quietly on her cell.

"I hate to be a party pooper, Brit, but it's after two in the morning," Tori finally announced. She pointedly leaned her head against his shoulder. "What do you say we go back to my place and catch up on our beauty sleep?"

Jenna finished her call and turned around again, her face more composed. He read the exact moment she noticed the too-large leather jacket she'd been clutching for warmth.

"Oh. Oh, yes," she stammered. "Please go and get some sleep. I—oh, here," she said, taking off the jacket and handing it back to Brit. "Thank you. Both of you."

Before he could respond, a nurse approached to tell the group that Ethan could now have visitors, briefly, but only one at a time. Brit watched grimly as Jenna hurried off with the nurse.

"Are you ready?" Tori's voice had a husky undercurrent as she scooped her purse and coat from one of the chairs.

"I'm not going anywhere until I've seen Ethan." Brit's tone was sharp and probably uncalled for, but Tori's clinging-vine performance was grating on him and he was even more disgusted with his own, earlier, lapse in judgment. "Look, I'm really beat and probably not very good company right now, so why don't I call you a cab? There's no point in both of us sitting around here being miserable. You might as well get some rest while you can."

"You know I can't do that, Brit, honey. I wouldn't dream of leaving you all alone right now. If you insist on waiting, we'll do it together." She sat back down and patted the empty chair next to her.

"Tori, it could be…"

"No, you heard the nurse say visitors could only stay a few minutes. Jenna should be out before you know it, then you can pay your respects and we'll be off."

Several minutes later Jenna returned and Brit shot to his feet. Though she still appeared exhausted, the fear in her eyes had disappeared. She looked surprised to see he hadn't left.

Brit closed the gap between them. "How is he?"

"Better, I guess. He looks so fragile, Brit. So…old and tired." She choked out a laugh. "Even now, he's in there making plans for the summer, assigning me tasks related to that damned project of yours. Says he'll add me to the payroll starting tomorrow." She blew out a breath. "Oh, and he ordered me home for the night. Told me I was going to need lots of energy to keep up with you and your—" Jenna stopped mid-sentence, an embarrassed look on her face.

A memory from their last time together shot straight to Brit's groin, and he fought to keep his expression neutral. *That's ancient history*, he reminded himself. *Over and done with.*

Jenna's eyes shifted to Tori. "Well, never mind. Da's asking for you. Hopefully you can convince him everything will still be there when he gets back."

Following Jenna's directions, Brit knocked softly on the door to Ethan's room. The professor lay dozing, pale and still amid a jumble of tubes and wires.

Worried that the older man needed his rest more than he needed company, Brit turned to go.

"Don't leave just yet." Ethan's surprisingly sharp eyes were fixed on Brit as he turned back toward the bed.

"How are you, Ethan?" Brit clasped the professor's hand between his own and squeezed gently.

"Embarrassed…exhausted…worried." Ethan's answer was more animated than Brit would have thought. "I've been thinking about that little incident yesterday morning."

"The doc says it had nothing to do with what just happened to you."

Ethan struggled to sit up. "I'm not talking about that."

Brit glanced at the heart rate monitor. "Whoa, easy there, partner. You're making this screen do the happy dance. Calm down or you're going to have nurses crawling all over this place."

"You're right." Ethan sighed and closed his eyes briefly before opening them again and spearing Brit with his gaze. "My intuition tells me that was no accident. Too many problems have plagued this project over the past several months and I'm not so naïve as to think they're all coincidental."

Brit nodded grimly. So much for keeping Ethan out of the loop. "You're right. Josh found the truss had been tampered with. Fortunately that was the only one in the bunch."

Ethan nodded. "That's something, at least. I realize I wasn't a target per se…this time…but we all know I'm the weak link in the chain. The longer this renovation takes, the better the chance that I won't be around to see it…which as you know would be a disaster for all concerned."

Brit didn't protest because, as always, Ethan was spot on. "I know what the stakes are, and you'll come through it fine," he finally said. "Despite everything, we're in the home stretch." He said the words with more confidence than he felt.

Ethan took another labored breath. "That's why it's imperative—*imperative*, Brit—that I bring Jenna on board as soon as possible to complete my work. She's the only one who truly understands what it all means, whether she'll admit to it or not. She's the only one." The old man rested briefly. "I would never share this with Jenna, worrier that she is, but if I had it to do over again, I wouldn't have had you hire Jason and those young men. I can justify it because they're scrappy. They'll take care of themselves. But Jenna. I absolutely *loathe* putting that darling girl anywhere near harm's way." He reached for Brit's hand. "So I'm begging you to keep her safe. Despite whatever's keeping you apart, please, *please* keep her safe."

Brit gave his partner a reassuring squeeze. "I promise, Ethan. Now quit with the doom and gloom. You just concentrate on getting out of this hospital."

Brit continued to hold Ethan's hand as the old man drifted into sleep, staying quietly by his side until the nurse arrived to chase him out. Ethan's words kept haunting him. Keep Jenna safe? Of course he would. But would it really come to that? More to the point, would he be able to protect himself from being close to *her*?

Despite Tori's protests, Brit dropped her off at her condo and found a motel on Franklin for the rest of the night. He'd already blown it by sleeping with the designer earlier that evening. The combination of fatigue, stress, and a double shot of Jameson on an empty stomach was always a surefire recipe for bone-headed decisions, and the head in his pants had won the day. Thank God he always kept a condom handy.

He didn't want to compound matters by leading Tori on. Even if he'd agreed to stay with her for the rest of the night, he knew exactly where his thoughts would be, and on whom.

Much better to sleep alone.

Chapter Five

"Arrogant bastard," Ralph Dorman muttered, peering over his glasses at the man holding court on the other side of the multipurpose room. He watched as the architect for the massive new Grove Center for American Art wrapped up his story with a self-deprecating grin, hands raised, palms up, in a classic "What're you gonna do?" gesture. The attentive cluster of local business owners at the Little Eden Chamber of Commerce mixer laughed delightedly along with several well-heeled outsiders.

Dorman was caught for a moment by the sheer presence of the man. Britland Maguire was over six feet tall, with the muscles of a stevedore. Word was, he liked working a construction site as much as designing the project to begin with. His good looks and self-assured air, coupled with the fact that he appeared to be on the sunny side of forty, added up to one formidable opponent.

Dorman was an architectural designer and

draftsman ("every qualification except the sheepskin," he told his clients). He was sixty-two and feeling every one of his years. An extra thirty pounds and a receding hairline didn't help matters either.

For the past fourteen years he'd served on the Little Eden town council, mainly to keep his name in front of the public. Although year-round residents gave him a fair amount of business, his major source of new commissions came from outsiders hoping his clout with local officials would help them push through their vacation remodels and new construction. They didn't seem to mind that he wasn't licensed, as long as he charged a bit less and got the projects through inspections.

He'd never admit it, of course, but if all he cared about was new design commissions, the new Grove Center for American Art would probably be as good for business as the original retreat had been over a hundred years earlier. That enterprise had taken Little Eden from a sleepy fishing village to a popular summer getaway for rich San Franciscans. But when The Grove closed in 1947, the town started to shrink, and declined during the decades after World War II. Now it was on the upswing again, complete with growing pains. Like other community leaders, Dorman tread a tediously fine line between appeasing the "no-growth" old-timers and those who favored keeping the property tax base growing through an influx of new residents—especially those with money.

"What the hell is he doing here?" Boyce Wheeler, one of those old-timers, groused from Dorman's side, gesturing furtively toward Maguire. His thin, scratchy voice grated on Dorman's nerves.

"I imagine he's come to dazzle the natives," Dorman said.

"It looks like he's making progress—and I don't like it one bit," Boyce complained. "You said they'd start having second thoughts by now. You told me you would handle it."

"Relax, Boyce. Have some patience." Dorman took a long pull from the wine glass in his hand.

How the skinny old man had managed to avoid the nut house for so many years mystified him, but he wasn't complaining. Keeping Boyce close and keeping him happy were all part of Dorman's long-range plan. Fact was, the eccentric senior owned several acres of prime coastal real estate and had no one to leave them to except his ingratiating niece—Ralph's wife, Myra. Staying with Myra in Bumfuck, California had been a trial, but, as Dorman's mother always used to say, "Good things come to those who wait."

Dorman watched Boyce yank at the decades-old tie he invariably wore for these events—a sure sign the rabble rouser was getting agitated. He smiled. Maybe he'd get lucky and Boyce would blow a gasket just by hyperventilating about this latest affront to his pet cause.

When The Grove's renovation had first been submitted for approval, Boyce Wheeler had established the Society for the Preservation of Earth, Air, and Resources, or SPEAR, and as president, he'd called his minions to arms. Dutiful members had donned their "concerned citizen" hats and showered the town planning commission with a monsoon of objections. To show his support, Dorman had also wielded all the civic power he dared to block the project.

Unfortunately the developers had dealt methodically with each obstacle; as a result, SPEAR's machinations had merely slowed down the construction schedule, not halted it. As the project unfolded, Dorman realized that stronger roadblocks were needed, but how far should he—or could he—take it? Time was becoming an issue for his private plans as well. He couldn't hold off New Venture Properties forever. They'd paid him well for an inside track once The Grove project failed and the land was turned over to Little Eden. They expected to see results. But until he could figure out a more effective strategy to halt the project, he first had to placate Boyce, and that alone was a pain in the ass.

Ever the politician, Dorman scanned the group of business owners with a friendly look. He smiled and gestured at the mayor across the room. Myra had come in with her garden club cronies and was talking to another council member. He forced a smile in his wife's direction but she ignored him. Frowning, he realized Boyce had spoken. "I'm sorry, what did you say?"

The old fart look extremely put out. "I said you're not exactly living up to your end of the bargain."

"Give it time, Boyce," Dorman assured him, taking another sip of his drink. "Give it time."

"You've had enough time already. Damn, I might

have known you wouldn't deliver." Boyce reached for a shrimp off Dorman's plate. "Well, it doesn't matter now," he sniffed.

Dorman looked at him sharply. "What does that mean?"

"I'm saying we tried it your way, and now we're going about things with a bit more...*style*."

What was the old man up to now? "Boyce, if you're planning something..."

Boyce caught Dorman's eyes with the kind of expression that made him wonder just how crazy Boyce really was. "Listen, I told you I didn't want The Grove to reopen, and I'm not going to let it reopen. I'm serious as a heart attack about that. I didn't get where I am by pussy footin' around. You understand me?"

No, you got where you are by inheriting a shitload of money, Dorman thought irritably. "Boyce, just remember who's in control here. This is our turf, not theirs. Sooner or later they'll get the picture."

"Oh, they'll get the picture, all right," Boyce said coyly. "Soon enough."

Brit Maguire had just finished a funny story about his short-lived college football career when he looked up to see Ralph Dorman and Boyce Wheeler across the room. They didn't look too pleased, which tickled Brit to no end. *Abbott and Costello must be feeling the heat from so much love in the room.* Brit was coming to realize that most of the folks in Little Eden either welcomed his new enterprise or were reserving judgment about it. Those solidly against the project were few in number, but had the loudest voices, and Boyce Wheeler had the loudest voice of all.

With a polite "If you'll excuse me," Brit made his way over to the no-host bar, assuming Dorman and Wheeler would seek him out. After all these months, he still couldn't figure out why Wheeler was so dead set against the reopening. Ethan and he were similar in age and they'd known each other for years. The retreat wouldn't impact Wheeler's neighboring property, except for the secluded cove they both had access to, and even that would rarely be used by the residents and guests, because it could only be reached by a steep deer trail.

On one level, Dorman's hostility was even more puzzling. You'd think a designer like him would be open to new developments, as long as they didn't screw up the neighborhood. But there was always that competition thing between professionals, so maybe that was it. He'd also heard Dorman was related to Boyce Wheeler by marriage. From experience, Brit knew family ties could be pretty tough to break.

Brit scanned the room. Where was Perris? He figured it wouldn't hurt to let the locals know The Grove Center Historic Trust was tired of taking it on the chin. Robert Perris was one of San Francisco's most lethal civil litigators, and thanks to the attorney's friendship with Ethan, he was more than willing to put a little fear into the opposition—with his usual flair, of course.

As Brit ordered a beer, a muffled cough to his left alerted him to Dorman and Wheeler's presence.

"Evening, Maguire." A vaguely condescending smile settled on Dorman's face as he offered his hand. "Quite a turnout tonight." The councilman took in the assembly. "Looks like folks came out in force to give you that big welcome you've been waiting for."

"Dorman," Brit nodded in return, his own smile perfunctory. "It's about time, don't you think? The road to acceptance in Little Eden hasn't exactly been lined with roses." He turned to the other man. "How's it going, Boyce?"

Boyce was reluctant to shake Brit's hand; Brit could almost see the steam escaping from his withered, hairy ears.

"I wouldn't be too sure this is all about acceptance," Boyce said, glowering. "Not everyone here is ready to blithely sing your tune. You people have got a lot to answer for, in my opinion, and—"

"Boyce," Dorman cut in sharply. "I think we can dispense with politicking for the evening." He tilted his head to indicate the people milling about. "As they say, there's a time and a place for everything. This certainly isn't it."

"Oh, I disagree." Despite the conversational tone of his voice and the genial smile on his face, Brit's steel gray eyes glinted with anger. "This might just be the perfect time and place to clear up a few things." He glanced over to see Robert Perris enter the room, impeccably dressed in his signature Armani suit and watered silk tie. The attorney exuded his usual competence and power, but tonight he was showing off something extra, or rather somebody. Jenna walked in with him, dressed to the nines and looking like she was made for his arm.

Brit's gut clenched. *What the hell is she doing here?* She was wearing one of those little black dresses, the kind that's a turn on for what it hints at but doesn't show. Her gorgeous blond hair was twisted into a prim little knot that begged to be let down at the right time, and by the right man—and no way was Robert Perris the right man.

"There you are, Brit." Perris strode up and shook Brit's hand. "Sorry I'm late. I told Ethan I'd bring Jenna tonight and the poor thing had to wait for me to finish a meeting." He turned to Jenna. "Jenna, I think you know Brit Maguire. Brit—"

"We know each other," Brit broke in. "Jenna, I'm surprised to see you here."

He noticed her chin rise a little as she answered, "Really? I thought Ethan spoke to you about that in the hospital. He asked that I attend in his stead this evening."

"No, he didn't mention it. And I'm not so sure you should be—"

Perris, who had ordered drinks for himself and Jenna, deftly interrupted Brit by extending his hand to Boyce Wheeler and Ralph Dorman. "I'm Robert Perris, legal counsel for The Grove Center Historic Trust, and this is Jenna Bergstrom. And who might you two gentlemen be?"

With surprised looks, Brit's two adversaries reluctantly pressed the flesh.

"Mr. Wheeler, I understand you've known my grandfather for many years," Jenna said.

Surprisingly, Boyce's face softened a fraction. "Yes, Ethan and I go way back. I'm sorry he's been ill."

"Thank you. He's feeling much better now and is being released from the hospital tomorrow. Perhaps when he returns to The Grove, the two of you can get together. Maybe talk over old times."

Brit had to admire Jenna's attempt at *détente*. Typical of a woman—trying to smooth things over when the men start beating their chests. Too bad it wasn't going to work. He turned to Perris. "Your timing couldn't be better," he said. "I was about to suggest to our illustrious councilman and his…supporter…that we discuss a few facts outside." He gestured to a sliding door leading to a small patio.

"Just a minute," Dorman sputtered. "I don't really think this is necessary." The councilman turned to Boyce, but the fire of battle seemed to have galvanized the rabble rouser; he was already heading for the doors.

Once outside, Boyce took the first shot. "I was just telling Dorman, here, about the shoddy inspections I hear are coming out of Sinner's Grove. It's disgraceful." He shook his knobby fist to emphasize his point. "Subpar work on one level usually means subpar work on others. I've had grave doubts about this project from the get-go."

Brit put his hands on his hips, an unconscious

gesture that broadened his already massive shoulders. "And from the get-go, you and your cohorts, with the help of the city, have tried to screw us over."

Dorman cut him off with a patronizing smile. "Surely you can accept that a project of this scale will affect the entire community and therefore must bear at least a portion of the burden, to ensure a positive impact."

"Cut the crap, Dorman," Brit shot back. "You know damn well we've done our share and more to get this project off the ground. We've complied with every outrageous demand of both the planning and the building commissions. We've bent over backwards and forwards to make you people happy, and still you stonewall us at every turn. You know we're already over budget and behind schedule, and you're doing all you can to make sure we miss the permit deadline so you can make us jump through even more hoops. No more, Dorman. We're finished bending over." Brit glanced at Jenna; she was totally tuned in to the conversation, even nodding her head slightly in support. He frowned at how good that made him feel.

"Now just a minute here," Dorman sputtered in anger. "You can't threaten—"

"Mr. Maguire hasn't threatened you. He's merely stated his intention to be more proactive in seeing that his rights are not violated in the future." The lawyer's courteous smile held no warmth as he gazed at Dorman and Wheeler. "I've gone over all the paperwork Mr. Maguire has given me, and I have to agree that you folks do seem to have gone a bit overboard on some of your requirements. Did you know, for instance, that over the past twelve months, you've required more environmental impact studies on this project than on all other new builds and renovations in this community, *combined?* Why is that, I wonder?"

"We haven't done any more than—" Wheeler's rebuttal died in an angry huff as Perris cut him short

"Mr. Wheeler, are you part of the governing body of this city? Could you or your organization perhaps have undue influence over elected officials? Might there be a conflict of interest here?" Boyce glowered as Perris nailed him with a probing stare. "Moreover, I find nothing in any of the documentation to support your rather slanderous accusation of shoddy workmanship."

"Well, you talk to the inspector," Boyce said, a hint of defensiveness coloring his tone.

"Oh I have," Perris said. "He too finds it strange that so many tests have failed a mere twenty-four hours after passing preliminary exams with flying colors, as if someone had known to sabotage the job site just prior to said inspections." He rubbed his chin thoughtfully. "Then there's the recent matter of a tampered roof truss. Had it not been discovered, people may have been injured or even killed. That's attempted murder, gentlemen." The attorney paused. He was met with frozen stares from both Dorman and Wheeler.

"Mr. Dorman, I've been trying to convince Mr. Maguire that you may simply have been, shall we say, overzealous in your efforts on behalf of the community," Perris continued. "Frankly, it's been a tough sell. Perhaps you might want to reassure him?" He looked over Brit's shoulder. "Ah, there's your city attorney now. I think I'll just say hello." He whispered something to Jenna before addressing the group again. "It was a treat talking to you. We'll be in touch soon on these matters, as you've requested, Brit. Gentlemen?" Shaking hands all around, the imposing attorney turned and sauntered away.

"Can't fight your own battles, eh, Maguire?" Dorman sneered once Rob was out of earshot. "Had to bring in a hired gun?"

"Our attorney might be willing to give you the benefit of the doubt, but I'm not." Brit's words were cool but lethal. "Since I can't settle this in the alley the way I'd like to, Mr. Perris will be personally addressing any other problems that arise. All we want is a fair shake, Dorman. Make it happen or start boning up on the legal definition of harassment."

Dorman smiled. From across the room he would have seemed the picture of congeniality. His words, uttered slowly and calmly, belied the look. "You think you can threaten me, Maguire? Hardly. You and your fancy lawyer mean nothing, *nothing*, around here. And sooner or later you'll get the message. I guarantee it."

Chapter Six

J enna had been watching the interaction of the men with equal amounts of admiration and trepidation. Ethan hadn't told her the extent of the troubles he and Brit had faced since the start of the restoration. No wonder her grandfather was feeling overwhelmed. She noticed Brit glancing at her now and again. His expression told her he didn't think she belonged there. Well, too bad.

At that moment a middle-aged woman walked up to the group. She had a round face and hair that had seen too many perms. The floral pink dress she was wearing made her hips look bigger than they probably were.

"Hello, Myra," Dorman said with a joviality that sounded forced. "I saw you earlier. Didn't your garden club meet tonight?"

"We finished early, so I thought I'd see what all the fuss was about. You're not making a fuss, are you, dear?" The steely look in her eyes signaled that

Dorman's wife was not happy with him. Jenna caught Brit letting out a tiny smirk.

"Hello, uncle." Myra pecked Wheeler's paper-thin cheek. "Have you taken your evening medication?"

"Hell if I know," Boyce grumbled. "Probably not."

"No problem. I always have it handy, just in case." Myra reached into her overly large handbag and handed two pills to Boyce, who grudgingly took them. A waiter passed by and she took a glass of wine off his tray. "Here, you can wash them down with this." Boyce obeyed and Myra looked around at the rest of the group expectantly. "Aren't you going to introduce me, Ralph?"

Before Dorman could remedy his *faux pas*, Jenna extended her hand. "Hello. You must be Mrs. Dorman. I'm Jenna Bergstrom. Ethan Wolff is my grandfather. You probably already know Brit Maguire."

"Yes, I'm sure we've met before. Nice to see you again, Mr. Maguire."

Brit nodded. "And you, ma'am."

Dorman looked thoroughly disgusted with the turn of events. "Yes, well, come along, Myra, Boyce. If you'll excuse us, we have other people to speak to this evening."

Jenna touched Boyce Wheeler's sleeve. "I'll tell my grandfather you asked about him," she said.

"You do that," the old man ground out and turned to go.

As Myra and the men left, Jenna was left alone with Brit on the patio. They both nursed their drinks, uncomfortable with the silence.

"Glad you came to the party?" he asked dryly.

"Ethan wanted me here to represent him, so I'm here."

"Well, a lot of good it did. Listen, this isn't a parlor game. These people are sharks, and they're no match for Ethan, much less someone like you."

"Someone like me?"

"Frankly, I don't know what's gotten into Ethan. I know he's frail and needs help. But why you? He's told me for years that you opted to go your own way and you've got your own life to live. He's right. You don't belong here, especially if you're going to bail on him. He doesn't need another stress in his life right now. He doesn't need someone who can't commit."

Jenna's eyes began to sizzle, her controlled demeanor on the verge of erupting. "I guess it's not up to you to decide that, is it? Ethan wants my help and I'm going to help him—whether you like it or not. So get used to it."

Brit took a step toward Jenna, then stopped himself. "So, what's the story with you and Perris? Are you with him now?"

"What? Robert and I—"

Brit held up his hand. "Sorry, I shouldn't have asked. None of my business. Shouldn't even be on my radar." He purposefully looked across the room as he took another drink.

Jenna let out a small sigh of frustration. If this is what working with Brit Maguire was going to entail, she might run screaming back to Saylor Academy at the end of it. "I've known Robert Perris and his family since I was a kid," she said softly. He's like a big brother to me."

Brit said nothing but nodded slightly to show he'd heard. A few more awkward moments went by. "I won't lie and say I'm thrilled to see you," he finally said in a quiet tone to equal hers. "But I do know how important it is to Ethan that you be part of the process, so I'll just suck it up." He turned and looked directly at her. "But so help me, if you hurt that old guy by disappearing on him…"

Jenna's eyes shot daggers at him. This conversation was happening on more than one level for sure. "I don't know how long I'll be able to stay and help my grandfather, but I've decided to move to The Grove while I do. And you know something, Brit? There's not a damn thing you can do about it. So yes, I'd say sucking it up is a good way to go." With that, Jenna walked across the room to Rob, hoping she looked poised and aloof, even though she felt anything but.

Brit watched Jenna glide through the crowd, drawing a number of glances and stares. She was cool and elegant, in a Princess Grace kind of way, and seemed untouchable. So different than the first time they'd met…

It had been Ethan's retirement party from Stanford University, and Brit, an associate with one of San Francisco's most prestigious architectural firms, had been a real cock of the walk. When he spotted Jenna, she'd been standing next to an older couple who turned out to be her parents. That night her killer body was held in check by a classy but sexy as hell red dress. And her hair. Man oh man. It was short, spiky, and platinum blond, tinted sort of pink on the ends. She looked like a Valkyrie right out of Marvel comics, and he remembered thinking maybe she could use some rescuing herself.

What followed were two of the most mind-blowing days Brit had ever spent with a woman. She'd flown in from New York City, having just graduated from art school. They'd hit it off immediately, *intensely*, and she'd been with him every step of the way. They'd talked and laughed and danced and *damn*, just fired on all cylinders. He remembered the first time she smiled at him and how he'd surprised himself by thinking, *I'd slay dragons for that smile.* Brit even held his libido in check when they spent their first night entwined in each other's arms, which said bundles about how special he felt she was. But the next night had been a different story entirely...

Don't go there. Nothing good will come from dredging up those thoughts.

Brit watched Jenna and Perris leave and waited a few more minutes before heading out to his own car, which he'd parked at the back of the town hall. He eased out of the parking lot, turning up one of the side streets behind Little Eden's main square. The moon was a sliver, leaving only the car lights to penetrate the darkness of the country road. Brit scanned the trees on either side and saw a pair of eyes reflected off his beam as he wound his way up the long hill.

Not a damn thing you can do about it. The words Jenna had flung at him stuck in his mind. She was right. Much as he would have preferred never seeing her again, the professor wanted and needed her to be close to him—and after all this time she'd agreed. He had no control over the situation, but why should that bother him? What they'd had together—if they'd ever really had anything—was a flash in the pan. It didn't make sense, but then, his reaction to her had never made much sense. Falling for someone so hard, so fast —it was crazy. He'd been crazy. Lucky for him she'd turned tail and run. And yet seeing her dredged it all up again—the lust, the hurt, the anger. All those emotions were instantly at home in him, as if they'd never left.

Lost in his thoughts, Brit accidentally drove past the main gate to The Grove. Rather than turn around, he continued on to the service entrance at the rear of the complex. Darkness shrouded the gravel road, and as he rounded a bend, he was surprised to see a pair of head-lights approaching him at high speed. "What the—" He barely had time to utter the words before the oncoming vehicle, a truck or an SUV of some kind, nearly ran him off the road. By the time he regained control, it had raced away into the darkness and he couldn't catch its license plate number. "Asshole," he muttered. He thought about checking with Don to see who on the crew drove dark trucks or SUV's, but real-ized it'd be easier to determine who *didn't*.

As Brit drove through the complex, he realized

immediately that something was off kilter. Street lamps that were purposefully kept on at night were dark; yet several of the new buildings were eerily lit. He drove over to the main exhibit hall and parked. Quietly he got out and walked around the side of the building.

Then he saw it.

Someone had taken the concept of "art complex" to a whole new level.

They'd treated the building itself as a canvas.

And used garish red paint.

"Is this the message you were talking about, Dorman?" Brit mused bitterly. He pulled out his cell phone and dialed 911. "I'd like to report yet another case of vandalism at The Grove," he said, acid lacing his tone. "Only this one puts all the others to shame. It's one hell of a mess."

Chapter Seven

Jenna had just signed Ethan out of the hospital when she got a phone call from Sherrie Phelps, Brit's office manager, about the vandalism. Telling Ethan about it was a mistake: he insisted they leave for The Grove immediately. Jenna talked him into at least stopping back at her apartment to throw some clothes in a duffel bag and explain the situation to Jason, who in turn called Parker and Kyle to bring their stuff pronto and meet at Jenna's to caravan out to the estate.

By mid-morning, they were off. Like clockwork, the weather began its eerie transformation once they crossed the Golden Gate Bridge. By then, the city's infamous fog began to dissipate, as if it simply ran out of the necessary steam to compete with the beauty of the Marin hills. By the time they reached the turnoff toward the Pacific coast, the sun was out in full force.

Unclear on the concept of caravanning, Parker and Jason had pulled ahead in Parker's black Lexus Coupe, with Kyle driving his own cherry red Mustang in hot pursuit. Soon after crossing into Marin County, both were long gone, and Jenna half expected to see one or both boys pulled over for speeding.

Keeping a steadier pace, she glanced at her grandfather and saw that he was catching forty winks. *Good. He needs all the rest he can get.* Despite Da's anxiety to reach The Grove as soon as possible, Jenna felt a perverse need to take her time. What were they headed into, really? Was her grandfather strong enough to handle it? Funny, but her main concern was for him; she had no worries at all about her own ability to cope. After what she'd been through over the past few years, she knew she could deal with just about anything as long as Ethan was all right. Just as she knew, instinctively, that Brit would lead them through the mess. Despite his obvious disdain for her, she'd felt his protectiveness and strength the moment she'd seen him again. He was...Brit.

Ugh. Don't go there. He's taken. End of story.

Jenna meandered through the various "boutique" towns that dotted the landscape heading west. Some were trendy, some funky, each had their own quirky personalities. Soon even those communities gave way to rolling hills, dairy farms, and government protected open space. Before long the air shifted yet again, as the ocean made its presence known.

Growing up, she'd always loved the signs that told her The Grove was near: the first gulls, the windswept vistas, the tangy smell of the sea. But this time, as they passed through the hamlet of Little Eden and wound their way up toward her family's old estate, Jenna realized a major change had occurred. The rundown retreat remembered warmly from her childhood was no longer in evidence as they drove through a brand new, spectacularly carved arch proclaiming the entrance to The Grove Center for American Art. "I guess we're not in Kansas anymore," she muttered.

Although it was still lined with weathered tanoak and laurel trees, the old dirt road leading through the complex had been replaced. Wider now and paved, it seemed to lead in several promising directions like the branches of a flowering tree. Scattered throughout the redwoods that comprised the original grove, Jenna could see that several pristine bungalows had replaced the weathered shacks of her memory. Built as lodgings for artists at the turn of the twentieth century, these had apparently been refurbished to provide spartan yet comfortable accommodations for the new generation of painters, sculptors, photographers, and other artisans who would come here to live and create.

To the left, up an incline, was the Great House, built by August Wolff for his beloved Lia in 1904. Once ramshackle and so forbidding that Jenna and her summer friends had dubbed it the "Haunted Mansion," the home had been restored to its original wood and stone magnificence. Jason, Parker, and Kyle, who had apparently dodged the Highway Patrol, were standing in the driveway, waving Jenna down.

"Oh, crap," she murmured. "This doesn't look good."

"What? What's going on?" Ethan had awakened from his nap. They both looked out the window and saw a squad car slowly drive by. "It must be even worse than Brit let on if the police are here," he said.

As the cruiser disappeared around the side of the building, Jenna turned to her grandfather. His face was tight with worry and though she knew she was wasting her time, she started to dissuade him from seeing what lay ahead.

"Jenna, stop looking at me like you're afraid I'm going to keel over any moment." Ethan's tone was firm. "I assure you, I'm made of far sterner stuff than you or Brit give me credit for. I'll be fine."

Before she could respond, Jason came bounding up, motioning for her to roll down her window.

"You should see the mess," he said. "Man, oh, man."

Jenna's stomach clenched. "Where is it?"

"Follow that police car, to the right. You'll see." He and his buddies trotted along in front of her car.

"The new section," Ethan said. "It's almost finished."

A short drive down a hill revealed the nightmare Jason had alluded to. Jenna parked the car and helped Ethan out, grabbing her camera out of habit. They looked around in disbelief. Located on part of what had long been an open meadow, the all-new structures of The Grove complex mirrored the Great House in style. Unfortunately several of the structures now looked like the aftermath of a bad artist's psychotic breakdown. Halfway through the exterior shingling process, both the shingles and the sheer walls of the buildings were covered in obscene red graffiti. Red paint had also been poured over a few of the roofs, such that it dripped morbidly down the massive oak pillars forming the buildings' main support. Windows had been smashed—even decorative corbels, exposed rafters, and beams had been desecrated.

"Oh my Lord," Ethan said quietly. "It looks dreadful."

"That ain't the half of it," said Jason, pointing. "Look over there."

They turned around to see a newly plastered swimming pool, its gleaming white surface marred with the same garish red paint.

"It's a horrible red, Da," Jenna said. She walked over to the edge of the pool and looked inside. Along the bottom and sides of the eight-foot chasm someone had scrawled the words "Protect Mother Earth" in elaborate script. Anger replaced the shock of seeing so much destruction aimed at part of her family's heritage. For the first time in a long time, she felt truly connected. *Now it's personal*, she thought.

"Quite a work of art, wouldn't you say?"

Jenna froze at the familiar, deep voice murmuring in her ear. She turned to see Brit, dressed in a ratty sleeveless shirt, paint-stained jeans, and scarred work boots. It was obvious by his prominent biceps, beard stubble, and matted hair sticking out from his 49ers cap that fashion sense had taken a back seat to hard physical labor. Was it only last night that he'd been dressed to kill and charming the locals at the Chamber of Commerce event? She couldn't believe the change in him, yet he still looked so...well, *yummy*. Jenna turned away in disgust at the direction her thoughts had taken.

"Award-winning," she said brusquely. "That is, if you have insurance. You do have insurance, I hope?"

"That's the least of our problems." Brit looked around and gestured to the teens, who were slowly making their way over with Ethan. "Didn't you get my message to hold off? How is he doing?"

Jenna sighed. "Stubborn. Determined. Weaker than he lets on. You know him. We did get your message, but he wouldn't hear of waiting. He insisted on coming. Says he's got too much work to do." She bit her lip as unexpected emotion welled up. "And now this. But thank you for the heads up so I could break the news to him before we got here." She glanced at a police officer interviewing two men who looked to be part of the crew. "But this is worse than I think either Ethan or I imagined."

"I know. The security guard—make that ex-security guard—was supposed to keep an eye on the place. Swears he must have fallen asleep. Didn't hear a thing."

"Do you have any idea who did this?"

"You were there last night. You know damn well who's behind this. I told you they were sharks." Ethan and the boys reached them and Brit turned to her grandfather. "Ethan, it's good to see you back on your feet, but are you sure you're doing okay? Jenna thinks—"

Ethan waved his hand dismissively. "Jenna thinks I'm a crazy old fool who should be spending every day in bed." He patted her arm. "I told you she's a worrier. But I'm all right. Truly."

Brit glanced at Jenna, who shrugged. "Well, I'm glad

you're back, although I wish it were under different circumstances."

"Brit, you remember my grandson, Jason. Jason Bergstrom, your very distant cousin Brit Maguire. And your newest employees, Parker Bishop and Kyle Summers."

"Pleasure," Brit said, shaking the young men's hands.

"We really appreciate you puttin' us on the crew," Kyle said, glancing at Jenna.

"Not a problem," Brit assured him. "You'll earn your keep." He pointed to a group of men talking next to the pool. "Parker and Kyle, you see that man over there wearing the hard hat? That's our foreman, Don Rodriguez. He's expecting you. He'll show you where to put your things."

Parker looked at Jason and Jenna before answering. "Uh, yeah, sure. Thanks."

"Catch you guys later," Jason said as his two friends walked away.

"And Jason?" Brit added, "if you don't mind, we've got a full bunkhouse so we're gonna put you in with your granddad for the time being. He'll also be your immediate supervisor, so whatever he needs done, you do, all right?" Jenna's eyes caught Brit's in gratitude; that's exactly where she wanted Jason to be.

Jason nodded. "I'm down with that."

Ethan, leaning on his cane, slipped his free arm through Jenna's. "And where would you like to have Jenna sleep?"

Jenna's eyes widened at her grandfather's remark.

She started to respond but Jason beat her to it by pointing to the contraption Brit was carrying. "What the heck is that? You look like a Ghost Buster wannabe."

"It's a power washer," Brit explained. "I've rented a couple of these plus some sanders to see if we can't get rid of some of this mess before we repaint."

Just then Jenna looked over Brit's shoulder to see a six-foot-tall, raven-haired, well-built man who looked to be in his early-thirties walking toward them. Although he was dressed casually in a sport shirt and khakis, she imagined he'd look equally at home on the cover of GQ—or with nothing on at all. Between Brit and this guy, how did mere mortals stand a chance?

Brit noticed her expression and turned around to see what had caught her eye. "Hey Gabe," he said. "Any news?"

"Not much." Gabe turned to Ethan. "Hello, Professor Wolff. Glad to see you're back in the saddle."

"Thank you, Gabriele. Gabriele de la Torre, I'd like you to meet my grandchildren, Jenna and Jason Bergstrom. They'll be working with me for the next few months. My dears, Gabriele is the local constable."

Gabe seemed amused by the professor's archaic vocabulary. "Good to meet you," he said, reaching out to shake hands.

Jenna noticed Gabe's subtle but unmistakable appraisal of her; unwittingly she glanced at Brit, who apparently had witnessed the same appraisal and was not amused.

"Gabe here is a detective with the Marin County

Investigation Division," Brit said. "But apparently he's doggin' it today. Didn't anybody in Little Eden or Bellam's Cove have a run on red paint?"

Gabe shrugged. "I wish it were that easy. We're having the paint analyzed, but we won't know the brand for another day or two. Unfortunately the vandals weren't dumb enough to purchase their supplies locally."

"Jesus, Gabe. You know as well as I do who did this. Have you even stopped by to chat with our good friend Boyce?"

The look Gabe gave Brit was grave. "I don't tell you how to do your job, *paisano*," he said quietly. "So, please don't tell me how to do mine."

Brit matched Gabe stare for stare. Finally, Brit shook his head. "I'm sorry, Gabe. It's just so damn frustrating." He took off his baseball cap and ran his fingers through his hair before shoving it back on. "Listen, can we at least get moving on this clean-up? You got everything you needed, right?"

Gabe looked around. "Yeah, we've dusted for prints and taken photos. You're good to go." He turned to walk back to his car, stopping to touch Ethan on the shoulder. "Really good to see you, sir. Does Dani know you're back?"

"No, we just arrived. I was hoping to call her later."

"I'm stopping by for lunch. I'll let her know you'll be calling."

"Thank you, son."

"No problem."

Jenna watched Gabe leave and turned to see Brit scowling at her. "What?" she asked.

"Not your type."

Since she'd been wondering more about Dani than Gabe, Jenna bristled. "What's that supposed to mean? How would you know what my type is, anyway?"

"You're right, I wouldn't know. But I can tell you he's not artsy enough for you. Wouldn't know his way around a SoHo gallery to save his life."

"And you would?"

"I didn't say I was your type either."

"Children," interrupted Ethan. "Please try and get along, will you? You're going to be working closely together, so you may as well make the best of it." He was smiling as he took Jason's arm. "Come along, my boy. Let's head back to my cottage so you and I can get settled in. Perhaps your sister will let you drive her car." He wiggled his eyebrows. "After that, I'll let you drive my golf cart. It's electric. Quite green and all that."

Jason turned to Jenna and held out his palm. "Keys, please?"

She fished them out of her jeans and handed them over. "You make sure Da gets settled and rests up," she instructed her brother. At his nod she walked back to the edge of the pool, determined to ignore Brit, even though she could feel him watching her. She began to take pictures with the intent that someday one of the images would find its way into her art. It told a grim story, but a compelling one. After a few moments her tongue got the better of her. "I thought questions about my social life weren't supposed to be on your radar."

"You're right," he said. "Old habits die hard. I'll work on it. But just so you know—he's in lust with Dani, so I doubt he'd be available anyway."

"Thanks for the heads up," she said dryly. She paused before adding, "You know, we've got more important things to worry about, like how we're going to clean up this mess."

Brit raised his eyebrows. "We?"

"Of course, 'we.' I'm here to help my grandfather, and if that means getting down and dirty with a power washer, then that's where we'll start." She turned toward the paint-ravaged buildings. "Let me take a few more shots and I'll help sand or scrub or whatever. Just tell me what you want me to do, and I'll do it." Once again she felt him watching her as she bent to take shots from every angle. Long-suppressed memories bubbled to the surface and she wondered what he was thinking. She felt rather than heard his murmur.

"Yes, ma'am," he said.

Chapter Eight

"It was the most enduring concentration of pure artistic talent the world has ever seen, and we're so privileged to be able to share it with the world at large."

Jenna's grandfather was holding court in the front parlor of the cottage he had lived in periodically for the past fifty years. Known as the "Firestone," it had been built along with the Great House as a retreat for The Grove founders' good friend and sometime business partner, William Firestone. Ethan and his late wife Nancy had spent many school vacations there, as had Jason and Jenna. Larger than the artists' quarters, it housed two bedrooms and a small office—a perfect size for Ethan and his grandson to share for one last summer.

Jenna sat on a chintz-covered sofa, her long legs tucked under her. Bone weary after a grueling day on the paint removal crew, her arms felt like overcooked noodles. Jason lay sprawled on the other end of the couch, his feet propped on her lap.

Across the room, Brit drummed his fingers on the arm of the easy chair he dominated, looking faintly annoyed that Ethan had asked him to come. And sitting next to the professor on the love seat was the young woman he'd just introduced as Dani Dunn. Petite, with dark eyes, short chestnut curls, and the faintest of accents, she seemed both exotic and like the girl next door. She appeared to genuinely dote on Ethan, treating him with the utmost respect. Dani, it turns out, was the great-granddaughter of a young painter from Italy named Luzio who had served as Lia's personal assistant in the mid-1920s. Jenna heaved an inward sigh. Even Dani had more of a connection to the original Grove than Jenna did.

Jenna glanced at Brit and grit her teeth. Working under his direction all day had been akin to torture. He hadn't exactly been a jerk, but he seemed to have gone out of his way to avoid interacting with her. He'd give her a job to do, then walk away, and when she'd finished and asked him to check, he'd been noncommittal, usually just nodding his head slightly before giving her another assignment. He hadn't made small talk, and she'd be damned if she was going to hold one-sided conversations. As a result, they'd worked closely together physically, but had seemed worlds apart. Her brother's guileless comment drew her back to the conversation.

"Honestly, Da, I've never understood all the hype. I mean, I know The Grove is cool and all, but wasn't it really just some super fancy art camp?"

Ethan smiled. "Perhaps on its surface, Jason, but in

truth, the most gifted artists of the early twentieth century conducted an amazing sociological experiment on these very grounds. San Francisco, which many people at the time referred to as the Golden City, already had a thriving art community. From those artists and others around the country, only a few were given the opportunity of a lifetime. Every year, for four decades, ten hand-picked individuals agreed to live together, in a sort of commune, if you will, which they called The Grove, to devote themselves entirely to their art—art which ran the gamut from painting to poetry, from weaving to glassblowing. They were financially supported in these endeavors by your ancestors, Gus and Lia Wolff, as well as by other patrons of the arts. Some of these individuals faded into obscurity after their sojourn here, their only claim to fame having been a resident at the retreat. But others went on to become artistic, even cultural icons. And remarkably, they all intersected here at The Grove."

"You mean 'Sinner's Grove.' That's what the local guys call it." Jason offered his observation with a smirk.

"That is indeed the local appellation," Ethan agreed. "It goes back well before the Wolffs moved here. Apparently a group of Dominican lay brothers lived up here and one of them fell in love with a village girl." He raised his eyebrows at Jason. "Some say she was a witch and cast a spell over the young man. At any rate, they ran away together, which didn't sit well with the Order, especially when the locals started calling the place—"

"—Sinner's Grove. Awesome!" Jason said. "So why

didn't they keep the name when they opened the retreat?"

"I'm not sure," Ethan said. "Perhaps—"

"—and we're here tonight because...?"

Jenna glared at Brit. How rude of him to interrupt! She was about to speak, but Ethan continued.

"I'm sorry, Brit. I know you're a bricks and mortar kind of man. But truly, I want each of you to understand what an opportunity we all have to shed light on the creative process here. We have it within our power to enlighten and inspire others who will not only support, but perhaps become the next generation of Picassos and Pollocks."

"And we're here to help you make that happen, Professor," Dani spoke up. "Why don't you tell them what you have planned."

"Essentially, each artist of The Grove was required to do two things. One was to conduct classes or share their philosophy with art patrons who would sometimes visit. The other was to submit one work of art representing his or her specialty, as payment for the year spent at the retreat."

"So that's ten artists a year, forty years. That's four hundred pieces of art," Jason said.

"Exactly. That's where Dani and Jenna come in. These priceless pieces have been in storage or on loan for far too long. Dani has already gotten started, but the two of you working together will be able to expedite the process of sorting, cataloging, and researching each artist and their contribution. The ultimate goal will be to create a comprehensive museum exhibit for these works as well as prepare a written retrospective for the viewing public."

"Art History 101," Jason offered.

"Oh, much more than that, Jason. We want to know each artist and how his or her contribution to The Grove fit into their overall body of work. Was it a seminal piece, a departure from the norm, and so on. How did life at The Grove affect the art and the artist? What do the pieces tell us about the individual and the times they lived in? We are so fortunate in that besides the actual artwork, we have running commentaries for each year, written by the artists themselves, about each other's creations. Between Jenna's art training and Dani's formidable computer researching skills, they will be able to add to those primary sources and place this most unique collection within its historical and cultural context for the edification of art lovers everywhere. It will be a legacy truly befitting the vision and generosity of Gus and Lia Wolff." Ethan looked at Dani and Jenna. He was beaming, almost quivering with emotion.

Jenna saw in vivid detail how much this whole process meant to him. Maybe it wasn't *her* legacy, but she was glad that events had led her back to help. "We'll do everything we can to make it happen," she said.

"Splendid! I knew I'd assembled the right team. This will be a labor of love for all concerned, I assure you."

Unwittingly, Jenna glanced at Brit, only to find him looking directly back at her. She quickly turned back to her grandfather and saw that he was beginning to fade. "Well—" she began.

"A moment please, Jenna. There's one more thing I would like to discuss," Ethan announced.

"We're all ears," Brit said flatly.

"Along with Brit and my own resources, our consortium of investors, called The Grove Center Historic Trust, has financed the lion's portion of the project thus far."

"The Money Men," Jason piped in.

"Precisely. The fact is that several of them have expressed an interest recently in seeing just what they're getting for their investment. So I have taken the liberty of arranging a bit of a tour."

"Given all the hassles we've been going through, not to mention last night's mess, do you really think that's such a good idea?" Brit asked. He did not look happy.

Da heaved a sigh. "Honestly, Brit, I'd rather wait a bit myself. But they do hold most of the purse strings, and I think, given the setbacks we've been dealing with, this might be the perfect time for a pep rally, so to speak."

Brit's tone was skeptical. "What kind of pep rally?"

"Oh, nothing too elaborate. An informal reception at the Great House, perhaps a night spent in one of the cottages…and a prototype of the museum presentation we're after."

"Sounds like a sneak preview," Jason said.

"Yes, that's it. I'm hoping our fine research team—" Ethan nodded at both Jenna and Dani "—will be able to come up with a template using a few of the first-year artists. Nothing in stone, mind you, just a tantalizing 'taste' of what's to come."

"When did you want this preview to take place?" Brit asked.

"I've set it up tentatively for about four weeks from now. I thought the second weekend in July might work. I hope that will give you two enough time?"

Jenna looked at Dani, who nodded.

"I don't like it," Brit said. "We're not exactly strolling to the finish line here."

"I know, but I do think our partners are getting restless. We have to reassure them that all is well."

"Even if it isn't." Brit stood and shrugged his shoulders. "But you want it, so we'll make it happen."

"Well," Jenna said brightly, pushing Jason's feet aside and standing up. "I'm all for getting an early start tomorrow, but right now I'm dead on my feet. If you'll just point me in the right direction, I'll head over to—"

"—the Great House. With Brit. You'll be staying with him."

Jenna stopped in her tracks. "Excuse me?"

Ethan smiled at his granddaughter. "Well, not precisely with him, but in the same building. Those are the only accommodations available, apparently. He'll show you."

"Wait a minute. What about one of the artist's bungalows? I could easily bunk in one of those."

"I don't think so," Da replied. "Tori tells me the cottage furnishings won't be delivered for another two weeks or even longer." He turned to Brit. "Perhaps you could —

"Cluck, cluck, cluck," Brit murmured, his eyes

locked on her. "Never figured you for a chicken." He stood up and headed for the door.

Jenna's eyes flashed. Throwing down a gauntlet, was he? After the way he'd treated her all day, she shouldn't be surprised, but damn it, it hurt. The invective she was about to volley died on her lips when Dani spoke up.

"Jenna, why don't you come over to the Havenwood for breakfast? You know where it is, at the end of Bayview? I can show you what I've done so far and we can figure out where we go from there. Say, about eight o'clock?"

"Um, sure, but would you mind making it Monday instead? I'm on the clean-up crew and we've got a ways to go."

Dani nodded. "Monday it is."

"Great." Jenna glanced at Brit. He'd stopped in the doorway and she caught his look of surprise.

"Come on," he said, holding the door open for her. "You can drive."

Heaving a sigh of frustration, Jenna looked over at her grandfather, who was chuckling. "What's so funny?" she muttered as she and Brit left the cottage.

"I haven't a clue," Brit muttered back. Apparently he'd heard her grandfather, too.

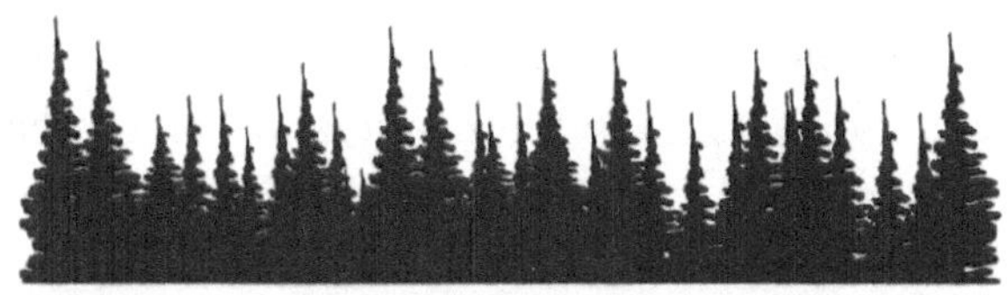

Chapter Nine

B oth Brit and Jenna were silent as she drove toward the Great House.

"Turn here," Brit finally said, motioning for her to turn onto a driveway that circled toward the back of the mansion. "I park back here so I don't clutter the front of the house," he explained. "Closer to the kitchen, too."

She parked her Honda Civic next to Brit's Porsche with the fleeting notion that his sleek car crouched in the shadows like a predator awaiting the hunt. Ridiculous. She grabbed her duffel bag from her trunk and began walking toward the house. Brit took it from her, daring her to complain with a raise of his eyebrows.

"This all you got?" he asked.

"I'm not sure how long I'll be staying."

"Oh. Right. I forgot." Brit's tone told her he figured the chances of her sticking around hovered somewhere between slim and none.

Jenna bit her tongue; she was too tired to fight

anymore tonight. "So, how come you're staying here and not in one of the cabins?"

"Space and privacy," he answered. "For as long as I'm here, I've basically taken over the third floor. In fact, my home office is in Lia's old studio. I've got my drafting table, CAD set up and weights in there—everything I need."

"What, no kitchen sink?"

Brit smiled at her tease. "That's next on my list." He fished a key out of his pocket and turned the lock. "After you."

Jenna preceded Brit into what seemed to be a glassed-in porch leading to the kitchen, which was dimly lit but looked huge. It had, after all, served the main dining hall of the original complex, located on the same floor.

It tugged at her a bit that so little looked familiar. With the exception of friendly dares to dart inside the old boarded-up structure, she'd had little access to the Great House during her childhood. Yet she could tell that much had changed. Stainless steel appliances shimmered indistinctly where the gauzy rays of the moon penetrated the windows. Granite and tile covered the counter tops and backsplash—colder, more impersonal somehow than the ancient butcher block and wood paneling she remembered. But this kitchen, she knew, would soon function much more efficiently than it had over a century ago.

As she wove her way along the darkened space, she was acutely aware of Brit following closely behind. At one point he touched her again, his hand warm on her back, to steer her in the right direction. She shivered involuntarily, hoping he wouldn't notice.

"Up these stairs," he said quietly as she reached the end of the long room. She followed his direction to a second floor landing, which was dimly lit. "Third door on the right."

Jenna stopped in front of the door and paused, finally turning around and facing her taciturn escort. He stepped back. She took a deep breath and let it out. "I don't understand you."

"What do you mean?" The sound rumbled from deep in his chest.

"I was just wondering why you were so…so prickly this evening. We seemed to have had a good day, and—"

"It was an excellent day. We got a lot done, and I wanted to tell you, I appreciate it. You worked hard, and I'm blown away that you're willing to come back for more."

Jenna smiled, amused for the first time that evening. "Don't sound so amazed," she said. "Don't you require a hundred percent from those who work for you?"

Brit's lips twitched. "I want it, but I don't always get it. So, I'm grateful when it comes my way, that's all."

"Well, you're welcome, I guess." *Boy, that sounded lame.* Desperate for something else to say, she added, "So you never said why you were so grouchy tonight. Even Ethan picked up on it."

"I was just thinking—worrying's more like it. I know it's impractical, but I'd much rather he handled the research aspects of The Grove off site, especially with the hassles we've had lately. And now with this preview he's got going…"

"You think the artwork might be in danger?"

"It's not the artwork I'm worried about. We can protect that…and yes, we've got insurance," he chided in reference to her comment from earlier that morning.

"What, you're worried about Ethan?"

The look Brit shot Jenna told her it wasn't only Ethan he was worried about. Her body immediately began to warm despite the coolness of the night.

"What happened last night was nasty, but it won't stop us from moving forward. And once Wheeler or Dorman or whoever's behind all this realizes that, they could try something worse. Because they definitely don't want The Grove to open." He looked at her intently. "And I don't want anyone getting caught in the crosshairs."

"I see." Shivering slightly again, Jenna turned back toward the door and reached for the handle; the door wouldn't open. "Um, do you have a key?" she asked over her shoulder.

From behind, Brit reached around as if he were going to embrace her. Heart flickering, she sucked in her breath, but let it out a second later when she realized he was just reaching beyond her for the door. He pressed the small lever above the knob that lifted the latch and pushed the door open.

"Ah," she said in a small voice. She entered the room and Brit followed. He turned on the light and looked around the cozy sitting room before turning back and handing her a skeleton key for the antique door knob.

"It's small, but nice," he said. "Ethan thought you'd find it comfortable…in case you plan to stay awhile."

Jenna kept her voice cool. "Like I told you at the reception, I'm helping my grandfather, for as long as I can, regardless of what you have to say about it."

Brit gazed at her for a moment, then turned to go. "Sleep tight," he said.

Jenna shut the door and surveyed the delightful little suite. The living area had a velvet-covered settee and two deeply cushioned armchairs set around a rosewood coffee table. Someone had placed a vase filled with yellow roses on top of it. A large, ornately carved wardrobe adorned one wall; inside was a small flat screen television. Next to it sat a dainty parquet desk that displayed a framed antique photo. The woman in the photo, she knew, was Amelia Starling Wolff. "At least you and I share a love of art," she whispered.

She continued her tour, smiling at the quaint claw foot tub and elaborate tiling in the bathroom. The bedroom was another treat for the senses, with a romantic four-poster adorned with a plush white down comforter. Of their own accord, her thoughts turned to Brit and what he might look like stretched out on that bed. She remembered his body, every inch of it, and wondered shamelessly if it would still look and feel the same.

She heard a soft knock on the outer door and momentarily froze. She and Brit were the only ones in this huge house, right? Had she conjured him from her imagination? The knock came again, louder this time, and Jenna chastised herself for being so skittish.

"Coming," she called. She opened the door to see Brit standing there, shirtless with a towel slung across his wide, muscular shoulders. He was also barefoot. He'd obviously just run down the stairs. Jenna almost moaned with lust.

"Sorry, I forgot to give this to you. It's a master key to the downstairs door. We'll be installing electronic security here in the next few weeks, which you may or may not be around for. In the meantime, don't lose it, because it fits a number of locks around the estate."

"Yes, sir," she said, giving him a mock salute as he turned to go back to his rooms. When he reached the stairs, he turned around.

"Jenna?" he called.

"Yes?"

"I meant it about today. You were great. It was unexpected and for that reason all the more appreciated. So thanks again…and lock your door."

Jenna used the skeleton key to lock the door from her side and leaned against it, waiting for her heartbeat to return to normal. Seven years ago she'd denied her heart out of fear that she would never belong, and that denial had cost her dearly. If she had a second chance, would she let the same fear stand in her way? She smiled ruefully. Who was she kidding, anyway? This time around the man only tolerated her because of her grandfather, and he was involved with someone else to boot. Following her heart this time around could be an even bigger mistake than before.

Yeah, *that* went well, Brit thought as he headed back up to his own suite. He had left the windows open and through them he could hear the muted sound of the sea far below. He could also smell the scent of laurel trees mixed with night blooming jasmine. Bad idea, he decided. It smelled like woman.

Women, he admitted, had their uses. But not since "The Jenna Interlude," as he called their long-ago hook up, had any woman gotten anywhere near his core.

Until now.

He'd expected a self-absorbed prima donna, a New York City elitist bemoaning her come-down in society. But Jenna had surprised him. She was the same down-to-earth woman he remembered, but with more depth. More character. Apparently the tragedy she'd been through with her parents' deaths had toughened but not broken her. Today she'd rolled up her sleeves and done what was necessary, whatever he needed her to do, no questions asked. She was game to help finish the job, too. Compared to the many high-maintenance women Brit had encountered in his lifetime, Jenna was an incredible breath of fresh air—not to mention sexy as all get out.

Maybe Ethan was right. Maybe Jenna cared more than Brit thought. But then, why had it taken her so long to help her grandfather out? God knows he'd been asking her to return to The Grove off and on for years. Even now she hadn't truly committed; she could leave the professor stranded in a heartbeat, as well Brit knew.

He walked through the suite to the bedroom beyond. Once inside he chucked his shorts and stepped into the spacious bathroom that held a shower—big enough for two, he noted grimly. As the water sluiced over him, his thoughts remained on the woman below him. That long, lean, sun-drenched look had always made him hot, and hers had only improved over time, damn it.

He vigorously shampooed his hair and rinsed under the showerhead. *Wish I could rinse away these feelings as easily.* Hell. What was he thinking? He ought to thank Jenna for running out on him so long ago. It had taken years to tamp down the longing mixed with betrayal that thoughts of her evoked. Experience had taught him that in all the ways that truly mattered, women couldn't be trusted, whether they were the girl of your dreams, a hot-blooded trophy wife, or even your own damn mother.

Brit stepped out of the shower, toweled himself off, and put on a clean pair of boxers before heading downstairs to the kitchen. Power washing was tough work and he was hungry. He searched the refrigerator and found all the ingredients for a killer pastrami sandwich, built one to his exact specifications, grabbed a beer, and headed back upstairs to his office. Ten minutes later, a review of the vandalism and the clean-up estimates had him frowning.

Unfortunately Boyce Wheeler's anti-development group SPEAR wasn't satisfied with throwing up a roadblock or two; this latest episode had gone way beyond their usual tactics. If Boyce thought he could get away with causing thousands of dollars' worth of damage, what else might he try and who might get hurt in the process? Brit wasn't content to let Gabe plod along with standard police procedures. With Wheeler's influence in the town and his connection to that slimy councilman Ralph Dorman, the investigation was likely to stall anyway.

No. What they needed here was an old-fashioned meeting of the minds. Brit decided to pay the head of SPEAR a friendly little visit, and the sooner the better. Maybe he could even get Jenna to come along and keep it civil, as she had at the Chamber mixer.

Jenna. The way she'd shivered around him, and tensed when she thought he was going to touch her—was she afraid? Did she want it? Did she want *him?* Damn. All he knew was that if he hadn't held himself in check he would have kissed her. Thoroughly. The thought of invading her mouth—and the rest of her body—made him hard as a post.

All of which posed a problem. Ever since the Jenna Interlude, Brit's policy was to avoid women whose expectations didn't match his own. He'd blown it with Tori and he wasn't about to do the same with Jenna.

But in Jenna's case, he wasn't worried about her expecting too much from him.

He was afraid history would repeat itself and he'd want too much from her.

Chapter Ten

Jenna walked into the light-filled foyer of the Havenwood Inn a little before eight on Monday morning. She'd been working her butt off with Brit and the rest of the crew, and was looking forward to focusing on her first love: art.

She recalled the old Queen Anne as one more dilapidated building that made up the village of Little Eden. Back in her childhood it had been a large, shabby storefront with rooms for rent upstairs. But today—wow. What had originally been a comfortable, family-oriented home had now come nearly full circle. Peeling paint and faded wallpaper had been replaced with warm, vibrantly colored walls framed by elegant crown molding and trim wainscoting. Instead of the dark, fussy furniture common to the turn of the century, the owners had opted for light, airy pieces, giving the small hotel a cottage-like feel. Flowers were evident everywhere, from the lush floral design area rugs to fresh cuttings displayed on several polished tables throughout the inn. Jenna immediately felt welcomed as she walked through the reception area to the cheery dining room beyond.

Since it was the middle of the week, she expected to be the lone customer, but in fact the room was nearly filled with diners. The handsome detective she'd met yesterday sat by the window. He was talking to a middle-aged woman and gesturing with his hands, kissing his fingers and flinging them out to show his apparent pleasure.

"Questa frittata è delizioso," he said to the woman. "Lei è incredibile, no?"

The older woman smiled indulgently. "Oh, our Dani's incredible all right. But you can tell her how good her frittata recipe is yourself."

"Sounds like I ought to order that," Jenna said, walking up to them and smiling.

"Jenna, good morning." Gabriele de la Torre rose as Jenna approached, but she waved away his chivalry.

"And a good morning to you, Detective." She turned to the woman and extended her hand. "Hello. I'm Jenna Bergstrom."

"A pleasure," the woman said. "I'm Nina Fabbi. My husband Paulo and I run the restaurant here. Welcome."

Jenna looked around the bustling dining room. "This certainly seems like the place to be."

"The food is incredible," Gabe chimed in. "I—" he looked beyond her and smiled the kind of smile women have swooned over for centuries. Jenna turned to see what, or who, had captured his attention. Dani had entered the dining room, exchanging greetings and goodwill with the restaurant's patrons as she navigated her way around the tables. This guy's got it bad, Jenna thought as she watched Gabe watch the young woman walk toward them.

"Good, you made it right on time." The warmth of Dani's greeting seemed tempered by a faint trace of uncertainty as she looked from Jenna to Gabe and back again. "Gabe," she murmured.

"*Buon giorno*, Daniela," he replied with a slow grin.

Jenna sensed the undercurrent between the two, but chose to ignore it. "I love the morning," she said amiably.

"Well then, let's head to my office." Dani gestured toward the doorway leading from the dining room into the lobby. "We can have something to eat while I show you what I've got."

"Sounds good to me."

"Enjoy the day, ladies," Gabe called after them.

"You too," Jenna replied. Dani glanced briefly back at Gabe but said nothing.

"I didn't know you worked here," Jenna said as she followed Dani down a hallway. "I thought you worked in computers. That's what Ethan said, anyway."

"I do, sort of. It's a long story." She held open the door to her office and Jenna went past her, noting immediately how warm and inviting—and messy— Dani's work space was. Dani motioned for Jenna to have a seat on the plush chenille-covered couch. On the coffee table perched a pot of tea, a heaping plate of scones with butter and jam, and a small carafe of orange juice. "Help yourself," she said, walking to her desk and leafing through some papers.

"I'd like to hear it," Jenna said.

"Hear what?"

"Your story."

"Oh. Well, I actually have a degree in hotel management, which involves a lot of computer work. I'm pretty good at it, so I used to earn extra money in college as an online researcher." She gestured around the room. "When I came back to work with my mom, I met your grandfather and agreed to help him out."

"Your mom owns this place?"

"We own it together. We bought it a few years back while I was in school and remodeled it over time. Mom used to be a flight attendant. She enjoys taking care of people. This turned out to be the perfect business for both of us."

Jenna relaxed against the cushy gold sofa cushions. Every furnishing in the room seemed casual and relaxed; how strange that the woman pacing in front of her seemed anything but.

"Your mom sounds cool," Jenna said. "How do you divide the work?"

"We don't anymore. She's flown the coop."

"She's gone? Why?"

Dani scrunched up her nose. "Love," she replied. "Love in the form of Mr. Herb Roscoe. He was a regular guest and used to travel for his company a lot. So, they got together and moved to Phoenix."

"You don't sound thrilled."

"Oh, I don't mind. Herb's a nice guy. I just didn't

expect to be running the place all by myself. My mom and I were—are—pretty close."

"That would be tough," Jenna said. "But hey, looks like there are some perks to the job. I mean, with regulars like Gabe…"

"How do you know Gabe?" Dani asked abruptly.

"I just met him yesterday," she explained with a smile. "But already I know something very important about him."

"What's that?" Dani sounded very curious. *Good.*

"That he only has eyes for one woman, and it certainly isn't me."

Dani blushed as Jenna's underlying message sank in: *don't worry, I'm no poacher.* Jenna could see the tension leaving the woman's face, but it was replaced immediately by a look of melancholy. "Well, you're welcome to him," she said.

What was the problem? Obviously Dani and Gabe were attracted to each other. Unbidden thoughts of Brit popped into her head, but she ruthlessly pushed them away. "Uh, no thanks," she said firmly. "I'm only here temporarily. Once I've helped Ethan out and Jason's off to college, I'll be looking for work elsewhere."

"You're an artist, right?"

"Yes. I've worked in galleries in New York—even had a showing a few years back. I'm thinking of spending some time studying in Europe. Broadening my exposure." She grinned. "Italy would be a good place to start."

Dani smiled wistfully. "It is a beautiful country, to

be sure."

"You're from there, right? When was the last time you were home?"

Dani had lingered by the curtained window and gazed outside. "A long time ago," she said quietly. "I like being here." She shook her head slightly, as if to clear her thoughts. When she spoke again, she was all business. "Let me show you what I've done." She retrieved a stack of file folders from her cluttered desk. "Ethan hadn't had much chance to classify the material, but he gave me The Grove's original accounting records plus the manifest for all the art work in storage. Toward the end of her career, Lia apparently worked with a man named Simon Wheeler, who was an attorney who lived on the adjoining estate."

"Wheeler? That must have been Boyce Wheeler's father."

"I think you're right. Anyway, he helped her organize and account for all the pieces owned by The Grove at the time it stopped operating." She pulled out a sheaf of papers, laid them on the coffee table and sat down next to Jenna. "So I made a spreadsheet showing the artists and their works, year by year."

Jenna looked at the charts and nodded. "This is great. It helps to get a sense of the scope of the project and how to tackle it."

"That's what I thought. Then I created more detailed charts for each year, beginning with 1905." She brought out more papers. "Here I incorporated various notes I found that were included with the manifest. There's some fascinating stuff in here, and some interesting characters." Dani paused and looked at Jenna. "May I ask you something?"

"Sure, go ahead."

"What do you know about Professor Wolff's father? That would be your great-grandfather."

Jenna frowned. It seemed petty to point out she wasn't connected to any of them. After all, this project wasn't really about her. She thought about the family history she'd learned from Da over the years. "I know Da had a stepfather who raised him, and twin half-sisters."

"No. I'm talking about the professor's biological father."

"Hmm. I guess I don't know anything about him. Why?"

"Did you ever stop to think about how your grandfather has the same last name as *his* grandfather?"

"Ethan Wolff...August Wolff...yeah?"

"The line is through Gus's daughter, not his son."

It took a moment to digest what Dani was saying. Then it dawned on her. "Married women rarely kept their maiden names back when Da was born."

Dani nodded.

"So...his parents weren't married?"

"We don't know that yet," Dani said, "but there's more." She leafed through one of the file folders, pulled out a faded newspaper clipping, and handed it gingerly to Jenna. In old-fashioned scrolled typeface a headline read "Original Grove Hopeful Returns: Is He Wooing the Ex-Boss's Daughter?" The article, written in the coy style common to society rags of the 1920's, alleged that a Mr. P.R., lately of Milwaukee, Wisconsin, had returned to San Francisco, seeking investors for a new type of photographic camera. While discussing the project with former employers A. and A. W., he'd cast eyes upon their lovely daughter G., a recent graduate of the Weems Academy in San Francisco, and they had struck up a *very* cordial relationship. The article had concluded with the titillating question, "Are wedding bells in the offing?" Jenna put down the article and sat back against the cushions.

"Da's never mentioned this guy," she mused. "The article's dated May twenty-third, 1926, and I know he was born in February 1927. So it's possible, I suppose. Wonder what his full name was."

"It has to be Peter Raines," Dani said. "The article said the man was a former employee, and he's the only person with the initials P.R. I found in their records, so I did an Internet search and found a Peter Raines in Milwaukee in 1925. He was one of the first Grove artists in residence, back in 1905, but he also served as Lia's assistant. He was a photographer and apparently he did a series on Lia which he contributed as his payment for the year. I can't wait to see the shots he took."

"So, if he was part of the original retreat, that would make him quite a bit older than Da's mother."

Dani visibly shuddered. "Maybe it was one of those May-December type relationships."

"Not my cup of tea either. Any idea what happened to him after he left The Grove?"

"The first time? That's where it gets a bit dicey."

"Not much to go on?"

"That wasn't the issue. I did find some material, but it's not the kind of information you'd want your descendants to know about."

"Sounds intriguing."

"Yeah, well, if you're into kinky stuff."

Jenna sat forward. "What do you mean, kinky stuff?"

Dani skimmed the notes she'd taken. "After his stint at The Grove, the next reference I found, several years later, has him on the staff of an underground sex magazine out of Omaha. Pretty sleazy stuff. A number of years after that he did a coffee table book, kind of a photographic retrospective called The Grove's First Year. Looks like that's the only artsy thing he ever did. Everything else was run-of-the-mill porn."

Jenna raised her eyebrows. "Not a very illustrious ancestor."

"Which is why you might want to check with your grandfather to see how far he wants us to take this."

Jenna sat for a moment while her grandfather's words came back to her. Perhaps another family secret to uncover, he'd said. "I have a feeling he already knows."

"Really? What makes you say that?"

"Well, he talked about solving a mystery about where he's perched on the family tree."

"I don't know," Dani countered. "Sometimes it's better not to stir the pot. Sometimes you're better off not knowing."

"I'm sure my grandfather would want the truth out

in the open, whatever it is," Jenna said confidently. "That's the kind of man he is."

Dani said nothing as she gathered up the charts and put them back into the folders, then pulled out an old photograph. "Look at this," she said, handing Jenna the faded print. "This photo was taken in June of 1906."

Jenna scanned the small photo, recognizing Amelia Starling Wolff by the artist's trademark flowing hair. The petite beauty was surrounded by nine men and women. "These are the artists who lived at The Grove for the first year?"

"Yes."

"Which one is Peter Raines?"

Dani grimaced. "None of them, as far as I can tell. I identified all the other men. Peter's simply not there."

"He was a photographer. Maybe he took the photo."

"Nope," Dani said, turning over the photo and handing it back to Jenna.

"'The First Class at The Grove. Photo by Gus.' So, what happened to Peter?"

Dani shook her head. "At this point I haven't a clue. All I know is, Peter Raines was one of the first artists to sign up for the full-year retreat. He'd lived and worked at The Grove since the previous June and he signed a list of survivors the day of the Great Earthquake in April of 1906. But after that day, nothing shows up for him until that Omaha reference I mentioned. It's like he disappeared from The Grove without a trace."

Chapter Eleven

I t took the weekend, and way too much overtime, to clean up the construction site, but today most of the crew was moving forward again. Brit peered over his office manager's shoulder as she updated the project schedule, pleased with what he saw. He watched her fingers fly over the computer keyboard, somehow fitting all the project pieces together into a unified whole. "What time did Don say he'd be back from Oakland?" he asked.

"Around three o'clock," Sherrie said. "Ethan was catching a ride with somebody to the San Rafael Library and Don was going to pick him up on the way back."

Brit checked his watch. It was eleven. "Listen. I've got to run an errand. Have him call me on my cell when he checks in, will you? And tell Jack to assign Parker and Bishop clean-up duty around the bungalows."

"Will do, boss."

Brit grinned as he headed back to the Great House to change clothes. Sherrie knew damn well she was the real boss around the Vintage Maguire field office; without her expert negotiating, cajoling, browbeating, and bird-dogging, his projects would never get beyond the drafting table. With Don Rodriguez in the field and Sherrie Phelps in the office, he had everything he needed to run a smooth operation. What he didn't need was Boyce Wheeler's SPEAR goons vandalizing the job site.

Although Gabe had warned him to stay out of it, Brit was determined to forestall any further incidents by meeting with Boyce Wheeler one on one, without councilman Dorman or any other agitators around. Maybe he'd get some insight into the old man's beef with The Grove. If Brit knew what the hang-up was, maybe they could work out a compromise. Maybe they could put the whole mess behind them.

He frowned. That was a whole lot of maybes. Still, he had to try.

He drove around to the back of the mansion. Once again he thought about recruiting Jenna to soften his edges, and as he turned the corner, his thoughts morphed into reality. Dressed in khaki shorts and a white sleeveless top, she looked like a summer camp counselor—clean, innocent, and fresh. She was leaning over the open door of her Civic, looking inside her car, so she didn't notice that he'd parked next to her. When she straightened, she saw him and abruptly stopped, caught in his stare. Her hair was loose and hung past her shoulders, thick with gold streaks. A warm gust of wind caught the mass and sent it dancing around her face. Using both hands, she caught the whipping tendrils, opening her body to him, as if to welcome him inside. Her movement, so graceful, so unaffected, stopped Brit cold. *I want this woman. I wanted her then. I want her now. I want to be with her. Around her. In her.*

He watched as she forced herself to break their connection. She leaned into her car again and pulled out several folders, hugging them to her chest in an almost protective gesture.

"How did the meeting with Dani go?" he asked, keeping his tone neutral.

"Fine. There's a lot to do," she said. She looked away and started to head into the house. Brit caught her arm gently. "I need your help," he said.

Fifteen minutes later they were on their way up the coast in Brit's Pilot, the beefy SUV he used for hauling both the tools of his trade and his clients. Somehow, he'd convinced her to accompany him on his visit to Boyce Wheeler. "I'm counting on you to keep me on the straight and narrow," he'd joked. Then he'd sweetened the deal by promising to show her where Ethan had kept most of the artwork for the past year. He'd even thrown in lunch plans. "You're in for a treat on all counts," he'd said.

She'd hesitated only slightly before saying, "You're on." And he hadn't realized just how important her answer was until she'd said yes.

Boyce Wheeler lived at Puerta del Mar, a late nineteenth-century estate featuring one of the most spectacular coastal views in northern California. It bordered The Grove complex, but no connecting road had ever been built between the two properties. They were virtually isolated from each other by rugged hills and jutting shoreline, linked only by a small, picturesque cove situated between them, accessed by a narrow deer trail. As a result it took Brit and Jenna almost an hour to drive to Puerta del Mar via the inland route.

"This place could use some remodeling of its own," Jenna remarked as they parked along a worn-out gravel driveway. In fact, the house seemed to be crumbling before their eyes. The painted siding of the Victorian-style mansion was cracked and weathered beyond repair; several slats were missing, while others hung haphazardly. The ornate oak door had been painted green at one point, but most of the color had since faded away, leaving a brown crusty barrier to the outside world.

"It's a shame, really," Brit murmured as he examined the pillars still bravely holding up the sagging front porch. "He shouldn't let a piece of history die like this."

A few raps on the rusted iron door knocker brought Mrs. Reynolds, Boyce's dour and ancient housekeeper, to the entrance. At the moment, her mouth was pinched in what he recognized clearly as distaste.

"We're here to see Mr. Wheeler," Brit informed her.

"Who is it?" Boyce's reedy voice demanded from within.

"That man from The Grove," the housekeeper called over her shoulder.

"You just tell him—"

"You can tell me yourself, Boyce," Brit cut in heatedly as he sidestepped the gaping woman and pushed through the open door, taking Jenna's hand in the process.

"Sorry. Excuse us," Jenna said.

Take it easy, Brit reminded himself. *Don't let the man get to you.* "I've come to talk things over, Boyce. Just talk."

Across the foyer, Boyce was standing at the arched entrance to his study. At the sight of them, he turned and shuffled back to his desk. Brit followed with Jenna in tow.

"You've got a lot of nerve, boy," Boyce said as he sat down.

"I'd say that makes two of us," Brit rejoined. Jenna tugged her hand from his and walked up to Boyce's desk.

"Mr. Wheeler—"

"You look more like Nancy today than you did the other night," he interrupted.

Jenna looked taken aback. "You knew my grandmother?"

"Of course. Lovely lady, she was. Sorry to hear that she passed. And I remember you from summers long ago. You used to ride your bike with your granddad into town. You'd be laughing as you tried to keep up with him. I remember."

Brit could see the confusion etched on Jenna's face. He could tell she was having trouble reconciling this seemingly harmless old codger who fondly remembered her grandma, with anyone so dead set against

The Grove. He couldn't reconcile the two personas either.

"Boyce, you've known Ethan and his family for years," Brit said. "You've been neighbors, for Chrissakes. Why are you so dead set against the renovation of The Grove? Do you think it's going to hurt your property in some way? Because whatever your beef is, it's getting out of hand. The latest bout of vandalism was way over the top."

Boyce smiled. "I'm sure I don't know what you're talking about. Why don't you two have a seat and I'll get us some refreshments." He reached over to an old-fashioned bell pull and tugged it.

"Don't bother," Brit said. "Look, your boys caused a hell of a mess, and for what? Do you really think you'll succeed in driving us out at this late date?" He looked at Jenna; she was doing her job, using eye contact and raised eyebrows to remind him not to boil over. Brit paused and took a breath, mitigating his tone. "I really don't get it, Boyce. Why are you so hell-bent on destroying Ethan's dream?"

Boyce's genial veneer cracked completely, like the paint on his walls, replaced with the twisted fervor he often failed to keep in check.

"Because he, and you—and you," he said, turning to Jenna, "have no right...no right to come here and trample over God's green earth with your cars and your parking lots and your buildings and your pollution and your energy-sucking, resource-chomping tourists!"

"But it's private property, Mr. Wheeler," Jenna said softly. "Just like yours."

At that last remark, Boyce's own eyebrows shot up along with, apparently, his blood pressure. "What I've done with my land is nothing compared to what you've done to yours!"

Brit looked around the dilapidated room with its magnificent view, and everything fell into place. "I think I finally understand," he said.

"What? What are you talking about?"

Brit glanced at Jenna before continuing. "You inherited this estate, and a hell of a lot of other valuable property. Didn't work a day to earn it, but you reap the benefits all right." He motioned toward the huge picture window behind Boyce's desk. "Nobody else has had that particular view for over a century—just your family, and you."

Boyce stood up abruptly, rigid with fury. "What of it? What does that have to do with anything?"

Jenna picked up on Brit's train of thought. "It has everything to do with it. You didn't mind The Grove when it was rundown and abandoned." She pointedly looked around the room. "You could commiserate then. But my grandfather worked his whole career to be able to bring it back to life for others to enjoy…and *that* you just can't stomach. Perhaps because you're not willing to do the same. Maybe you just don't want to share what you've been given."

Boyce inhaled sharply. "My reasons for what I choose to do, or not do, are my own. But I'll tell you this. The Grove should never have opened in the first place. They should have taken a hint from the name 'Sinner's Grove.' It was a blight on nature from the beginning." He stood up and gazed out his window. "My grandparents loathed the idea of your quote unquote 'retreat.' People wandering around the woods, onto our property. Making noise. Trampling. Scaring the birds and the wildlife. I'm just glad my grandfather didn't have to endure it for long, God rest his soul."

"If your family felt The Grove was such an eyesore, why didn't you just sell out and move someplace else?" Brit asked.

Boyce glowered at them. "Oh, your people would have liked that, wouldn't they? It was bad enough my grandmother had to—" He paused, as if he'd already said too much. "Never mind. Let's just say I will never, never desecrate this land like you did yours." He gestured around the room with his claw-like hand. "My grandmother never should have rebuilt this place after the earthquake. When I go, I've told my niece I want this monstrosity bulldozed. And if I could, I'd do the same for The Grove. Ashes to ashes. Dust to dust." The old man was breathing rapidly now. "I can't be responsible for my actions, or anybody else's actions where the end justifies the means." He paused again, working to get himself under control. Then, as if he'd flipped an internal switch, his voice audibly calmed. "Of course, I'd never break the law, you understand." He sat down again, his expression once again benign; only his eyes reflected how angry he really was.

A series of brisk knocks broke the tense silence; all

eyes turned as the door to the study opened and Mrs. Reynolds walked in.

"Excuse me, Mr. Wheeler. Mr. Dorman and the others have arrived for your luncheon meeting. I have sent them to the back veranda per your request."

"Tell them I'll be there momentarily," Boyce told his housekeeper, who nodded and left.

"Planning your next attack against The Grove?" Brit asked, earning a frown from Jenna for his sarcasm.

"I'm sure you'd love to know," Boyce said with a Cheshire-cat grin that looked macabre on his wrinkled face. He rose from his desk and walked toward them. "I'm sorry we'll have to forego refreshments. Another time perhaps." He looked Brit in the eye, his voice brittle but filled with conviction. "You'll find neither Ralph Dorman nor I scare easily, Mr. Maguire. Now if you don't mind, I have a meeting to attend."

Brit was thoughtful as they walked back to his car. Boyce seemed both fanatical and measured; the two characteristics didn't seem to mesh.

"I think we were just thrown out," Jenna mused. "Mind telling me what we accomplished?"

"Not much," Brit admitted. "But it always pays to know your enemy." He concentrated on pulling out of the driveway before continuing. "Did you see how wigged out he got? I don't think there's any line he wouldn't cross, whether it broke the law or not."

"It was kind of scary. The guy is definitely teetering

on the edge." She looked back at the ramshackle old house. "And yet he seems to be in control as well. I wonder what that meeting was all about?"

"SPEAR business, no doubt. That means it can't be good news for us." He left it at that as he turned onto the main road leading to Bellam's Cove.

Jenna looked surprised. "I thought we were going to the storage facility."

"Remember, I promised you lunch, sweetheart, and I'm going to treat you to the best fish and chips this side of London." He noticed she didn't react to his endearment, choosing instead to ignore him and drink in the rolling landscape along the way. They spent the rest of the trip in companionable silence, stopping at Addie's Eatery for her famous lunch special. Over fresh cod fried in the lightest of batters, served up with mouthwatering sweet potato fries, Brit filled Jenna in on the difficulties The Grove Center Historic Trust had faced in its quest to open the new art complex. She understood enough to ask the right questions and seemed genuinely interested in the answers. Just as they were getting ready to leave, Jenna's cell phone rang.

"Oh. Hey, Declan." Jenna looked at Brit, said "Excuse me," and walked away from the table, still talking on the phone. At one point she laughed, the sound bouncing back to slap him in the face.

Damn. He was an idiot. Of course she'd be seeing somebody. Or someone would be interested in her. What did he think—she'd been pining for him all these years? He certainly hadn't pined for her. Much.

He paid the bill and stepped outside to wait for her, vowing not to mention the call—a vow that lasted all of two minutes.

"Declan?" he asked when she finally joined him at the car.

"Declan O'Connor. He's a reporter for Channel Seven. He taught a class at Saylor this past semester."

"Good friend of yours?"

Jenna shrugged. "Sort of."

"But…he'd like to be a better friend, is that it?"

"Something like that."

"Ah." Brit let the subject drop. He'd never been a glutton for punishment, and it was downright painful thinking of her with another man. But how many signs did he need to tell him that he and Jenna weren't meant to be together?

On the way back to The Grove they talked of everyday matters and Brit remembered how easy she'd been to talk to. That's it. Maybe they were just meant to be buddies. Maybe he could stay friends with a woman he wanted to strip naked whenever he saw her.

Right. And maybe the 49ers would all wear pantyhose during their next game.

Just inside the main entrance, Brit took the road leading to the meadow where all the vandalism had taken place. By now, the buildings were almost back to their original, pristine condition. He parked next to the museum building and waited for Jenna's reaction. It didn't take long.

"Wait a minute. I thought the artwork was secure. Are you telling me the jerks who poured paint all over this building could just as easily have ruined a multi-million-dollar art collection by walking inside?"

"Not exactly." Brit shot Jenna a lazy grin. He led her through the public area of the building and down a hallway before unlocking a door marked "storage." Once they were inside, the door closed soundlessly behind them. Situated in front of an interior door was something that looked like an ATM machine. Instead of a keypad, however, it had a flat translucent tabletop that resembled a slide viewer.

"Watch and learn," Brit said. He placed his broad hands palm down on the screen. An electronic voice said, "Welcome, Mr. Maguire."

"Jenna Bergstrom. Guest. Grove 949." He motioned for Jenna to put her hands down on the screen.

"Guest approved," the voice replied. After an audible *click*, the vault-like interior door swung open.

Jenna tossed Brit a puzzled look. "How does it know to accept me? Am I part of a database?"

"You are now. But the code tells the system you're acceptable. Without it, the program knows something's not right and it won't open."

"I'm impressed," she said. "Should I call you Ali Baba?"

He nodded. "Sounds about right. Wait 'til you see the treasure."

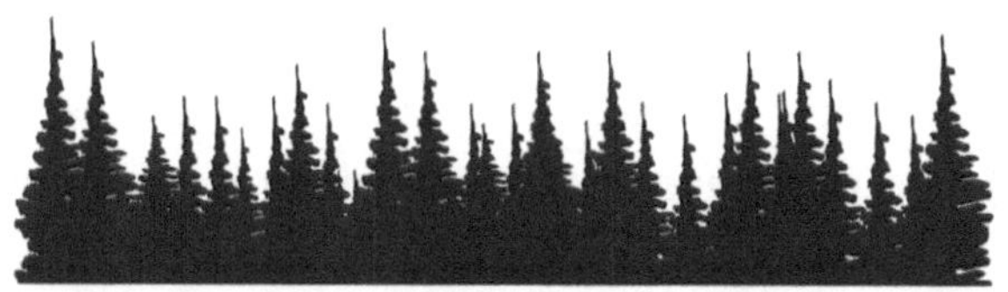

Chapter Twelve

With mounting anticipation, Jenna let Brit lead her through the doorway of the inner chamber.

The room they entered was pitch black until Brit said the words "Lighting, please." At once the storage area was bathed in a soft, filtered light.

Wow. Jenna stood transfixed as row after row of shelves, slots, and drawers were revealed. *An art historian's dream.* She shivered and rubbed her arms.

"The temperature is kept at sixty degrees for the paintings," he explained.

"No. It's just...well, it's straight out of Indiana Jones," she said, a hint of wonder coloring her voice. "I mean it's all right here, but who would ever think...?"

"Pretty amazing, I know. The artwork was stored elsewhere for decades, and when we got the go-ahead for the project, this fireproof storage room was the first structure we built. Ethan had the whole inventory moved over just as it had been originally stored, and once it was secure we added the rest of the museum around it."

"How did Ethan afford this? I know he's always done some art consulting on the side, but this…it must have cost a fortune."

Brit looked around. "You're right, it's not cheap. But it's protecting a fortune, so it's worth it. Some of our investors have deep pockets, and some of them, I'll admit, are more than a little mysterious. It took him a long time to build the consortium, otherwise the center would have been built years ago. But you know Ethan. He says it will all come together 'in due time.'"

Jenna nodded. "Sounds like him." She made her way down the softly lit aisle, transfixed as she reverently touched the meticulously labeled shelves. The artifacts —everything from paintings and sculptures to woven fabric and furniture pieces—were carefully stored according to the year they were created. Her steps faltered and she paused.

Brit walked up behind her and gently clasped her shoulders. "What's wrong?" he asked.

She looked back at him, her eyes glistening with tears. "Da told me stories about this collection when I was little." she explained. "I can't believe it's really, truly here. His legacy."

"Your legacy."

"No," she whispered. "Not mine."

"What do you mean?"

"Look, it's…it's not important." She looked around the room in an effort to compose herself. He gazed at her for a moment longer and when she finally met his eyes he nodded slightly and gave her shoulder a sympathetic squeeze. It fortified her. "Let's see if we can find those commentaries Ethan talked about." She scanned the storage area marked 1905. "This might be it," she said finally, reaching for a book-shaped object encased in a soft felt covering. "Yep." A quick scan of the shelves found the next several years' editions as well.

After collecting the books she needed, Jenna stopped to flip through several canvases stored vertically in the shelf above her. They were filed alphabetically by artist. "Look, here's a Winterfeld!" she cried, pulling out a nude of a voluptuous woman.

Brit was looking at the bronze bust of a young man; he turned to see Jenna's discovery. "He hit it big in the Roaring Twenties, didn't he?"

"Yes, but he killed himself when the Depression wiped out the market for his work."

"Too bad. It's probably worth a gold mine or two today."

"Yes, he—ouch!" Jenna cried out and clutched her hand.

"Here, let me see." Brit moved closer and reached for her hand. Her finger was bleeding copiously.

"I must have cut it on the stretcher," she muttered, wincing as it began to sting. "Good thing I've had a tetanus shot." She looked at her slender hand encased in his, and felt...protected. Cared for. That was the wonderful part of being with someone strong, she thought.

Brit reached into his back pocket for a handkerchief, and carefully, tenderly, secured it around the wound. "It's clean," he said quietly.

Jenna looked at him, her eyes widening as she recognized the stark hunger etched across his face, the closeness of his body, the intense need she had to press against him.

"This isn't a good idea," she whispered.

"Yeah, I know," he said. Then he slowly, deliberately wrapped a hand around her nape and took her mouth.

She moaned softly, opening to his entreaty, and he took the kiss deeper, cradling her injured hand against his chest as he molded her body to his. God, he felt good. Perfect, in fact. She lost herself for a few moments longer before summoning the strength to step back from him.

"I can't do this," she said.

Brit was having trouble shifting gears. "What?"

"I said I can't do this." Her voice was slightly stronger now. Staring at him, she held her ground.

"Why not?"

"For starters, I don't think your lady friend is into sharing." She turned from him, but he took her by the shoulders.

"Look at me, Jenna," he said gruffly, waiting until she complied. "Tori is not my lady friend, as you put it. My relationship with her isn't what you think it is."

Jenna looked at him with surprise. "Are you saying you haven't slept with her?"

He paused. "No, I'm not saying that exactly, but really, she means nothing—"

"Oh," Jenna said, her eyes widening. "So you just

sleep with women who mean nothing to you." She nodded. "I get it. You see, you want, you take. Must be nice."

Brit's eyes glittered. "That's a cheap shot—especially coming from you."

Jenna felt the needle-sharp stab of his rebuke. She had no comeback because, damn it, he was right. Seven years ago, she had led him to believe their budding relationship was more than a weekend fling. She'd gone back to New York, leaving him to think she'd tie up loose ends and return. Then she'd left him hanging without a word of explanation.

"You're right. I'm sorry. As you said before, our personal lives should be off each other's radar." Her voice was deadly calm now. "I think we ought to go." She turned to leave again and this time he didn't stop her.

She had just reached the door when his voice called from behind her. "Wait. I'd like to show you something." He led her to the far end of an aisle where a huge painting was stored apart from the other artwork. Its protective cover had recently been removed and currently a sheet was draped over part of it. "Ethan showed me this the last time we were here." He drew off the sheet to reveal a life-sized portrait of Amelia Starling and August Wolff.

Jenna let out a small gasp. They were gorgeous. She bent to look at the signature. *Luzio Furlan.* "Dani's great-grandfather," she murmured. In the painting, Lia appeared to be in her late forties to early fifties, Gus a decade older. They were standing in front of the Great

House. They looked centered, vital, and very much in love.

"Gus and Lia had something," Brit said. "They belonged together."

Jenna stood contemplating the portrait for several minutes. Gus and Lia did belong together. Theirs was a love story for the ages. What would she give to have the same thing with Brit? She turned back to him. "I don't know where I belong or with whom," she began. "As for The Grove, the only thing I'm sure of is that right now Ethan…Da…needs me. Where that leads, or where that leaves us, I haven't a clue. I can only take it one day at a time."

Brit nodded. "I couldn't agree more. But add this to the mix." With those words he gathered her in and took her lips in another searing kiss—hard, possessive, and full of unbridled lust.

Jenna responded naturally, completely. It took her last shred of willpower to finally break away. When she opened her eyes, she saw that he was as shell-shocked as she.

"Let's go," he said.

They didn't speak on the short drive back to the Great House. They'd pulled around the back to their usual parking space when Brit's cell phone rang. He checked the screen and answered.

"Hey, Sherrie. What's up?" As he listened, his expression turned somber. "Jesus Christ. Was Ethan hurt?"

"What's happened?" Jenna cried.

"Just a minute, we're almost at the office." Brit

swung the Pilot around and headed back to the construction trailer. He turned to her. "Wasn't Don bringing Ethan home from the library today?"

Fear surging through her, Jenna nodded. "That's what he told me. Why? What's going on?"

"Don's been in a car accident," he said, careening into his allotted parking space and slamming the car door before heading up the office steps. Jenna followed suit and they both met Sherrie, who rushed out crying hysterically. Brit took her in his arms. "It's okay, honey. He's strong. He's going to be okay." He gently took her by the shoulders to calm her down. "Now tell me what happened."

"Ethan? Did they say anything about Ethan?" Jenna caught Sherrie by the arm. She could feel her own hysteria amping up.

"I don't know. I don't know. They only mentioned Don. They said he went down an embankment," Sherrie said, gulping between sobs. "Out on Fifty-Seven. Thank God, some…somebody saw the skid marks and stopped to check. His truck was at the b-bottom of the hill. They've taken him to the hospital in Bellam's Cove. And Brit? They're saying alcohol was involved!"

"No way," Brit said, his jaw clenched. "No fucking way."

"I know, I know," Sherrie whimpered. "I told them it wasn't possible." She looked at him with her heart in her eyes. "They don't know if he's going to make it!"

"Oh, my God," Jenna whispered. She met Brit's eyes. "We've got to find out about Da." She pulled out her cell, started to punch in her grandfather's number, and stopped halfway. "What am I doing? He never has his cell nearby." She started running down the hill toward his cottage. "I'll call you if he's there," she called over her shoulder.

Within minutes Jenna was pounding on her grandfather's door.

No answer. She peered into the window and saw no activity. "No, please, no," she whispered. She ran back up to where Brit was still comforting Sherrie while talking on the phone. She caught his eye and shook her head. Tears began to fall.

"Yeah, Jack? Don's been in an accident and I need you to take over. Sherrie and I are headed over to Bellam's Cove Hospital now...Right...Call my cell if anything comes up. I'll keep you posted...Hey, have you seen Ethan today?...What? Okay, thanks, man." He put the phone away and gave Jenna a nod. "Jack says he saw him during the lunch hour playing cards with Kyle on the deck of the bunkhouse. Ethan told him he'd decided to work at home today."

Still heaving from her run, Jenna leaned forward with her hands on her knees. She took a minute to catch her breath and then looked up at the sky. "Thank you, God," she uttered.

"We need to go right now," Sherrie announced in a barely controlled voice. "I'll drive. Just let me get my purse." Looking determined, she hurried back to the office.

"I'll ride with her, make sure she's okay," Jenna said.

"Thanks, I appreciate it."

"You know, Da could have been in that car, Brit. Something could have happened to him." Jenna crossed her arms to keep her anxiety in check.

"Yeah. Something could have happened. As you said, thank God it didn't, at least to him. But Don… God *damn* it! I swear, if this turns out to be anything but an accident…" Brit didn't finish the sentence, but the anguish on his face said it all.

Something could have happened. The accident had to be just that—an accident, right? It was just a coincidence that all these other bad things had happened to Brit and his crew. It had to be.

Except that Jenna's gut told her something entirely different. She hoped she was wrong, but if she wasn't, then no one was safe at The Grove.

Anger started brewing inside her. She took several deep breaths to relax herself. Because if somebody was truly out to harm anyone, including her grandfather, the problem wouldn't be restraining Brit. It would be restraining *her*.

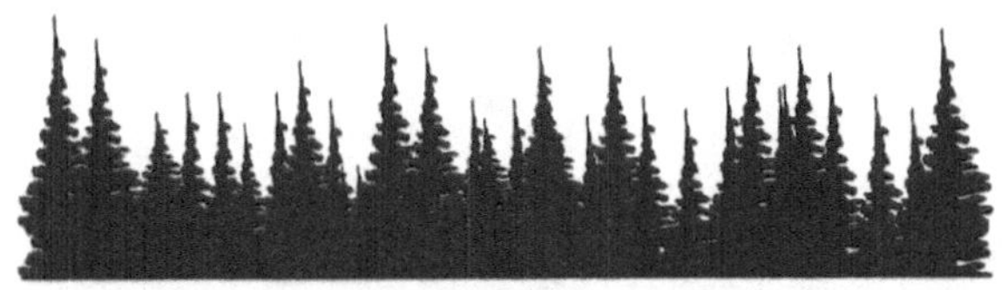

Chapter Thirteen

This is *not* a good habit to get into, Jenna thought as she sat once again in the waiting room of an ER. She watched helplessly as Brit paced back and forth, waiting for news about his foreman. Finally the surgeon appeared, looking solemn and tired.

"How is he?" Sherrie asked, jumping up from her seat next to Jenna. When the doctor hesitated, she added, "He's my partner. We live together. I'm on his emergency form."

"Hello. I'm Dr. Janek." The man smiled briefly at the three of them. "Mr. Rodriguez had some internal bleeding, but he came through surgery with no complications. He's not out of the woods yet, however. We have to give him some time."

"Excuse me," Brit said abruptly. "He's my foreman. Was he conscious at all when they brought him in? Did he say what happened? There's just no way he would have been drinking. He—"

"He had no alcohol in his system, although I understand there was plenty of it on the front of his shirt and around his mouth. He apparently did try to say something at the scene, which I believe one of the EMTs wrote down after they stabilized him. A detective was here earlier. You'll have to talk to him about that."

"When will he wake up?" Sherrie asked.

"The anesthesia from the surgery will wear off in another hour or so, but there's no telling when he'll regain full consciousness. He's severely concussed and the body tends to reserve its energy when that happens. When he's able to receive visitors, I'll let you know. Until then we'll just have to wait and see. If you'll excuse me…" The physician left the group, pulling off his surgical cap as he walked resolutely down the hall.

At that moment Gabe de la Torre entered the waiting room. "How's Don doing?" he asked the group. "By the time I got here he was just heading into surgery. Is he awake yet?"

Brit didn't waste a minute. "No, but the doctor said Don said something when the ambulance got there. Do you know what it was?"

Rather than answer, Gabe gestured down the hall. "Come on, let's get something to drink in the cafeteria and sort this out."

Brit was about to retort when Jenna put a gentle hand on his forearm. "He's right, Brit. We all need to calm down a little bit. Let's start with the facts."

Brit glanced at her, took a deep breath, and nodded. "Yeah, okay."

After they'd gotten coffee and sat down, Gabe

pulled out his notepad. "I just talked with the first responders. It looks like Don went off Highway Fifty-Seven between eleven thirty and three in the afternoon. A driver noticed the skid marks at three ten and called 911. When the EMTs reached Don, they smelled alcohol."

Sherrie shook her head. "Impossible."

Gabe looked at her with a touch of sympathy and continued. "He was barely breathing, but they stabilized him. He did mention something before he lost consciousness…" Here Gabe flipped the page over and read, "Ran off road."

"'Ran off road?' That's obvious," Brit said. "He was telling them that somebody ran him off the road."

"Or that *he* ran off the road," Gabe countered. "Look, once we've taken evidence from the scene, we'll see what's what. And it may be that we'll have to wait for him to wake up and tell us what happened."

"I have a pretty good idea what happened, Gabe."

"What are you saying?" Gabe's question was sharp and full of warning.

Brit looked to her; oddly flattered, Jenna nodded back, encouraging him to go on. She only hoped he wasn't going to get a tongue-lashing from Gabe for sticking his nose where it didn't belong, because there was no way Brit would put up with it.

"Jenna and I went to see Boyce Wheeler earlier this afternoon," he began.

Gabe glanced at Jenna, his eyes hooded. "I don't think I'm going to like this."

"It was a friendly conversation, for the most part,"

Jenna explained. "Boyce even talked to me about my grandmother."

Gabe leaned back in his chair, skepticism apparent in every gesture. "So, what, you two were just in the neighborhood? Just wantin' to chew the fat with your kindly old next-door neighbor?"

"You know damn well why I went over there, Gabe. Look, don't blame Jenna. I dragged her along. And I'm glad she came. She saw what a loose cannon he is. He admitted he doesn't want The Grove to open, and I think he'd do whatever it takes to reach that goal."

"Even attempt murder? Come on."

"Okay, maybe he didn't do it himself, but I'd bet my last dollar he ordered it done. Somehow he must have found out that Ethan was going to be in that car, and—"

Gabe held up his hand. "Wait a minute, you're losing me, here. The paramedics said Don was alone in the car. What does Ethan have to do with it?"

"Thank God nothing, at least this time around. Look, it's a long story. Suffice to say Ethan's health and well-being is key to the re-opening of The Grove. Something happens to him, we've got problems you can't even imagine. Boyce Wheeler must know that, and so does Ralph Dorman. The two were headed into a meeting when we left."

Gabe looked at Jenna. "You buying any of this?"

Jenna shrugged. "Boyce didn't admit to anything, but Brit's right. He was almost foaming at the mouth, he was so set against The Grove."

Gabe jotted some notes down on his ever-present

pad. "Okay, I'll follow up with this. There's still no hard evidence that this was anything other than an unfortunate accident. But if the signs do point in another direction, you two may end up providing the very alibi SPEAR, or at least Wheeler, needs to beat the rap."

Brit snorted. "Just our luck."

Gabe looked down at the cell phone that was clipped to his waist; apparently it was vibrating. He noted the number. "Sorry, I've got to run," he said, standing up to leave.

Brit reached for his sleeve. "That bit about the alcohol? Like Sherrie said, it doesn't make sense. Don used to have a problem, but I've known him for ten years and he's been sober at least that long."

"Brit's right," Sherrie said. "We don't keep anything alcoholic in our house. Don wouldn't drink. He just wouldn't."

"It's suspicious, I admit. The EMTs said his shirt was soaked and there was residue in his mouth; they also found an empty bottle of Jim Beam in the car. But none turned up in his system."

"You took fingerprints, I hope."

Gabe's look narrowed. "Telling me how to do my job again, Maguire?"

"You know this whole thing stinks to high heaven, and I'm not talkin' about cheap whiskey." Brit leaned across the table. "These assholes are getting serious, Gabe."

"I know...Christ, I know. Which is all the more reason for you folks to take it easy and don't go looking for trouble. Watch each other's backs." He clasped Brit's shoulder. "We'll get to the bottom of all this, I promise." Gabe glanced at Sherrie and Jenna as he turned to leave. "Ladies."

Gabe had almost reached the entrance to the cafeteria when Tori swept by him, making a beeline for Brit.

"Oh, my God, I got over here as fast as I could. I've been looking all over for you. How is he? Is he going to be okay?"

Brit shot Jenna a look, his expression shuttered. "We don't know yet. We're waiting for him to wake up."

"I'm glad I got here, then, to keep you company." Tori settled herself in the chair that Gabe had vacated, seemingly oblivious to the looks being exchanged at the table.

"I'm glad you're here, too," Sherrie said. "I've got to finish up at the office and call Don's sister in Minneapolis. I'll return as soon as I can, Brit, but if you get any news before then, you call, okay? I'm talking the minute you hear something!" She gathered her purse and the sweater she'd laid on the back of her chair. Jenna noticed her hands were shaking.

"Would you mind giving me a ride back to The Grove, Sherrie? I'd be happy to drive," Jenna said, glancing at Brit. "I have to get back and check on my grandfather anyway."

"Give my love to the professor," Tori said before turning to Brit. "You look beat, honey. I'm going to get some coffee. You want another cup?" Brit watched Jenna as she got up to leave.

"No, thanks," he said.

Jenna and Sherrie headed for the exit. As Tori walked over to the coffee station, Brit called out, "Jenna."

With an "I'll meet you in the car," Sherrie continued walking outside while Jenna paused.

"Look, about earlier—" Brit started.

Jenna looked down at her finger, which was still bandaged with his handkerchief. "Oh, sorry," she said, unwrapping it. "Oh, yuck, it's a mess. I'll clean it for you."

"That's not what I meant," Brit said, irritation lacing his voice.

"Hey, gotta go."

"This isn't the end of it, you know." The determined look on Brit's face told her he was dead serious —and he wasn't talking about the problems with SPEAR.

Jenna gazed at him and felt a catch in her throat. She hid her emotions with a half-smile. "Like the song says, you can't always get what you want." She felt him watching her as she hurried out to meet Sherrie in the parking lot.

"You sure you don't want to stay here?" Jenna asked Sherrie, who was already behind the wheel. "Maybe I can tie off some loose ends in the office for you?"

"No, thanks. I'd go insane just waiting. I need to be doing something." Despite her raw emotions, Sherrie seemed calm enough to drive. "You think Don's going to be all right?" She posed the question anxiously while Jenna buckled up.

Jenna nodded. "I don't know him all that well, but he seems like a pretty tough cookie to me."

Sherrie chuckled as she dug in her purse for another tissue. "Oh, Don's a hard-headed son of a gun, all right."

"Then there's every reason to believe he'll get through this." Jenna watched as Sherrie took a deep breath and pulled herself together. "And I'm sure the police will get to the bottom of it," she added. "Gabe seems like he's very, very good at what he does. I like him."

Sherrie looked surprised. "Don't tell me you've got an eye for Gabe? I could have sworn you and Brit were…you know."

Jenna felt her face redden. "Brit and me? You're kidding, right?"

"Girl, I may be close to sixty, but I've still got *some* hormones left. There's a regular power surge between you two."

"You sure you're not talking about Tori?" Jenna asked only half in jest. "They seem to be… um…together."

Sherrie chuckled. Talking about her boss's love life was apparently a good distraction. "That's what Tori would have everybody believe, but sayin' it's so doesn't make it so."

Jenna looked out the window. "It's none of my business anyway."

"Poppycock," Sherrie said, patting her hand. "The

current's flowing in both directions. He wants you in a mighty big way."

"Yes, well, I'm not too keen on being electrocuted."

"Oh, I imagine that boy could do some pretty shocking things. Don says he fell in love years ago, but was hung out to dry, which is why he's a bit gun shy. But you're different."

"I'm not so sure about that," Jenna murmured. She didn't dare pursue that line of conversation. As they fell silent, she willed herself to put her feelings for Brit aside; they were simply too confusing at the moment.

Instead, she focused on the events of the past few days. If Don's so-called accident really was a deliberate act, that meant whoever had it in for The Grove was willing to cross any line to stop the project. But it didn't make sense. What would hurting Don accomplish? Everyone who knew Brit Maguire knew he'd find a way to keep going.

But Da might have been in that car. He was the driving force behind the project and his well-being was critical to its success. If he died now, both the reality and the spirit of The Grove would die with him. Maybe that's why he was so adamant about Jenna understanding what he was trying to accomplish. She felt tears begin to pool and hastily wiped them away. This wasn't an interlude between one phase of her life and the next. It wasn't a pleasant summer spent in the company of her dwindling family. Now she understood. This was a matter of life and death.

Chapter Fourteen

Several days later, Jenna stood in the doorway of the construction office, not wanting to intrude as she watched Sherrie reach for another tissue and wipe her eyes. Brit's office manager turned slightly and saw her.

"Sorry," Sherrie said, smiling through her tears. "Can't seem to stop the waterworks."

Jenna walked over and put her arm around her friend. "What's the latest?"

"Don's still in a coma and the doctors don't know when he'll wake up," she said, her voice wavering. "They moved him to a rehab hospital in Bellam's Cove, so we've just got to wait it out."

"And that's the hardest part." Jenna gave Sherrie a squeeze. "Patience is a virtue, but it's also a pain in the butt."

Sherrie laughed. "You got that right. Now, what can I do for you?"

"I just wanted to see how Kyle and Parker are doing

—maybe hear what the crew thinks of them, if you've heard anything."

"The boys seem to be holding their own," Sherrie said. "The regulars call them the 'grunts'—boy, does the crew love having somebody else do the scut work! I haven't heard any complaints, other than you've gotta tell them precisely what to do. Neither of them are what I'd call 'self-starters.' Your brother, though, he seems willing to do whatever's needed. And he's great with your granddad."

"I know. That's one of the bright lights in all this. Jason seems to be taking a load off Da's plate, which needed to happen. I worry about Da taking on too much."

Sherrie nodded. "I'll tell you who else I'm worried about these days, and that's Brit. Talk about a self-starter."

"What *doesn't* he do?" Jenna asked in exasperation. "I hardly ever see the guy, and we're living in the same house. Granted, it's a huge house, but still."

"Tell me about it. He's filling Don's shoes as well as his own, trying to keep the crew moving at the same pace, but it's hard. I don't know when he has time to eat, much less think."

"Plus he's annoyed that Dani and I are working on site. He'd much prefer having the collection safely stored someplace else."

Sherrie gave Jenna a look that seemed to be filled with layers. "He never worried about the artwork before you came on board, and I don't think he's worried about it now. He wants you to be safe. End of story."

Jenna felt her face redden and turned away. "Uh, well, speaking of which, I'm headed over there now to meet Dani, if anybody asks."

Jenna walked determinedly toward the museum building, thoughts of Brit stuck in her head. Was Sherrie right about his special concern for her? Brit had implied as much the night she'd moved into the Great House, but she'd told herself he was worried about everyone, not just her. The two of them rarely even spoke to one another other, but when they did... when they did, she sometimes caught him looking at her with such...intensity. And what's worse, she found herself looking at him the same way. She shivered involuntarily—a phenomenon that seemed to have increased since she'd moved to The Grove.

Shaking off her thoughts, she let herself into the building and shut the door behind her. Regardless of Brit's fears, she'd come to enjoy collaborating with Dani and working up close and personal with the collection. They'd already developed a prototype that could be used to create The Grove's year-by-year artists' exhibit. Focusing on the retreat's first year, they'd sketched out profiles of the original resident artists, using the commentaries and other sources to bring them to life.

"You'll love this," Jenna said to Dani later that morning. She'd uncovered an entry written by the watercolorist Marcus Edelman about fellow artist George Winterfeld.

"He's talking about Winterfeld's nudes. 'They're too abstract,' he says. 'I know your *Nude Study #14* is supposed to represent the ripe fecundity of the archetypal female, but damnation, man, she looks absolutely nothing like Mandy, who, as we all know, is every *pasha's* ideal *houri*. Given the choice, what red-blooded man would choose to go to bed with a dimpled lump like yours?'"

"Whoa, that Mandy must have been something," Dani said, grinning.

"She's mentioned a number of times in the first year's commentaries. I gather she was the resident life studies model."

Jenna's new security clearance gave her access to the pieces that would eventually be shown to the public. Using the 1947 manifest, she and Dani successfully located most of the first year's selections. There were a few glitches, however. Two works created during that period weren't on site. One, a chalice made by the ultimately world-renowned glassblower Frieda Mallock, was listed as "loaned to Smithsonian Museum." The other, a pair of bronze figures depicting Persephone and Hades, created by the iconoclastic sculptor Mason Tanner, had apparently been "loaned to family." Despite his premature and bizarre departure, the photographer Peter Raines had also left behind a contribution—several artistic photos of Lia. Unfortunately, the negatives for those photos were missing as well. Jenna passed the information along to Dani, whose job it was to track down the missing pieces and see about reclaiming them. They would deal with the lost negatives later.

To get some perspective on her grandfather's heritage, Jenna decided to start at the beginning, with the matriarch Lia Wolff herself. As the daughter of a well-connected family in New York City, she had displayed a talent and a passion for painting at a very young age. A disastrous first marriage found her heading west for a whole new life—even sporting a new last name, "Starling," which became her professional moniker. That life had ultimately brought her together with Klondike King August Wolff.

As she read the accounts of her family's forebears, Jenna recalled the many "Gus and Lia" stories she'd heard from summers past. Her grandfather would always end such tales with, "Your great-great-grandmother was one of a kind, just like you." Jenna remembered being absurdly pleased whenever he'd told her that because, like Lia, she too had developed a passion for art early on. She'd felt a strong connection. Even now, knowing she wasn't related to Lia biologically, Jenna was surprised to find she still took pride in the comparison.

Since she was researching Lia extensively, Jenna took charge of organizing the artist's impressive body of work. Those stored pieces would eventually be displayed in the special Amelia Starling Wolff Gallery within the museum.

The collection ranged from childhood sketches and art school projects to studies of the poor children of New York City's Mulberry Street and the hard-working immigrants of San Francisco's Chinatown. There were also extensive sketches and paintings created during her worldwide tour with August Wolff in 1903. In addition to Lia's commissioned work, some of which Jenna hoped to procure for the exhibit, the artist's greatest fame had come from her magnificent study of individuals touched by the Great Earthquake of 1906, and later, returning soldiers from World War One.

The manifest listed a few works by Lia on loan, much as it had shown for the first year artists Mallock and Tanner. But the commentary for 1906 had produced an intriguing bonus: talk of a unique painting by Lia that was completely different in style from all the others. Jenna made a note to go through the paintings in the storage facility to see if it had inadvertently been left off the manifest.

After several days of delving into the lives of the Wolffs, Jenna felt in her bones that Lia and Gus had been deeply in love with one another, and had created a daughter out of that love. That daughter in turn had created other children, one of whom had grown up to be her grandfather. She still had much to learn before she could attempt to answer her grandfather's questions, but an idea took root and began to grow.

There was a story here, a story of struggle and accomplishment, of greatness and giving. And sadness, too. It was her family's story, if not her own. Did she have the right to tell it? Her pulse quickened as she mulled the possibilities. It occurred to her that maybe she *was* connected. Maybe not by blood, but by spirit, passion, and yes, love. So much love.

Perhaps that was enough.

Feeling better than she had in a long time, Jenna hummed a little tune as she locked up her office and headed back to the Great House on the hill. The sun was nearing the horizon; it was the time of day artists and photographers referred to as the "golden hour."

The construction site was virtually deserted; most of the workers had no doubt left for the day. But Jenna heard insistent hammering and decided to investigate. Following the sound, she headed down one of the paths that led away from the public buildings and deeper into the grove, eventually coming upon one of the renovated artist's cottages set in a clearing. A man was perched on the roof, hammering, while another stood on a ladder handing shingles up as needed. Jenna drew closer and saw the sun's final rays glinting off Brit's hair and the sweat on his back as he swung the hammer in hard, sure strokes. She swallowed and once again tried to fight her feelings for him, knowing it was a losing battle. She noticed belatedly that Kyle was handing materials up to Brit.

"Hey," she called up. "Getting kind of late. Sure you can see what you're doing up there?"

Kyle immediately jumped off the ladder and trotted over to Jenna. From her experience with him at the Saylor Academy, she knew Kyle had problems gauging the personal space of others. It had never bothered her before, but here, in this setting, she found she had to fight the urge to step back from the young man's imposing bulk.

"Hello, Ms. Bergstrom," Kyle said. "I've been meaning to talk to you." He leaned in. "About what happened between us."

Jenna couldn't help it. She stepped discreetly back. "Water under the bridge, Mr. Summers." She gestured up at Brit. "How are you liking it here?"

Kyle followed her eyes up to Brit, who had stopped hammering and was looking down at them. Never had she been so happy that someone else was near. Especially Brit.

"Oh. Oh, sorry, Boss. Got distracted." Kyle trotted back toward the ladder, but Brit waved him off and climbed down instead.

"I can see why," Brit said, walking up to them. "Ms. Bergstrom," he acknowledged with a subtle smile. He pulled off his work gloves and stuffed them in his back pocket before grabbing a shirt that had been hung carelessly on a tree branch. "Something we can do for you?"

"No. I was just headed back and I heard the hammering. I thought it was kind of late to be working, is all."

"Well, your timing is perfect. Mr. Summers here is going to clean up the job site and I've got to change before heading over to visit Don. I'll give you a ride."

Jenna caught the unhappy look Kyle shot Brit. She was about to walk back toward the main path when Kyle touched her shoulder. "I really do need to talk to you," he said.

Brit caught the interplay and must have noticed

Jenna's discomfort. "Not tonight, son. Maybe tomorrow."

As they headed back toward Brit's Pilot, Jenna thanked Brit for taking on the boys. "And I really appreciate you having Jason work directly with Ethan," she said. "He's been a great help already."

"Not a problem. What's the story on Kyle and Parker?"

"Jason's been kind of a mentor to them, if you can believe that. They're both good kids. Both have issues. Parker's kind of a loner, and Kyle—well, let's just say Kyle has difficulty with boundaries. And I think they both suffer from a bit of 'affluenza.'"

"'Affluenza'? What's that?"

"Kids with too much money and too little supervision."

"Ah. So, what does Kyle want to talk to you about?"

"Nothing, really. He…he got out of line on the last day of school. I had to call Security."

Brit stopped in his tracks. "What? Then why on earth is he working here?"

"It wasn't my idea," Jenna explained. "Jason had asked Ethan about it long before school let out and you all arranged it."

"Well, I can just as easily unarrange it. You don't need to feel uncomfortable around him. Just say the word."

Jenna shook her head. "No, it's all right. I really think it was just last-day jitters on Kyle's part. Sometimes kids like him get squirrelly when there's no structure."

They'd reached the car and Brit opened Jenna's door. "What about Parker?"

"Oh, he's a bit of a lost soul, I think. He's quiet but I think the proverbial still waters run deep. He and I had a long talk one afternoon about how much he loves the ocean." She smiled at the memory. "He said he'd like to be either a marine biologist, or a surf bum."

Brit grinned. "Yeah, that pretty much sums up the mind of a seventeen-year-old."

Jenna looked up at him. "The voice of experience, I take it?"

They'd reached the Great House and parked in the back. "I could tell you stories," he said, "but I won't. I'm already late for visiting hours."

"With all you've got going, when do you find time to sleep?" Jenna couldn't help the hint of vexation in her voice. Like Sherrie, she was worried about him, too. The last thing they all needed was for Brit to come down sick from pure exhaustion.

Brit looked at her and raised his eyebrows. "Damn, I knew there was something I forgot to put on the schedule." With that he squeezed her shoulder and headed up the stairs two at a time. In a matter of minutes she heard the shower running.

"You're a good man, Charlie Brown," Jenna murmured as she headed to the kitchen for an evening snack.

Before dropping off to sleep that night, she thought about the date she'd set up with Declan for the following evening. She and the reporter had agreed to meet halfway, in Sausalito, for that steak he'd promised. So why did she feel, deep inside, that she was about to two-time Brit? That was absurd. All day long she'd been driving herself crazy by comparing images of the two men. She simply couldn't allow herself to think that way. She and Brit were housemates, nothing more, and Declan was simply a nice, attractive man who was interested in her. She'd be a fool to second guess the situation. Better to just let fate take its course.

And fate did.

The next evening Declan stood Jenna up for their date. She tried his cell phone several times but got no response. Irritated, she drove back to The Grove and spent the evening watching television, mentally chastising herself because she was more curious about where Brit was than what had happened to Declan. She'd turned on the local news at nine p.m. when she noticed the ticker at the bottom of the screen:

> KTRN news reporter Declan O'Connor
> mugged on way to car; severely beaten.

"Oh my God," Jenna cried, grabbing her purse and car keys and racing out the door.

Chapter Fifteen

Some days just suck, and that's the truth, Brit thought as he finally pulled up to the Great House at eleven thirty that night. For once, the job wasn't to blame. Work on the construction site had gone well, in fact. Aside from Don's absence, the crews were firing on all cylinders. They'd made pure forward progress without having to clean up or fix up any man-made disasters. Slowly but surely The Grove Center for American Art was becoming a reality.

The problem was Jenna. Or rather, the fact that he'd been thinking about her all day. That morning Sherrie had been chatting it up with her, apparently, and learned she was going out with that reporter tonight. Of course Sherrie, with a gleam in her eye, had told Brit all about it as soon as she saw him.

"You'd better act fast if you want to keep that one," she'd advised. "She's a keeper, and you aren't the only one who sees it."

Brit had scoffed at her teasing, but her words had

stuck with him. Like Gorilla Glue. He fought the urge to ask Jenna outright about her date. No way was he going to mention any other men to her. That subject was supposed to be completely off-limits.

Like hell it was.

So he'd gotten through the day, telling himself it was no big deal that she was going to dress up for the guy, that he was going to take her out and probably charm the pants off her. *Don't go there. Redirect.* He gave himself points for not seeing what Tori was up to; instead he and some of the crew members went over to Bellam's Cove for pizza, beer, and pool. So what that he couldn't concentrate and lost twenty bucks on the game? No big deal. Afterward he'd headed over to the rehab center and sat awhile with Don. The staff knew Brit by now and didn't care if he came in late. It didn't matter anyway because Don was still out like a light.

So now it was getting on toward midnight and shouldn't she be home by now? It's not safe for a woman alone, driving at night.

But she's not alone, is she? the jerk voice inside him said. *She's with one good looking, glamorous TV reporter, and she'll probably be with him all...night...long.*

Fuck.

Brit took a shower and sat at his desk, trying to focus on scheduling. Nope. Then he tried paying invoices. Crap. Nope. Finally he turned to playing Minecraft on his computer in survival mode, where you had to build elaborate structures to keep the monsters at bay. But even that didn't keep him occupied for long. Christ, he didn't have to play at building stuff as a defense against the bad guys. These days that was his life.

It was almost one in the morning when Brit gave up the ghost and hit the sack. Obviously Jenna was spending the night with the guy. He didn't want to give a damn about that idea, but he did, and it rankled. Which is why he was still awake when he heard the ring tone that told him he'd gotten a text. He reached for his phone and read:

I'm spending the night at my apartment in the city. Declan was mugged and I'm visiting him in the hospital tomorrow. Jenna

"Whoa," Brit muttered, before texting back:

All right. RU OK? Let me know if I can help in any way.

Jenna texted back:

Fine, just tired. CU tomorrow.

Brit put the phone on his night stand and lay back, staring at the stars he could see outside the large picture windows. A whole series of thoughts careened through his head: Was Jenna with the guy when it happened? How badly was the guy hurt? Did he know his attacker? And finally, the one thought that couldn't be ignored: *Thank God she didn't spend the night with him.*

Lying there, Brit felt like the biggest prick in the

universe. But he couldn't help it. He felt sorry for the guy, but most of all, he felt relieved.

Third time's a charm, Jenna thought, clenching her jaw as she walked into Declan's hospital room the next morning. She'd stopped by the night before, but he'd been sleeping. Thank God his wounds weren't life threatening. He was scheduled to be discharged at eleven a.m. so she'd left him a note saying she'd drop by to see him before he left. Afterward she'd gone back to her apartment, packed more clothes for The Grove, and tried to sleep without much success.

Now Declan was sitting on the side of the bed, dressed and ready to leave. A man in a blue sports jacket stood to one side checking his phone messages while the nurse tried to cajole the Irishman into following hospital protocol.

"I'm not riding in that wheelchair, ma'am. Sorry to disappoint," he said as Jenna walked into the room.

Jenna put on a smile. "Why walk when you can ride?"

Declan gave her a lopsided grin; his face was swollen, sporting two black eyes and a large bandage down his right cheek. "You're kind to pop round and say hello," he said, barely moving his mouth. "You're a sight for sore eyes—literally."

She kept her tone light. "It's the least I can do for someone who was willing to buy me a steak."

"I'm afraid it'll have to be chocolate shakes for a

while." He shrugged his wide shoulders and pointed to his chin.

The man in the sport jacket slipped his phone in his pocket, walked over, and stuck out his hand. "Glen Nebbers, KTRN Public Relations." He handed her a card, then turned to Declan and grinned. "Not bad, old boy."

"Be nice," Declan said. He turned to Jenna. "Glen was going to run interference with the media and then give me a lift home. Any chance I could hitch a ride with you and leave him to deal with the teeming hordes by his own sweet self?"

Jenna smiled, grateful to be of some use. "I would be delighted." She glanced at the nurse hovering nearby. "Your chariot awaits," she said to Declan with mock severity, pointing to the wheelchair.

Declan looked at the nurse, who nodded in a *See, I told you so* kind of way. Jenna rolled him down the hall and out the door, and was surprised to see a group of local reporters and several photographers gathered in their path.

"Do you know who did this?" one reporter called out. "Why were you mugged?" another added.

Jenna heard the *click click click* of several cameras and realized she'd be in the shot.

"News at Eleven," Declan muttered.

The public relations rep turned to the reporters who were following them. "Please give Mr. O'Connor some space here. He needs to get home and rest. I'll be happy to answer your questions."

"Thanks for running interference, Glen," Declan said.

"Not a problem. Now skedaddle while I feed the jackals. I know how insatiable you reporters are." He smiled and turned to Jenna. "Good man," he pointed out.

Leaving the gaggle of media types behind, Jenna and Declan reached Jenna's car and she helped him into the passenger seat. He was quiet as they drove, speaking only to give her directions to his Richmond district flat. Jenna wondered what he was thinking.

"Would you come up for a bit?" he finally asked.

"Of course. I want to make sure you've got everything you need," she said.

They entered Declan's apartment and Jenna was struck by how eclectic it was. The paintings and art objects made it clear that he had traveled all over the world. Jenna noticed pictures of what looked like family members standing in front of a house in a setting that could have been staged by Ireland's Tourist Bureau. Jenna picked up a picture of Declan with two older people. "Your parents?"

"Yes," he said. But he was preoccupied. "Have a seat, will you, Jenna? I'd like to share something with you."

"Okay," she said, looking at him carefully. "Are you all right?"

Declan smiled and ran his finger down her cheek. "Sure and I'm fine, lass." Then he turned serious. "I've been debating whether or not to tell you this. I left it out of my report to the police. I figure if you give me the go ahead, I can call and tell them I just remembered something more. But I wanted to ask you first."

Jenna could feel her heart starting to beat faster. "What is it?"

"This was not a random mugging," he said. "I was targeted."

"That's terrible!" Jenna cried. "Why would anyone want to hurt you? Were you reporting on something?"

Declan paused as if gathering courage. Finally he shook his head. "No. It has nothing to do with work. It's because I've shown an interest in you."

"What?!"

"Look, none of this is your fault, so don't take it upon your lovely shoulders, but the gouger who beat me up was a hired thug. He was methodical. He knew the damage he wanted to inflict. And just before he cut me with his knife, he said, 'This here's a message you need to hear loud and clear. My client says for you to stay away from Jenna, or the next time you'll lose something more than your pretty face.'"

Jenna was stunned. What was this all about? Who would do such a thing? "But I'm not even seeing anybody," she said.

"I don't understand it either. It's not as if you and I had ever...you know. But he specifically mentioned you, and I wanted you to be aware of it."

Jenna sat for a moment, speechless. She'd had a few casual relationships over the last few years, but none had ever been fueled by jealousy; there were no ex-boyfriends wishing to monopolize her time. She was clueless. But that, she realized, was the least of it. They hadn't yet found this thug, and that meant Declan might still be in danger. *Oh my God.* Those pictures they just took! It could be plastered all over the papers that she and Declan were together. "I shouldn't be here," she said, getting up. "You…you shouldn't be seen with me. And the news people…the photographs."

"Bugger the photos," he said. "And don't worry about me. I'll make sure it doesn't happen again. I just want you to be safe."

Jenna involuntarily thought of Brit. "I'll be fine," she said.

"All right then. Do you want me to give the police your name? If I do, be aware they'll no doubt want to interview you, and it will likely get leaked to the press. A story like this shouldn't have legs, but it will simply because of the tabloid nature of it."

More unsavory news associated with The Grove? No way. Da didn't need any more hassles than he already had. "No. I…I'd appreciate it if you kept my name out of it, at least for now. Until I can figure out who might be behind all this."

"I thought as much. And while I would rather not give them the satisfaction, I'm going to stay away from you—more for your sake than mine. I wouldn't want you in the line of fire, so to speak."

"Don't worry. There's no way I'm going to spend time with you while some nutcase is out there trying to hurt you," she admonished him. "But we'll stay in touch, yes?"

"You can count on it. And you can bet I'm going to do some digging on my own. Maybe it has something to do with the problems your family has been having with The Grove."

Jenna frowned. "How do you know about that?"

"News gets around, lass. Especially in the media biz. Listen, I must admit I am a bit knackered at the moment. I appreciate the ride home, but I'm going to lie down for a while."

"Oh. Oh, of course. Is there anything I can get for you? Do you have enough to eat? Is there someone who can look in on you?"

Declan smiled, although the gesture looked painful. "Yes, I have plenty of Jameson and soda bread, so all is well. And my neighbor will check in on me—she does it whether I'm sick or not, so I think I'll be all right."

Jenna couldn't help the tears that began to form. "I am so very, very sorry," she said. She hugged him and made him promise to call her the minute he had more information.

On the way back to The Grove she went over the possibilities. Did any of this have to do with SPEAR, the anti-development group? If so, how? And why? What did they hope to gain by frightening her or those she was close to? Did they think she'd turn tail and run, or maybe convince her grandfather to give it up? Once again she came up empty. But coming on the heels of what had happened to the foreman, and the danger she sensed her grandfather was in, this latest crime brought it home like no other. Fear began to coil itself around her, but she took a mental machete to it, hacking it back. She would *not* give in to a victim mentality. No way in hell.

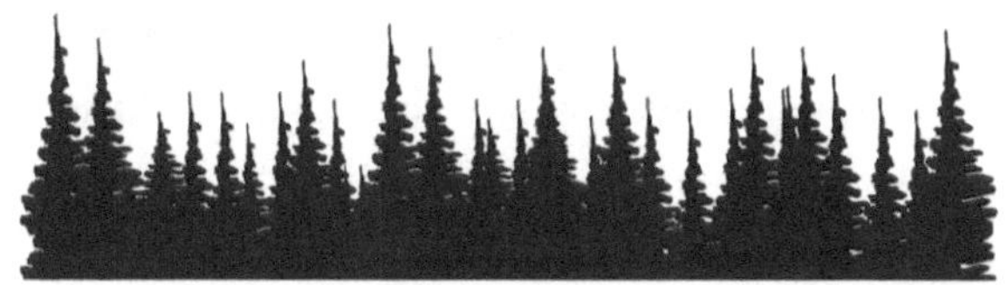

Chapter Sixteen

Days passed and Jenna kept in touch with Declan. Although no suspect had been caught, at least the reporter was on the mend. Jenna talked with Brit about the incident but didn't mention the personal nature of the attack. He'd probably want to keep her in a plastic bubble, which would only have pissed her off. And frankly, with everything else on his plate, she couldn't bear to give him one more thing to worry about.

Instead she focused on what she could control, namely her work on the exhibits, and discovering more insights about Peter Raines and his relationship with Ethan's mother, Giselle. One evening after work, she stopped by the Firestone Cottage to share with her grandfather what little she'd learned so far. He sat and listened thoughtfully.

"My mother never talked about my biological father," he said when she was finished. "Ever. She loved my stepfather dearly, and by the time I was old enough to care about such things, they'd had twin daughters, so we had a full, happy home life. Honestly, for years I thought my stepfather *was* my father, or at least I told myself that was the case. The name 'Peter Raines' came up only once, when she was dying. We were in essence saying our good byes when she began talking about him. I suppose she felt guilty about keeping such important information from me all my life."

"One of those deathbed confessions, huh?"

Da smiled faintly. "I suppose. But even then she didn't actually say he was my father. She said she'd known a man by that name, who had once worked for her mother."

"That's right. Raines did work for Lia. What did she say about him?"

A faraway expression on his face, Da seemed awash in memories. After a few moments he spoke. "She wasn't clear-headed at the time," he recalled. "I remember leaning over to hear her more clearly. She said something like, 'He shouldn't have left her. Mama would never betray Papa with Sandy…he shouldn't have left me. I would never betray him…" Da looked at her and shrugged.

"That's it?"

"That's it. You can see why I didn't pursue it. It all seemed so vague. At a minimum I thought, 'Well, she had an affair and the man left her.' But now, Jenna, I find I truly want to know. Assuming this Peter Raines fellow was indeed my father, why did he disappear, as you say, after the earthquake, reappear twenty years later to woo my mother, and then disappear all over again? It simply doesn't make sense."

Jenna took one of her grandfather's hands in her own. "Are you open to knowing, no matter what we find?"

Ethan looked at her with sad, knowing eyes. "You, more than anyone, must understand the feeling of being left in the dark for so long. The light, when it's shed, can be so bright it's painful, but at least you can finally *see*."

Full of resolve, Jenna spent the next few days pouring over all the data she had accumulated regarding the characters at the original Grove. The name Mandy cropped up often; she was mentioned by many of the artists in her role as life studies model, but she also wrote commentary of her own. Apparently she was more than just an employee. One such reference by Winterfeld included Mandy's last name, Culpepper.

"Now here's a connection worth noting," Dani said after running a name search. "Mandy Culpepper is none other than Mrs. William Firestone."

"Whoa, really? As in our Firestone Cottage? As in *the* Firestones? Very old name. Very old money. Will was in business with Gus around the time The Grove was built."

Dani had pulled up an obituary from the *San Francisco Chronicle*. "It says Amanda Firestone was known for both her 'literary success and philanthropic largesse,' which lasted over seventy years."

"What does it say about her time as a model at The Grove?"

"Not a darn thing. But she does have a wing named after her at the Bay Area Textile Museum."

Mandy had been at The Grove from the beginning. She knew all the players. She was a model, but a writer, too. Maybe she had some personal papers worth looking into. "I know it's a long shot," Jenna said, "but are you up for a field trip?"

Dani smiled. "I'm ready when you are."

The Firestone clan was huge. After several phone calls and curt interviews with reluctant family members, Jenna and Dani had finally caught up with a cooperative source. One of Mandy's many grandchildren was the curator of the Amanda Firestone Costume and Clothing Collection. The woman explained the scope of her work via speaker phone.

"You really must come down and see the collection," she said with evident pride. "My grandmother absolutely *ruled* the Bay Area fashion world for well over half a century."

"That would be starting about when?" Dani asked.

"Well, she became a Firestone in the summer of 1906 and shortly thereafter began to set the tone for society. She was quite singular, you know."

"Oh, we know," Jenna chimed in. "But actually, we

were more interested in her activities prior to her marriage. You know, when she worked as a model for the artists at The Grove."

"Oh."

The "oh" on the other end of the line may as well have been the sound of a door slamming shut. Jenna glanced at Dani with raised eyebrows. Yet another dead end?

Dani tried again. "So…would you have any papers from your grandmother dating back to that time period, ma'am?"

"Well, no, I wouldn't. The family doesn't pay too much attention to what went on prior to my grandmother's marriage…except for Baby Reggie, of course."

Dani frowned. "Baby Reggie?"

"Oh, she's not really a baby, not anymore. But we all call her that. She's the last of the last, you know."

"Meaning?" Jenna asked.

"Well, grandmother was quite prolific, as you probably already gathered. Grandpa must have been a randy old billy goat. She produced nine children, all of whom reached adulthood and all of whom in turn produced relatively large families themselves. The Firestone clan is quite extensive."

Dani gestured to the list of names she'd gathered and smiled at Jenna. "Don't we know it."

"So Reggie was the last child of the last child. She's the youngest of the third generation. Also the black sheep, if you must know. But that's neither here nor there. She'll have some idea of what you're looking for, I'm almost certain."

The following morning, having been given directions to "Baby Reggie's" home workshop, Dani and Jenna headed for Atherton, a wealthy enclave down the Peninsula from San Francisco.

"Looks like being a Firestone has its perks, no matter where you are in the pecking order," Jenna joked as Dani drove through the arched gateway of a multi-million-dollar estate. Precisely manicured lawns and an expertly trimmed rose garden set the stage for a spectacular Victorian-era mansion painted a deep lavender and trimmed in forest green. A gardener clipping an eight-foot-tall privet hedge watched as they slowly cruised by. "Wait a sec." Jenna rolled down her window. "Excuse me, sir, can you tell us if Ms. Regina Firestone is home?"

The man smiled, a wide toothy grin in his sunburned face. "Keep going, around that way," he said, pointing. "You'll see her place. Can't miss it. It's the one with all the pretty flowers."

A short time later Jenna and Dani glimpsed a bright yellow cottage through the trees. As they pulled up in front of the flower-laden porch, they could hear the mournful howl of a hound dog somewhere in the yard that seemed to correspond to a hissing-type sound. No one answered the front door, so they walked around the back and saw a tall, slender woman wearing welder's goggles and a leather apron, holding a blow torch and bending over a large metal basin. Every time she turned on the torch, the dog, a rotund basset hound, would begin to howl. The dog was either singing along or in great distress, it was hard to tell.

"Just a little bit more, Mr. Big," the woman called out, oblivious to her visitors.

Jenna and Dani waited until the woman had finished with the torch. She then poured something from one container to another inside the basin. Afterward she flipped a lever that caused the tub to spin furiously for several seconds. As it slowed down, she took off her goggles, picked up a long-handled pair of tongs and lifted a small cylinder that had apparently been spinning within the tub. She bent over and plunged the cylinder into a bucket of water, causing another hissing sound and complementary howl from Mr. Big. As she straightened, the dog noticed Jenna and Dani and dropped the howl in favor of a deep ferocious bark.

"Knock it off, Mr. Big," she admonished the hound. "We don't like barking dogs."

"Is it safe?" Jenna called out, only half in jest.

The woman grinned, lovely dimples framing her exquisite face. "Yes, but watch your ankles." She took a small object out of the cylinder and began brushing it with an old toothbrush dipped in the bucket water.

"Looks complicated," Jenna remarked, gesturing to the odd assortment of tools and machinery surrounding them. "What are you making?"

The woman took off her apron and hung it on a hook near her back porch, then shook out the glorious auburn hair she'd tied back while using the torch. "I'm just recasting some silver into a new ring design I'm trying out. What do you think?" She offered the ring to Jenna and Dani for their perusal.

"Stunning," Dani said, turning the ring over. "Now I can see why handmade jewelry is so expensive."

"Damn straight," the woman said with a smile. "I'm Reggie Firestone, by the way." She extended her hand.

"I'm Jenna Bergstrom and this is Dani Dunn. We're working for The Grove Center Historic Trust."

"Janice called ahead and said you two might drop by. Sounds like a fabulous project you're working on."

"It is. But we've hit some snags in our research and we thought perhaps you, or really your grandmother, might be able to help us out."

Reggie raised her eyebrows. "That sounds intriguing. Let's go inside out of the heat."

A few minutes later the three women were settled in the cozy parlor of the cottage, ice teas in hand. Mr. Big had claimed the ottoman in front of the buttery leather chair Reggie sat in. Large, bold-hued pillows accented a lived-in sofa and love seat. Small tables and shelves held an assortment of collectibles, including books, rocks, colored stones, carvings, and jewelry displays. Family photos abounded, as well as some of Reggie herself in hiking or caving gear. From the looks of things, the supposed black sheep of the Firestone clan had traveled a great deal, but still appreciated the comforts of home.

"You've got a wonderful place here," Dani said. "Is this part of the Firestone estate?"

Reggie's eyes gleamed. "One of many, I'm afraid. I'm just a tenant, however. This place belongs to my Uncle

Toby, who bought it from the rest of the family years ago. He rents the cottage to me for a bit under market value, which goes even farther because I don't have to rent separate workshop space. In return I keep Mr. Big occupied whenever I'm in town. He and I are buds, aren't we, Biggie?" She fondly scratched the basset behind his ears. The dog was obviously in love.

"What exactly do you do?" Jenna asked, taking a sip of her tea. She'd noticed a couple of framed certificates on the wall as well as some trophies. Reggie was apparently accomplished as well as beautiful.

"I'm a jewelry designer by trade. Have you ever heard of 'Fire Stones'?"

Dani sat up excitedly. "Oh! I've heard of your work. My mother lusts after it. Her boyfriend bought her one of your necklaces for Christmas last year and I think that's what convinced her to move in with him."

Reggie laughed. "I hope that's a good thing."

"Yeah, sort of." Dani smiled.

A short time later the portly hound lumbered up onto Reggie's lap while Jenna and Dani perused a scrapbook she had given them.

"You look a lot like your grandmother," Jenna noted, flipping through the pictures.

"That's what everybody says, but I don't see it. I mean, come on. She was a beautiful woman."

Jenna looked up in surprise; it was obvious the woman wasn't aware of her own exquisite looks. "If you don't mind my asking, you're the only descendant who seems at all interested in your grandmother's life before she got married. Why is that?"

Reggie shrugged. "It seems everybody else is content to believe that Grandmamma sprung to life fully formed after she married into the Firestone clan. But she was a Culpepper before that, and that's always intrigued me."

Jenna glanced at Dani, wondering how she should bring up the potentially sensitive topic of Mandy's prenuptial career; Dani must have read her thoughts.

"Go for it," she said.

"So, um, did you know what kinds of…activities… your grandmother did at The Grove before she got married?" Jenna looked for any sign of revulsion on Reggie's part, and found nothing but a bemused expression.

"You mean, did I know my little ol' grandma had a voluptuous body that artists loved to reproduce in whatever medium they could get their hands on? Yep. Honestly, it's a sore spot between me and the rest of the family. They'd prefer to keep that little fact to themselves, but I don't see anything wrong with the world knowing the full story of my grandmother, including her life before she married Grandpa Will."

As the women conversed, Jenna found herself liking this woman more and more. Reggie was incredibly down to earth for having such patrician roots. She could have coasted on her family's standing in society, but chose to live her life on her own terms. Jenna had done that to a certain extent herself after she'd discovered her own roots; it wasn't an easy path.

Dani finished looking through the scrapbook,

which had been filled with the good works of Amanda Firestone. "She was an incredible woman."

Reggie nodded. "I know, and she deserves a full accounting of her life. Which is why I'm glad you two tracked me down. I've been lobbying to add a special exhibit to her wing at the textile museum—one that includes her time at The Grove."

"Well, maybe we can help each other out," Jenna said. She brought out copies of excerpts from the commentaries she'd taken from the storage facility and handed them to Reggie. "We think you'll find this interesting reading."

Reggie flipped through the pages and paused a moment before replying. "I may have something of interest for you too." She deposited Mr. Big with a thud and retreated to the back of the cottage. Her chubby protector stared balefully at them, as if daring them to make one false move.

"If Mandy's the writer Da said she was, we may have hit the jackpot," Jenna murmured.

Dani inhaled deeply. "I've got goose bumps, like I used to get when I'd finally discover the answer to some obscure question through an Internet search."

Reggie returned minutes later with several small notebooks in hand. They were obviously old and well worn. "Grandmother filled dozens of these over the course of her lifetime, starting when she was about fifteen, I think. They became much more ornate over time, but all of them are filled with notes and observations and even scenes that later became part of her children's stories."

"She left them to you?' Jenna asked. "You must have been pretty young when your grandmother passed away."

"Strange, I know."

"Why do you think she did that?" Dani asked.

"I've often wondered. Maybe she considered me special because I was the last grandchild she knew she'd have. And I must admit I was pretty precocious. Surprisingly, I remember having conversations with Grandmamma during her last years. I don't know, maybe she saw something of herself in me."

"How did you come to be interested in jewelry?" Jenna asked. "Your grandmother was known more for her fashion sense than her jewels, wasn't she?"

Reggie smiled. "Yes and no. One of my earliest memories is trying on her 'fancy baubles' as she would call them. She received many of them from my grandpa, of course, but certain ones she'd hand to me and say 'this one was from before.' I never knew what she meant, so I attached greater significance to them. I guess I've been trying to answer that question ever since in one way or another."

Dani eagerly flipped through one of the commentaries that she and Jenna had brought along. "Lia insisted that the artists chronicle their thoughts and opinions on life at The Grove. Hence, the commentaries. I think this might help," she said, handing the passage over to Reggie, who read it aloud.

"March eighteenth. It was a large piece of citrine and Mandy laughed as she placed it between her breasts. I swear a shaft of light caught the facets of the stone and beamed down as if to say 'Here lies heaven, gentlemen.'"

"Wow," Reggie murmured. "And to think she was a ward of the Wolffs when she did that."

"Really?" Jenna couldn't mask her surprise. "Hard to believe they'd let her pose in the nude like that. Then again, she definitely doesn't seem like a conventional type."

Reggie nodded, obviously pleased with the explanation. "Maybe I inherited more from grandmamma than her red hair."

The women chuckled and Dani flipped through Mandy's notebooks. Suddenly she looked up. "Reggie, at the risk of sounding presumptuous, could we borrow a couple more of these? Since the Wolffs were her guardians at some point, she probably remained close to them even after she married your grandfather. Specifically, we're interested in the years 1906, 1926 and 1927."

"They're actually by number, not by year, so I'm not sure which notebook covers which year. You're welcome to go through all of them if you like, but may I ask why?"

"We're trying to piece together a story-within-the-story," Jenna explained. "Hopefully your grandmother's writings for those years will help us do that."

Reggie nodded and brought out a box half filled with the notebooks. "I've got about thirty of them in here. That should take you through that time period." She handed Jenna the box. Inside were a collection of journals, some plain, but others quite ornate, encased in beautifully tooled leather in red, burgundy, and deep green.

Reggie grinned, her natural beauty radiating through her simple demeanor. "You sure can tell that grandmamma went up in the world, can't you?" Her lighthearted expression soon turned earnest. "I hope her notebooks will be helpful to you. The problem is she seemed to write down *everything*, from the day's grocery list to her favorite children's names. A stream of consciousness almost, like she'd be sitting there and come up with a scene for one of her stories and write it down, and on the next page she'd be talking about what the cook should make for dinner. And some of the descriptions she wrote about Grandpa Will and the things they did..." Reggie stopped to dramatically fan herself. "Well, you'll see."

"Would you...do you need a receipt or anything, showing that we borrowed these?" Dani asked.

Reggie looked at her with clear, green eyes. "You wouldn't screw me over, would you?"

"No, of course not!" Dani looked aghast.

"Didn't think so." Reggie grinned at Dani and Jenna. "We're on the same team, ladies. Have at it."

Jenna's answering smile faded as she and Dani headed back to the car with the box of notebooks. She realized they might be that much closer to uncovering a story steeped in turmoil. Even though her grandfather very much wanted to know the truth, that didn't mean it wouldn't hurt him. A lot.

It was a sobering thought.

Chapter Seventeen

After a light dinner at the inn's restaurant, the women decided to work in Dani's office for a few more hours before Jenna called it a night. She drove back to The Grove, parking around the back of the Great House as usual. Brit's Porsche was parked there, but not his Pilot, which meant he was either still working or visiting Don. The sun had set and the imposing redwoods had begun their nightly transformation into stygian guards, offering their services to the forces of darkness...

Enough of Fright Night. Jenna firmly tamped down her growing nervousness and walked toward the back door. Normally a motion sensor turned on the porch light, but apparently it wasn't working. She reached into the outside zippered pocket of her purse where she kept the master key.

It wasn't there.

Jenna's uneasiness surged back with a vengeance. She stopped and looked around warily before unloading the contents of her bag. Had she dropped it into the main compartment? Maybe. The key had to be in there *somewhere*. Out came her car keys, wallet, skeleton key for the room, tissue pack and hairbrush, a few rubber bands and a notebook. She shook everything and the purse itself. Finally the key fell out. Breathing a sigh of relief, she entered the darkened sun room. "Anybody home?" she called out. It was a stupid thing to say, she realized, but somehow hearing her own voice helped calm her jitters.

She made her way quietly through the dimly lit kitchen and headed up the stairs to her suite, feeling more and more like those stupid heroines in scary movies who walk toward the closed door at the end of the hall even when the audience is shouting "Don't do it!" Why wasn't Brit home yet? Even asking the question bothered her—she should be perfectly able to deal with her own insecurities.

At the second floor landing, Jenna noticed she didn't have any closed doors to worry about after all. Just the opposite, in fact. The doors along the hallway were all slightly open, including the one to her suite. That was not normal. While she rarely locked her door with the skeleton key Brit had given her, she did close it firmly every time she went downstairs. Had she forgotten to do that in her rush to leave that morning? She flipped on the light and dropped her purse and sweater on one of the armchairs in the sitting area. On her way to the bathroom she happened to glance at the little writing desk and gasped.

The antique photo of Lia Starling was gone.

In its place, within the same frame, was a close-up photo of Jenna, smiling. Across her face someone had drawn a thick black slash.

A small white envelope was propped up against the frame. With shaking fingers Jenna opened it and pulled out a card which read, simply, "It's dangerous here. If you stay, you might get hurt.—M.C."

Jenna's pulse began to race. Someone had access to this house. Someone bad. She looked around wildly. Could they still be here? Could they still be *in her room*? She noticed the door to her bedroom was shut. Had she shut it? Was someone behind it? She tried to remain steady, but started to shake, her lungs gasping for air. No. If someone were out to harm her, why would they warn her? *Okay. Okay. Stay calm.* She turned around and walked quickly back across the sitting room, half expecting an arm to grab her from behind. None did, thank God. Reaching the hallway, she raced toward the staircase and was halfway down the dark flight of steps when she saw a figure coming up toward her. She screamed, turning around and running back the way she'd come, her heart ready to leap out of her throat.

"Jenna wait—what's wrong?" The man took the stairs two at a time to catch up to her but she kept running.

"Wait...*wait*," he said, catching up and grabbing her arm.

"No!" she screamed, blindly fighting him. He had to duck, but finally captured her flailing arms and wrapped his own around her, holding her close. He backed her against the wall, using his entire body to subdue her. "Sweetheart, it's me," he said slowly. "It's Brit."

Still heaving, Jenna looked at him with wild eyes. Then it registered. This was Brit.

She was safe.

He could tell the moment she recognized him. Her eyes lost that feral look and she seemed to melt in his arms. He immediately loosened his grip and placed her arms around his neck. He continued to hold her firmly around the waist and rubbed a hand soothingly down her back.

"What happened?" he finally asked. "What spooked you?"

"I—I..." Jenna sighed and burrowed into his neck.

"Come on, baby. Talk to me."

Jenna took a deep breath, then pushed gently away and took his hand. "Come with me."

They entered her room and she went straight to the little desk.

"Look," she said, pointing to the photo.

He looked at it closely. "What the hell?"

"Now read this." She handed him the note.

As he read the warning, Bret felt outrage begin to build and join forces with his instinct to protect. What kind of coward would resort to scaring a woman like this? Had Wheeler or Dorman really sunk that low? He saw Jenna begin to wilt as her adrenalin leveled off—

just as his was kicking into gear. "Why don't you have a seat and we'll figure this out, okay?" He guided her to the sofa, careful to keep his voice even and his anger from spilling over. The thought of Jenna in any kind of danger was simply untenable.

Unthinkable.

He began to pace. "First of all, was anything taken from the room, or messed up in anyway? Was someone looking for something, maybe?"

Jenna shook her head. "No. Nothing that I can see. Just the picture and the note. But who is this 'M.C.'? Do you know anyone with those initials?"

"Not offhand, no."

"Maybe it has to do with the opening of The Grove?" she asked. "This SPEAR group or whoever?"

"Gotta be," Brit said. "Unless you've got some enemies I don't know about."

Jenna shook her head. "It's weird. It's just so *intimate*. I mean, who would go to the trouble of taking a picture of me?"

Brit stopped and looked down at her. "Plenty of men, believe me. But it's obvious someone wants to make sure you get the message up close and personal."

Jenna worried her bottom lip for a moment before looking up at Brit. "Maybe we should get the police involved."

"Oh, I'm gonna call Gabe, all right." He ran his hands through his hair. "Right now, though, I want you to stay here while I take a little tour of the house to make sure we're alone."

Jenna's eyes grew wide. "Omigod. You think he might still be here?"

"Doubtful, but it won't hurt to check."

"But what if he's armed?"

"Sweetheart, he better hope he's armed to the teeth, because anything less and I'm going to rearrange his anatomy." With that, Brit got up and quickly checked her bedroom and bath before heading back out. "Lock the door behind me," he added.

"Okay, but…"

He turned around and waited.

"Come back when you've finished, okay?"

Brit looked pointedly at the little sofa; Jenna couldn't miss his meaning.

"I'll sleep here," she offered. "You can have my bed."

Brit gazed at her for a moment before answering. "Tell you what. You put your jammies on and when I come back, we'll go to my suite. The sofa converts to a bed in there."

She smiled at him, and he remembered the way he'd felt the first time she'd done that seven years earlier. Only this time there really might be a dragon to slay.

"Okay," she said. "And Brit?"

"Yeah?"

"Thank you."

Brit nodded. As he closed the door he considered the delectable creature on the other side of it. *My God, when I find out who's behind this, I am* not *going to be responsible for my actions.*

He searched the ground floor of the Great House in earnest, part of him hoping he'd actually find the bastard and deal with at least one part of this unholy mess in a very concrete and satisfying way. Stepping outside, he stood for several moments on the front porch, listening to the darkness. He heard nothing, which was disappointing, but no surprise.

Back inside, he checked all the downstairs windows, but saw no signs of forced entry. The doors also appeared secure.

The second floor appeared undisturbed as well, so he headed up to the third floor. Nothing was amiss until he reached his bedroom. There he saw the contents of his nightstand strewn all over the bed. He usually kept a few wrapped condoms in the drawer and they'd been cut in two. A pair of scissors had been stabbed into one of his pillows several times and were now stuck there. "Fuck," he muttered. He quickly snapped a picture on his phone for Gabe to see and then scooped up the drawer's contents and threw away the debris. Then he pulled out the scissors and stuffed the pillow in his closet. Jenna didn't need to see any of that.

Once he saw that nothing else was out of place, he trotted back down to the second floor. Jenna met him at her door wearing a well-worn, oversized Steinmann Art Institute T-shirt, a pair of ankle-length tights, and a look of heart-stopping vulnerability.

"Did you find anything?" she asked.

"Uh, nope. Nothing was jimmied or broken. Frankly, I don't know how they got inside unless they picked a lock. Or used a key. But all the masters are accounted for at the end of every day. Only a few of us carry them twenty-four-seven. You still have yours, I hope."

Jenna nodded. "That's how I let myself in."

"Well, my guess is they've done what they intended to do, at least for tonight. I'll call Gabe first thing in the morning. We'll get to the bottom of this. I promise."

They headed up to his suite and Brit insisted Jenna take his bed, while he made up the sofa sleeper in the sitting area. As she said good night, her entire being radiated the message that while she was afraid, she nevertheless trusted him to take care of her.

No matter what it took, that's what he intended to do.

He watched the boss man standing on the porch, peering into the dark like he had x-ray vision or something. He wouldn't see a damn thing. Did he think the danger had passed? Did he think he could keep her safe? *Think again, asshole.*

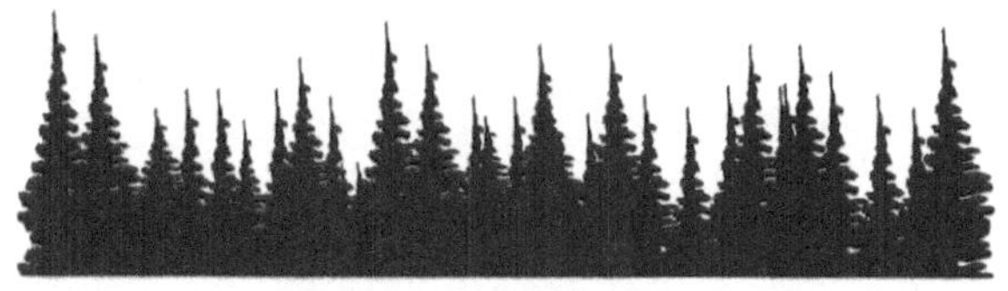

Chapter Eighteen

W arm and relaxed after a surprisingly restful sleep, Jenna awoke the next morning to sunlight streaming in through a dramatic bank of picture windows taking up the south and west walls of the room. The views from the mansion's third floor master bedroom were spectacular, encompassing rugged sea-drenched cliffs, pastoral hills, and the towering redwoods of The Grove itself. No wonder Brit had claimed this space; it was magnificent.

Somewhat like him, she thought ruefully. Strong, fearless—and yes, she had to admit, romantic, too. The previous night, after checking the house, Brit had come back to her room and escorted her upstairs to his own suite. After offering to change the bed linens for her—an offer she politely declined—he'd gallantly retreated to sleep on the sofa in the outer room.

Jenna rolled over and luxuriated in the softness of his king-sized bed. There was something so intimate about sleeping where he'd slept, and wrapping herself in the same cocoon he'd made for himself. She could smell a hint of his shaving cream in his pillow, and for a moment she pretended he'd spent the night with her, holding her, keeping her safe in his arms. It had been so long since she'd been pampered, had let herself be pampered, and it felt *so* good to imagine it, even if just for a moment.

She sighed. Time for a reality check. She'd been targeted by some anti-development weirdo, it had freaked her out, and Brit was merely humoring her by having her stick close to him for the night. Once they figured out how to secure the house, she could go back to her own quarters. That was for the best, right?

Her mind wandered back to the kiss at the storage facility. She could still recall his lips on hers, warm and firm and insistent; his large hand caressing her neck; the way he purposefully molded his body to hers. He'd gotten into it every bit as much as she had. There was no mistaking the passion flaring between them. That's what made it all so complicated.

She reached for her purse and dug out her hairbrush, beginning her morning ritual as she gazed out the picture window at the pounding surf below. The waves reminded her of her own roiling emotions. For so long she'd worked at feeling strong and self-contained, able to lead her own life and forge her own identity. But lately she'd begun to feel *connected,* as if she were part of something larger than herself. But that was scary too, because if you got too close to something—or someone—then you ran the risk of losing them, and losing your heart in the process. Which was better? To protect yourself from heartache by not getting too close, or taking a chance on something wonderful?

And now she could throw physical terror into the mix. It was one thing to protest a development; something else entirely to harm those associated with it. Who had attacked Declan and who had left the warning in her bedroom? Was it the same person? Maybe it was someone who worked here at The Grove. Or someone who worked for Boyce Wheeler's SPEAR group. Could he really be that heartless? Or was it all a sick joke? Damn it, she did *not* like having more questions than answers! She finished brushing her hair and bundled it up into her usual no-nonsense ponytail. Enough is enough, she decided. She was not—repeat —*not* going to give this creep the satisfaction of scaring her to death. She'd take precautions, for herself and for Da. And Brit said he'd get Gabe up to speed. They'd find out sooner or later who was responsible and that would be the end of it.

As for her relationship with Brit, the way wasn't so clear. She had no clue what his expectations were. Heck, she didn't even know what *she* wanted. She only knew how he made her feel, which was wonderful.

Feeling better after her mental pep talk, Jenna returned to her room, got dressed, and headed down to the big kitchen, anxious to start focusing on something other than her own scattered feelings. As soon as she entered the room she was surrounded by the delicious aroma of butter and blueberries. Brit had obviously come and gone, but on the counter he'd left a plate of mouth-watering muffins and a note that read, "I picked these up at Lindy's Bakery this morning. Help yourself." Next to the plate was a carafe of hot water and an Earl Grey tea bag in a pretty ceramic cup. Jenna bit her lip, trying not to smile.

Because during that magical time seven years ago, she had told him that unlike most people who had to have their morning coffee, *her* absolute favorite way to wake up in the morning was with a blueberry muffin and a steaming cup of Earl Grey tea.

Jenna didn't have the opportunity to thank Brit for his hospitality because she barely saw the man for the next several days. Because he wore so many hats, he was too busy to say hi, much less have a conversation. He did make sure Gabe interviewed Jenna about the intruder, however.

The detective and a forensics specialist met her at the Great House the morning after the break-in. While the technician dusted for fingerprints and bagged the evidence, Jenna filled Gabe in on everything she knew. She even gave him Declan's cell phone number and told him what Declan had told her about the mugger, although she begged Gabe not to make that public, or tell anyone else about it. Gabe assured her they'd run any prints they found on the photo, frame, and warning note, along with the mansion's entry points, and if something turned up he'd contact her immediately. He arranged for a patrol car to make the rounds at night, and he let her know she could call him any time day or night if she felt threatened in any way.

In reality Jenna did feel more secure. Brit changed the locks on the Great House and had an alarm system installed for good measure. Even more comforting was the unspoken agreement with him that she would continue to stay in his suite. They fell into a routine of sorts: Brit would leave early, always putting hot water on and leaving some sort of breakfast goodie for her. She in turn found herself making sandwiches and dropping them off with Sherrie to give to Brit when he stopped by the office. The first time she brought them in, Jenna felt a bit defensive and tried to explain her actions to the older woman.

"I just thought I'd help out, him being so busy and everything. And the fact that he's given up his room for me, well…you know how it is."

Sherrie, who knew all about the sleeping arrangements, merely raised her eyebrows and went back to work, leaving Jenna feeling foolish that she had said anything about it at all.

Brit had taken some of his clothes out of the bedroom closet and left her a note inviting her to hang her things in their place. She figured he was just being considerate, and suppressed the image of their clothing hanging intimately side by side. It's only temporary, she told herself. Nothing to get worked up over.

Nevertheless, at night Jenna found herself listening for Brit to come home, which he invariably did late, often after visiting Don. Brit was simply working himself to the bone and she worried about him.

One night, unable to sleep, she quietly opened her door, intending to slip past Brit and head downstairs to the kitchen. As she tip-toed by, she saw that he was sprawled face down on top of the sofa bed, still completely dressed. *Poor baby, you must be totally wiped out.* She knelt down by him and gently untied and tugged off his boots, then took a plaid stadium blanket she'd found on a nearby chair and pulled it over him. He barely moved a muscle. "Some guard dog you turned out to be," she murmured. She couldn't help herself; she ran the backs of her fingers across his stubbled cheek. Suddenly he reached out, took her hand and kissed it.

"Ruff," he whispered.

Jenna jumped up and backed hastily away, her heart thumping. "Very funny," she muttered. She was going to say something else, but realized he'd fallen back asleep. She shook her head and returned to her bedroom, thoughts of a midnight snack all but forgotten. As she slipped under the covers, she couldn't help but grin.

Fortunately Jenna had enough on her mind to keep from dwelling on either the intruder or her feelings for Brit. Her days were filled with the challenge of fleshing out the workable prototype for the museum exhibit in time for the upcoming Investors' Preview. Dani joined her most afternoons. Using schematics of the exhibit space as well as the artwork dimensions, they created a flow chart showing how a visitor would experience the four decades of The Grove. The plan was to present a graphic timeline of each period showing notable events in the arts, politics, and society. The timeline would set the context for a description of the artists who inhabited The Grove year by year. Selected individual pieces would be displayed and highlighted on a rotating basis along with a brief analysis of the artist's contribution and his or her background. With the push of a button, visitors would be able to hear audio clips from the era, and discreetly placed computer screens would enable them to call up a more detailed profile of each contributor.

While researching the painter Sander de Kalb, Dani uncovered an inconsistency in Peter Raines's story. Raines, the mysterious photographer, had supposedly told Ethan's mother Giselle that he'd left The Grove just after the Great Earthquake because he hated the fact that Lia, Giselle's mother, had been having an affair with de Kalb. Having learned about Gus and Lia, Jenna didn't buy the photographer's excuse. Dani's discovery made it clear that Raines had at the very least been misinformed.

"I haven't yet figured out Mandy's notebooks, but look at this," Dani said one afternoon while she and Jenna were busy at their respective computer screens. "I found an article from 1904 that says de Kalb was a member in good standing of the San Francisco Apollonians."

"Never heard of them," Jenna said, swinging her chair around. "Why's that important?"

"Just that the Apollonians were named after Apollo, the Greek god of beauty. Let's just say they had a keen appreciation for the male form."

"Ah…in other words, the last thing de Kalb would have been interested in was an affair with Lia Wolff."

"Yes, that would be one way to put it." Dani flipped through a spiral-bound notebook on her desk. "I dug a little deeper, too. Turns out Sandy had a partner. I think the code words back then were 'close friend.' The guy must have spent some time at the retreat, because one of the entries in the 1906 commentary talks about 'looking forward to seeing Sandy's Roger again.' I couldn't find any de Kalb relative named Roger, so it's a pretty safe bet he and Sandy were a couple."

Jenna tapped her pencil thoughtfully. "So then why did Peter Raines lie about the reason he left The Grove? And why did that lie include Sander de Kalb?"

"I'm not sure about the first question, but my guess is he used de Kalb because Lia had been linked to him prior to her marriage."

"Linked? What do you mean?"

Dani flipped through her notes. "It seems Amelia Powell—that was her married name—was divorced by her husband in 1899 for adultery. She was supposedly having an affair with Sander de Kalb, whom she'd gone to art school with."

"Huh, I never heard that. But I don't get it. Why would she have an affair with him if he was gay?"

"I don't know if we'll ever know the real story on that one, but something tells me there are layers to it. Turns out Lia's sister ended up married to Lia's ex-husband, and apparently they all got along just fine later on. I found an announcement that says they even attended Lia's marriage to Gus."

Jenna stretched her arms above her head. "Odd, to say the least."

While they'd been talking, Jenna had been looking through the photographic work by Peter Raines entitled *The Grove's First Year*. The prints he'd left as payment for his tenure at The Grove were only a fraction of the shots he actually took for the book he later published. She was struck by the number of pictures of Lia: Lia in repose, Lia painting, Lia laughing. Every shot of the woman was somehow…reverential, as if…as if…"Wait," Jenna said finally. "What if Peter, not Sandy, had a thing for Lia?"

"You mean, like an affair?"

"No, I can't imagine Lia two-timing Gus, not from everything I ever heard or read about them. That's why Peter's story never rang true for me. No, I'm thinking maybe Peter—"

"—held a torch for her."

Jenna nodded. "Here, look at these photos." She turned the book around so Dani could see what she'd been noticing in Peter's retrospective. "See how lovingly he captures her in every shot?"

"You're right," Dani said. "But why would he leave before the end of his year?"

"I don't know. Maybe he couldn't stand it anymore, loving her and knowing nothing would ever come of it."

Dani nodded slowly as she closed the book. "Yes, I imagine that could be very painful," she said quietly.

Jenna looked at her new friend, immediately picking up on Dani's reflective tone. There's a story here, she thought. But aloud she said, "Do you mind if I use your notes on Peter Raines? I think I'll dig a little deeper into his life…what happened after he left, and what brought him back after twenty years. Maybe we'll get some answers."

"Be careful what you wish for," Dani warned.

Chapter Nineteen

A short while later, after calling it a day and seeing Dani off in her car, Jenna headed back toward the Great House on foot. It was a perfect summer evening; the afternoon's warmth hadn't yet been overtaken by the usual coastal fog. The mixture of bay leaf and honeysuckle left a potent scent in the air and Jenna couldn't help but remember bygone summers when play extended into the evening hours with hardly a break in stride.

She glanced across the parking lot to the large grassy area referred to by the construction crew as "the quad." The lawn had been planted a few months earlier and was now a favorite spot for workers to gather and relax during lunch and often at the end of the workday. Tonight, apparently, an impromptu soccer game was just about to begin, but they were short a few players. Jason called over to her.

"Hey, Sis, come on! We need a ringer!"

Jenna laughingly shook her head.

"Come on, Ms. Bergstrom, please be on our team!" Kyle and Parker were part of the group of young athletes, and Kyle wasn't shy about shouting out encouragement.

"What's the matter, not up to the task?" Jenna's spine tingled as she heard Brit's whispered taunt just behind her. She turned to look at him and he slowly smiled. At that moment something inside her clicked. She was sick of being serious and responsible all the time. Why not take a break and have some fun with a really sexy guy? Right here. Right now.

"I will if you will," she shot back.

"You're on," Brit said. "Bergstrom," he called to Jason, "Your sister's on your team. Make sure she doesn't break a nail, now."

Jenna grinned. She knew Brit was deliberately goading her. She also knew she was going to enjoy kicking his butt.

With good-natured grumbling on both sides, the makeshift game began. Jenna and Brit squared off as forwards and went after the ball—and each other—as if they were mortal enemies. Hips shoving, torsos swiveling, legs tangling, they fought each other for possession as if a championship were in the offing instead of a summer afternoon pickup game.

Brit was powerful, using his larger physique to block and dominate. But Jenna's years of playing childhood soccer easily came back to her. She was quick and skillful, using her slender body to find openings and maneuver around her nemesis. Though she was aware of others on the field, and in fact passed the ball to

Jason, Parker, or whoever else was open on her team, she knew, instinctively, that only one man mattered, just as she knew he sensed the same thing about her. The unfettered joy of it all caused her to laugh out loud, which of course Brit apparently took as an outright challenge, grinning his acceptance of the gauntlet she'd thrown down.

Jenna had just stolen the ball from Brit when Kyle came up on Brit's right side, attempting to block him from going after her. Distracted, Brit didn't see Parker come up on his left side and clip him.

"Hey, watch it," Jenna warned, since there was no referee to call Parker on it.

"Oh, sorry." Parker moved quickly back into his proper position.

Several shots on goal, headers, and corner kicks later, the game was tied. Light was fading fast and twilight was turning the competition into a good-natured free-for-all. Undaunted, Jenna and Brit continued to play hard and fast, their sheer delight in squaring off against each other evident to all. At one point Jenna was dribbling the ball, getting ready to pass it to Kyle, when Brit moved in to intercept it. Suddenly Parker ran into him, crying out, and falling down on the field.

"Parker? Are you all right?" Jenna rushed over to the young man, who lay on the ground grabbing his ankle and moaning. She knelt down by him. "Let me see," she said, reaching for his leg.

Brit also stopped to see if he could help. "Hey, you okay?"

"Um, yeah. I think it's okay. I just wasn't ready to get hit that hard."

"What are you talking about, Parker? You ran into Brit, not the other way around."

"She's right, dude," Kyle said.

Parker glared at Kyle before giving Jenna a slight pout. Brit shared a look of mild disbelief with Jenna before turning and walking away.

Jason ran up to lend a hand. "Yeah, that was smart. Way to win points with the boss."

"It was an accident," Parker explained in a petulant tone. Jenna had been kneeling over his leg to examine it when he reached out to touch a strand of hair that had come out of her ever-present ponytail. She looked up in surprise.

Kyle swiped Parker's hand away. "Hey what are you doin', man? You don't touch her like that."

"I know, dude. I, uh, I—thanks, Jenna."

Jenna could feel the undercurrents, and they weren't healthy. She abruptly got up. "Nothing's broken, thank goodness," she said briskly. "Fun game, guys. Gotta run." She looked over at Brit and decided the hell with it, she didn't want their interaction to end, especially on such a sour note. With Jason, Parker, Kyle, and the rest of the ad hoc team members looking on, she raced across the field to him with an extra soccer ball and dropped it in front of him like a sleek, happy retriever presenting a ball to its master. Laughing, she began their strange courtship dance anew, teasing him and daring him to take the ball away.

Hot, sweaty, and pressed up against a beautiful woman—what more is there? Brit gladly went along with Jenna's blatant flirtation. She'd all but dared him to steal the ball from her and he'd happily obliged. With possession trading back and forth, he had progressively backed her up the hill until they reached the driveway of the Great House. Laughing and taunting each other, they were so focused on their game that they failed to notice they weren't alone.

"Looks like fun. Can anybody play?" Tori was leaning forward against the railing of the front porch, her low-cut blouse displaying her impressive cleavage to its best advantage. Her grim expression, however, didn't match the sweetness of her words.

Surprised by her presence, Brit lost his concentration and bumped into Jenna, causing her to stumble backward until he caught her deftly around the waist and drew her against his body. She looked up at him briefly before turning to Tori.

"Hey, Tori."

"I thought we had a date, darling." Ignoring Jenna, Tori's eyes blazed at Brit.

Shit. "No, Tori. We didn't have a date. You wanted me to look at your color schemes and I forgot all about it. Sorry."

Tori's voice dripped sarcasm. "Yeah, you look devastated." She moved across the porch and down the steps toward them.

Brit instinctively held on to Jenna, but she pried

herself away and turned to glare at him. "Uh uh, you're not putting me in the middle of this," she mumbled to him before raising her voice. "If you'll both excuse me…" With that, she walked resolutely around the back of the mansion, leaving Brit to deal with the lady scorned.

Tori walked up to Brit, stopping when she was close enough to brush her breasts against his chest.

"You're running out of chances, darlin'," she murmured.

Frustrated, Brit ran his hands through his hair. "Look, I'm sorry, Tori, but you should have taken the hint a long time ago." He glanced up at the floor that held his bedroom and Jenna, then looked back at Tori and raised his eyebrows.

"I get it," Tori said bitterly. "I get that you're a bastard who doesn't give a damn about other people's feelings." She raised her hand to strike him, but Brit easily caught her mid-swing.

His expression hardened. Enough was enough.

"There's no need for name calling. Listen. I slept with you. Once. I guess I talked myself into thinking you were into hooking up without strings, just like I was. I shouldn't have done it, because I don't have those kinds of feelings for you, and for that I apologize. But hear me loud and clear: there's never going to be anything more between you and me."

Tori continued to glare at him, gesturing toward the house. "Why? Are you telling me blonds are more fun?"

"It'd be easier to say yes, but the fact is, Jenna has nothing to do with it. Again, I'm sorry. Now if you can't put your resentment aside and maintain a professional demeanor around here, I'll have to let you go."

"We'll see what my daddy has to say about that," she hissed. "You wouldn't want to piss off one of your deepest pockets."

Brit cocked his head. "Really? Do you honestly think threatening me with the likes of Garrick Winston is going to change my mind? I don't care who your daddy is."

Tori stared at him a moment longer, then appeared to wrap her dignity about her like a cloak. She walked passed him, then paused and looked over her shoulder.

"We really could have had something," she said. "But you blew it, and for what? A different piece of tail? I heard she's only here for a little while to help the professor. Then she's heading off to jump start her art career. What are you going to do then?"

After Tori left, Brit sat down on his favorite front porch chair. The evening had turned cool, and the slight sweat he'd worked up earlier playing soccer caused him to shiver. Coastal fog had begun to slither in, its tendrils conspiring with the fading light and increasing wind to lend an air of foreboding to the compound. An evening that had begun simply, delightfully, with a certain promise, was now murky, rife with unknown menace. Brit shivered again. *Hell*, he thought, annoyed that he'd let the atmosphere get to him. He couldn't regret that Tori believed he still had feelings for Jenna; much as he tried to downplay it, it was true. Just as it was true she was headed elsewhere in the near future. What was he going to do about that? What *could* he do? Groaning, he pictured Jenna upstairs in his suite, no doubt furious with him. Even the thought of her angry turned him on.

Yeah, the wind was blowing, all right. And a nasty storm was on its heels.

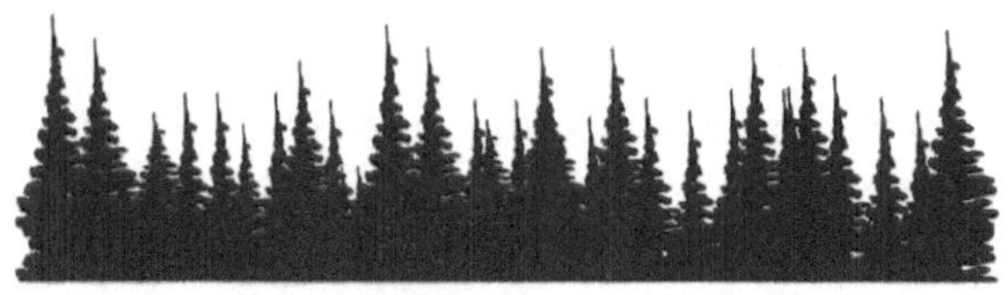

Chapter Twenty

He'd been sitting on his bunk playing Halo 2, fighting Covenant hunters by enticing them to charge, then sidestepping and trying to melee them in the back. Only he was blowing it and Master Chief was getting smashed every time. All because he couldn't keep his mind on the fucking game. *Shit.*

He shut down his laptop in disgust. Like a looped audio track, it kept running through his mind: Jenna's sexy laughter as the night swallowed up her and the boss man after the soccer game. His jaw tightened and his arms tensed as he fought to keep the bile inside. Just then Jason stuck his head in the door.

"Hey, what's up, bro?" Jason asked him.

"Just chillin'. Playin' Halo." Except I've got a hard-on for *your sister that won't quit.*

"A group of us are gonna shoot some hoops at the rec center. You in?"

"Nah, I'm gonna hit the sack."

"You're missin' out, but suit yourself," Jason said as he headed toward the parking lot.

"Yeah, whatever," he muttered. A half hour later he left the bunkhouse, thinking he'd scope out the mansion again. The boss man had put in an alarm system. What a joke. Didn't they know he could get around just about any type of security if he wanted to?

It felt good to be alone, nothing but him and thoughts of Jenna. Nobody else mattered. They were scum. He viciously kicked an empty soda can that someone had left by the side of the path. But Jenna was...Jenna was *everything*. And the way she was flirting with the boss man was disgusting. Sickening. Didn't she care that he'd screwed that designer lady? Not that Tori wasn't a hot piece of ass, but man, how could Jenna even put herself in the same category? She was so much better than that.

He'd almost reached the path that led to the cove when he heard two voices filter through the gloom. He quietly stepped closer so he could see them better. One of them was Lester, a dumbass on the construction crew. The two men were talking in low tones.

"Look, I pay you to keep me posted on Boyce's plans, but you screwed the pooch on this one. Why didn't you tell me he was planning to run their man off the road?"

"He never said nothin' about it, that's why," Lester said. "Can't tell you about an order if he don't give the order."

The other man scratched his jaw. "Yeah, he swears up and down he didn't have anything to do with it. I've confronted him several times on the matter, but he won't budge. He even blames me for it. It doesn't make sense."

Lester shrugged. "I don't know what to tell you, Mr. D. Maybe it was just an accident like they said."

The guy called Mr. D. poked Lester in the chest. "Listen. I don't trust Boyce and because you're his man, I don't trust you. If that foreman comes out of that coma and fingers SPEAR, don't expect me to cover for you. And if he dies, well…"

Lester smiled. His teeth were crooked and tobacco-stained. "You worry too much, Mr. D. Ain't nobody gonna pin anything on SPEAR or you or anybody else. But hey, you gotta admit it sure messed with everybody's mind around here."

"I don't give a shit about their minds. I give a shit about this project failing. And so far, that's not happening. Now what about that other business we talked about?"

"The old man's totally on board with causin' some major shit when the investors show up. He thinks it's another of his brilliant ideas, like the paint job. When Saturday night rolls around, they'll get a show, all right."

"Yeah? What have you got planned?"

"Not sure yet. I'm workin' on it. But whatever it is, it'll throw them sumbitches on their asses. You can depend on that."

"I am depending on that. You've gotta pull off something big. Dramatic. Nothing chicken shit. But nobody gets hurt. *Comprende?* And the next time Boyce puts you or any of your cronies up to something, you run it by me. I don't want to be blindsided like that again."

"Sure thing…Um, Mr. D.?" Lester looked around, then held his hand out.

Mr. D. pulled out a couple of twenties from his wallet and handed them over. "Look, I've gotta run," he said. "I've been here too long as it is."

"Hey, you're the one who don't wanna be seen with me on your side of town," Lester reminded him. The moron grinned and gestured to his heart. "Hurts my feelings, you know?"

Mr. D. didn't crack a smile. "Just check in at the usual time. And keep your mouth shut."

"Right," Lester said. "No calls, no emails, no texts. Clean as a whistle."

The two men went their separate ways. Mr. D. had parked his SUV away from the lights, and Lester headed toward the employee parking lot. Soon they were both out of sight.

He returned to the bunkhouse, glad to be one of the few occupants. Lighting a joint, he lay on his bed, going over the conversation he'd just overheard. Lester and Mr. D. obviously had it in for The Grove. Which meant they didn't like Brit Maguire. *Which means we have something in common.*

In need of more facts, he opened his laptop again and booted up. He began researching The Grove Center Historic Trust, SPEAR, Little Eden, and any other connections that cropped up. An hour or so later he again shut down the computer, armed with a good sense of the major players and what they all wanted from each other. Two names, Boyce Wheeler and Ralph Dorman, kept showing up. He'd bet a month of his daddy's dividend checks that Dorman was "Mr. D."

His thoughts began to churn, filling with possibilities, options, and strategies. It didn't look like Jenna was going to take the hint and leave, but if The Grove folded, that would pretty much ruin Brit Maguire. And if he went down, there's no way Jenna would still go for him. The old man was dyin', Jason would be off to college, and she'd be all alone…except for little ol' him.

An idea began to form. If Lester and Mr. D. wanted to stir up trouble for the fat cats, he was more than willing to help. *And Lester, my man? You'll be the star of the whole fucking show.* He snickered. Did they really think adding security was going to stop him? They didn't know Jack. No, they didn't know *him*. Nobody did. Except Jenna. Now all he had to do was convince Mr. D. his plan would work—minus a few details, of course.

He finally drifted off to sleep imagining Jenna, naked and writhing, inviting him to her bed.

Two evenings later, Ralph Dorman walked by the usual group of council members and hangers-on with the well-practiced air of a man with a purpose.

"Oh, Mr. Dorman—"

"Can't talk now," he said with a dismissive wave of his hand. "I've got a client meeting to get to. Good night." Client meetings were the excuse he always used to deflect the yakkers after Little Eden's weekly council session. Sometimes he really did see clients, but in fact the last project he'd worked on was designing a mother-in-law unit over a garage last month. A garage, for God's sake! Thank God the kickbacks from New Venture Properties were still coming in, although he could tell the developer was getting restless about when he'd deliver on his end.

Because it was Myra's Bunco night, Dorman had arranged his usual hook-up with Wanda in Bellam's Cove. But right now he was dying for a cigarette. He scurried out the back door of the city hall and reached for his pack of Marlboro Lights. Just then he heard the faint click of a lighter, and a voice that murmured, "Want a light, Mr. Dorman?"

"Jesus, you scared the crap out of me, son." Dorman peered at the young man in the shadows. The kid was wearing a hooded sweatshirt pulled down low, and sunglasses, even in the dark. "Do I know you?"

"No, sir, but I know you…and I think I can help you out of some difficulties you're having."

Dorman looked around, not sure what to make of this creepy character, and feeling a bit vulnerable since no one else was anywhere near.

"Difficulties?"

"With The Grove."

What in the hell was he talking about? "I don't know what you mean."

The young man's voice was low, calm, and assured. "I think you do. You see, I work with Lester."

Oh shit. "Lester?"

The stranger sighed. "We can play games and waste time, or we can get to the point, *Mr. D*. I work at The Grove and let's just say, I know about your and Lester's little chit chats."

Despite the cold, Dorman was beginning to sweat. "I don't know what—"

"Cut the bullshit...*sir*. I know what you and that Wheeler dude and his SPEAR buddies are up to. Now I can blow the whistle on all your sorry asses, or I can do what I *really* want to do...which is to help you. I can, you know. Help you, that is. I have free run of the place, more than Lester. I've got access to keys he doesn't have. I've got—"

"Wait a minute." Dorman held up his hand in an effort to get his breathing under control. This punk obviously knew something or he wouldn't have dared approach Dorman. Shit. Shit. *Shit*. Maybe he could bluff his way out of this. "Son, I don't know what you think you know, but let me assure you—"

The kid closed the distance and got right in Dorman's face. "Listen, asshole. I recorded the little talk you had with Lester the other night. I know you're looking to blame each other for driving Rodriguez off the road. I know about the whacked out paint job. I know you're planning some cluster fuck to scare the shit out of the investors, and you're relying on a moron like Lester to make it happen. I've done my research and I know you want The Grove to go away. Well so do I, so either we work together...or we don't."

Dorman fought a rising surge of panic and began to

rationalize his way through this alarming new set of facts. Okay, so the kid knew something. If he'd really recorded the talk with Lester, that could ruin *everything*. But he didn't seem to have blackmail in mind; in fact, he sounded like he wanted to get his hands dirty, too. *Hell, maybe we can turn this to our advantage. Maybe we've got the makings of a scapegoat in case something goes wrong.* But what was in it for the kid?

"So, if I may ask, why are you invested in the demise of The Grove?"

"Let's just say I'll be happy to see the walls come crumbling down around Brit Maguire."

Dorman, intrigued, cocked his head. "Maguire, huh? What'd he do to get you so riled up?"

"I just don't want him around...certain people, that's all."

Dorman considered the young man while he took a drag on his nearly burnt-out cigarette. "What, you got the hots for that little redhead? What's her name...Tori Winston?"

"Shit, no. She's a slut. Besides, he's not with her anymore."

"Ah." Dorman took another educated guess. "It must be Ethan Wolff's granddaughter, then. They look like they might want to do the nasty, if they haven't already. She's a nice piece of ass if ever—"

In a flash the young man had grabbed Dorman by the lapels and shoved him against the back of the building. "You shut the fuck up," he growled. "You ever say or do anything to harm her and you're road kill, you got that?"

His hands raised in surrender, Dorman quickly sought to get the conversation back on track. The kid was thinking with his dick, and guys who did that could be manipulated. He smiled. "No offense, young man," he said. "I just…now I know why Maguire's on the top of your shit list. Hell, I don't blame you. He gets way more tail than he deserves."

The kid's eyes blazed and then hardened. Dorman realized with a growing sense of dread that despite his young years, the punk was probably capable of doing just about anything without batting an eye. "What's your name?" he finally asked.

"My name's not important. What's important is that the best place to stage your little ruckus on Saturday is at the equipment barn. Lots of gas, lots of potential for a really big boom. You tell Lester I'll make sure the building's open. He needs to soak the perimeter inside the barn when everyone's watching the slide show at the museum. Make sure he gets it good and soaked around the gas drums, and leads a trail to the side door in the back. He'll know which one I'm talking about. It opens from the inside. Then when they're all hanging around afterward and walking back to their rooms, all he has to do is light it near that side door and get the fuck out of there. Maybe he can even leave some cigarettes so it'll look afterward like some dipshit fucked up. You got all that?"

As he listened, Dorman's admiration—and fear—of the kid continued to grow. "Yeah, I got it," he said. "If I see this man Lester you've been talking about, I'll be sure to pass along your message."

The young man looked at Dorman and smirked. "You do that," he said.

Dorman watched as the punk turned back toward the darkness of the night. Just before he disappeared, he heard his voice one last time.

"We're in this together, Mr. D….to the end."

Dorman turned and walked toward his car, his hands shaking as he pulled his keys out and opened the door. Jesus, what had he gotten himself into now?

Chapter Twenty-One

"Okay, now this is creepy." Dani said. She and Jenna had just pulled into the parking lot of a neglected strip mall in the industrial section of Santa Rosa. Jenna parked in front of a non-descript storefront adorned with nothing but a plain green door with a small sign on it. A large white marquee with black letters proclaimed "Live Nud s Every Wknd."

"Remind me what a 'nud' is again?" Jenna asked facetiously.

As she'd promised several days earlier, Jenna had delved deeply into Peter Raines's past. The experience had not been pleasant; in fact, by the time she'd come up with a solid lead, she'd felt unclean. They'd taken the afternoon off to see where the lead would take them.

Dani's initial inquiries had proven, sadly, all too true. Peter Raines had spent the lion's share of his professional career as a photographer of women for both tabloid and pornographic display. Much of his published work was merely suggestive, but magazines like *Smut Gazette* and *Lusty Ladies* were hardcore and therefore underground enterprises—usually just one step ahead of the law. Peter Raines's photos could be seen in those publications up until a year or so before his death from alcoholism in 1934. It seemed as if The Grove had been his one and only attempt at artistic excellence.

Dani sighed as she took in the bleak surroundings. "I still can't figure out how you even thought to connect Peter, Lia, and porn. They seem about as different as night and day."

"The wonders of the Internet at work again," Jenna said. "I just kept thinking of all those pictures Peter took of Lia and wondered if maybe he tried to profit off them in some way. I mean, she was almost a rock star in the art world back then, so maybe he tried to cash in and she got mad, and that's why he left. Then I got to thinking about how he ended up in the porn business and thought, hey, what if he took some other photos of Lia that were, I don't know, racier than the ones we saw, and tried to sell *those*. So I googled *Peter Raines, Amelia Starling Wolff,* and *pornography* and came up with a link to this guy's website."

"I'm sorry, but anybody who spends a lifetime creating a database of old porn magazines has got to be an *idiota* of the first order."

"With a name like 'Bobby Tickler,' I wouldn't be surprised." Jenna grabbed her notebook and locked the car. She waited while Dani knocked on the door. After several raps, it was opened by a very tall man with extremely pale hair and almost snow-white skin.

"Yes?"

"Um, hello. I'm Jenna Bergstrom and this is my colleague Daniela Dunn. A Mr., um, Tickler, is expecting us."

The imposing albino gazed at them without emotion before ushering them inside the dimly lit club.

"Ms. Tickler is in her office. Follow me if you please," he announced in the precise diction befitting an aggrieved English butler.

Jenna and Dani looked at each other behind his back. "*Ms.?*" Jenna mouthed.

They were directed into a spacious room with a window overlooking a sweetly landscaped courtyard in the back of the building. Sitting behind the desk was a slightly overweight woman who looked to be in her mid to late sixties, with straight, jet-black hair spiced with gray. Dressed in a light blue polyester top with matching pants, she could have been anyone's youthful grandmother, and in fact had several family photos prominently displayed on the credenza behind her. She rose as they entered.

"Hello, I'm Roberta Tickler," she said jovially, extending her hand. "You must be the intrepid researcher who emailed me."

Jenna couldn't help but smile. "One and the same. I'm Jenna Bergstrom from The Grove Center Historic Trust and this is my colleague Daniela Dunn."

"A pleasure. Won't you sit down?" She instructed her imposing assistant to bring in some Diet Cokes before turning back to Jenna and Dani. "I trust that will suit you, although neither of you look like you need to watch your waistlines. I, on the other hand, must be ever vigilant." She patted her stomach for emphasis. "Now, I understand you're in search of some old photos."

Jenna pulled out her notebook. "Yes. In your email you mentioned you'd be happy to check your database to pull up any references or photos regarding the painter Amelia Starling Wolff in any of the…of the…"

"You can say it, dear: porn mags, smut rags, filthy garbage. We've just about heard it all." She smiled benignly.

"Um, pornographic publications, then."

Ms. Tickler chuckled. "You ought to try out for the diplomatic corps. At any rate, I inputted the names you gave me and came up with a couple of hits."

Dani had been looking around at the framed graphics of old-time porn magazines hung on the wall like awards. "Pardon my curiosity, but may I ask how you came to have all this information? I'm not sure how big the pornographic print industry was in the twenties and thirties, but it must have been quite an undertaking to catalog it all."

Roberta nodded sagely. "Ladies, you have no idea how prevalent it was then, and of course, continues to be today. This happens to be a family business, and being something of a historian myself, I undertook the project several years ago. My life's work, as I see it, is to create the world's first definitive encyclopedia of worldwide porn."

"Wow. That sounds quite...quite ambitious," Dani said.

Jenna caught Dani's glance and retained a passive expression even though she wanted to laugh. She and Roberta were two birds of a feather, weren't they? Both trying to research and weave part of the tapestry of American cultural history. "So, what did you come up with?"

Roberta took a file folder out of her desk drawer and opened it. "The first one was for a publication in the twenties out of Kansas City called *The Terrible Tattler*. Nothing hardcore in it, mind you. I'd compare it to the typical tabloid you find in today's supermarkets—just titillating enough to make it into my database. This issue featured some photos of Amelia Starling Wolff in a park or woods or something. The headline read 'Famed Artist Goes Wild in the Wild.'" She pulled out a copy of a photo and showed it to Jenna and Dani; it was one of the pictures that Peter had taken during his stint at The Grove.

So that's why he kept the negatives, Jenna thought. He was going to milk them for whatever they were worth.

"The other one..." Roberta paused and frowned as she looked at what her file contained. "The other one isn't quite so innocent, I'm afraid." She brought an entry close to her face and took off her glasses. "It's easier to read without them sometimes," she murmured. "Go figure." She scanned the page and looked up at Jenna and Dani. "This was taken from an industry insider's 'tip sheet.' It says here that in 1933

Raines submitted a photo which he called *Lia in Ecstasy* to a hardcore publication in Omaha, but the magazine apparently chose not to run the photo."

"Why wasn't it published?" Jenna asked. Her insides had begun to churn.

"Believe it or not, even the most hardcore magazines of that era had *some* standards," Roberta explained. "If they felt a woman was posing for a photograph against her will, they wouldn't touch it. Maybe they were afraid of getting sued, or being an accessory to a crime. Or maybe they just drew a moral line in the sand. I like to think it was the latter, of course."

Jenna's stomach lurched. *Against her will?* What was going on here? "May I see the photo?"

Roberta turned the file around so that Jenna could see it. It was a digital reproduction of an old photo that had been scanned into a computer file. The photo was small, grainy, and of course black and white. But none of those limitations could mask the content, which was of a petite, naked woman with long, flowing dark hair, lying across a bed naked with what looked like some kind of diaphanous scarf covering one breast, leaving the other exposed. She was looking at the camera with a stunned expression that sent chills down Jenna's spine. If it wasn't Lia Wolff, then it was her double. It was disgusting.

Dani looked at the photo, a look of sheer loathing on her face. Breathing harshly, she said, "So you're sure this was never made public?"

"I can't be one hundred percent certain, of course.

I'm limited by the scope of my database. But you can feel pretty confident that once this notice made the rounds of the industry, no one was willing to take a chance on publishing it."

"May we…may we take this photo?" Jenna asked.

"Of course, dear. Go ahead and take the whole file. I won't be publishing anything from it." She handed the material over, a concerned expression on her face. Jenna rose to go and noticed that Dani was still taking deep breaths, staring at her hands in her lap.

"Dani?" She touched her friend on the shoulder.

"What? Oh. Oh, yes. Thank you, Ms. Tickler."

"Call me Roberta." Just as Jenna and Dani rose to leave, the ghostlike assistant returned with the soft drinks. "One for the road," Roberta said, motioning for the man to give them each a can.

"Thank you, Roberta. You've been quite helpful," Jenna said.

"If it's any consolation, some of the world's most famous people have crossed our paths at one time or another. Everyone has a dark chapter or two they're not that proud of."

Jenna nodded and ushered Dani out the door. Back in the car they buckled up and Jenna gripped the steering wheel. "Holy moly."

Dani had finally calmed down somewhat. She turned to Jenna. "Do you think he…forced her to pose?"

"We don't even know for sure it was her. It could have been staged to look like her," Jenna said, even though her instincts screamed otherwise. She paused, dreading her next thought. "Or...she could have wanted it."

The look Dani gave Jenna was beyond fierce. "No way."

"We probably won't know for certain unless we find the negatives and see more shots."

Dani shook her head. "They weren't with the stuff stored under 1905–1906. Of course, why would they be? It's not as if Peter would say, 'Hey everybody, I just violated my mentor, and here are the negatives to prove it.'"

Jenna let out a choked laugh. It was absurd—so horribly, disgustingly absurd. "Well, we know he kept at least some of his negatives for years, so perhaps we can track those down somehow."

Dani touched Jenna on the shoulder. "We don't need to keep doing this, you know. We can just...just leave it right here."

Jenna shook her head. "No," she said forcefully. "Everyone deserves to know the truth about themselves and where they came from. If I stop now, I'll always know more about Peter Raines than Da does, and I shouldn't hold that power over him." She paused, forced a smile. "But hey, maybe we'll find something to vindicate the man. Ever think of that?"

"Yes.... Of course." Dani's response was muted, but Jenna could hear the skepticism in her voice loud and clear.

While Jenna started the ninety-minute drive back to The Grove, Dani reached for the notes Jenna had brought along and flipped through the pages. "Okay, we know Peter Raines dropped out of sight after he signed the earthquake survivors' list. From that day forward there are no more photos of Lia by him, no commentaries by him, no mentions of him by anybody at The Grove, except a few comments that more or less said 'Good riddance.' And he wasn't in the year-end group photo. If he forced her to pose for obscene photos, wouldn't the police be after him? He wasn't hiding all those years. Why wasn't he caught, and even worse, why did he return to the scene of the crime? Granted, it was twenty years later, but still..."

"Maybe he figured if she hadn't turned him in for so long, she never would," Jenna surmised. "Or there was a statute of limitations or something. Or maybe he was just an arrogant prick."

Dani snorted. "That I can believe. So he comes back, gets rejected again, this time over money, then, according to the article we read, proceeds to seduce his victim's daughter. Comes back ready to sneer in their faces and force them to welcome him into their happy family, but suddenly changes his mind and leaves again, this time for good."

Jenna continued the litany. "He goes back home to Kansas to lick his wounds. Continues working in the porn industry. Tries years later to sell a smutty photo of Lia, fails at that..."

"And drinks himself to death at his father's farm by 1934," Dani concluded.

Outside of Santa Rosa, Jenna turned onto the freeway headed south. "I can't remember—was his father still living?"

Dani checked the notes. "Apparently so. He didn't die until 1939. So he would have had five years in which to pack up his son's effects."

"And done what with them?"

"Put them in the attic?"

"Maybe. Is the farm still in the family?"

"Easy enough to find out." Dani pulled out her iPhone and called up the Internet. Referring to the address she'd jotted down in her notes, she tapped several keys. "County Records," she said in response to Jenna's quizzical look. "The answer is no," she announced after several minutes. "The farm was sold in 1940 and has had, looks like six or seven owners since then. So my guess is the attic, or barn, or wherever old stuff was stored, has been cleaned out several times by now."

Jenna drove silently, thinking over the scenario. Peter's father must have been devastated by what his son had become, especially knowing how talented Peter was when he was younger, when he'd been an artist at The Grove. Remembering that time might have filled the father with pride. Or maybe not. Could be he was mad that his son had become a photographer and not a farmer. Who knows—perhaps he just got rid of all the evidence of his son's sordid profession. She couldn't help but voice her fear. "What if the father just destroyed it all?"

"Then we're up against a pretty thick brick wall," Dani said. "The possibilities are fairly cut and dried. Either his father stored Peter's things and they're still at the farm someplace—a long shot, but we can always try to track that down—or he sent items to another relative and we can try to track that as well. Or he destroyed it, in which case, it doesn't really matter."

Jenna kept thinking of the poor father. How would he hold on to some shred of pride in his son? Then it struck her. *By donating the fruits of his son's artistic labors.* Of course. And what better place to donate the material than to The Grove! "I've got a hunch," she said excitedly.

"Let's hear it."

"What if, during the period between Peter's death and his father's death, the father actually boxed up the negatives and shipped them to The Grove?"

"Hmm."

"Think about it. We haven't inventoried the decade of the thirties. That's when it would have been sent."

Dani frowned. "Wouldn't Lia have known right away what it was?"

"Not necessarily. She was in her sixties by then, and the studio was in its heyday. They must have had a lot of stuff coming in and going out of there. Maybe no one thought to bring it to her attention."

By this time they had reached Little Eden and Jenna pulled over in front of the Havenwood Inn. Dani got out and leaned inside the passenger window. "You want to come in for a quick bite to eat?"

"I'd love to, but I think I'll explode if I don't check out my theory."

"Would you like me to come up there with you?"

"No, that's okay." Jenna grinned. "I wouldn't want

you to hear me swearing a blue streak if I don't find what I'm hoping to find."

"All right, but you call me the minute you've checked the inventory—the minute!"

"Yes, ma'am. And Dani? Thanks for coming with me today."

"Are you kidding? I wouldn't have missed 'Bobbie Tickler' and her albino butler for the world." She grew somber. "I'm torn. I want to know what happened, but not if it's too painful to bear, especially given the stress the professor's already under."

"I know. But he says he wants the truth, no matter what it is, and I've got to respect that."

Dani nodded and tapped the window ledge. "Call me," she reiterated.

Jenna drove up the hill toward The Grove with a jumble of emotions racing through her. She felt she was on the brink of solving the mystery of why Peter Raines left The Grove, at least the first time, so many years ago. But the answer was unthinkable.

She drove through the grand entrance to the estate and couldn't help but look around to see if Brit was still working. No sign of him. She parked next to the new museum building and let herself inside, entering the storage room and placing her hands on the security scanner.

"Welcome, Jenna Bergstrom," the voice said.

As always, the futuristic technology intrigued her.

"Lights on, please," she commanded softly once she was in the secured area, and it was immediately bathed in its usual soft glow.

Having spent some time cataloging the collection for the museum exhibit, Jenna now knew her way around, so she went directly to the section housing the artwork for 1934, the year Peter Raines had died. In that section of the room several paintings hung in their special vertical holders, a shelf held a few sculptures, and three clearly labeled boxes showed decorative art pieces as their contents. Nothing looked like it might contain photographs or negatives.

Jenna made the same inspection for the years 1935–1937 and found nothing that remotely resembled a box of negatives.

But for 1938 she hit pay dirt.

Leaning against the wall behind a shelf housing artwork was a very old-looking, medium-sized box. The tape covering the box was yellowed and pealing, and the writing on the address label was so faded as to be hardly legible. Jenna looked closely and noticed the return address first. She saw "Salina, Kansas" and her heart began racing. *This is it.* Oddly, the package wasn't addressed to Amelia Wolff or to The Grove; instead it was made out to "Miss Giselle and Mr. Ethan Wolff *care of* The Grove." Maybe that's why no one paid any attention to it, she thought. Either they didn't know Ethan, or planned on giving it to him the next time they saw him or Giselle, which was probably not that often, since by that time Giselle would have been married and living elsewhere.

With mental apologies to Da for snooping, she lifted the package and set it up on a table. Peeling off the old tape, she opened the box. Inside were several folders full of film sleeves, one or two glass negatives, and a smaller box containing camera accessories and what looked like a large pocket watch. On top of the items was a thin, sealed brown envelope addressed to "The Wolffs." It was attached to a larger envelope that wasn't sealed. Jenna took out the contents of the larger envelope and found several old newspaper clippings from the *San Francisco Chronicle* as well as some tabloid-type publications from the late 1920s and 1930s. All of the articles had one thing in common: they mentioned the Wolff family.

"Maybe Peter Raines had a heart after all," Jenna murmured. She put the material back in the box and carried it out of the secured storage area. When she opened the door from the outer storage room to the hallway, Kyle was standing right in front of her.

"Hello, Ms. Bergstrom," he said softly.

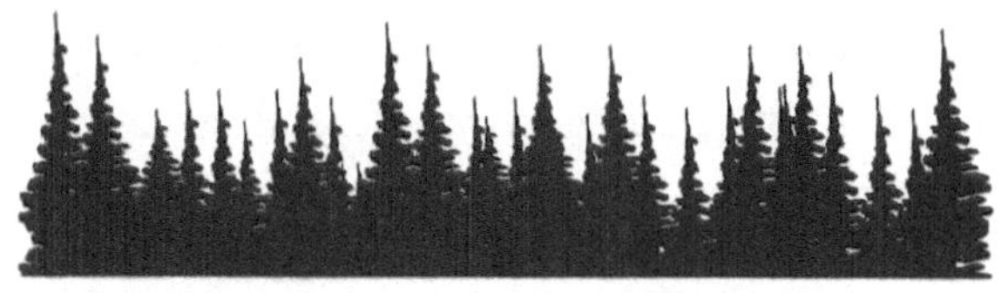

Chapter Twenty-Two

Jenna's heart leapt through her throat and she almost dropped the box. "Kyle! What are you doing here?"

"Parker said you were in here. I wanted to make sure you're okay. It's getting late, you know." He took a step toward her. "Here let me take that." He gestured to the box she was carrying.

Jenna felt like recoiling, even though rationally she knew that was the wrong response. Maybe he had a crush on her. So what? He was only seventeen—albeit a *big* seventeen. But the feeling of panic persisted and she wondered if Brit were anywhere nearby. She forced her voice to sound neutral. "No. I mean, how did you get in the building? You need a key this time of day."

Kyle shrugged his shoulders. "The outer door was open. I just walked in."

He had to be lying. Thankfully the art collection was still protected by electronic security, but somehow Kyle had found a way into the main museum building, whose door she'd shut when she'd entered earlier. Unless someone else had come in and left the door unlocked, which was highly unlikely, that meant Kyle had to have a key. And if he had a key, maybe he was the one to leave that cryptic note in her room. But how did he get one? Brit said the keys were all accounted for, and master keys couldn't be duplicated...could they?

Now was not the time to challenge the teen, but she had to let Brit know about the breach as soon as possible. In the meantime, Kyle Summers wasn't someone she wanted to remain alone with. "Oh. I guess I left it open," she lied. "Well, here, thanks." She handed him the box and they left the building, heading down the path to Ethan's cottage. Thankfully it was still light out and some of the other workers were milling about. She began to calm down.

"About the last day of school," Kyle began.

"I told you, that's old news. Really."

"No, I gotta say this. I was a complete idiot and I don't blame you for bustin' me. Sometimes I just...well, I just need to think before I speak, that's all. You're a nice person and you don't deserve that shit—I mean that kind of treatment."

Jenna looked at him in confusion. Was she wrong about this guy? "Well, I'm glad you're working on that."

"Oh, I am. I still think it, though. I mean, about you and all, but..."

"TMI, Kyle."

He sniggered. "Too much information. I get it."

They were approaching the Firestone Cottage and

Kyle switched gears as teens do so well. "Hey, you think Jason might want to shoot some pool?"

"Yeah, maybe so," Jenna said. They reached the porch and Jenna tapped lightly on the front door. "Ethan…Da?" she called through the screen.

"Inside, my dear," came the response.

"I've got Kyle out here. He wants to know if Jason can go shoot some pool."

Instead of Ethan's voice, Jason himself came to the door. "Hey, bro. Let's have at it. Lucky's in Bellam's Cove?"

"Sounds good, man. Uh, here, Ms. Bergstrom." Kyle handed her the box.

"Well, thanks for your help, Kyle."

He looked at her intently. "Anytime, sweet lady."

Jason rolled his eyes. "Sweet lady? Dude, you sound like some reject from a Borat routine."

Jason didn't catch the angry look Kyle gave him as they headed toward Kyle's car, but Jenna did. Maybe it *was* time to let Kyle go. But at the moment, other matters were more important than a teenage crush—unless he'd been the one to take it too far and invade her room.

She found her grandfather in his usual chair, reading from a stack of letters and articles. He raised his glasses to the top of his head and looked over at her. "How are you, Jenna?"

She put the box by his feet and bent to kiss him on the forehead. "I found something, Da," she said quietly. "It might answer some questions."

"I can tell by the look on your face they aren't necessarily the answers I'd like to have."

Jenna sighed and pulled up a dining room chair. "Dani and I visited an unlikely source this afternoon. A porn historian, of all things."

Ethan chuckled. "The sacrifices one makes for one's profession. It was 'revealing,' I take it?"

"Ha, ha." Jenna smiled briefly, but her heart wasn't in it.

Ethan's voice sobered. "Tell me, my dear. I'm ready."

She explained Peter's seeming obsession with Lia and theories about why he might have left The Grove so suddenly. She described how logic led her to the storage room and how she'd found the box that now lay at his feet. "I couldn't help but open it," she admitted.

Ethan took her hand. "That's all right, my dear. You make a superb detective. So tell me, what is in the box?"

"A letter addressed to you and your mom, for starters. You would have been around eleven, I think. It was sealed, so I didn't open it. Here."

He took the letter; she noticed his hands were shaking. Ever the researcher aware of primary sources, he took a letter opener and gingerly slid it under the sealed flap, taking care not to tear the envelope other than to open it. He pulled out a thin piece of paper and, putting his glasses back on, began to read:

Dear Miss Wolff and Young Mr. Wolff,

I don't ritely know who you are or what connects you to my son Peter, but I am sorry to tell you that the cursed rot gut finally took my boy and he went to his Maker these four years past. It took me awhile to decide what to do, but now I got the sense my time here on this earth is ending, so I am sending you his fotografy trappings becus for some reason he must have took a liking to you and your famly. I can tell that becus I found these papers with his things. Peter never did have no famly of his own besides me, so I rekon he mite have looked on you that way, although he never said nothin' to me about it. If that's so, then you ought to have what belonged to him. He was a good boy at heart and I still miss him somethin terrible.

Yours truly, Abner F.Raines"

Da said nothing as he pulled the newspaper clippings out of the larger envelope.

"They're all about my family," he murmured. He went through them one at a time and paused after he'd finished the last one. Plucking a tissue from the table next to his chair, he quietly lifted his glasses and dabbed his eyes. Jenna could feel her own tears rolling down her cheeks as she leaned over and hugged this man who was indeed her beloved grandfather.

"You see, he loved you," she whispered.

"Perhaps. Or perhaps it was just idle curiosity." He looked at her with sad acceptance in his eyes. "We'll never know, will we?"

"No, I suppose not," she said, thinking of her own birth mother. "But we can hold on to that, can't we?"

Da touched her arm gently and glanced down at the open box. "So, what legacy did my dear old father leave me?" He began to reach down.

With a grimace, Jenna stayed his hand. "Those are mainly negatives, Da. Some, we hope, are from his time at The Grove. But some…"

Ethan looked at her, courage and wisdom in his forthright gaze. "Some are what, Jenna?"

It was now or never. "Some are pornographic, and some, we suspect…we fear…might be evidence of a crime he committed against Lia Wolff."

"What crime?"

"We think he might have taken obscene photos of her against her will."

"My God," Ethan said, leaning back into his chair. "Are you sure?"

"No, we aren't. The little evidence we were shown is inconclusive. But if you want to find out for certain, then we'll have to find someone or some place that can print these negatives, and do it discreetly."

Ethan closed his eyes for a moment or two, as if he were gathering strength. "I have someone in mind for the job," he finally said.

"You do? I swear, you seem to know someone who can do just about anything."

Ethan smiled faintly. "I do, don't I? It must come from being on the planet so long—you're bound to run into all sorts of people from all walks of life."

"But you're one of the few people I know who can charm them into doing your bidding." Jenna hoped her banter would lighten Ethan's mood, which had darkened considerably since she'd arrived. But it couldn't be helped. He'd asked for the truth, and she was going to give him what he wanted. She just wished it didn't hurt so much. "So, who is this person?" she asked. "Is he or she in the city?"

Ethan smiled. "It's a he, and unless I miss my guess, he's about as far from the city right now as one could possibly be. He lives in northern Idaho and travels a lot. But he is the only one for this job, and I'll wait until I can contact him. In the meantime, we must push on. The Investors' Preview is just a few days away, you know."

"I know, and don't you worry. Dani and I have the prototype almost finished. I think you'll like what you see."

Da reached over and patted her hand. "I have no doubt of that, Jenna my love. Never had. Never will."

Brit heard Jenna enter the back door and his fading energy kicked up a notch. He continued stirring the saucepan full of chili, hoping she'd stop by to see what was cooking. When he heard her footsteps entering the kitchen, he smiled and took a swig of his beer.

"I made an extra potato," he said casually, not looking up. "Care to join me?"

She walked over to the stove and peered into the pot. "Looks like you're having chili."

"I am—on my potato." He grinned. "Gourmet all the way."

Jenna put her purse on the counter. "Tell you what. I'll make a salad and we'll make it a five-star meal."

"I like the way you think," he said. "Beer or wine?"

"With chili? Beer, of course. What have you got?"

"Oh, a brewery snob, huh?" Turning the chili on low, he walked over and opened the subzero refrigerator, his arm high on the door. "I've got Stella, Heineken, Bud, Payback, Anchor…"

Jenna scooted under his arm to peer inside. "Oh, you've got Payback Porter? I love that." She leaned over to check the lower shelves and bins, pulling out salad ingredients. Brit couldn't help but enjoy the view. He reached beyond her to pull out the bottle and poured the dark, chocolaty brew into a glass.

One of the granite countertops in the industrial-size kitchen had a built-in chopping block and Jenna used it to prep the salad. Brit checked on the potatoes, stirred the chili, and found himself grinning at the domestic pair they made.

"What's so funny?" she asked.

"Nothing. Just…how'd your day go today?"

"Some good, some bad," Jenna said. She told him about searching for the truth about Peter Raines, how it led to the box of negatives, and the sad history that might come to light as a result of what she'd found.

"That sucks," Brit said. "How's Ethan doing with it?"

"All right, I guess. I think he's at the point where he'd rather know the truth, no matter where it leads."

"Yeah, truth is good." He took another drink of his Heineken. Why did it suddenly taste so delicious?

"And…there was something else," she said, a note of caution in her voice.

"Uh oh. That doesn't sound good."

"Kyle was waiting for me when I came out of the

storage room. When I asked how he got in the building, he told me the door was open, but I know for certain I closed it when I went in."

"Nobody else around?"

"Not that I saw."

"Which means that somehow he might have a key."

Jenna shrugged. "Or someone came in after me that I didn't see. I just don't know."

"Did he seem defensive, like you caught him where he shouldn't be?"

"Not at all. He was looking for me, in fact. He said Parker told him I was inside, and he specifically wanted to talk to me."

"Like the other night on the job site," Brit mused.

"Exactly. He apologized for his outburst on the last day of school. Maybe I'm a lousy judge of character, but he sounded totally sincere to me."

"Do you think Kyle could have been the intruder the other night?"

Jenna frowned. "I honestly don't have a clue. Obviously the initials don't match up, but that would be pretty stupid on his part if they did. I think Kyle might have a crush on me, but would he go to so much trouble? I suppose if I left, and he quit his job shortly afterward, that would tell us something. But it could just as easily be someone who doesn't want me caught in the middle of all the problems with The Grove, or worse—someone who wants to scare me and my grandfather off. But do you honestly think it could be Mr. Wheeler? Somehow I just can't picture it." She sighed in apparent frustration.

Brit gave her shoulder a brief, reassuring squeeze. "No telling who it is at this point. Maybe Gabe will come up with something. In the meantime, how would you like me to handle the kid? I can fire him, I can ream him, or I can keep an eye on him, see if he does something out of line. If it were me, I'd can him." He hesitated. "But you make the call."

Jenna sent Brit one of her luminous smiles that made it all worthwhile. She put her hand on his arm. "Thank you for leaving it up to me, Brit. I hate to give Kyle the shaft for something I have no proof of. So my gut tells me to just keep an eye on him. I do think he's a good kid at heart."

Brit shook his head. "I had a feeling you'd go soft on me." His eyes softened. "But the lady has spoken." As he served up dinner, he brought up a brighter topic. "So, how's the presentation coming? I assume you and Dani have that well under control."

Jenna grinned. "We do, as a matter of fact. I think Da's really going to like what we have so far." With lively gestures she described the prototype exhibit and some of the many facts about the artists they'd uncovered. Just listening to her, Brit felt his own dampened enthusiasm begin to reboot. No matter what she was willing to admit, he could tell that Jenna Bergstrom *loved* what she was doing. He raised his bottle and tapped her glass. "To a successful Investors' Preview," he toasted.

"Here, here," she said with delight.

After dinner they worked together to clean up the

kitchen. Then Jenna made a suggestion that just about blew him away.

"Listen, you've been very kind to give up your bed just so I'd feel secure," she started. "And I do. More than you know. And tonight I'm willing to move to the sofa bed, or even back to my own room, if you want. But… the Giants are playing the Padres in—" she looked at her watch "—about fifteen minutes, and the TV in your bedroom is a lot bigger than mine. So would you mind, terribly, if I watch the game with you before I go to bed?"

A feeling of déjà vu swept over Brit and he almost staggered with it. He remembered vividly the first night they ever met. How easily they'd connected, on so many levels. How *right* they felt together. Just like tonight. Was this going to end the same way? He hesitated and Jenna picked right up on it.

"Oh. I'm sorry. Forget I even asked. That was a truly dumb idea. Listen, I'll just—"

"No, that's a *great* idea," he said. "I was just thinking about…making popcorn. That's it. If you can't have hot dogs, you gotta have popcorn. You go up and turn on the game. I'll nuke some and bring it up."

"You're sure?" She looked vulnerable. She looked sweet. Damn, she looked good enough to eat. The hell with the popcorn.

No, no, don't go there.

Twenty minutes later, Brit and Jenna were ensconced on his king-sized bed, propped up on pillows, watching the game and eating popcorn out of the same big bowl. As often happened when he was too comfortable watching sports on TV, Brit let his fatigue take over. By the time he finally turned off the TV with the remote, Jenna had already fallen asleep, her head on his shoulder, her arm laying gently across his chest. He pulled a comforter over them and switched out the light. Their very first night together, seven years ago, they had tumbled into bed and spent the hours wrapped in each other's arms just like this. He hadn't taken her then and he wasn't about to take her now, even though every instinct in him cried out to roll Jenna beneath him, wake her with kisses, and make her his. Eventually, weariness slowed his blood enough that sleep gained the upper hand. The last thought Brit had before dropping off was *I am right where I want to be.*

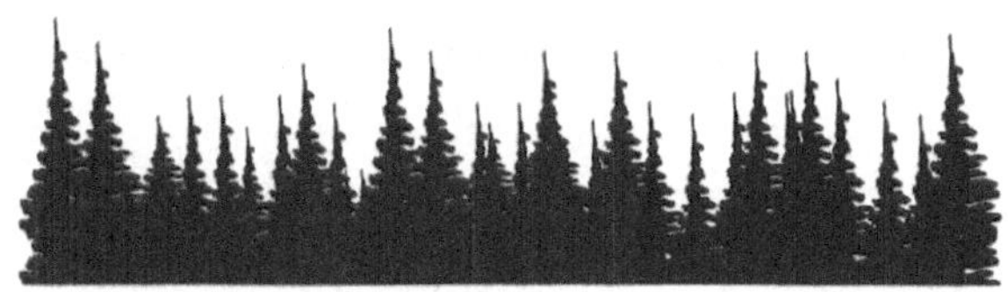

Chapter Twenty-Three

"As you've seen here tonight, the perfect nexus of art, commerce, and public good took place on these very grounds for nearly half a century, producing some of the world's most intriguing expressions of art, sculpture, and design. Soon, through your continued support, The Grove Center Historic Trust will re-establish that synergy for a new generation of artists and art lovers. We can all be proud of what we're accomplishing here at The Grove. May I have the lights on, please?"

Jenna heaved a sigh of relief and watched her grandfather bask in the applause coming from the small but select audience seated in the media room of the museum building. The PowerPoint presentation she and Dani had created had gone off without a hitch. They'd artfully combined vintage photos of the old retreat and its resident artists with images of both the renovated and new buildings nestled amidst the setting's timeless natural beauty.

The presentation was the climax of a busy day spent touring the grounds, followed by a catered dinner. As a result, the "money men," as Jason called them, seemed reassured, or at least cautiously optimistic that their investment would soon begin to pay off. Not financially, of course—that would take time as the art complex became known as a destination in its own right. But at least the major donors would reap the benefits of increased public goodwill. Jenna noted wryly that Brit had designed an impressive "Founder's Wall" that greeted visitors as soon as they arrived at the center.

As Ethan sat down, Brit rose and walked to the podium. Dressed in a linen sport jacket with a peach dress shirt and cream-colored tie, he looked handsome, assured, and downright *delicious*. He glanced at Jenna and smiled briefly before addressing the group.

"I'd like to thank Jenna Bergstrom and Daniela Dunn for putting together that excellent presentation," he said, eliciting another round of applause from the group. "They, along with the professor, are truly the heart and soul of this endeavor. As you saw in their prototype museum exhibit earlier today, they will bring history alive in this beautiful place. We are lucky to have them as part of The Grove Center team."

Jenna blushed, hoping no one noticed. She tried to cover it by raising her wine glass in a playful salute to Dani, who sat across from her. Dani grinned back.

God, what a feeling! How long had it been since she'd felt truly part of something bigger than herself? Part of a team. Part of a *family*. She gazed at Brit and realized he had a lot to do with it. He wanted her close to him and he wasn't afraid to let her know it, even if it was mainly because of the threat they faced.

Although the Great House was now protected by the new alarm system, Brit had insisted she remain in his suite—for *his* peace of mind, he'd said. They continued to sleep in separate beds, but the undercurrent between them that Sherrie had kidded her about was constantly humming. Jenna was in fact finding it hard to fall asleep at night, knowing he was so close. More than once she'd fantasized about sleep-walking right into his muscular arms.

"So there you have it," Brit continued. "Over a hundred years ago, two visionaries created a welcoming space for artists who in turn produced some of the most outstanding creative expressions of the twentieth century. With the opening of The Grove Center for American Art, that tradition will continue, but with the added mission of giving the public an opportunity to experience both the past and the present through exhibition, instruction, and interaction with resident artists. Now, before we adjourn, I'd be happy to answer any questions you may still have."

Jenna glanced around the room and saw satisfied looks on nearly everyone's face. The one exception was Garrick Winston, Tori's father. Earlier in the evening, the Texas-born financier had cornered Jenna, making it plain he'd be more than happy to partake in some extracurricular activities. Jenna had gracefully fended him off.

Now, however, Winston was showing a different

side. Someone had been filling him in on the various setbacks the project had experienced and he wasn't convinced that all was well.

"It looks like you spit polished the place up pretty good," he said. "But I understand you've had problem after problem, and even some vandalism. Sounds like the locals aren't too keen on this project getting off the ground."

Brit looked the powerful, older developer squarely in the eye. "Well, you're half right," he said. "It's true we've had problems. Some have been run of the mill, others not so common. And it's true that a small minority of the community hasn't yet realized the advantages that a revitalized Grove will bring to the area. But each and every hurdle has been dealt with successfully. We believe we're changing the hearts and minds of most of the naysayers and we're confident we'll meet the targeted Grand Opening in early October. We need your continued support—" he paused to look around at the other investors "—*all* your support, to see this project through. I hope you'll have enough faith in all of us here at The Grove to make that happen." Brit once again scanned the room. "Are there any more questions?" Heads shook and no one responded. After a moment he closed with, "All right then. That concludes the planned portion of our evening. I'd like to invite everyone to the library of the Great House, where after-dinner drinks will be served."

After Brit finished speaking, he began making his way toward Jenna but was waylaid by Tori, who had also commandeered the arm of her father. Jenna couldn't make out what they were saying, but it was obvious by their body language that Tori had suggested a rendezvous of some sort that Brit, gesturing to Jenna, had refused. Both Tori and her father caught Jenna's eye; neither of them looked happy. Without thinking, Jenna rose and walked over to rescue Brit.

"There you are," he said, putting his arm possessively around her. "How'd I do, sweetheart?"

Jenna's eyebrows rose at the feigned intimacy, but before she could say anything, Tori's father cut her off.

"So, that's how it is," he said in a disgruntled tone. "Might have known it'd be you, Maguire." He turned to his daughter. "Come on, girl. It's obvious you got no dog in this hunt now."

"Daddy, I—"

"I said come on. And Maguire? You'd best make nice with the locals or the money'll dry up faster than a witch's tit." Tori reluctantly turned to leave with her father, but the look she gave Jenna over her shoulder was a combination of frustration, sadness, and longing. She must really care for him, Jenna thought. Strangely, she felt no jealousy, only empathy. It's painful to care for someone if the love isn't returned.

Jenna glanced at Brit. "That was pleasant."

"That was necessary," Brit countered. "My next tactic was going to involve a very large club."

Jenna smiled and turned to go, but Brit caught her by the elbow.

"We need to talk," he said quietly but urgently.

Jenna gestured to the group of investors filing out of the room. "What about them?"

"Dani and the professor are holding court. This can't wait." He took Jenna's hand, all but dragging her out a side door of the media room, down a hallway, and into one of the new offices. Shutting the door, he pressed her up against the wall. It was dark, but there were no blinds in the windows and a three-quarter moon shone through, illuminating the two of them.

"What are you doing?" she asked, her breath hitching.

"Something I've been dying to do all week." He angled his head and captured her lips in a fiercely sensual kiss.

Wrapped in the cocoon of moonlight and secure in his arms, Jenna opened herself to the exquisite feeling of Brit's lips softening gradually over hers as the triumph of possession gave way to tenderness. She heard a soft whimper, and knew it belonged to her. *This*, her mind railed. This is what you've wanted all along. *Stop. Running.* The walls she'd tried to maintain crumbled as she gave herself to the kiss. She wriggled her arms free and drove her fingers through his dark, unruly hair as his mouth slanted over hers again and again, demanding access she gladly yielded. Their tongues dueled and savored, in turn, as waves of pleasure cascaded throughout her body. His slightly unsteady hands roamed over her body, settling finally on her backside as he pulled her snugly between the *V* of his thighs and against his solid shaft. He lifted his head slightly and began exploring her face with tiny kisses, first her eyebrows and lids, the soft skin behind her ear, the corner of her mouth. He paused, breathing in her scent from the crook of her neck.

"It's been the sweetest kind of hell having you in my bed and not touching you." His voice was deep, guttural.

"You're touching me now," she said breathlessly.

He groaned. "It's not enough. Not nearly enough. "

Panting, she tilted her head to give him greater access to her neck. "I want—"

"What do you want? Tell me," he demanded.

"I don't know. It's complicated. I—"

"No, it's simple," he said. "You want me. And I sure as hell want you." He paused long enough to skim his hands down the sleek sides of her turquoise cocktail dress before bringing them around to cradle her breasts. "Do you remember anything about the night we made love?" he whispered.

Jenna, too agitated to speak, merely nodded.

"I remember...*everything*," he murmured, continuing his sensual assault. "I remember a golden girl...sweet, intelligent...funny. I remember your beautiful breasts...your delectable rear...and the way you wrapped those long, gorgeous legs around me." He gently stroked and squeezed each part of her body as he described it. "And I remember how hot and tight and wet you were for me...only for me. God, Jenna." The last words were cut off as he took her mouth again, drawing her tongue into an age-old dance of intimacy.

Jenna was lost as she found herself responding to this man exactly as she had done seven years before. As his hand found the edge of her dress and began lifting it higher, she moaned, willingly lifting one leg to wrap around his waist, wanting nothing more than the feel of him entering her body.

At that precise moment a huge explosion shook the building, rattling the windows and causing a fireball to light up the night outside the window, filling the room with the harsh light of reality.

Chapter Twenty-Four

"What the hell?!" Brit turned around when a second explosion followed on the heels of the first. He immediately wrapped his arms protectively around Jenna.

"My God, was that a bomb?" she cried. She couldn't believe what was happening. She quickly dropped her leg and straightened her dress, fear turning her passion into panic.

"I don't know," Brit said grimly. "Let's find out."

They ran out of the building, passing several workers and a few investors rushing in different directions with terror-stricken faces. The street lights had not gone out, and Jenna saw her brother across the lawn.

"Jason! Do you know what happened?"

"It looks like the equipment barn blew up!" he called as he ran in that direction. "I just called 911."

"Anybody hurt?" Brit yelled.

"Don't know yet!"

Brit took Jenna by the shoulders. "Go back to the Great House. I'll check it out."

"Not in your life," she shot back. "I'm staying with you."

Brit nodded curtly and started running toward the maintenance area. Thankful she'd worn flats to the presentation, Jenna easily kept up with him. As they crested the hill, Brit stopped short and stuck out his arm to keep Jenna from running past him. "Too dangerous!" he yelled.

She grabbed onto his arm to stop her momentum. *Oh my God—this is hell on earth.* The front two-thirds of the huge barn was a fireball shooting flames a hundred feet in the sky. And the heat was so intense, she felt as if even her blood was boiling. Smoke was everywhere, sucking the oxygen from the air. Men were shouting and running back and forth, trying to be heard over the roar of the inferno. *Please keep Jason and Da away from this*, Jenna prayed, her breathing harsh and labored.

"How's it looking, Jack?" Brit called out to the man he'd pegged to help manage the crew.

"Not good." Jack, looking disgusted, tossed a hose on the ground where it joined several others coiled haphazardly in the gloom like somnolent snakes. "Whoever did this cut the hoses. We can't get any pressure, so we're down to a bucket brigade until the fire trucks get here."

"Everybody accounted for?"

"I think so, but it's pretty crazy right now. Maybe we oughta do a head count."

Brit looked around in frustration. In the distance sirens could be heard. "Good idea," he said. "Maybe—"

"Mr. Maguire! Mr. Maguire!" Parker Bishop and Kyle Summers ran up to the group.

"What's wrong?" Jenna cried.

"I think…I think—" Parker seemed to be particularly anxious.

"Spit it out, man," Brit barked.

Jenna tugged on Brit. "Give him a chance to calm down!" she scolded.

"We think…we think maybe that guy Lester's still in the building!" Kyle's voice was tinged with panic.

"How do you know?" Brit asked, his tone sharper than steel.

"We were on litter patrol down around the lower bungalows. Parker said he saw him go inside."

"How could you see in the dark?" Jenna asked.

"I think it was him, but I don't know for sure," Parker hedged.

"The light wasn't that good, but we saw *somebody* go inside and close the slider. You can tell when that big sucker closes," Kyle explained. "I didn't think much of it and kept working."

"Me too," Parker said.

"No, you were on the phone, dude, remember?"

Parker nodded. "Yeah, that's right. My dad called. And then, *Kablam!* So we started running back here."

Brit didn't waste a second. "Anybody seen Lester?" he yelled to the members of the makeshift fire crew.

A chorus of "no's" came back.

"Jack, you got a master key on you?" he called out.

The man shook his head.

"Get one!" Brit yelled. He then headed toward the back of the barn.

"Where do you think you're going?" Jenna cried, grabbing his arm.

"If he's in there, there's a chance he's in the back and can't get out," Brit said. "He may not be able to get to the side door. We've got to get it open and help him out."

"But you're not going in after him, right?"

Brit paused and looked at Jenna, running his fingertip down the side of her cheek. "Don't worry." With that he took off, glancing back once before he turned the corner of the building.

Speechless, Jenna watched his retreating figure as if in slow motion. She noticed vaguely that Kyle and Parker had walked up on either side of her. Kyle put his arm around her shoulders.

"It's all right," he said soothingly. "We're here."

Jenna turned and looked up at the large, muscular young man. He had the same glittery look he'd had the last day of school. Then she looked at Parker. He was staring at Kyle and his eyes burned ferociously, just as they had that same day. Fear, slippery and cold, slid over her.

"We need to help Brit," she said neutrally, hoping her voice wouldn't betray the anxiety threatening to overtake her.

By the time she worked her way safely around to the side of the burning barn, several burly workmen were in the process of battering the side door with what looked like a large fence post. The door was already starting to buckle from the heat. When it finally gave way, smoke billowed out and Jenna watched in horror as Brit tore off his jacket, tie, and shirt, soaking the latter in a nearby bucket and wrapping it around his nose and mouth.

"Don't go in there—please!" Jenna cried.

Brit looked at her briefly, his eyes communicating what words could not. Then he disappeared inside the carnage. Moments later another deafening explosion ripped apart the air.

"Nooooo!" Jenna screamed. Tears streaming down her face, arms wrapped around herself to keep from falling apart, Jenna stared in shock at the burning, crumbling building, her only words a mantra-like "please God, please God, please God."

She felt someone—Parker, perhaps—urge her back from the heat of the fire, but she couldn't seem to move. Her entire focus was on the jagged hole into which Brit had run. She couldn't believe he was gone. Wouldn't believe it. He was going to walk out again. Any second now. Any second. Any second.

And a moment later, he did.

Brit emerged from the building spitting ash out of his mouth, carrying the limp, mangled body of Lester Small in his arms. Lester was wearing gloves and it looked like they'd melted onto his hands. He was burned in several other places and Brit cringed at the pain he must be feeling—or would be feeling, if he were conscious. *Come on man, don't give up on me.* Using his own dampened shirt to protect Lester's soot-blackened face, Brit could feel the hot sting of embers on his back. The smoke he'd inhaled was beginning to work its way back out of him, fighting with his lungs as they tried to take in the cleaner air. He could feel the adrenalin seeping out of his body and he began to lose his grip. Thankfully several men rushed forward and took Lester from him. At that moment Jenna rushed up and threw her arms around him. Even through the smoke he could smell her sweet scent. He automatically wrapped his arms around her as they both sank to the ground.

"I thought…I thought…" Jenna whispered.

"Shhh, it's okay," he managed before erupting in a fit of coughing.

Her eyes wide with concern, Jenna pushed back and looked at him. "Can you breathe? Oh, God, you can't breathe, can you? Somebody! Anybody! Help us over here!"

Despite his struggle to take in enough air, Brit smiled. He was alive and the woman he craved was going bonkers on his behalf. Life was good.

The fire trucks had arrived and a paramedic rushed over with a portable oxygen tank. He wasted no time fitting a mask over Brit's face. After inhaling the rich concoction for a few minutes Brit felt his airways begin to normalize. As the paramedic checked his vital signs, Brit gestured to the still unconscious Lester stretched out on the ground nearby. Other paramedics were working on the man, but there didn't seem to be any response from him. Brit caught the eye of his rescuer in silent question; the emergency worker shrugged his shoulders.

"You may have risked your life for a dead man, buddy," the paramedic said. "What the hell were you trying to prove by running into that mess to begin with?"

Jenna, who was shivering, ganged up on him. "He's right. You were an idiot. An *idiot!*" She emphasized her point by throwing her arms around him again, dislodging his mask in the process.

Brit took the mask the rest of the way off and smiled grimly up at the paramedic, who looked bemused. Brit rubbed Jenna's back and murmured hoarsely, "Had to do it, sweetheart. You know that." Jenna, her face still buried in his neck, nodded. He took another hit from the oxygen.

"You're going to have to take a ride to Bellam's Cove Hospital to get those lungs checked out," the crew member said. "You okay for a minute or two 'til we're ready to go?"

At Brit's nod, the man went to help his partners, who were still trying to revive Lester.

Moments later, however, Brit heard the words he'd been dreading since the explosion first occurred.

"Time of death 10:45 p.m."

Lester Small was gone.

Chapter Twenty-Five

"What in the heck are you doing here?" Sherrie asked as Brit walked into the project office on Monday morning. "Last I heard you were headed over to the Emergency Room to get those impressive lungs of yours checked out."

"And so I did," Brit replied, his voice resembling someone with a thirty-year smoking habit. "They stuck a scope down my throat, tested my blood, and declared me fit to come back and give you as much grief as I want, as long as I don't raise my voice in the process. Once the ringing in my ears stops, I'll be good as new."

"Thank God for small favors." Sherrie fussed with the papers. "So…did you stop by the rehab center?"

"Of course I did. Don's holding his own." Brit reached over and gently squeezed Sherrie's shoulder. "Don't give up on that old goat, now. He's a fighter. Always has been. They say his mind is just giving his body a long overdue rest."

"I know," she said, reaching up to touch Brit's hand. "But why is it taking so long?"

"Beats me. All we can do is wait it out."

Sherrie sighed. "Oh, I almost forgot. Gabe de la Torre wants to talk to you. He's got some preliminary information about the explosion on Saturday."

"Was it an accident?"

"He didn't give any details. Said for you to call him. Here's the number," she said, offering him a slip of paper.

"Unfortunately, I've got it on speed dial, but thanks." Brit headed for his office, then paused and grimly asked, "Did the investors get taken care of?"

"Sure. Professor Wolff and Dani made sure most of them got off yesterday morning. Garrick Winston waited around awhile longer hoping you'd come back. Said he 'had some words for you,' whatever that means. But even he got fed up and left yesterday afternoon with Tori. The good news is no one complained that we cancelled the golf tournament."

"Christ, they better not have."

"Well, they might have been understanding about that, but they definitely weren't happy with the turn of events. I wouldn't be surprised if we have a few who bail on us, and I'll bet the first one on the list is Garrick Winston."

"You're probably right. Let me see what I can salvage."

Brit sat down at his desk in the trailer and stared out the window. He could see parts of the museum complex down the hill, framed by gracious redwoods and a rich blue sky. Looking at it in the bright warmth of a summer morning, it was impossible to imagine the horrific destruction that had occurred only two nights previously. Yet it had. A man was dead, and many more could have met the same fate. Thankfully no harm had come to any of the investors...or, God forbid, Jenna.

Despite the turmoil of the past thirty-six hours, Jenna had never been far from his thoughts. Physically, however, he'd barely seen her. Apparently she'd made sure Ethan was taken care of, then been on hand while Gabe and his crew gathered evidence. Since the docs had insisted Brit stay away from the smoky site for at least a day, Jenna had helped Jack coordinate the clean-up efforts. Although she'd continued to sleep in Brit's bedroom, she was sound asleep when he'd come in. He'd felt so whipped himself that if he hadn't been worried about coughing all night, he would have crawled right in after her.

It dawned on him: *I can count on her. She's been right there, through all of it. Ready to work by my side, wherever she's needed. Ready to pitch in with no excuses.* The thought of her leaving again filled him with a panic he'd never before experienced, not even the first time she left. *She's become a part of me*, he realized. Hell. Now what?

He didn't know what to do about it. "So what else is new?" he muttered. Dealing with The Grove's problems was like spinning in a vortex, with no sense of control or means of escape. The sense of powerlessness was overwhelming. What he felt for Jenna was equally confusing, except he wasn't sure if he wanted to escape or not.

Forcing his thoughts elsewhere, Brit dialed Gabe and got him on the first ring. "Hey Gabe. It's Brit. What have you got?"

"Nothing good, I'm afraid. Tell me again where you found Lester."

"He was lying toward the middle of the barn, totally messed up. Bleeding. Out cold. I guess he didn't have time to get to the side door because he could have gotten out that way."

"Why was he in there to begin with?"

"I don't know. He shouldn't have been. We'd closed up for the night and he didn't have access."

"Except that he did. Your boys said they saw him closing the big sliding door."

"Yeah, but that requires a master key, and I can't believe somebody left it open."

"In which case somebody's either got a key, or they picked the lock. You know everybody on your crew?"

"Not as well as I should, apparently."

"Well, with no signs of forced entry at the Great House, it's the only way to explain the break-in there as well."

"So you're saying it could have been Lester?"

"Could have been. Problem is, Lester didn't have a key on him, and we didn't find anything resembling one anywhere near him. We did confirm that accelerant had been used around the inside perimeter of the barn, leading to a couple of fuel drums."

"Lester's our man, then."

"Maybe. Maybe not. But here's what's weird."

"What, aside from the fact that SPEAR sent its own version of a suicide bomber out to blow up The Grove?"

Gabe's voice turned cold. "We don't know that, Brit, and I'm not going to have you jumping the gun over this."

Brit leaned back in his chair. "Yeah, yeah. What's weird?"

"Looks like Lester might—*might*—have been carrying a gasoline can. At least we found one near where you say you picked him up. But it was full with the lid screwed on tight. There were a couple more stacked in the back of the building, but it doesn't look as though they'd been touched."

Brit took a moment to absorb the information. "That means the place blew before Lester had even started to douse the place."

"If that was his intent. We've got to run the prints, but right now it's looking like whatever Lester's purpose for being in the barn, it blew before he could finish his business and leave, or maybe someone knew he was going to be in there and double-crossed him. Could be SPEAR wasn't even involved. Maybe…"

"Maybe what?" Brit asked.

"Maybe, someone else found out the plan and tried to get back at SPEAR by killing one of their minions and having the whole mess blamed on that group."

"Now wait a minute. If you think—"

"It doesn't matter what I think," Gabe interrupted. "It matters what the evidence shows. But I'm telling you off the record that you've got layers upon layers going on here, and maybe even a loose cannon in your midst."

Brit blew out the air he'd been holding and was rewarded with a coughing fit. "Sorry," he croaked after taking a pull from his water bottle. "Still got some crap left over from Saturday night."

"Yeah, well, that's the least of your problems. We're still analyzing what we've got, but in the meantime, I'm just sayin' watch your back, *amico*."

"Point taken. Thanks for filling me in. I'll catch you later."

Brit hung up the phone and thought about what Gabe had told him. He had no doubt that SPEAR was behind the attack on Saturday night, and it appeared as though Lester Small, who'd been working on the crew for months, was the mole. Looking back, he realized Lester was in tight with the security guard whom Brit had fired the morning after the painting spree. And they were both relative newcomers to Little Eden. Damn, maybe he should have practiced a little profiling before hiring the guys. Too late now. The damage was done, and didn't Lester pay the ultimate price?

Brit tried to think like Gabe and not assume anything without the facts to back it up. That lasted all of two minutes. In his gut, Brit knew Lester was up to no good. So who knew he was going to be in the shed at that particular time, and did someone at SPEAR double-cross him or did Brit have another loon on his crew who thought he was doing The Grove a favor by handing out his own brand of justice? Brit tapped a pencil as he considered the possibilities. If Wheeler had a hand in it, there's no way he would have shown himself in enemy territory on the night of the Investors' Preview. Maybe he paid somebody, but what would he gain by killing his own guy? And Dorman? Same logic. Both of them had to know it would come out that it was arson. If the evidence did point to SPEAR, a dead body sure wasn't going to win them any points. So, if Dorman or Wheeler weren't behind it, who was?

Something about the whole deal just didn't add up. What was he missing? Brit heaved a sigh of frustration and put his conjectures on hold. Right now he had to shore up the investors' confidence that had been shattered on Saturday night. If there was any confidence left, that is.

Five days later, Brit was having trouble scraping up enough confidence to pay the phone bill. Garrick Winston had been the first and most vocal of the defectors.

"You almost got us killed, son," he pronounced on that Monday afternoon. "You gotta be nuts if you think I'm going to continue pouring my hard-earned money down a rat hole, and a booby-trapped rat hole to boot."

Nothing Brit could say would persuade the developer, who had managed to convince four other prominent investors to jump ship with him. Several days of protracted but unsuccessful meetings had left Brit and the professor with their own invested capital and that of a handful of other brave souls, but even with insurance proceeds, it wasn't nearly enough to see the project through to completion. Finding new money would take time—time that they simply didn't have, thanks to an odd codicil to Lia Wolff's last will and testament.

Since her daughter Giselle had gone on to marry a very wealthy man, Lia had, apparently with Giselle's blessing, bypassed her daughter and spread the Wolff fortune among her three grandchildren by Giselle, as well as the offspring of her and Gus's children from their previous marriages. Millions of dollars' worth of investments had been distributed to various members of the family, while Ethan, as the first grandchild of both Gus and Lia, had been given her most prized possession, The Grove. To ensure that her legacy was carried on in some manner, she'd stipulated that if Ethan couldn't or wouldn't reopen the estate in his lifetime, it would revert to the city of Little Eden. Lia had no doubt assumed they'd turn it into a park or nature preserve, which would probably have been okay. But Brit recalled the conversation he'd had with Ethan when the professor first approached him about taking on the project.

"Separate the land from the art, and eventually the art itself will dissipate," he'd explained to Brit. "Only our family understands the critical connection between the two. Only our family can keep it all together." No wonder Jenna was so important to Ethan's master plan; he needed the center to open, and he needed someone who shared his passion for art to carry on The Grove's legacy.

So far Jenna had been fantastic about helping Ethan, but Brit still wasn't sure if she truly wanted to take over for her grandfather. Despite what it might mean for their own relationship, Brit had to admit she had every right to her own career. Hadn't he broken away from his family for the same reason? Jenna had spent time in New York; maybe that's where she planned to return after she helped reopen the estate. But given their latest woes, that could be a moot point. If Ethan passed away before the center opened, it wouldn't matter whether Jenna wanted the job or not.

As if things couldn't get much worse, Gabe had called to confirm that Lester's prints hadn't shown up on any pertinent evidence, so the only crime he could be accused of at this point was being in an unauthorized area. As usual, no link to SPEAR could be proven. Even if Lester *had* set the explosion—which Gabe pointed out there was no proof of—to the casual observer it looked like the actions of a lone kook whose karma had caught up with him.

Brit decided to break the bad news about the investors to Ethan in person. He would have offered whiskey, but Ethan couldn't drink, so Brit took along a beer for his own fortification instead.

He found the old man rocking on the front porch of his cottage, a lightweight blanket draped over his frail legs. Despite the warmth of the afternoon, the professor seemed chilled, as if his body were slowly giving up the fight to keep him vital.

Brit knew instinctively that even if The Grove failed, his own company, Vintage Maguire Restorations, would weather the storm. But the thought that after so much work, his partner, cousin, and very good friend still might not live long enough to see his dream realized made Brit want to punch something—or someone—at the injustice of it all.

He leaned against the porch railing, explaining to Ethan just who had jumped ship and why, and trying to look more optimistic than he felt. He swigged his MGD and gestured with the bottle. "We can keep the doors open for maybe a month to six weeks, but after that it's anybody's guess."

"Not the most promising position in which to find ourselves, is it?" Ethan mused.

"No, sir. What galls me is knowing that Dorman and Wheeler must be celebrating right about now. The thought of that really ticks me off."

Ethan shook his head. "Oh I can't imagine Boyce being too happy about losing one of his loyal followers. I do believe there's a vestige of a human being underneath all that enmity."

"You could have fooled me. So, any ideas on how we pull this one out of the fire, professor? No pun intended."

Ethan's smile was fleeting. "You mean before I kick the proverbial bucket?"

"I didn't mean…ah shit," Brit muttered, draining his beer and setting it on the porch railing with a thump.

"It's all right, my boy." Ethan chuckled as he put his glass of tea on a nearby table. "And if it's any comfort, I am a lot more hardy than the evidence suggests. As I recall, I've reminded both you and Jenna of that on many occasions." He gingerly rose from the rocker. "It so happens I do have some ideas, which I am going to ruminate on from the comfort of my bed. In short, it's time for me to take a little siesta and I suggest you take one, too."

Brit snorted. "No time for that, I'm afraid."

"Then how about a nice hike down to the cove? I hear it does wonders for restoring one's equilibrium." Ethan opened the door to go inside, but added over his shoulder, "The scenery there is quite lovely." He made show of looking at his watch. "And has been since about a half hour ago."

Surprised, Brit looked at the professor, who shrugged his shoulders innocently.

"Just a thought," Ethan said, closing the door behind him.

Chapter Twenty-Six

Brit hesitated. He'd often wondered if Ethan thought himself a matchmaker when it came to Brit and Jenna. Maybe he figured this was one goal he could achieve before it was too late.

But was the goal realistic? Brit frowned. He knew from bitter experience that things didn't always turn out the way you wanted or expected them to. The thought of rediscovering Jenna, just to lose her again, made his blood run cold. No. He wouldn't think in those terms. He'd think about today, and only today.

He practically ran back to the Great House and grabbed his backpack, loading it with a bottle of wine, some plastic glasses, napkins, and a half-eaten box of Wheat Thins. A quick scan of the refrigerator produced a chunk of cheddar cheese and a Granny Smith apple. Not too sophisticated, he admitted, but it would have to do. He stopped by the linen closet on the first floor and pulled out a beach blanket, stuffing it in on top of the food. Halfway out the door he turned and ran all the way back to the master bath, where he plucked two wrapped condoms from their box under the sink. *Ever the optimist.*

Within minutes he was jogging along the deer path that led down to the sheltered swimming cove situated between The Grove and Puerta del Mar. Winding, narrow, and overgrown in spots, the trail was rarely used by people; only those who knew about the beauty and serenity at the end of the trek bothered to navigate it.

He'd made it two thirds down the slope when he spotted her through the trees. She was facing the sea, sitting on the sand just out of reach of the waves that were gently lapping the shore in front of her. Her arms were wrapped around her drawn-up knees and a slight breeze caught her hair, which was long and loose, flowing down her back. A wave of longing flowed over him and he fought it, knowing that whatever he was able to get from her would probably never be enough.

It will have to be, he thought. He tamped down the tightening in his groin, a state he'd suffered from off and on since they'd been interrupted the night of the Investors' Preview. He took a deep breath and made his way toward her.

Jenna felt Brit's presence even before he spoke. They'd both been so busy they'd hardly seen each other since the night of the explosion. The truth is, she'd ached for him. Had she wished him into existence?

"Ethan told me you were here," he explained. "Do you mind?"

She shook her head, feeling strangely shy. "Be my guest."

"I brought sustenance." He laid out a blanket and the contents of his pack. Taking out his pocket knife, he cut up the apple as well as the block of cheese. Grinning sheepishly, he presented her with the impromptu appetizer and a glass of white wine. "Only the finest."

"I'm impressed," she said with a smile.

He leaned over and kissed her lightly on the lips. "I'm glad."

Jenna sighed and turned back to the waves to calm her nerves. So much had happened in such a short time, both good and bad, that the feeling of losing control threatened to swamp her. It was a sensation she'd hated as a teenager, and she'd fought against it ever since. Brit Maguire was the kind of man who seemed to competently handle virtually every situation he found himself in. She envied that trait.

With a grace that seemed unusual for someone his size, he stretched out beside her and drank his wine, calmly watching the waves flirt with the shoreline. Beginning its descent toward the horizon, the sun and its heat felt gentle, even life-affirming. She was reminded that only days ago Brit had risked his life by charging into another very different kind of heat.

"How are you feeling?" she asked, needing to reassure herself that he was all right.

He reached for a cracker. "Physically, I'm fine. But I won't kid you—we're in a heap of trouble here."

Jenna nodded. "I figured as much." A moment later, to her dismay, a kaleidoscope of images assailed her: Ethan, and the dream he might not live to see; Jason, and how far he'd come; her parents, the last time she'd seen them; and Brit, the man she realized she was falling in love with all over again, whom she'd almost lost. It was simply too much. She couldn't stop herself as her eyes began to overflow.

"Hey," Brit said softly. He took her chin and gently began wiping her tears, first with his thumb and then, reverently, with his lips. "It's okay, sweetheart. We'll get through this." His kisses were soothing, but she soon realized she wanted more. Much more. For whatever reason, she was meant to love this man. Her arms slipped around his neck as she leaned into him and hungrily covered his mouth with her own.

Brit paused and took her by the shoulders. "Are you sure, Jenna?"

She hesitated only slightly before whispering, "Just love me. Please."

Jenna's trepidation melted into need as Brit took her mouth in one long, drugging kiss.

"It's about time," he whispered, and leaned away. With rough movements he stripped out of his T-shirt and let it drop to the sand. Jenna bit her cheek as she watched the long muscles of his work-hardened body ripple and bunch to the caress of the light off-shore breeze. God, he was beautiful. He'd been so handsome when they'd first met, young and strong and cocky as only a man in the throes of burgeoning success could be. She'd thought him perfect then, but she'd been wrong. The bright edges of youth had been burnished by time and experience, bringing character and strength to the imposing man beside her. He wore it well. His lightly furred chest was broader now, deeper, too, and bronzed by long hours in the sun. Brit was not afraid to work alongside his crew; the ropey muscles encircling his arms were a powerful testament to the benefits of swinging a hammer for hours on end.

Brit's face was an homage to masculinity as well, mostly unchanged by the years except for a certain maturity around the intense gray eyes. The jaw was a little firmer, the angles more defined. And the mouth… oh God, the mouth. A punch of heat flashed low in her belly at the vivid memory of Brit using that mouth to drive her into oblivion. As she stared, fixated, the mouth curled into a self-satisfied grin, and Jenna knew, with embarrassing clarity, that he was there with her, sharing the erotic flashback.

She sighed as he closed his arms around her and immediately claimed her neck as his own, with kisses that sent her toes curling. He smiled against her hair while his hands went to work on her clothes. "Do you remember this?" His hands demonstrated by cupping her breasts as his thumbs teased the aroused nipples straining against the constricting fabric of her blouse. "And this?" His hand roamed downward to settle possessively against her mound.

Jenna sucked in a breath as her brain time-warped seven years into the past. Memories surfaced that had haunted her for months after she'd returned to New York and cut off ties with him. She'd dreamed of him, of his hands and mouth on her body. Of his cock *in* her body, working her with slow, deep strokes. It mortified her to think of the number of times she'd awakened in the dead of night, her body sheened in sweat and aching for release. Eventually the dreams had faded to nameless yearning and, finally, ended altogether. And then fate had sent them careening back together like two full-bore locomotives heading straight toward each other on the same track.

"Damn it," he muttered, snapping her back to the present. He'd managed to wrestle the blouse from the waistband of her jeans, but his fingers were making little headway with the few tiny buttons he could reach. When she leaned back to give him better access, he groaned with gratitude. She let him struggle for a few moments longer before brushing his hands aside.

"Let me." Her voice was husky and her own hands none too steady, but she managed to finish the job without tearing anything. As she began to shrug out of the blouse, his big hands covered her own.

"Oh, no. My turn." His tongue teased the whorls of her ear as he eased her hands away and made short work of removing the offending garment. Then he dropped his gaze and froze.

Foregoing her usual sports bra, Jenna had decided to lift her spirits by wearing what she considered her "dressy" lingerie. The bra was white and lacy, though far from virginal, and supported her breasts while exposing a lush expanse of delicate skin. She rarely thought about cleavage, but now, at this moment, she was glad her breasts were full and displayed to their best advantage.

"Jenna, you take my breath away." His voice was warm chocolate, his eyes still focused on her breasts. Honey, hot and sweet, pooled in her core. She reached for the waistband of her jeans, but his hands were there first. In less than a heartbeat, he'd popped the button and dispensed with the zipper.

"Hips up," he commanded softly, scooting lower for better access. When she complied, he slowly pulled the soft denim down over her hips. A thin whistle of appreciation slipped past his lips. "Jesus, Mary, and Joseph," he breathed. She remembered now—she'd worn the matching thong.

Brit lowered his lips to the small triangle covering her womanly secrets. Her back bowed as he held her hips immobile on the blanket, nibbling and licking at the thin barrier while his agile fingers played their own game of hide and seek, arousing, inflaming. His tongue scorched a path across the gentle swell of her belly, dipped down into the velvet hollow where it joined her hip. He used his teeth there, on the delicate skin stretched so tautly over her hipbone, scraping lightly, as if testing the texture, the taste of her. She pleaded with him as the heat began to take her. Begged, more like it, but he shushed her with whispers and a brush of his lips, calming her even as she realized he was fighting for his own composure.

As he pulled away, an errant gust of wind slid in to fill the void, pebbling her feverish skin. She hugged her arms to her chest and watched through heavy-lidded eyes as he kneeled beside her, removing her shoes and jeans with stiff, jerky movements. When he finished, he sat back on his heels. The imposing erection pushing against the zipper of his shorts was impossible to overlook.

"Now I need you to take your bra off for me."

The chill dissipated quickly as she warmed to the smoke in his words. She slowly flipped the front clasp, spilling the pale globes into her hands. She held them up to him, an offering. "For you," she whispered. She whimpered as he placed a reverent kiss on each nipple. When she reached for him, he captured her wrists, bringing her arms to rest on the blanket above her head.

"Not yet, love. I need to see you first." He kissed her forehead. "I need to touch you." His mouth skimmed down one arm, scattering kisses over her wrist, the inside of her elbow, the side of her breast. "You make me burn, Jenna. I've been burning since the minute I saw you again."

His tongue ran up and over an areola, circling once, then twice, promising more before darting away to lavish attention on the small hollow at the base of her throat.

She groaned in frustration and Brit clearly sensed her need, bending to lap at one enticing nipple before suckling it powerfully.

Yes, oh yes! Every hormone in her body quivered in expectation as he drew her into his hungry mouth, feasting first on one swollen peak and then the other. Every nip and tug sent shock waves whipping down her spine, straight to the very core of her being. His broad hand cupped her mound, pressing rhythmically with every deep pull. She bucked, hard, as one of his fingers snaked its way beneath her panties and through the damp, swollen lips of her sex to take up the rhythm. The climax hit her with the force of a one-two punch, the shock of it tearing the breath from her lungs.

She sensed more than felt when he moved away again. Boneless and replete, she fought through the euphoric haze fogging her brain. Her breath caught in her throat as his face finally swam into focus. His breathing was ragged and fast, his restraint obviously costing him. *She'd done that.* Feminine satisfaction thrummed through her veins, clearing the cobwebs and firing her blood. She wanted more.

"Now the panties." He dipped his head to indicate the only barrier protecting her from total nakedness. "Please…" The skin over his cheekbones was tightly drawn and his hands fisted on his knees as he sat back to watch.

Without taking her eyes off him she reached down to pull off the tiny wisp of lace covering her mound. Then she lay back, waiting. Wanting.

Brit quickly shucked his shoes and clothing, stepping out of his khaki shorts and revealing a fully engorged erection. He positioned himself in front of her, resting on his haunches. He was completely comfortable in his nakedness and she couldn't help but stare. *Oh. My.*

She rose up to her knees to face him. She wanted to

bring him the same pleasure he had just given her. "Do you mind?" she asked, pushing him gently to his back.

Brit did as she asked. She ignored his cock for a moment, enticing though it was as it bobbed hopefully in her direction. She traced the tan lines across his thighs, outside in, where her fingers met scant inches below his testicles. She glanced up, but his eyes were closed, his lips drawn in a near grimace.

Cupping her hands, she carefully hefted his sac, rolling the weight against her palms. "Amazing," she murmured. She squeezed gently and heard him hiss. "Sorry. Did I hurt you?"

"No, you didn't hurt me." He ground his teeth. "But you're killing me here."

"I hope not." She swirled her tongue over the leathery pouch and he hissed again. Tenderly, she kissed each lobe, then let go.

"Jenna," he growled, his voice half warning, half plea. "We need to—" He choked to a stop as her lips closed over the velvety crown of his penis.

She'd never done this with any man before, but with Brit it seemed the most natural act in the world. She licked and suckled him for several moments, heard him moan, and smiled. "I hope I'm doing this right."

"Oh baby, it's way too right." He stopped her before she could put her mouth on him again, and laid her back down. He raised her knees and spread her legs wide before him. She could not be more vulnerable, yet she felt no shame. She trusted him completely. Wanted to give herself to him completely.

He reached for his shorts and rifled through the

pockets, pulling out a foil packet, which he placed on her chest, perfectly centered between her breasts. "Guard that with your life."

She sucked in a breath at the lovely friction of skin-on-skin as Brit scooted backwards down the front of her body. He paused long enough to drop a kiss on each nipple and one in the center of her stomach before homing in on his target. "God, Jenna. You have no idea how often I've fantasized about seeing you like this…of tasting you again." He nuzzled the downy fur covering her mound, reveling in the sweet smell of her arousal. "Do you know how gorgeous you are here?" His tongue dipped between the lips of her sex, teasing the distended bud peeping from between the folds. "I could eat you alive." Intent on his goal, he drew on the tiny pearl, attacking and retreating until she was writhing beneath him. Her hands worked frantically in his hair as she fought for release. Any moment she would come. With one last lap of his tongue, he lifted his head and met her dazed eyes. "Not yet, baby. Not without me." A sheen of sweat covered his face and chest as he crawled, panther like, right back up the way he'd come.

He tore the foil pack open and quickly donned the condom. She expected him to climb on top of her and simply take what he wanted, but he surprised her. Instead, he lay on his back and rolled her on top of him. She straddled him, planting her hands squarely on his wide, sweat-glazed chest. Below her, his erection bobbed between her widespread thighs. She looked up to see him watching her with lambent eyes.

"Now," he said. "Ride me, Jenna."

For a moment she feared the size of him, the strength and intensity of him. But an instant later her fear passed and she knew it was time. Their time. He met her half way, his hips surging upward as she came over him. His fingers dug deeply into the soft swells of her buttocks as he guided himself into her. There might be gentle bruises tomorrow, but it was a small price to pay for the mind-numbing sensations careening throughout her body. They moved together, his thick cock spearing her, thrusting inside of her until her vision blurred and all she could do was hang on. The orgasm, when it came, was blistering, a conflagration that burned through her soul, turning her bones to liquid. Through her own keening cry, she heard a deeper voice, a shout of primal exaltation. He thrust a few more times and let out a groan, holding her tight to him as he pulsed inside of her. Afterward he guided her down so they lay side by side on the blanket, her head nestled in the curve of his shoulder.

His eyes were closed against the brilliant sunshine and she watched as the corner of his mouth tipped up in a satisfied, barely-there smile. He fondled a lock of her hair that he'd woven between his fingers. After a few moments he opened his eyes, turned, and looked deeply into hers. "I didn't think anything could surpass that night so long ago," he said quietly. He paused a moment before adding, "I was wrong."

Jenna didn't respond. She couldn't. She was filled with a jumble of emotions that she dare not reveal. What would happen next? Could they try a relationship again? Would he even want to? Or was this just "scratching an itch," as Sherrie said weeks ago? Jenna didn't want to think that's all it was. She didn't want to think, period.

Brit tipped her chin up and took her lips in a kiss so full of desire that she shivered with the power of it. She returned it with equal fervor, telling him without words that she felt the same way.

Chapter Twenty-Seven

Dressed again in his shorts, Brit lay on the sand, using his pack as a makeshift pillow. Jenna stretched like a cat next to him and sat up, once more watching the waves. She looked the way he felt: content. As if this were right where she should be—making love with him outside, on a gorgeous beach, in the middle of the day. The notion warmed him. Considerably. She looked over her shoulder at him. "Lia used to come down here for inspiration, to think and to paint. Did you know that?"

Brit shook his head. "No, but I can see why she did. It's incredible here." He was looking at her, not the sea.

"I feel closer to her here, which is odd, considering."

"Considering what?"

Jenna looked at him for several moments before gazing out at the water again. She let out a breath. "I'm not who you think I am."

Brit sat up, brushing the sand off his legs. His mouth curved up in a faint grin. "That sounds ominous. Are you going to tell me you're a Russian spy, or maybe from the planet Krypton?"

"Nothing so dramatic, although it's important, at least to me."

"Tell me," he said softly.

"When I was fourteen, my parents were at a holiday party, so being a typical kid I was rummaging around their closet looking for hidden Christmas presents. I came across a box full of papers and inside was my birth certificate."

"Doesn't sound so ominous," Brit said.

"Except that it showed I wasn't born Jenna Louise Bergstrom. I was actually somebody else." She turned to him and spread her arms as if to take a bow. "Meet Alliyma Cusi."

"Whoa. What?"

"Yeah. Turns out my father had an affair with an artist named Diana Cusi. She was a blond, blue-eyed American but had married a Peruvian and kept his name. She got pregnant, but didn't really want the baby. My dad talked her into carrying me to term and then he took me off her hands."

Jenna looked forlorn; having a mother who habitually tried to smother him, Brit couldn't imagine not feeling wanted. He took her hand and kissed it. "She was a fool," he said.

"I don't know. Whatever she was, she didn't want to be a mom. Apparently she signed over the papers and immediately left for South America. She still had a thing for Peru, I guess. My dad said she died over there when I was five."

"I'm sorry," Brit said. "But you got the better end of the deal, sounds like. A mom and a dad."

Jenna shook her head. "At the time I was way too immature to get that. So I took my feelings out on my mom—my adoptive mom. I gave her hell. It didn't dawn on me until much, much later the torture she must have already gone through having to raise the result of her husband's cheating."

"I doubt she would have considered it torture. Still, why do you think she was willing to raise you?"

"My dad told me they'd been trying to have a baby for years and he blamed the stress of that on his looking elsewhere. I guess my mom figured this was the only chance she was going to get to have a child, and half a genetic match was better than none. Luckily she finally did get pregnant with Jason when I was ten." Jenna hugged her knees. "The fact is, I'm in no way related to Ethan or Lia Wolff or anyone else in this family except Jason, and ever since I learned that, I've thought of myself as…well, different."

"So all the talk of 'family legacy' and you carrying on The Grove tradition must have made you feel…"

"Like a fraud. Like…like somehow I wasn't worthy. So I began to create my own identity—one that couldn't be taken away from me by a piece of paper."

"I take it that's why you drifted away from your family?"

"Yes. Stupidly, I figured I was no longer a member of the Wolff tribe, so I left."

They sat in silence for several moments, but Brit knew they had to address the elephant in the room.

"I came after you, you know."

Jenna nodded. Wiped a tear from her cheek. "When Allen told me, it was all I could do not to hop on a plane and fly back to you."

Allen. So that was the punk's name. He could still remember taking a cab to the address in Manhattan that Jenna had given him when they'd parted. Even now he could picture the guy's sneering face as he shut the door in Brit's face. Even now Brit felt his temper flare. "But you didn't fly back," he said curtly.

She looked at him, a plea for understanding in her eyes. "No. I didn't."

Brit took a deep breath and let it out, ready to hear the worst. "Why not?"

Jenna echoed his sigh, hesitating as if to gather the right words. "You grew up belonging, right? To your family, your social group, to every place you wanted to fit in. Am I right?"

Brit nodded slowly. "Yeah. Guilty as charged."

"The thing is, you represented everything I felt I'd lost, and part of me—the part that wasn't in lust with you—resented that. You were a member of The Club, and I…well, I wasn't. You fit in so well that if I'd stayed with you, I'd have always felt like a hanger-on, an appendage."

"There's no way you would ever take a back seat to me," Brit said.

Jenna smiled sadly. "But I thought so at the time. And I'd told myself over and over again that if I couldn't be a full-fledged member of The Club, I'd start my own club. In my mind, that couldn't have included you. But rather than explain it to you, I chose to run away. The feelings I had for you were so intense. I had never experienced them, so I couldn't understand them. And I for sure didn't want to be swallowed up in them. I knew my feelings would weaken my resolve, so I took the coward's way out. Does any of that make sense?"

Brit shrugged. "I've never walked in your footsteps, so I can't exactly relate. But I *can* understand wanting to create your own world, on your terms. I can understand that very well." He paused, frowning at the memory. "So what happened with that guy Allen? Weren't you living with him?"

Jenna reached for her bra and T-shirt. Maybe she felt vulnerable, but damn it, he had a right to know.

"Allen was part of my new construct—the identity I'd created for myself. He was a bad-boy type, and didn't artists hang out with bad boys? We hadn't gone out long and he was pushing to have me move in. I was flattered. It was heady to think someone was head over heels about me." She looked down, fussing with the bottom of her shirt, obviously embarrassed. When she looked at Brit again, she wore a grim smile. "As it turns out, it had more to do with high rent and a roommate who had just moved out. It was so lame of me to give you that address. I've thought about it many times and wondered if maybe I did it subconsciously to let you know how things stood without having to spell it out. Again, cowardly."

"How long did you live together?"

"We didn't. Fortunately, when I returned, I stayed

with a college friend long enough to learn Allen had been sleeping around behind my back. So no, I never lived with him. He was angry about it, which is probably why he led you to believe I *was* living there, to get back at me through you. Poetic justice, huh? And not too long after that, the accident happened."

Brit could feel the sorrow settle over Jenna's shoulders. He sat up, drawing her closer to him. "Tell me what happened."

Her smile was wistful. "I'm sure you remember my parents from Ethan's retirement party. The original beautiful couple, weren't they? My dad was a golden boy, all grown up. My mom, well, she liked basking in his glow. And after the affair that led to me, she wasn't going to give him any more opportunities to stray." She hesitated, ran her fingers through her hair.

Brit gave her shoulder a slight nudge. "Go on."

"Oh, well, 'it was a dark and stormy night,' as they say. My parents were on their way home from a fundraiser down on the peninsula. They'd both been drinking, and neither of them should have been driving, but I guess my mom felt she had a little better control of the situation." She shook her head. "Obviously not."

"I remember Ethan saying your father was killed outright."

"Yes, both he and the driver of the other car—a nice young man with two little kids waiting at home for their daddy." She was shivering now. "Mom never forgave herself, of course. Despite everything, Dad had been the center of her universe, and then he was gone, along with somebody else's husband and father. She'd come out of it alive but with a serious back injury that caused her a lot of physical pain. She needed some heavy duty medication, which I think in the end suited her just fine."

"So Jason was, what, eleven or twelve when it happened?"

"Twelve, and certainly not ready for his perfect little world to collapse. But it did, like a house of cards, really."

"I heard about the lawsuit."

Jenna snorted. "Who hasn't?" She made a sweeping gesture. "'Famed Society Matron Sued for Wrongful Death in Drunken Auto Collision.' Yep, headlines like that'll really make your day, especially when you lose the case and just about all your assets in the bargain."

"That bad, huh?"

Jenna's tone turned matter-of-fact, as if she weren't emotionally involved. Maybe it's easier that way, he thought.

"Eventually my mom lost the house in Campbell and most of their savings. The apartment in San Francisco was leased, so at least she was able to keep that. Jason went from being a suburban prince to the odd kid out at a public middle school in the city. Mom was out of it a lot of the time, so he was…was pretty much left on his own." She paused again.

"Then what happened?" Brit asked.

She let out a long breath, as if she were expelling poison. "Turns out Jason was joining Mom in her nightly 'therapy' cocktails, only she didn't know it.

Then one night she either lost track of her medications, or made the decision to stop the pain once and for all, because she took a combination that pretty much ensured she'd never wake up. And she didn't."

"What about Jason?"

"He was the one who found her. And it made such an impression that he tried the very same thing a few weeks later. Fortunately I was around to get him help in time." She shook her head in disgust. "Too bad I was a day late and a dollar short with my mom."

"What would you have done differently?"

"I...I would have gotten out of my own self-righteous universe. I would have come back sooner. I would have cared for her and Jason. I would have told her...I would have told her I love her and to not give up." Jenna's voice hitched and she stopped, letting the tears fall freely down her beautiful face.

Brit shifted, took her gently by the shoulders and insisted that she look at him. "Maybe you could have helped her, but maybe not," he said. "Your mom must have been carrying around a hell of a lot of guilt, and sometimes that's too big a load for anyone to carry. And you did live clear across the country."

"Convenient, huh?" Her tone was laced with a kind of desperate sarcasm. "When I heard about the car accident I flew back from New York right away, but I didn't stay much beyond my dad's funeral. I remember one night I took Jason out for pizza. I figured it was ample 'quality time' and I was so magnanimous I even let him pick out the toppings." She laughed bitterly. "How monumentally selfish I was. I said I had to return to New York because of my job, but..." Her eyes filled again with tears. "But the truth is, I just didn't want to face it, face what was happening. I told myself my brother was old enough, my grandfather would be there...and that...and that my mom wasn't my 'real' mom and didn't need me." She looked at Brit beseechingly. "Remember what you said to me, the night of the Chamber event? You said I wasn't good at committing. You're right. Just like I ran out on you, I ran out on them." Her tears then turned to sobs.

"Oh, baby." Brit gathered Jenna in his arms as the grief she'd obviously held in for so long came pouring out. She clung to him and he stroked her back soothingly, saying nothing, knowing that when you feel that lousy, especially about yourself, nothing anyone can say is going to make it any better. Only time does that.

After several minutes Jenna managed to get her emotions under control. She slowly pushed herself away from Brit and used the hem of her T-shirt to dry her tears.

"Damn, that felt good," she joked.

Brit smiled. "You say you don't think you're connected enough to the Wolff family to be involved, but look at me: my family connection to this enterprise is pretty weak at best. I'm a descendant of Lia's son from her first marriage. That family had absolutely nothing to do with The Grove. Not a damn thing."

Lia leaned her head on Brit's shoulder. "I know, but some of Lia's blood does flow in you, so you got in under the wire. From the time I found out my true parentage, I no longer felt that connection—or at least I told myself there wasn't one."

Brit put his arm around her again. "You do realize you're being ridiculous. You have more of Lia Wolff in you than any of the rest of us. Your passion for art, your creativity…"

"Ethan—Da—said the same thing. He says I'm the best one to take over when he's gone. Only recently have I begun to think that maybe there are other kinds of bonds besides just DNA."

"Couldn't have said it better myself," he murmured, leaning over to kiss her.

The afternoon was waning, and with it, the tide. Brit felt slightly melancholy knowing their interlude was coming to an end. He gazed at Jenna as she finished dressing and stood up. She pointed in the direction of the rocks and held out her hand to him. "Let's see who got left behind."

They walked slowly along the rocky outcropping, peering at shallow indentations filled with seawater, algae, and the occasional creature who'd missed the outgoing tide. A half-submerged, knobby-skinned sea star clung stubbornly to the side of a rock, sharing space with a cluster of mussels. A violet-hued anemone waved its slender tentacles, hoping to catch some prey. Brit prodded it with his finger, causing it to close upon itself in response.

Jenna grinned and addressed the flower-like creature. "I know just how you feel. I can't help but respond to him either." She glanced at Brit and smiled.

I want her again, Brit marveled. He took her hand and brought it to his lips, then casually held it as they worked their way across the rocks. After some time they reached the large natural sea wall that formed the far end of the cove. Jenna leaned back against it and fixed her eyes on him.

"Okay, now that I've bared my soul—among other things—it's your turn." She drew him toward her. "I expected you to be a partner in that big fancy firm you worked for. *And* I assumed someone would have snatched you up right away, that you'd have three kids by now. But none of that happened. Why?"

Brit rubbed the back of his neck, turned, and looked out to sea. How much should he tell her? Some of the story was personal, some of it damn embarrassing. But as he looked back at her expectant face, he realized that if she'd been able to lay herself wide open, he owed her no less.

"It's a long story," he began.

"I'm not going anywhere."

"Can I hold you to that?" slipped out of his mouth before he could stop it. She looked surprised and he smiled ruefully. "The truth is, when I finally accepted that you wanted nothing to do with me, it pretty much threw me for a loop. I wasn't used to having that experience with women."

Jenna's own smile faltered. "I didn't intend to hurt you."

Brit shook his head slightly and held up a hand.

"No, you had your reasons—not that I totally understand them. But when I called the professor and he filled me in on what was going on with you, I admit I went a bit nuts." He pulled away, putting his hands in his back pockets. "I was really pissed at you, of course, but I was also a little worried that I was losing my touch. So I started, um—"

"Nailing anything in skirts?"

He nodded grimly. "Pretty much."

"Must be a guy thing," she said. "But understandable, considering what I'd done." She cocked her head. "But what did that have to do with changing jobs?"

Brit regarded her seriously. She deserved to know all of it. He exhaled. "One of the skirts happened to be the trophy wife of the senior partner."

"Uh oh," Jenna said, her face impassive.

"It gets worse," he said. "We went after each other like crazy for a few months, and then she announced abruptly that her husband knew all about us and if I didn't leave the firm immediately, he was going to see that my career ended up in the tank."

"Oh, my God. So, what did you do?"

"I left the firm, of course. But you want to know the funniest part?"

"There's something funny about all this?"

"Oh it's funny, all right. Turns out my boss never had a clue about our affair. The little woman was just getting ready to divorce him and figured if our relationship came out, she'd get a much smaller slice of the pie. Instead, she hired a top notch attorney and reamed the poor guy without him ever suspecting a thing."

Jenna touched Brit's arm. "Sounds like you feel bad about what you did to him."

"Yeah, I do, but my bad karma came around and bit me in the butt, didn't it? I lost my job, and found out later that none other than my own mother was behind it all."

"*What?*" Jenna's lovely eyes looked puzzled.

"My mom's a real ball buster. Dear old Evelyn is chairman and CEO of Britland Development Corporation and she'd been trying to get me to move back East and join the family firm ever since I left home. I'm not kidding when I say I know what it's like to want to break free."

"But your own mother? What on earth did she do?"

"You talk about a club—the CEOs of major corporations are all into each's other's business. She heard my boss's wife was thinking about divorce, so she struck a deal with Candilynne—"

"Candilynne? Someone actually goes by the name Candilynne?!"

"Yes, I confess. I'm an idiot. So my mother, who knew me all too well, apparently, struck a deal with Candi to seduce me first and then ensure that I was out of a job. In return, Evelyn arranged for a top notch divorce lawyer and said trophy wife was off and running."

"Why would your mom do such a thing to you?"

"To get me to crawl home with my tail between my legs, I suppose. Only things didn't quite work out that way. I decided to form Vintage Maguire Restorations instead."

Jenna grinned. "You showed her."

"Damn right. Anyway, it's taken a few years, but Mom's actually come around to accepting the path I've chosen. She's visited me several times. In fact, she now takes all the credit for me striking out on my own. But one could argue it was you who pointed me in that direction."

Jenna looked thoughtful. "So in short order you get screwed over by me, a married woman you were having an affair with, and your own mother. It's a wonder you don't hate all women by now."

Hate? Hate was the farthest thing from Brit's mind at the moment. As he gazed at Jenna, he didn't dwell on the betrayal he'd felt after their time together, only about the wonder of the time they'd just spent on the beach, and of the evenings before that. He didn't know how to respond to Jenna's supposition, so he showed her the error of it simply by holding out his arms. She walked into them and laid her head on his shoulder.

"I'm so very sorry," she said.

"Not to worry," he murmured, breathing in the fresh scent of her. "I've learned to live for the moment…like this one."

They remained absorbed in each other, neither of them willing to jinx the moment with questions like "What now?" Brit reveled in the soft warmth of Jenna's skin, the feel of her curves nestled against his body. Too soon, she sighed and pushed slightly against him. "We'd better get back. I promised Ethan I'd stop by later on this afternoon and he'll be wondering what happened to me."

Oh, he's got a pretty good idea. "You're right," he said. "Back to the real world."

Together they made their way back to where they'd lain and gathered the remnants of the picnic. They walked back up the trail quietly hand in hand, but as they neared the crest, Jenna spoke up.

"I don't understand. What's so terrible about The Grove that someone would want to close it down so badly? It just doesn't make sense. Why—" Jenna stopped in mid-sentence and Brit saw that she was staring up at someone who stood at the top of the ridge. The person, wearing some sort of a hood, was staring back at them.

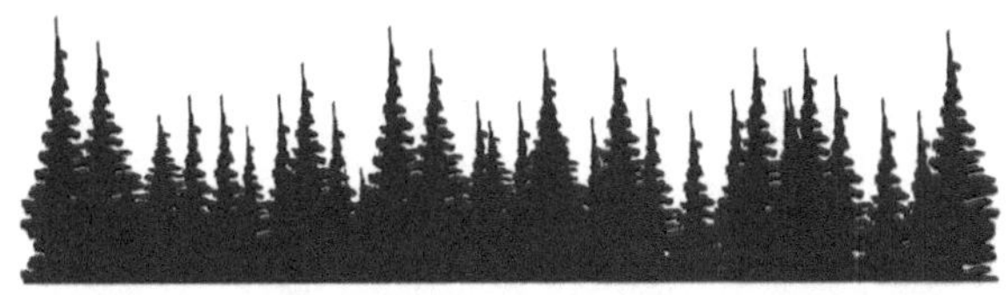

Chapter Twenty-Eight

"Who's that?" Jenna asked.

"Can't tell with the hood on." They watched the figure turn and beat feet away from them.

Jenna felt herself blush. "You don't think…?"

Brit put his arm around her waist and kissed her forehead. "No, I don't. What happened between us belongs to just us. No one else."

Jenna said nothing, but rested her head briefly on Brit's shoulder for the support he offered. Nothing was truly resolved between them. No words of commitment or a future together had been spoken. She still didn't know if Brit would ever truly forgive her, or if today was all they'd have. But she wasn't going to think it to death, especially in light of what lay ahead.

"What do you think's going to happen?" she asked.

He seemed utterly tuned into her mindset. "With The Grove? We hang on, I guess. Try to find new backers. Hope that Ethan stays well enough to see the project through."

"And if he doesn't?"

"I don't even want to go there. Right now the most important thing is making sure he, and you, stay out of danger. We still don't know precisely who's got it in for us."

"What about—"

They were headed back toward The Grove when Jason came running up to them.

"Hey, Da said you guys were on a hike, but what took you so long? Come on. He's got some news to share."

"You see what a little R&R can accomplish?" Ethan grinned unabashedly at Brit and Jenna as they all sat in the parlor of his cottage. He'd insisted on refreshments before he divulged his secret, and Jason, in keeping with his ad hoc role as majordomo, had served them all lemonade and brownies. Brit realized he'd worked up an appetite with Jenna and devoured two of the chocolate confections in short order. A glance at Jenna triggered another hunger, one not so easily satisfied. One day at a time, he told himself. Take it slow. Problem was, there weren't all that many days left if they couldn't get The Grove back on solid financial footing. He caught Ethan's eye and the professor winked at him. *Winked at him!* Apparently the old guy was referring to something other than his own R&R, which irritated Brit all the more.

"Out with it, Ethan," Brit said impatiently. "You look like the cat that ate the canary."

"Do I?" Ethan said, gleefully ignoring Brit's rancor. "Well, I suppose I must let that proverbial cat out of the bag, then." He paused, no doubt for effect.

"You're driving us crazy here," Jenna admonished.

"All right then. My news is simply this: I have secured the financing needed to complete The Grove Center for American Art."

"No shit?" Jason asked.

"I'd put it more decorously, young man, but in essence, yes, I am telling the truth."

Jenna rush over to give her grandfather a hug. "That's fantastic, Da, but how? Where'd you get the money?"

"Ah, now that, I'm afraid, I can't divulge at this time. Trust me on this, however: our silent partner is quite reliable. He has to look into a few matters related to the project, but he has already promised to come through for us."

Brit couldn't hide his skepticism. "You're sure about this?"

"Quite. I've known this fine young man for several years. I had only to describe the latest problems we've been having and he stepped up to the plate in more ways than one. He is quite wealthy, but more than that, he's impeccably trustworthy, more like a member of the family, really. Unfortunately he has no taste for the limelight, which is why he prefers to remain in the background."

Ethan reached for a sheaf of notes which he used to

describe the way he saw the project unfolding from that point forward. Brit, Jenna, and Jason listened intently. Brit was amazed, as always, that this gentle soul, battling his own physical decline, could have such unflappable energy and enthusiasm.

"Gabe assures me that the investigation into the explosion continues. In the meantime he is assigning police protection for the center around the clock until those who masterminded that heinous crime are apprehended."

Brit scoffed. "I could save the taxpayers a lot of money. All Gabe needs to do is pay a little visit to Boyce Wheeler and get to the bottom of SPEAR's latest activities."

Ethan rubbed his chin. "I fear you may be right. But that's something we must leave to the authorities…we *must*, Brit."

"We may have to, but I don't have to like it." Brit glanced at Jenna and rose from the couch. "Now that we're back in business, I need to play catch up. Jenna, you okay?"

"Yes. I'd like to go over some notes with Da. I'll be along later."

"Take care, then," he said. "If it gets too late, give me a call and I'll come escort you back."

Jason grabbed his jacket. "Wait, I'll go with you. I wanna fill the guys in on the news. Looks like they'll be able to keep their jobs after all."

As Brit and Jason headed down the path, Jason confided in Brit. "I've been kinda worried about Parker," he said. "He's been totally in the dumps lately. I think he and Lester might have been friends."

Jason's words triggered a memory. *We think...we think maybe that guy Lester's still in the building...*Parker said he saw him go inside. They'd been picking up trash, Kyle said. *In the dark.* Grunts or not, that just didn't make sense. Brit remembered looking back at Jenna just before he headed to the back of the building. The boys were flanking her. One of them—which one?—had his arm around her. He couldn't remember and it was infuriating.

They found Parker and Kyle lying on their respective bunks tapping on their laptops. Both were wearing headsets that made them look like customer service reps in a call center, except they were mumbling. They glanced at Brit and Jason briefly before turning back to their screens. *I guess human interaction's not enough incentive to mess up their game,* Brit thought cynically.

Jason glanced at Kyle's screen, looked at Brit, and shrugged. "They're playing League of Legends and they're on the same team, so there's no way they're gonna stop until the game is over. Just a sec." He jogged over to the center of the bunkhouse where a large whiteboard was used for employee notices. Grabbing one of the markers, he pulled off a flyer that was posted on a nearby wall. On the back of the flyer he wrote GOT MONEY FOR GROVE FROM MYSTERY MAN! YOU STILL GOT JOBS! He flashed the card in front of each of them. Kyle smiled briefly, gave a quick thumbs up and returned his hands to the keyboard and mouse; Parker barely acknowledged Jason by nodding and kept tapping away as well.

And this is the hope for the next generation? Brit caught himself mentally whining and put a stop to it. *I'd have been doing the same thing at seventeen.*

"So much for sharing the good news," Jason groused.

"Eh, well, they don't quite have your perspective," Brit said. "Come on, I'm going to pick up a sandwich at Lindy's before I get down to work. You want to join me?"

"Sure," Jason said, looking pleased.

"Good. While you're at it, you can tell me all your sister's most embarrassing moments growing up so I can tease her about them. And tell me about your buddies, too."

Jason laughed, which was the diversion Brit had hoped for. He was determined to find out more about Bishop and Summers. They both seemed to have a thing for Jenna, and that couldn't be healthy.

"Milk it, baby. Milk it," Dorman panted as Wanda Ramsey rode him. The frizzy-haired waitress had big thighs and her breasts were beginning to sag, but she sure knew how to work a man's Johnson. Dorman had compared notes with a few of his golfing buddies who shared his penchant for raunchy sex and they'd all agreed: Wanda was one of the best.

"Yeah, baby. Uh huh, baby," she cooed as she bounced up and down on him, holding her hands on her broad hips and thrusting out her breasts as if she were performing bareback under the Big Top. Dorman was just about to explode when there was a knock on the motel room door.

"Shit," Wanda croaked in her Virginia Slims' voice. "Wayne doesn't know I'm here. What about Myra?"

"Hell, no," Dorman grounded out. "Uh, just a minute!" he called. At that moment he heard the sound of a key being inserted in the lock. The door opened and the creepy kid he'd met after the city council meeting stood there in the same hoodie, wearing the same shades, snapping pictures of them with his cell phone.

"Sweet Jesus," Wanda rasped, so surprised that she didn't even bother to dismount or hide herself.

"What the hell?" Dorman hissed. "What do you think you're doing?"

The young man stood there, calmly watching. "Getting some nice fat pussy, huh, Mr. D.? Myra put a lock on her goody box?"

"God*damn* it," Dorman growled, practically pushing Wanda off and quickly finding his pants. He'd be damned if he was going to deal with this asshole naked. "For God's sake, give us some privacy. I'll meet you outside in five minutes."

The kid smirked and turned to go. "Yeah, wouldn't want to intrude on such a romantic moment. But make it quick," he added, his voice suddenly cold. "We've got important business to discuss."

A moment later Dorman had gotten Wanda dressed, pressed a fifty in her hand, and shuttled her out of the room. On her way out she gave the kid a once over as if she were sizing him up as a future client. What did he expect from a slut, anyway? Dorman quickly dismissed her from his thoughts and motioned the kid inside.

"Shit, at least tell me your name," he said, reaching for a pack of cigarettes on the nightstand.

"It's Chief to you," the punk said.

"Okay then, *Chief*. What's this all about, and how did you know where to find me?"

The kid snickered. "You must eat your prunes every morning, 'cause you're a real regular kind of guy. Twice a week you have meetings back in Little Eden and then, if you don't have anything else going on, you high tail it over to this motel. The clerk on duty likes his blow so he appreciates a little extra cash now and then. So I ask what room you're in and can I pay you a little surprise visit and he figures he's not giving up any national secrets." The young man stepped closer. "In case you thought you were pulling a fast one on your old lady, Mr. D., it ain't rocket science."

"Fine," Dorman snapped, lighting up and hoping his hands weren't shaking enough to be noticed. "So, what brings you here?"

Instead of answering right away, the kid took his time ambling around the room, checking out the mediocre prints on the wall, peeking into the bathroom, and looking out the window at the parking lot beyond. It was late in the evening. A car door slammed and Dorman could hear strident female laughter, the kind he had come to recognize as belonging to one of Wanda's perennially shit-faced coworkers. For a second he felt ashamed of the company he was keeping. He quickly rationalized it, however, reminding himself that soon he'd be moving on to bigger and better venues. That is, unless this wiseass little dick thought to take him down.

"Come on, I haven't got all day," Dorman said, injecting more bravado into his command than he felt. "If you've got news, then share it or get the hell out."

"Do I detect a bit of temper?" Chief asked sweetly. "If I were you, I'd be a little more polite to the person who holds your reputation by the balls." To emphasize his point he waved his cell phone back and forth.

Dorman willed himself to count to ten before responding. It was obvious the punk wanted to rile him, but why? "I'd say after last Saturday night, we've joined a mutual admiration society," he said.

"I don't know what the fuck you're talking about," the kid countered.

It was Dorman's turn to snicker. "Yeah, well, your plan worked like a charm, except for one thing: you didn't count on Lester being too stupid to double-check his escape route *before* he set off the fireworks. What happened? Did you unlock the door for him too late? Didn't give him enough time?"

Suddenly the kid stopped and looked directly at

Dorman, his eyes blazing some sort of unholy fire. "My timing was perfect," he said quietly.

It took a moment, but Dorman finally realized what the kid was implying. *Oh shit. This is one scary creep.* He swallowed. "So, um, what did you need to see me about?"

"It's about your master plan to ruin The Grove. You still want the place to go belly up, right?"

"Yes, of…of course. You know that. And you've got the same goal. You told me so yourself."

"Yeah, well, I thought last Saturday was the way to go. Place goes up in smoke, somebody dies, investors freak out. Bye bye apple pie." The kid resumed his pacing. "Except they found another Deep Pocket—this one rich enough to see the whole project through. And the fuckers aren't even giving out the name so we can scrag that dude too."

Dorman stared at the stranger called Chief and couldn't help but marvel once again at how spectacularly cold the bastard was. He quickly sobered, however, as the kid's news registered. "You mean they're back in business? Somebody's really stepped in with the cash?"

"It finally sinks in. So I'm putting you on notice, Pecker Head. Either you come up with a foolproof plan in the next few days, or I will. And if we go with my plan, I can guarantee savin' your balls will be at the bottom of my list."

Chapter Twenty-Nine

"You're not going to believe this," Dani said, swinging her chair around to face Jenna. "I think I cracked the code of Mandy's notebooks."

Since Ethan's announcement that a new investor had been found for The Grove, Jenna and Dani had been working diligently on the museum exhibit material and Jenna was confident they'd meet their deadline to have the signage, brochures, and catalogs printed in time for the art center's Grand Reopening in early October.

But discovering the truth behind her grandfather's parentage was proving more difficult. The negatives had been sent to a trusted photographer friend of Ethan's up in a place called Hayden Lake, Idaho. She was concerned the man wouldn't know what to look for, and if he found something, it might be too awful to reproduce. But the material belonged to her grandfather, after all, and if he felt confident in this guy, then she probably should, too.

Meanwhile, she and Dani had brainstormed possible keys to the odd collection of writing produced by the artists' model Mandy Culpepper, with no luck until now.

Jenna leaned back and tossed her pencil on the desk. "What have you got?"

"So we already know that Mandy, after she became Amanda Firestone, wrote a number of popular stories, like those ones about the Chinese immigrant children, and this one, *Westwind Farm*." Dani handed Jenna the oversized storybook.

"I remember this book. I read it when I was little." Jenna flipped through the pages. "It's all about this wonderful little society where the animals all have human traits, for better or worse."

"Yeah, and what made it interesting was that not all the stories are happy ones."

"But somehow you could relate to them," Jenna said. "Yes, I remember." She handed the book back and smiled. "I guess I'd put the collection somewhere between Beatrix Potter and George Orwell, if that's possible."

Dani scooted her chair closer and gestured with her hands. "So after looking through her notebooks and comparing it to her published work, it's pretty obvious her character sketches and scenes served as a kind of rough draft for her later short stories. But did she just dream these characters and their situations up or base them on real life? I'm thinking she was a creative thinker, but also a diarist of sorts."

"How do you mean?"

Dani reached for one of the earlier notebooks Reggie Firestone had lent them. She opened a page and read. "'Alphonse the rooster crowed loudly this morning, flapping his wings and letting his strength be known to everyone in the barnyard. But Lysandra the mother hen was having none of it.' From what we know of the dynamics of Gus and Lia, doesn't that sound like it could be them?"

Jenna took the journal and began to scan passages at random. "You're saying the animals she writes about represent real people?"

Dani shrugged. "Why not? She was a very down-to-earth woman, apparently. Very creative. And who knows, maybe she felt by writing in a kind of code she could record precisely what she was observing without hurting anyone's feelings or talking out of turn. And hey, she was only fifteen when she started. Gus and Lia were her guardians, remember."

"Okay, let's say you're right about this. How do you determine who's who? Gus and Lia sound somewhat plausible, but what about, say, Sandy de Kalb?"

Dani motioned for Jenna to give her back the journal. She thumbed through several pages to find one marked with a Post-it Note. "'The barnyard's newest member has been with us only two weeks and already I love him. Sinbad is such a beautiful cat—a slender male calico with a distinctly female way about him. The way he moves, the way he licks his paws. He is graceful, kind, and gentle. It's a pity he only has eyes for Romeo, a tabby from the neighboring farm.' We know that Sandy de Kalb was slender, dark-haired, and gay. He had a lover named

Roger, who lived in San Francisco, and he was also known to be a true gentleman. Mandy's entry describes him to a T. Who else would you like to hear about?"

Jenna pursed her lips. "What about Peter Raines?"

"You won't like it very much." Dani turned to another page. "'I saw Pierre today. The sly little fox was slinking along the backside of the henhouse. He insinuates himself everywhere, trying to disguise his true nature. Lysandra doesn't see him licking his chops, but he is hungry, of that I'm certain.'"

Jenna contemplated Dani's theory. Maybe Mandy's simple allegory held the key to what had gone on at The Grove. The idea seemed bizarre, but possible. "You're right," she finally said. "It does sound like Peter. But once Mandy became Amanda Firestone, she no longer worked at The Grove. So who did she write about after she left?"

Dani grinned and again held up Amanda Firestone's famous book. "I'm sure her society friends made great characters for *Westwind Farm*." She thumbed through the pages. "Ah, here's one: 'Mrs. Pigglesworth trotted into the room, her high pink forehead crowned with a large band of feathers plucked from Fannie's bottom and dyed with blackberry juice until they'd reached a bright purple hue.' Now tell me she isn't making fun of some condescending society matron who's part of her newfound social circle."

Jenna laughed delightedly. "Good point. What a great way for her to let off steam without 'ruffling feathers,' as they say."

"Ha. Ha. And the good news is, it looks like she did stay close to the Wolffs long after her marriage."

"How can you tell?"

Dani flipped to another page of notes. "I skimmed through the later notebooks and compared character names with those in her earlier ones. Sure enough, I've spotted Alphonse and Lysandra, along with a new character, a sprite little bird by the name of Glindabelle."

"Giselle, I take it?"

"That's my guess. I also scanned for Pierre, and his name turns up again too." She handed Jenna a piece of paper along with the journals. "Here's my take on who's who. I thought you might want to check it out, see if you agree."

"Thanks. I just wish we had some hard evidence to go on and not so much conjecture."

"Hopefully the negatives should provide that. 'Patience is a virtue' and all that."

"I know, but it's still frustrating." Jenna straightened her desk and got up to leave. She noticed that Dani looked like she was just settling in. "Hey, don't you have an inn to run?"

"With ten rooms and a great staff, it almost runs itself. Besides which, I don't do much else—besides this. Speaking of, I'm going to work a bit more on the inventory."

"Good enough. I'll see you tomorrow, then...and Dani?"

Already immersed in her quest, Dani had to be

prompted with a tap on her shoulder before looking up. "Yes?"

"Thanks again for caring about all of this. About my grandfather. And about what happened. It means a lot to him, and it means a lot to me."

"I am honored to help your family, just as my great-grandfather was," Dani answered softly. "Truly. Now go. I think you have someone waiting for you, am I right?"

Jenna felt herself blush and waved her hand dismissively to cover it up. As she left the office and headed toward the Great House, she barely noticed the chill in the evening air or the last vestige of light as darkness began to settle. Instead, the puzzle that she and Dani were working on nagged at her. They knew Peter Raines had trod a dark path—one that might have included an unsavory crime. Soon they'd know the definitive answer to that particular question. But there were others, such as why had he come back? And why had he left again so abruptly, after leaving the daughter of his alleged victim pregnant? Had Gus and Lia bought him off? Did he have a sudden attack of conscience? Jenna's head was starting to spin with the *what ifs* and *maybes*. She tried her usual trick of mentally shelving thoughts and worries that she could do nothing about.

The problem was that images of a certain sexy architect immediately filled the vacuum. Dani was right; no doubt Brit *was* waiting for her, as he had been every day this past week. She gave in to the now familiar sense of anticipation that had begun to course throughout her body.

Thinking of Brit and what they would do to each other in the dark thrilled her more each day because she knew from experience just how incredible it was going to be. Somehow, he knew when to be tender, when to demand, when to let her lead. He had kissed and nipped and suckled and licked virtually every inch of her body, and he had taught her how to do the same to him. Sometimes they had taken each other fast, and sometimes excruciatingly slow, but always, at the end, he enveloped her with his large, muscular body and she felt desired, protected, even cherished. Just thinking about Brit's lovemaking caused her skin to flush and her nipples to peak.

She had no doubt that for now, Brit desired her. But the question hovered nearby, marring those otherwise perfect moments: would he be interested in building a future together?

She'd known from the night of the explosion that she was still in love with him. The intense attraction she'd felt seven years ago was no fluke, no passing itch that she could scratch easily with someone else. She was destined to love Brit, and she could no longer run from those feelings. But could she admit as much to a man if he wasn't prepared to love her back?

She thought of the way she'd treated him so long ago, and the hurt his own mother had inflicted upon him. It didn't take a shrink to know that's not how you teach a man to trust you enough to share his feelings.

And that assumed he even *had* feelings that ran deeper than simple lust.

He'd said he'd learned to "live for the moment." That could mean a lot of things, one of which was he'd learned not to worry about long-term relationships. Maybe that's the way she should approach their situation as well. But could she? Could she simply love him until she couldn't be with him anymore because he'd decided he was no longer interested?

Thoughts like those consumed her so that as she neared the front veranda of the Great House she didn't even notice a figure slowly rocking back and forth in the shadows. The rhythmic creak finally alerted her that she was not alone.

"Brit?" she called softly.

"He's not here, Jenna," the murmur came back.

Fear slammed through her and she stopped, paralyzed, not knowing if she should run. The figure rose and walked down the steps toward her. "What's the matter?" Parker asked, stepping into the pale glow of the porch light.

"I…uh…you scared me, that's all. I…wasn't expecting anybody to be sitting up there." She swallowed hard and forced herself not to make a scene. Where was Brit?

As if he'd read her mind, Parker reached out to touch her arm. She couldn't help it; she flinched. "Is he supposed to be here?" he asked softly, shifting his gaze briefly to the mansion.

"I…don't know. We just share the space. I'm not sure of his schedule."

"Can I come in and talk with you for a while?"

Hell no. "Uh, well, I'm pretty tired," she said. "What did you want to talk about?"

"Oh, this whole fuck up with The Grove here. You know. Lester getting killed and all. It's kind of bummed me out."

"I can understand that. It's pretty crazy around here. If you're worried, perhaps you should…I don't know…maybe think about finding another job."

Parker inhaled sharply. "It's not me I'm worried about. It's you."

"Me? Why?"

He looked at her intently. "It's dangerous around here. When Kyle and I saw the explosion the other night, we both got really worried about you. Something could happen. You know. Something bad."

Jenna's breath started to hitch. *Remain calm.* "Look, Parker. I'm flattered that you're…concerned for me, but really, you're too young to be worried about things like that. I can take care of myself."

Even in the dim light Jenna could see Parker's eyes turn glacial. His entire being seemed to form a ball of repressed fury. She thought he might fly into a rage, but he surprised her.

"I'm older than my years," he said cryptically.

Jenna tried for a note of condescension that she hoped would bring him down to earth. "No, you're not. You're just a kid. Good night, Parker."

She half expected him to rail at her, but he didn't. He merely smiled and said, "Goodnight, Jenna. Sweet dreams…and stay safe." He then disappeared into the darkness.

Jenna stood on the veranda, taking a moment to bring her heartbeat back to normal, when her cell phone rang. She noted the caller and breathed a sigh of relief. "Declan! How are you?"

Brit passed Parker on the path leading up to the Great House. The kid seemed angry about something. Brit's thoughts immediately turned to Jenna and he picked up his pace. He was nearly at the front steps of the mansion when he heard Jenna exclaim "Declan!" The tone of her voice sounded like she'd been waiting forever for his call. In an instant the cool of the evening turned downright cold. Brit acknowledged her with a wave of his hand but walked around to the back and let himself in. He went over to the utility sink at the far end of the kitchen and sluiced water over his face and arms, drying off with a paper towel. He'd put in a long, hard day, made tolerable by the notion that Jenna would be waiting at the end of it. Maybe he ought to rethink that kind of mindset.

He was halfway through a bottle of Stella Artois when Jenna came rushing through the back door and into the kitchen.

"Thank God you're here," she said with a sigh and made to go into his arms. He stiffened and she stood back, surprise etched on her face. "What is it?" she asked. "What's wrong?"

"Nothing," he said, stepping away and taking another swig of his beer. He walked over and opened the refrigerator, bending down to survey the contents. "Got a date tonight?" he asked, trying to sound nonchalant.

Jenna marched over to him. "What? What are you talking about?"

Brit pulled out some leftover chicken, straightened, and looked at her impassively. "Sounds like you and Declan are hooking up. Just wanted to know if it was tonight."

Jenna, hands on hips, looked at him incredulously. "You're kidding, right?"

I wish I were. "Look, I'm sorry. I told you early on, stuff like that shouldn't be on my radar. My bad." Brit's insides were roiling. *Redirect. Redirect.*

Jenna eyes grew wide, but after a moment they softened. She drew in a breath and put her hand on his forearm. "Well, it damn well ought to be on your radar," she said quietly. "It would certainly be on mine." She hesitated. "But as it turns out, I am meeting Declan tonight, and I need you to come with me."

"What? I hate to tell you, sweetheart, but I gave up threesomes awhile back."

"Oh!" Jenna punched him on his arm. "That is too much information, and I am serious! Declan's been digging into our situation here, trying to get to the bottom of who attacked him, and has some information he says we might find useful. That is, if you're interested at all in hearing it." She confronted him, hands on hips, eyes blazing.

Shit. This is why I hate rollercoasters, Brit thought. He paused and then reached for her, placing his large hand on her waist. "I told you I'm an idiot," he murmured in her ear, just before kissing it.

"Yes, you are," she whispered. She reached her hand behind his neck and pulled him down, opening her mouth to him and demanding that he do the same. Within seconds, the kiss turned nuclear. Brit lifted her onto the kitchen counter and insinuated himself between her widespread legs. She braced herself on the counter while he devoured her, reaching for the buttons on her shirt, all the while nibbling and kissing and suckling and letting her know he was ready to take her right then and there.

"Wait…*wait.*" Jenna stopped his hands as they were about to unbutton her jeans. She was already shirtless, her breasts heaving, about to overflow her bra.

Damn, the power this woman has over me. He stopped, resting his forehead against hers and breathing hard. "Okay, I'm listening," he ground out.

"I told Declan we'd meet him at Remington's at seven, which means we have to leave in the next few minutes to get there on time."

"You told him 'we'?"

Jenna took Brit's face in her hands. "Yes, I told him 'we.' Is that all right?"

"Quite all right," he replied solemnly, then sighed. "Let's get going."

Chapter Thirty

They reached Remington's in San Rafael a few minutes after the hour. It was a popular restaurant known for its succulent steaks and intimate atmosphere. Jenna spotted Declan sitting at the bar, sipping what looked like a whiskey straight up. He wore jeans and a dark green sweater. His black hair was disheveled, and he still had a white bandage on the side of his cheek. An iPad was sitting on the bar in front of him.

Two beautiful young women "dressed for the hunt" walked up to him and started talking. One seemed particularly aggressive and leaned to whisper something to him. He nodded and took another sip of his drink. He didn't seem particularly thrilled with the company, but knowing Declan, he was charming them in spite of himself. Jenna glanced at Brit, who gave her a look signaling, *I'm not impressed.* Jenna quirked a smile. *Of course not. You're a male and he's the competition.*

Just then Declan spotted them and stood up, grabbing

his iPad. "Jenna, lass," he said, walking up to her and kissing her on the cheek while Brit stood by impassively. Declan then turned to him and offered his hand. "You must be Brit Maguire. Declan O'Connor, at your service."

"I understand you've got some information for us," Brit said.

Declan grinned at Jenna. "So much for the niceties. Can I buy you two a drink?"

"I'll get it. Why don't you two get a table? Jenna? Porter?"

At her nod Brit went up to the bar while Declan pointed her in the direction of a table in the back. "He's not thrilled with me," Declan mused.

"Brit? Oh, he's…preoccupied, that's all. Lot's going on. He's really a great guy."

Declan gazed at Jenna. "Don't know about that, lass, but lucky? That I'll give him."

Twenty minutes later, having already ordered steak sandwiches for Brit and Jenna, and soup for himself, Declan laid out what he'd discovered.

"After Jenna filled me in on what's been going on, I looked into all the major stakeholders for The Grove Center for American Art, including your Trust, the Little Eden town council, the SPEAR group, and any other names that cropped up," he said. "Lots of layers to weed through, but the picture's coming into focus."

Jenna was thrilled to have one more mind working

on the puzzle; Brit was less enthusiastic. She watched as he leaned negligently back in his chair.

"Persistent bugger, aren't you, O'Connor?" he said.

Declan smiled. "It's part of me job, boyo. I started with the question of who stands to gain if The Grove fails to open. Some interesting connections cropped up." He booted up his iPad. "Have you ever heard of New Venture Properties?"

Jenna shook her head, but Brit spoke up. "Yeah. They're a big outfit out of Los Angeles. They focus on resorts, golf courses, things like that."

"Right you are. Apparently they've been waitin' in the wings for a certain property in West Marin to become available, once it's taken over by the town of Little Eden. They're first in line to purchase The Grove, which the city is all too ready to unload in order to improve its balance sheet."

"So they know about the codicil to Lia's will," Brit said.

Jenna couldn't mask her irritation. "That damn codicil. What was Lia Wolff thinking? I'm convinced the pressure my grandfather's been under because of that will was part of what landed him in the hospital."

Brit took her hand across the table. "It's also one of the reasons he wants you back in the fold."

Declan was scanning his notes. "Ah. How about Pacific View Design, LLC?"

Both Jenna and Brit shook their heads this time. "Never heard of them," Brit said. "Are they from around here?"

"You might say that. They're 'on retainer' with New Venture, which is the usual cover-up for a kickback."

"So who are they?" Jenna asked.

"The principle partner is Ralph Dorman."

"Why, that cocksucker—sorry, Jenna. So Dorman uses his power on the town council to stall the renovation as long as he can, or even stop it altogether. Why? In the hope that Ethan won't live long enough to see it through? That's friggin' cold."

"That's outrageous," Jenna agreed. "What can we do about it? I mean, that's got to be flagrant conflict of interest."

"Yes it is," Declan said, "and it certainly provides a motive, but I'm afraid you need something more than that to put a stop to it." He scrolled to another file on his tablet. "Now as to the mugger mentioning you, Jenna—"

Brit popped up in his chair. "What? What are you talking about?"

Declan shot Jenna a disapproving look. "Ah, you didn't tell him, I take it?"

Uh oh. Jenna shook her head. "I didn't want to worry him."

Brit looked offended. "Didn't want to worry me? For Chrissakes, Jenna, I'm already way beyond worried!" He turned to Declan. "What exactly did this asshole say to you?"

"Just that I was to stay away from Jenna or I'd lose more than my pretty face. Come to think of it, that's something *you* might say."

Testosterone's flowing now, Jenna thought. She put her hand on Brit's arm, but he counterpunched anyway.

"Listen, if I wanted to warn you off, buddy, I'd tell you myself. I wouldn't send in any surrogates." The two men's eyes locked on each other.

Jenna sighed and Declan was the first to offer détente. "Anyway," he continued, "I've been thinking we might be dealing with two different scenarios here."

"What do you mean?" Jenna asked.

"It seems like the warning I got about you was personal. They didn't mention The Grove or anything connected to it. Just you. And maybe whoever left that note for you was coming from the same place. So I asked myself, other than Mr. Maguire here, whom I assume is honorable enough to do his own dirty work —" Brit tipped his head in agreement "—who else might want you all to themselves?" He paused and grinned. "Besides me own bad self of course."

Jenna ignored the quip. "I don't know," she said, perplexed. "I haven't gone out with anyone…"

"But you do have admirers, don't you? A couple of swains by the name of Parker Bishop and Kyle Summers, as a matter of fact. Didn't they fight over you on the last day of school?"

"Oh come on," Jenna started. "No way would they—"

Brit held up his hand. "No, he's got a point, Jenna. Has anything turned up on them?"

"Sorry to say, neither of them is as innocent as you might wish they were, lass. They've both got records their rich daddies have tried to suppress. Kyle exposed himself to one of his cousins, and Parker was cited for carrying an illegal weapon."

"Oh my God," Jenna said. "But they're working at The Grove this summer. Surely you don't think they would…would…"

"Hire someone to mug me? I have no idea, but I have to follow the logic. If not them, then who?"

"Maybe some nut job who took a fancy to her when she moved to The Grove," Brit suggested.

Jenna rolled her eyes. "You make it sound like someone would have to be a nut job to take a fancy to me."

"Hardly," Brit and Declan muttered at the same time. Surprised, they looked at each other and chuckled.

Brit then looked at Jenna. "Sounds crazy, but I think it's entirely possible Kyle or Parker could pull something like that off. One of them—I can't remember which—seemed all too eager to comfort you when I went in after Lester. And what about Kyle getting close to you in the museum building?"

"I'll see what else comes up on that score," Declan said. He reached for his wallet. "Look, I've got to run. I'm on the night shift. They're probably hoping nothing happens that'll put me on the telly, not with this mug." He pointed to his bandage.

"I'll get the bill," Brit said.

"No, my treat," Declan insisted.

Jenna reached for her purse. "Oh for heaven's sake. I'll pay the bill—and don't argue, either one of you!"

While Brit and Declan waited outside the restaurant for Jenna, Brit took a moment to size up the Irishman. *He's got good taste in women, I'll give him that.* The two men exchanged cell numbers and Declan assured him he'd send any additional information he uncovered their way.

"And Brit," the reporter added, "Remember what you said about me being persistent? I am that. Rest assured, if you step away from that lovely lass for any reason, she won't be alone for long."

Brit returned Declan's look with a steely-eyed glare of his own. "I wouldn't hold my breath…boyo."

Declan smiled faintly. At that point Jenna walked up and Declan kissed her on the cheek.

"We'll figure this out, I promise, lass," he said, and walked to his car.

"Goddamn it," Brit muttered, watching Declan drive off.

Jenna turned to him, a worried look on her face. "What is it?"

"I fucking like the guy."

Jenna laughed and put her arm through Brit's. "What's not to like? I'm convinced you're twins, separated at birth."

They talked about the information Declan had uncovered about Kyle and Parker. Brit wanted to let both boys go immediately, but once again Jenna objected, saying it wasn't fair to accuse them of wrongdoing with no proof.

"I don't like it," he said. "But you're the boss." He got behind the wheel of his Porsche and headed back toward West Marin; however, instead of continuing on Sir Francis Drake Boulevard toward Little Eden, he decided to turn onto Main Street in the hamlet of San Anselmo. "Do you have to be back at The Grove tonight?" he asked.

"No, I suppose not. Why?"

"There's something I've got to do."

At ten o'clock, the streets of the little town were beginning to thin out. Brit parked in a small lot next to a well-kept building with a sign that read "San Anselmo Hotel." He took Jenna by the hand and entered the side door of the establishment, which led to a small front parlor. "Anna? Ben?" he called quietly.

A tall, distinguished looking man came out from the back. "Ah, Brit, how are you doing, young man?"

"Great. Listen, I'm sorry for the short notice, but my fiancée—Jenna, meet Ben. Ben, Jenna—and I need a room. Any openings?"

A shocked expression on her face, Jenna took a moment before answering. "Um, wait. We're—"

"—beat," Brit said impatiently. "Exhausted. Asleep on our feet. So, what do you think? Are we in luck?"

Ben gave Brit a look that said he didn't believe a word of Brit's story, but then shook his head and smiled. "Yes, you're in luck. The Eagle's Nest is open." He handed Brit a key and turned to go. "Lock up and turn out the lights," he said.

Once they were alone, Jenna punched Brit on the

shoulder. "Are you kidding me? Is this some kind of standing bachelor pad where you bring your—"

"Hell, no," Brit said. "Listen, I lived here for several months while the Great House was being renovated, and Ben and Anna treated me like family. Now my mother and her entourage stay here every time they come to see me. She says it's the last outpost of civilization...thinks Little Eden's the middle of nowhere. Come on."

He took her by the hand and quickly went up a flight of stairs to a delightful third floor room with windows overlooking a forest of tall trees. Once he had Jenna inside, he turned and locked the door, stopping briefly to look at her. "I'm sorry, but I've been waiting all day to be with you, and then in the kitchen, and seeing you with Declan...baby, I just had to do this." And with that he stepped up to her and speared his hands through her hair, taking her mouth voraciously, with the strength and the power of a passion too long denied. He stopped long enough to peel off his shirt and then went at her again, backing her up to the cozy full-size bed covered in a beautiful pastel quilt. "Now you," he said.

Jenna, immediately compliant, seemed to surge with energy in response to his desire for her. She quickly took off her top and bra, letting her breasts spill out for his pleasure. Pulling Brit on top of her onto the bed, she grinned. "Exhausted, huh? Asleep on your feet, is it?"

Brit smiled just before he took her right nipple into his mouth. "I will be...in about an hour."

Roughly ninety minutes later, after one quick and another, much slower round of lovemaking, Brit lay spoon-fashion behind Jenna, his hand cupping her breast, breathing the deep sleep of someone who works their body hard and has earned a rest.

Just before drowsiness got the better of her, Jenna thought fleetingly of the word Brit had used with Ben. *Fiancée*. She tried it on for size. It fit well, but it was just a disguise. A ruse. The reality was something else. She just didn't know what.

Chapter Thirty-One

The receptionist at the Sheriff's substation in Lagunitas looked like she was about sixteen, with fire-engine-red hair and a dainty little nose ring that made Brit wince. She did know how to wear a pair of jeans, however. When Brit asked to talk to Gabe, she escorted him down to Gabe's office.

"Detective de la Torre? Mr. Maguire is here to see you." She stood in the doorway, gesturing to Gabe, who was sitting at his desk getting ready to toss a mini Nerf basketball into a plastic hoop that was strategically placed above his computer. He missed.

"*Merda,*" he muttered.

"It's hotter than hell in here," Brit said. "Let's go someplace else and cool off."

"Sounds good to me. Uh, that'll be all, Kelly." Kelly had been staring at Brit, which was unnerving to say the least. "She's into muscles," Gabe explained once she'd left. Brit merely raised his eyebrows.

Ten minutes later the two men were stretched out

alongside the creek that ran through town, under the shade of a decades-old bay laurel tree whose branches offered at least some relief from the day's inferno. Brit pulled a large zip lock bag of ice from his backpack along with a couple of Miller Genuine Drafts. Gabe checked his watch.

"Come on, you're off duty in, what, ten minutes?"

"Yeah, what the hell." Gabe reached over for one of the beers.

"I've got some information you might want to follow up on, but first I need some answers," Brit said.

Gabe nodded. "Fair enough, as long as it's off the record. I've got enough hassles without getting my butt in a sling over loose lips."

"Understood."

Gabe gazed out at the languidly flowing water. "Trouble sticks to The Grove like flies on shit," he began.

Brit smiled grimly. "Tell me something I don't already know." He took a swig of his MGD. "Question is, what are you gonna do about it?"

Gabe shrugged his broad shoulders. "Nothing I *can* do at the moment. The evidence is spotty. Look, here's what we know." He counted his fingers for emphasis. "One, Lester was good buds with your security guard, who up to now's been playing deaf and dumb. But I think Lester's death's got to old Gid, so hopefully he'll give somebody up soon. Two, we got a search warrant for Lester's apartment. Turns out he was a cash and carry kind of guy, but we did find a cash receipt for the red paint used in your little art demonstration."

Yes. Now we're gettin' somewhere. "Okay then, there's your proof it was Boyce Wheeler's call."

Gabe shook his head. "Not so fast. There's no evidentiary link to Wheeler, Dorman, or SPEAR, except that Lester was a member of that group." He continued his countdown. "Three, we're still waitin' on Don to get his version of what happened. There were some partial boot prints at the scene, and we're seeing if at least the size matches Lester's foot."

Brit could feel his temper starting to rise. He should have brought Jenna along to calm him down, but she was a distraction unto herself. "Okay then. Anything related to the explosion?"

"Yeah, indirectly. I told you earlier we didn't find any prints, which we wouldn't have found for Lester anyway because he was wearing gloves. Turns out there were dried flecks of the same red paint on them that turned up on that gas can I told you about. In a different mood, I might even appreciate the symmetry of all that evidence, but seeing as how Lester's dead, I don't derive much satisfaction from it."

"Especially since you and I both know Lester wasn't smart enough to be the 'lone gunman.'"

Gabe took a swig from his own bottle and nodded. "I'd have to agree with you on that one."

"Christ, you know he was a stooge for SPEAR."

"No, we don't know that…or at least we can't prove it yet. But we can prove one thing: Lester Small was either the unluckiest SOB who ever lived…or he was murdered."

Gabe's words caught Brit by surprise. "Murdered? Explain."

"Evidence shows the accelerant used to start the fire was lighter fluid, not gasoline. And we know the explosion originated in the corner of the barn that held the large fuel drums, which isn't where you found him."

"So you're saying Lester probably went in there to start a fire, but someone beat him to it."

"I'm saying Lester went in there and *then* someone beat him to it."

"You mean someone else was in there?"

"Nope. Didn't need to be. Among the debris near the point of origin we found the makings of a very small, very crude incendiary device."

Okay, *now* this was getting scary. "Wait a minute. Someone planted a bomb in the equipment barn?!"

"No. Nothing that sophisticated. Just a simple rig using several nine volt batteries, some shredded steel wool and a disposable phone. It was pretty clever, actually. The perp used the vibrating phone to make the connection between the batteries and the wool, which created a spark. And a spark is all it took because the area around the fuel drums was already saturated."

"So you're saying Lester had nothing to do with starting the fire."

Gabe shrugged. "Like I said, he was either at the wrong place at the wrong time, or else someone set him up. What I want to know is, who would have screwed him over? Somebody from SPEAR? Doesn't make sense."

"Maybe he was getting lippy," Brit suggested. "Maybe Wheeler or Dorman didn't want him to talk."

"It's a possibility, but my gut tells me Wheeler isn't that ruthless. He wasn't faking it at Lester's funeral. I think his grief was real. Now, Ralph Dorman's another story."

"How do you mean?"

"A few weeks ago we got an anonymous tip to keep an eye on both Dorman and Lester. I put a P.C. in there—"

"P.C.?"

"'Plain clothes.' We figured it couldn't hurt to keep tabs. Sure enough, Dorman shows up at the next SPEAR meeting, which he often does, apparently, to keep the group filled in on what the city's doing to make sure you guys at The Grove are jumping through all the bureaucratic hoops. Anyway, our guy spots Lester slinking up to Dorman outside after the meeting. Dorman looks around like he doesn't want anybody to see them, then he starts giving Lester shit and walks away. Fast forward to the funeral, Dorman's acting the part of concerned civic leader, but I happened to be there, too. The guy kept checking his watch and texting. His distress was barely skin deep. Still, we've got no direct link between him and SPEAR, and no direct link between SPEAR and the crimes."

Brit took some ice from the bag he'd brought and rubbed it on the back of his neck. "Look, you know there's a connection. If nothing else, Dorman's related to Wheeler through marriage. Can't you get a warrant and check Wheeler's files or something?"

"No can do. We thought we'd go that route based on the vocal opposition SPEAR's had to the project from the get-go. But Judge Franklin says there's not enough probable cause. He's part of the old guard anyway—even warned us against starting a witch hunt. Says SPEAR is just asserting its First Amendment rights and there's no harm in that."

"What if you can show motive, like good old-fashion greed, for stopping The Grove?"

"What have you got?"

Brit laid out the facts Declan had dredged up, including the link between Dorman's company, the city of Little Eden, and New Venture Properties. He also explained the codicil to Lia's will.

Gabe jotted down the information. "I'll look into it. But unless we can prove a quid pro quo…"

Brit's frustration bubbled up again. "Jesus, seems like you guys spend more time figuring out what you can't do than what you can."

"Pretty much," Gabe agreed. "But if you ever found yourself in a tight spot, accused of something you didn't do, you'd appreciate the checks and balances."

"Maybe, but come on, there's got to be something else. Anything on the photo or the notecard?"

Gabe shook his head again. "Nowadays anybody can print just about anything, including their own photos and stationery. With no fingerprints it's almost impossible to track down."

"Well, so far that stacks up to a big fat zero."

Gabe pointed with his now empty bottle. "For now, maybe, but I've been at this awhile, Brit, and I can tell you that sooner or later somebody will screw up, and when they do, the pieces of the puzzle will all start falling into place."

Brit considered whether to bring up the matter of Kyle Summers and Parker Bishop. Both he and Jenna had felt uneasy regarding the boys' whereabouts on the night of the explosion, so he'd asked his acting foreman where they *should* have been. Jack recalled that he'd told the grunts to sweep the area between the museum complex and the Great House, since that's where the investors would head after the program.

"But they were picking up trash way down by the bungalows, in the dark." Brit pointed out.

Jack had grinned. "Hey, for once they did something without me asking."

Maybe they'd finally learned what it meant to be proactive little worker bees, Brit thought...but maybe not. What the hell; it couldn't hurt to fill Gabe in. "Okay, here's something else to add to the mix. I hired a couple of kids, friends of Jason's, to work the construction crew this summer. Kyle Summers and Parker Bishop. I think they've both got the hots for Jenna. They've been kinda squirrelly around her. Puppy love kind of shit, but it still gives her the willies. One night Kyle even shows up inside the Museum, waiting for her. He claims the door was unlocked, but she swears she closed it. Both boys have got records, too. Maybe somehow they broke into the Great House to leave that message for her."

"Yeah, or maybe, as you said, Lester did it. Wouldn't he have had more access to the keys than those kids?

He could have made a copy himself and used it to get into both the Great House and the equipment barn."

"Yeah, except you said he didn't have a key on him. And whoever set that fire had to have access to the barn, too." Brit scrubbed his hand over his face in frustration. "Goddamn it, Gabe. I don't know how you stay in this line of work. It's infuriating!"

"Yeah it is. But let me tell you, when you finally nail the bad guy, it's *sweet*."

"I hope to hell that happens sooner rather than later." Brit drank the rest of his beer and put the bottle in his pack along with Gabe's empty bottle, then got up to stretch his legs.

At that moment Kelly the receptionist sauntered up to the two men. "Uh, Detective de la Torre?" she said, twirling one of her red curls between her fingers. "There was a call for you. Someone at a rehab center said for you to call right away. Something about some guy waking up."

Brit caught Gabe's eye. "I'll see you there."

Brit, Sherrie, and Jenna were already at the nurse's station, getting ready to visit Don, by the time Gabe arrived. *Now maybe we'll get some answers*, Brit thought. He watched Gabe turn on the charm as the detective pulled out his badge for the nurse on duty.

"I understand Mr. Rodriguez has regained consciousness," he explained with a smile. "I'd like to talk with him immediately if that's possible."

The head nurse, who looked like she took no prisoners, gestured to Brit and the women. "You willing to pull rank over them?"

"'Fraid so."

"So be it." She pointed him in the direction of room 114. "Soon as the doctor finishes with Mr. Rodriguez you can go in. But no more than a few minutes. That's the rule."

"Yes, ma'am," Gabe assured her. "Five, tops."

"I'll be watching," she warned, tapping her watch and failing in her attempt to remain stern with him.

Brit chuffed. Women were always putty in Gabe's hands. Didn't matter what age. He just had the knack, plus he had that Italian thing going. Funny how it didn't work on Dani, though—maybe because she was Italian too and saw right through him. Plus, much to Brit's relief, Jenna didn't seem bowled over either. He nodded, acknowledging Gabe's signal that he wouldn't take long. Sure enough, five minutes later he walked out again. He gave Brit a thumbs-up sign as he hurried out of the building.

Brit tracked down the nurse, more impatient than ever to see Don. "May we go in now?"

"Yes, but I'll tell you the same thing I told the detective: five minutes is all you get. Mr. Rodriguez is still quite weak."

Brit and Jenna stood at the door while Sherrie ran over to Don's bed and leaned over to hug and kiss him. Brit glanced at Jenna and smiled. *It'd be nice to have a woman who loved you like that.* Then he thought about the incredible night they'd just spent together. *Damn.*

After a few minutes of murmured words, Sherrie straightened up and walked back to Brit and Jenna, drying her eyes.

"I told you he was a stubborn cuss," Brit said.

"Well, you better get over there. He wants to talk to you before they throw us all out."

"I'm so happy for you, Sherrie," Jenna said. She waved to Don across the room.

"Come on, let's let Brit and Don hash it out," Sherrie said. "I told him I'd get him a cup of strong coffee anyway."

The women left and Brit strode over to Don's bedside. He couldn't help but note the contrast between the robust, no-nonsense man Don had been and the thin, pasty-skinned patient who currently occupied the bed. Still, it was a blessing he was even alive, much less actually awake.

"Hey, Don," he said.

Don smiled weakly. "Shit, you're not gonna fire me for layin' down on the job, now are ya, *jefe*?"

Brit chuckled. "Yeah. I'm writin' you up for jumping out of a moving vehicle while falling down a ravine." He walked over and squeezed Don's hand. "Glad you made it back."

"You and me both. Hey, give me a sip of that agua, will ya? Sleepin' all day works up a thirst."

Brit held the glass of water close so Don could sip from its straw. "So what the hell happened?"

"Thanks, man," he said, indicating that he was through drinking. "Honestly, I don't remember much about what happened. I know I was driving along on

Fifty-Seven, just listenin' to the radio, when, bam—I must have gone over the side."

"Report says you were drinking."

Don's eyes blazed and he shook his head. "No way. That's bullshit. I gave that up years ago."

"I didn't believe it either," Brit said. "They said you had a lot of it poured over you, but none in your system."

"Yeah, Gabe mentioned that. Brit, I think somebody set me up."

"It's looking that way. Hey, what'd you mean when you told the paramedics, 'Ran off road'?"

Don grimaced. "I sure as hell didn't run myself off the road. I know that for damn sure."

"I *knew* it. That's what I told them."

"And like I told Gabe, I'm pretty sure I saw the same car following me pretty much all the way home. A black SUV."

Brit went on alert. "You sure that's what it was? I think that's the same kind of car that almost ran me over the night of the vandalism. Remember I told you about that? What do you mean, it followed you all the way home?"

Don ran his hand across his almost bald pate. "I was over in Oakland picking up some pipe fittings, and I see the car on my rear but I don't think anything of it. I mean, how many black SUVs are there? But it keeps showing up. It's behind me on the bridge, and everything, but still I don't think anything of it. And then I get to Fifty-Seven and...and...I dunno, I was driving around a curve, I think, and—"

"And then you take the plunge?"

"Somethin' like that. That's all I remember, really. So tell me, how are things going at The Grove?"

"A lot's happened," Brit said. He was about to go into detail when the nurse came in to shoo him away.

"That's all for now, gentlemen. Mr. Rodriguez needs even more beauty sleep, if you can believe it. You can visit again in a few hours."

"Better not cross the Dragon Lady," Don joked.

"Ha, ha. Now scoot," the nurse commanded.

"Yes, ma'am." Brit briefly touched Don's shoulder. "Glad you're back, man. Get stronger, 'cause we need you. Badly."

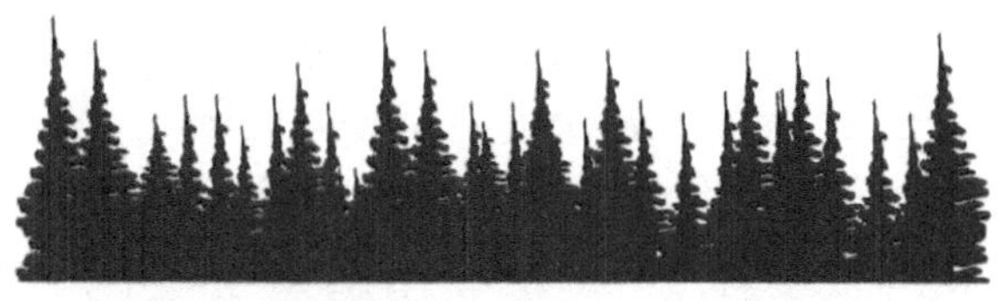

Chapter Thirty-Two

"Look, Ed, I—" Dorman had to stop while Ed Tarpin, the president of New Venture Properties, continued ranting on the other end of the line. The developer was putting Dorman on notice that if things didn't turn around, and soon, they'd be looking for viable projects elsewhere. Oh, and did he mention if Dorman didn't return the fucking twenty-five grand they'd advanced him, he'd be eating his lunch through a straw?

Hunkered down in a corner booth in the Wayside Café, Dorman was getting his ass chewed via cell phone while he waited for Wanda to bring him his usual Manhattan—stirred—and spicy nachos. He tried again.

"Yeah, I know, Ed, but—" No use. The asshole was bound and determined to use Dorman as his whipping boy and there wasn't a damn thing Dorman could do about it.

Wasn't that just hunky dory. Who in the hell would

have thought Wolff would find another major donor, and so frigging fast! Little Eden's city attorney had checked out all the angles. As long as The Grove reopened as a functioning enterprise, there'd be no way the town could break Lia Wolff's will.

Dorman held the phone away from his ear and rolled his eyes. When was this jerk going to run out of gas, anyway? He made one last attempt. "Uh, excuse me, Ed, but I've got to head into a meeting…yes…yes I know. Yes, I'll keep you posted…all right. Goodbye."

Disgusted, he snapped the phone shut just as Wanda walked up with his drink. For the first time that evening he noticed her face, which was sporting a black eye barely covered with makeup. "What the hell happened to you?"

Wanda leaned down so that only he could hear. "Your little prick friend and his camera is what happened to me. Wayne happened to get a print in the mail and a note saying he could see the video on Peepers.com."

"Jesus, can you tell if it's me in the picture?"

Wanda just looked at him, a sneer distorting her already swollen face. "Yeah, thanks for the sympathy. I'm touched." Looking disgruntled, she headed back to the kitchen.

My God, Dorman thought, that punk, that "Chief" or whoever the fuck he is, is capable of some very nasty shit. The image of Lester, frying in that shed, came to mind, and fear started to grip him. He quickly downed his drink. "Calm down," he muttered to himself. "You can figure this out."

Wanda came back and practically dropped his nachos in his lap. He held up his empty glass and signaled for a refill, which she reluctantly brought a few minutes later. The usual chips smothered in jalapeños and chile con queso didn't go down well; he started to feel a combination of heartburn and nausea.

It's all Boyce's fault, he reasoned. Boyce and his obsession with bringing down The Grove. He was the one who'd pointed out the weird codicil of the will; he was the one who'd insisted The Grove not see the light of day. Okay, so vandalizing the place was one thing. He could even see the value of blowing up a building or two as long as nobody got hurt. But running somebody off the road with the intent of killing them? Taking the chance and getting one of your own men killed? What was Boyce *thinking*? And now there's this sociopathic moron horning in on the action, doing his little power trip with the cell phone video and thinking he's now got Dorman by the short hairs. *Think again, scumbag. I didn't get this far to be trampled under by the likes of* you.

Dorman had one more drink, gave Wanda a twenty-dollar tip, and got up to leave. Obviously he wouldn't be meeting her after her shift. Shit.

The parking lot was half empty and dimly lit, which is why Dorman didn't see the first blow coming. It hit him in his midsection, sucking the air out of him and causing him to sink to his knees.

"Wh-what's—?" The next blow was a kick to his

ribs. He moaned, falling onto his back, but not for long, because his assailant grabbed the front of his shirt and lifted him just enough to backhand him across the face.

"That's for doin' the nasty," the man said, punching Dorman in the eye. As his eye began to swell shut, Dorman made out a stocky guy with a big head covered with a sheer black stocking. Then the man administered the *coup de grace*: a swift kick to the balls.

"And that's for takin' it public."

Dorman immediately curled to the fetal position and had one fleeting thought before passing out: *I guess Wayne recognized me after all.*

Sometime later Dorman awoke back in his own living room, lying on the sofa with a cold bandage on his forehead. He vaguely remembered waking up in the cramped back seat of a car as it was moving. At first he thought Wayne might be taking him out in the woods someplace to kill him, but he soon realized his wife, Myra, was driving. When they reached their home, she'd managed to get him inside and onto the couch. He glanced at his watch. Apparently he'd passed out again, because it was now past midnight.

Myra came back into the room from the kitchen carrying a glass of water and a bottle of Advil, which she set on the coffee table near him. Even though she had a passably pretty face, she was one of those fleshy women; always had been. After twenty-three years of marriage, she'd grown into her grandmotherly persona. It suited her well.

She was always organized and always busy. She played Bunco and belonged to the Little Eden Historical Society. She volunteered at the retirement home and was president of the garden club. He'd never really been attracted to her, but the fact that she was Boyce Wheeler's heir was a major asset. They rubbed along well, doing their own thing, and he saw no reason for that to change, despite this little dust up. It wasn't as if it were the first time, after all. Time to start making amends.

"Myra, I—"

"Shut up," she said simply. She sat down on the recliner across from the couch and steepled her fingers, staring at him.

"It's not what it seems," he tried.

Myra's expression was bland, but the look in her eyes, from what he could see out of only one of his own, seemed as cold as…well as cold as that young punk's.

"You've really done it this time," she said.

"I can explain. You see, somebody jumped me, and—"

"Don't bother. Wanda called and asked if I wanted to come and pick up a sack of garbage that was taking up space in the parking lot. I asked her which parking lot—the café or the motel?"

Dorman winced, as much from the words as the pain working its way throughout his body. He stalled for time by taking four pain pills with a sip of water.

"She means nothing to me," he offered.

Myra's smile was twisted. "Do you really think I care?" she asked. "I'm talking about the call from Detective de la Torre of the Marin County Investigator's Office."

This does not sound good. Dorman struggled to sit up. "What are you talking about?"

"Apparently you didn't check your cell. The good detective wants to talk to you about where you were on the day The Grove foreman had his accident. He seems to think you might know something about it."

Wait a minute. Wait. A. Minute. Things were moving a little too fast. "Hold it right there. I didn't have anything to do with that! I heard it was an accident, pure and simple."

Myra tilted her head and looked at him. Her voice was tinged with sarcasm when she said, "You and I both know it wasn't an accident. Somebody forced that man over, just like Lester blew up that shed. Except now the powers that be think *you're* involved somehow. You, the upstanding city council member. You, the pillar of the community. You, the politician who usually has the smarts to dip his wick down the road to keep things discreet."

Listening to Myra, Dorman got the distinct impression she wasn't speaking out of hurt or jealousy or even anger, but sheer disgust. Strangely, he felt insulted. But he couldn't afford to alienate her—not now, when so much was at stake. He decided to lay it all out and try to get her on board.

"Look, it's no secret your tree-hugging uncle is dead

set against the reopening of The Grove. *He's* the one who's been behind all this. The vandalism, the foreman's so-called accident, the explosion at the equipment shed. Lester was his man, and he took one too many chances, that's all."

"Uh, no, that's not all," Myra said. "There's the little matter of New Venture Properties."

Dorman swallowed. He was beginning to realize he'd underestimated his seemingly docile spouse.

"New Venture Properties?"

Myra stifled a snort. "You're not really going to sit there being dumb *and* clueless, are you?"

Dorman's hand clenched the glass of water he'd been holding. For a moment he loathed his wife, but inwardly he counted to ten. Patience, his mother always said. Patience. "Okay, okay," he finally admitted. "There was a codicil to Lia Wolff's will: if The Grove doesn't reopen in Ethan Wolff's lifetime, the city claims the property. And if Little Eden owns the property, it can turn around and sell it to New Venture Properties to be developed." He hesitated, then blew out a breath. "And if New Venture has the land, it can call on Pacific View Design to create the executive golfing community it plans to build."

"Oh, so you'd actually *do* something for the kickbacks you've been getting? And here I thought Pacific View Design was just a shell."

Dorman swallowed painfully. How did she know about the money he'd taken from New Venture? He thought for sure he'd covered his tracks regarding the payments.

His wife sniffed. "And when were you going to tell me about this little project you'd signed on to?"

"Oh. Well, I wanted to surprise you when it was a done deal. No sense getting your hopes up until it happened."

"Right," Myra said. "You were just looking out for the Little Woman." She got up and started to pace across the room. She seemed to be thinking out loud. "So does New Venture know about Wolff's new capitalization?"

Dorman looked up. He didn't think Myra even knew what the term 'capitalization' meant, much less how it applied to The Grove. Besides…"How did you know Ethan Wolff got new financing?"

Myra waved her hand dismissively. "I know about all of it—the will, New Venture Properties—everything. I've known from the beginning." She stopped and looked at him, her pale blue eyes sharp as ice. "I just wanted to see how long you were going to keep me in the dark."

Jesus, this was a side to his wife he'd never seen and truth be told he kind of liked it. My God, was he starting to get a hard on? "Myra, if I'd known—"

"Doesn't matter now," she interrupted. "Our first order of business is to deal with your police problem." She got out the notepad she always carried with her and began writing on it.

"Well that, I can tell you, is a complete red herring. I had absolutely nothing to do with whatever it is they want to pin on me."

"Fine, then it shouldn't be a problem to clear it up. I

suggest you get a good night's rest and we head over to the station first thing tomorrow."

Dutifully he got up to go to bed. As he left the room she was still jotting notes in her little book.

The next morning Dorman and Myra sat in Detective de la Torre's small office in Lagunitas. Dorman continued to stare at the photograph the officer had handed him, showing the license plate of his SUV taken at a bridge toll booth.

"I'm telling you, Detective. I did *not* drive my car over the San Rafael Bridge at, what does it say, one twenty-eight in the afternoon, on June twentieth. That's impossible. My car was parked in front of my office all afternoon."

"Can you substantiate that claim, with a witness, perhaps, or records that might show where you were during that time frame?"

De la Torre might be young and good looking, but as far as Dorman could tell, he was a self-righteous, sanctimonious prick who didn't fully comprehend who he was talking to. He tried intimidation. "Young man, are you aware of my standing in the community? I really don't think the city attorney, or the citizens of Little Eden, for that matter, would appreciate having to prosecute a case of out and out harassment, but I assure you, it can happen."

The detective simply smiled. "That sure would be a waste of taxpayers' money," he agreed. "Which is why a simple answer to my question should help clear matters up." His voice turned cold. "Why was your car seen crossing the bridge if you weren't in it?"

Dorman thought frantically through a number of scenarios. Then it dawned on him and he turned to his wife. "Myra, you borrow my car sometimes. You know, when you need to transport larger items, like plants or furniture or what not. Did you perhaps trade cars with me that day?" He turned to the detective. "Sometimes Myra will come by and swap cars for an hour or two, and I'm so busy in my office, I won't even know she's done it."

Myra contemplated his question for a moment. "No, dear," she finally said. "I borrowed it last Thursday, remember? I had to bring those small pear trees back and they wouldn't fit in the back of my Prius. But the time before that? Oh, my goodness, I can't remember."

The detective nodded and looked at Dorman. "Say, if you don't mind my asking, what happened to your face?"

Dorman touched his by-now swollen cheek. "As it happens, I *do* mind," he ground out. "Let's just say I had a run in with a door."

"Fair enough. So, for the record, you deny having driven your car across the San Rafael Bridge on June twentieth at approximately one twenty-eight in the afternoon."

Dorman was getting more and more agitated, a state his wife must have noticed because she put her hand gently on his arm. He took it for the warning it was meant to be.

"I most certainly do. Look, Detective de la Torre, all I know is that I never took my car that day. Perhaps someone swapped my plates or took my car and went on a joyride for a few hours."

"Perhaps," de la Torre said, pulling a card out of his wallet. "Tell you what. If something jogs your memory, or if you come up with some record that substantiates your whereabouts on that day, please give me a call, day or night. In the meantime, we're going to have to impound your car while we check for fingerprints and other evidence."

"What?!"

Myra's grip on his arm tightened. "That will be fine. We'll have to go home and get it, however. Let's go, dear," she said.

"I'm sorry, ma'am, but we'll be coming to get it immediately."

"Uh, it's…" Dorman looked at Myra and hesitated.

Myra didn't miss a beat. "That's fine, detective. You'll find it in the parking lot of the Wayside Café. Do you know where that is?"

The detective smiled. What a condescending little cockroach. "In Bellam's Cove. Yes, ma'am, we surely do."

Outside the station it was all Dorman could do to keep from blowing a gasket. "The nerve of that prick," he muttered.

"Come on, you have bigger fish to fry," Myra said.

She got behind the wheel of her car and was silent for much of the drive home. Finally she spoke up. "Our primary problem at this point is the fact that The Grove is on track to reopen before Ethan's death, something you've made clear you don't want to happen. I'd like to hear what you're going to do about it."

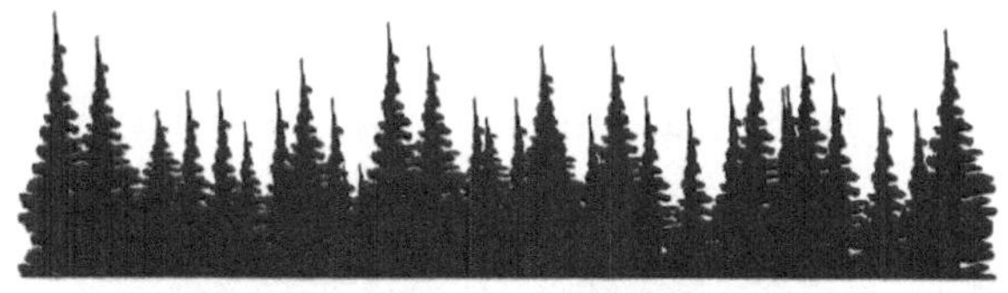

Chapter Thirty-Three

Thanks to Ethan's mysterious financial backer, construction picked up again quickly at The Grove. Brit continued to work sixteen hours a day, and Jenna was lucky to see him in passing whenever she dropped off her usual lunch fare at the construction trailer. Sherrie was in wonderful spirits now that Don was on the mend, and even Ethan seemed to be operating on recharged batteries.

While Dani concentrated on organizing the inventory, Jenna continued to flesh out the backgrounds of The Grove artists for the museum exhibit and catalog. At the end of each day she allotted some time to pursue the mystery of Peter Raines. Prints from the negatives might prove evidence of a crime, but there had to be some context to it, and Jenna was determined to shed light on whatever had happened so long ago. What she found added more pathos to an already sad tale.

It unfolded as she finished a review of news articles for the months in 1926 corresponding to Peter Raines's return to The Grove. The retreat was in its heyday and was often mentioned in society news columns and art magazines. With perseverance she'd been able to piece together a timeline of Peter Raines's activities. Like the society rag had said, he'd returned in February or March and approached Gus and Lia about investing in a new portable camera design, one that would rival the Kodak Brownie that was so popular at the time. Apparently Gus and Lia weren't interested, but Jenna was able to confirm the story, albeit in bits and pieces, that Raines had indeed courted, seduced, and abandoned Giselle Wolff.

The narrative she found woven through Amanda Firestone's later notebooks bore this out. By replacing the animals' names with the real people she and Dani had agreed matched the characters' descriptions, Amanda and Lia's close and ongoing friendship came across clearly. Throughout her journals, Mandy had portrayed herself as a plain brown mouse named Mitzie. There were many entries of talks between the two women.

"[Lia] came to see me today," one passage read in early May of 1926. "She was very upset that [Peter] had met [Giselle] while her little bird was home for a visit. She doesn't trust him, and when I asked her why, she became very distraught, which wasn't like [Lia] at all. I always sensed something had happened between [Peter] and her the day of the Big Shake Up, and asked her about it again. She kept repeating, 'I don't know. I'm just not sure' through her tears, and said, 'I've never said anything to [Gus].' I implored her to tell her beloved mate, that he was a fine rooster and would know what to do."

An entry a month later revealed a much more upbeat exchange, in which Lia told Mandy she'd taken her friend's advice and felt as if the weight of the world had been lifted from her shoulders. At first Gus was enraged, she said, but eventually calmed down when she explained she had no proof. They agreed to boot Peter out of their lives forever, "whatever the consequences."

"I can only conclude that [Peter] hurt [Lia] in some terrible way," Mandy wrote. "Her painting directly after the Big Shake Up gave a hint of it, but I saw a glimpse of it only once, and couldn't say for sure if my suspicions are correct. But it doesn't matter now. What matters is that [Lia] and [Gus] together are far stronger than either could ever be apart. That is what I have learned from my wonderful [Will]."

Jenna grew pensive. Gus and Lia were destined to be together, and even something as terrible as what she suspected happened to Lia wasn't enough to break them apart.

Maybe fate had stepped in for her and Brit as well. She smiled at the thought.

"You look happy."

Jenna looked up to see Dani standing at the entrance to their office, ready to work for the afternoon. She had a wistful smile on her face and a bag in her hand.

"I am," Jenna said. "For the time being, anyway." She watched, gratefully, as Dani pulled out two ciabbata sandwiches and two lattes; it was one of the many perks of working with a restaurant owner. "Thanks, by the way."

"No problem. But what do you mean, 'for the time being'?"

Jenna leaned toward Dani's desk, her expression losing some of its buoyancy. "I guess I'm waiting for the next crisis to hit The Grove. Wondering if the center will really open when it's supposed to…and if it does, what I'll be doing next."

"What do you mean? You and the professor and Brit will be right here, working together. I mean, come on. You and Brit…" Dani finished her sentence by raising her brows.

Jenna smiled gamely at her friend. "I don't know. I guess I'm finding it difficult to 'live in the moment,' as Brit says."

"Ah, you're wondering how long the two of you are going to last?"

Jenna nodded. "We don't talk about it, but I imagine it's in the back of Brit's mind that I might do the same thing that I did to him seven years ago."

"You two used to go together?" Dani couldn't hide her surprise.

"Not exactly. We met, came together like fireworks, and then I bailed. I was struggling with family issues and his and my coming together—it was just too intense."

"And now?"

Jenna smiled. "Still intense. But I'm in a better place, so I can handle it now. Truth be told, I'm ready for the next step, but I can't blame him if he isn't. It's hard to forgive someone when they hurt you like I hurt him. I suppose in the end it all comes down to trust."

"I agree," Dani said pensively. "In the end, trust is everything."

Jenna looked at her friend and colleague. "Tell me to shut up if you want, but I've got to ask, why aren't you and Gabe burning up the sheets? When we first met, you said I could have him, but it's obvious you two are connected somehow. What gives?"

Dani turned back to her computer screen, plainly uncomfortable with the turn of the conversation. "Let's just say he could do a whole lot better than me and leave it at that," she said. "Now I hate to change the topic, but I've uncovered a problem with the inventory that I'm afraid we're going to have to deal with sooner rather than later."

Jenna decided to leave well enough alone. "What have you got?" she asked.

"It's what we *haven't* got. Some of the artwork is either lost or stolen."

"What?!" Jenna swung her chair around in disbelief. "What are you talking about?"

Dani pulled a hard copy file out of her laptop case and handed it to Jenna. "This is the 1947 manifest, signed by Lia, so I used it as my baseline. Some pieces for each year are physically missing, and the manifest says they were loaned out to either museums or to the families or friends of the artists. Now, I can't tell if these notations were made before or after Lia signed the document, but either way there should be no problem, right?"

"Sounds like all we have to do is retrieve them."

"You'd think, except that virtually all of the locations listed say they've never heard of the pieces to begin with."

"Wait. You're saying the artwork isn't where the manifest says it should be?"

"Yes, and I've double-checked to make sure the places didn't inadvertently lose the pieces. None of them have, and anyway, it would be too coincidental if they had all somehow misplaced the items they'd been given."

"So where would the pieces be?"

"I have a pretty good idea of where most of them are. Well, not exactly where they are, but that they're *somewhere*."

"I'm not following you," Jenna said.

"Okay. Once I realized the pieces were missing, I began looking for them within the art collecting community. I was hoping it would be a simple matter of tracing them to their most current owner and proving that the artwork had been taken from The Grove collection."

"Sounds reasonable," Jenna agreed.

"Problem is, most of the trails end at a blank wall: the 'anonymous collector' category. In the art world, those buyers are apparently elusive at best. Many of them seem to get their pleasure from owning world-famous works of art that only they can look at."

"The old 'I know something you don't know' routine," Jenna offered.

"Precisely! And these collectors are proving extremely difficult to track down."

"But who took the artwork from The Grove to begin with?"

"That's another problem. I worked backward through the record of each piece's ownership."

"The provenance," Jenna said.

"Exactly. The ones I checked all entered the market, invariably with an 'anonymous seller,' at a time when the demand for that genre or artist was at a peak. I guess when something's really hot, some collectors are willing to overlook where it came from—they just want it. This happened at different points, which is strange because I can't imagine the collection has been systematically broken into time and time again. I mean, why wouldn't they steal everything at once? And of course there wouldn't have been any record of a theft, since the collection wasn't active during those years. The family just assumed it was all in storage, or at least somewhere safe, and for the most part, it was."

"Sounds like the thief, or thieves, knew enough about the value of each piece to sell it at the best time. Any way to figure out when the first missing piece entered the market? Say, if it was the 1950's, then you'd know how far back the thefts began. That might shed a little light on what happened."

Dani nodded. Apparently she'd thought the same thing. "I'm going to have to catalogue all the missing pieces before I can do that. I've only dealt with the first four years and already I've found five missing pieces." She leaned over and touched Jenna's arm. "I'm wondering if we should talk to Ethan about this. Maybe he'll give us a clue as to how to proceed."

Jenna thought about how upbeat her grandfather was at the moment; news like this might set him back. "It may come down to that, but let's hold off for now. Find out the extent of the problem so we can have as many facts as possible. Then we'll let Ethan know and follow his lead. He may not want this to come out now, not if it'll cause even more problems for The Grove."

Dani looked skeptical. "Are you sure?"

"Think about it. On top of everything else, we'd be facing a scandal regarding the theft of millions of dollars' worth of art. We don't need that right now. And we've got time before the Grand Reopening. What if we work to get the pieces back, and in the meantime, we can design the exhibits around the missing pieces. They simply won't be highlighted like the others. We can insert the art as we recover it, or rely on the descriptions alone if we don't. Either way, it will at least give Ethan one less thing to worry about. Besides which, I have something else to add to the mix, something that, unfortunately, fits right in."

"I'm not going to like this, am I?" Dani said.

Jenna pulled out the notebook she'd brought with her. "I took detailed notes on the Commentary for 1906. There's so much here we can use. But there were a couple of entries that referenced a painting that Lia had done." She looked down at her notes and read, "Unlike anything we've ever seen here at The Grove."

"Really? What did it look like?"

"There aren't too many details, since apparently Lia was quite secretive about it. Only Mandy and a couple of the other artists happened to get a glimpse of it. I guess it was pretty disturbing."

"What? Why was it disturbing?"

"Well, it was quite gothic, which wasn't her usual style, and the feeling of the painting is that a young woman is, and I quote, 'in the throes of a passionate experience.'"

"What *exactly* does it show?"

"Apparently there's a young woman with long dark hair lying across a bed in what seems to be a dungeon. There's a shadow leaning over her. Her hair is in disarray and you can't tell if she's enraptured by what's being done to her, or else unconscious or in pain." Jenna rocked back in her chair. "I'm really torn about this. It's apparently a very provocative work and would make a great addition to the Amelia Starling Wolff wing of the museum. But what if it represents something that happened between her and Peter? And even that might be beside the point."

"Why is it beside the point?" Dani asked, an odd expression on her face.

"I checked all throughout the storage facility and, just like the art pieces you've been bird-dogging, this one is nowhere to be found."

Dani had grown quiet, but Jenna could tell she was visibly upset. What was going on?

After a long pause Dani said, "Well, add that one to the list," in a light-hearted tone that didn't match the look in her eye.

"No kidding." Jenna sat up straight and turned to her monitor. "I think our job just got a whole lot more complicated."

"I think you're right," Dani said, and Jenna noticed her friend had pushed her lunch away.

Chapter Thirty-Four

"I thought you said he'd be here," Dorman grumbled as he and Myra stood outside the crumbling mansion of Puerta del Mar. He had just rapped on the rusted-out door knocker a second time to no avail. "Where the hell is Mrs. Reynolds?"

"I wouldn't know. Boyce told me this afternoon he was staying in this evening. He's around." Myra reached into her purse and pulled out a brass key ring in the shape of a dollar sign. It took her a moment to flip through all the keys, but finally she found the one she was looking for.

"I didn't know the old goat gave you a key," Dorman said.

"He didn't." Myra swiftly unlocked the old oak door and opened it, knocking as she did so. "Uncle Boyce? Yoo hoo! Anybody home?"

There was no answer as the two entered the gloomy foyer. Boyce didn't believe in wasting electricity on anything as frivolous as decent lighting, and for once Dorman was glad. Since being roughed up two nights earlier, he'd been particularly sensitive to bright light.

Myra walked immediately through the arched entrance to Boyce's office at the far side of the hall. "Not in here," she announced. Dorman followed her and watched as she briskly examined the papers stacked on Boyce's desk.

"With all his money, why didn't he ever fix this place up?" Dorman looked through the arched window to the fading sunset beyond. "It could have been a real showcase."

Myra glanced at Dorman in surprise. "Didn't he ever tell you? Once he dies, I have instructions to tear this house down. He can't stand the place."

"Damn, what a waste."

Myra gave Dorman a knowing look. "Have you ever known me to waste anything, Ralph?"

Dorman thought of the many nights of leftovers he'd been forced to endure; he pictured the outdated dresses that Myra wore year after year. And the uncomfortable thought crossed his mind that perhaps Myra had stayed with him all this time because she didn't want to waste money on a divorce. "Uh, no, I haven't," he said. "So, if you're not going to tear it down, what are you going to do with it?"

"Depends on what the market will bear," she said. "It could roll over into the golf resort, perhaps serve as an outlying clubhouse. Or maybe it's a separate community. We'll have to see."

"You're awfully confident that's all going to

happen," Dorman chided. "But if The Grove opens, we're shit outta luck."

Myra frowned at Dorman's profanity. "And you'll likely lose a kneecap or two. Ed Tarpin doesn't mess around."

My God, how did she *know* shit like that? Dorman feigned nonchalance. "I'm just saying…"

"Look, all Boyce has to do is follow instructions and The Grove will come tumbling down. Now where is he?" Myra strode down the long hallway toward the back of the first floor, looking in various rooms. Dorman followed. They made it to the kitchen, where they noticed the door to the cellar was open and a light shone from below.

"What's he doing down there?" Dorman wondered out loud.

"Probably calculating the increased value of the aging cabs he's got down in the wine cellar. My great-uncle was quite the collector."

They headed downstairs and sure enough, a glow indicated that Boyce was inside the separate room that had housed the Wheeler family's extensive wine collection for decades. Myra entered the room first and stopped so abruptly that Dorman almost bumped into her.

"What the hell?" he muttered.

Myra had stopped because the far wall of the twelve by fifteen foot storage room, which normally supported a floor-to-ceiling rack of expensive wines, was in fact a giant sliding door. It was currently open, revealing a small opening to another room beyond.

"Did you know about this?" Dorman said to his wife.

Myra seemed not to hear him. "Why, that little sneak," she murmured. She walked forward and once more Dorman followed. He peered through the doorway to see another room even larger than the wine locker, only this one was in essence a small art gallery. Several paintings, sculptures, and decorative objects were displayed on special pedestals and cabinets. Each piece of artwork was lit to accentuate its best features. Boyce was at the far end of the room, apparently so absorbed in the unpacking of a box that he failed to hear Myra and Dorman behind him.

"What are you doing, Uncle?" Myra asked. Her voice sounded innocent and sweet, and it dawned on Dorman that his wife was quite a good actress.

Boyce froze, then slowly turned around. His eyes looked feral, and he was sweating profusely. "How did you two get in here?" he asked, his voice reaching a particularly grating level of squawk.

"The front door was open," Myra said smoothly. "We called for you but you didn't answer."

Dorman looked around the room. "What is this place, Boyce?"

"It's none of your business, that's what it is," Boyce snapped. "Now the two of you, get out of here."

Myra had paused to examine a few of the pieces. Her quick intake of breath as she read one of the display labels caused both Dorman and Boyce to look at her.

"What?" Dorman asked.

Myra turned to her uncle. "How did you do it?" she asked.

Boyce looked like a deer caught in the headlights. "Do what?" he croaked.

"You know what," she replied calmly. "These pieces are from The Grove collection."

"You're kidding," Dorman said, striding over to one of the cases and peering closely at a bronze urn and the label next to it. "Damn. You stole this from them?"

Boyce began to breathe heavily, his face turning red. "I did not steal from them. I'm trying to give them *back*!" he ground out.

Dorman stifled a snort. "Oh yeah, I can see *that*."

"Be quiet, Ralph." Myra was still looking at Boyce, who was growing more agitated by the moment. "What do you mean, Uncle?"

"I mean my father stole these and more from the Wolffs over sixty-five years ago. How do you think we got our grubstake?"

Myra didn't sound like she was faking it this time. "What do you mean? I thought...I mean, the real estate—"

"Bah! My grandfather was barely hanging on when he bought this place before the turn of the century. Then the Wolffs moved next door with all their newfound money and bohemian ways and he couldn't stand it, thought they were yokels. He drilled that home, and my father grew up feeling the same way."

"All right. Your grandfather was an elitist and thought they were tacky. So what?" Dorman didn't see what the old man was so wigged out about.

Boyce glared at him. "So he goes and gets himself killed during the big quake, that's what! He leaves my father, who's only seven, and my grandmother nothing but this property, this so-called 'Puerta del Mar,' which had been almost totally destroyed."

"How'd they hold on to the place if they didn't have money?" Myra asked.

"The Wolffs, of course. Those Frisco hillbillies turned out to be bleeding hearts, too, and they took my grandmother on as a charity case. She felt so bad, she signed over half the property, which infuriated my father once he was old enough to understand what she'd done."

Dorman couldn't believe what he was hearing. "What do you mean—half this place isn't even yours?"

"Bet you thought we owned everything down to and including the cove, didn't you? Well, we don't. We've only got an easement. But ol' Gus and Lia, they didn't make a big deal about it. They helped my family fix up the house, kept Grandma going, even paid for my father's law education down the road. They probably figured he'd be eternally grateful." Boyce sniffed disdainfully. "Grateful like a snake."

"Get to the point, Uncle. The artwork."

Boyce looked at Myra, exasperation written all over him. "What I'm saying is, my dear father, while helping Lia Wolff catalog and prepare all this artwork for storage, actually siphoned off the best pieces for himself. That's what paid for our first investment properties. *That's* what built up the Wheeler fortune."

"How'd you find this out?" Dorman asked.

"Same as you. Stumbled across my dear old papa one day, checking on his inventory. It had decreased, of course. Went down every time he deemed the market was right for a piece. He followed the ups and downs for each artist whose work he'd stolen. Knew when to unload it for top dollar."

"This is incredible," Myra said. "So what did you mean by saying you're trying to give them back?"

Boyce began to work himself up again. "Why do you think I've been opposed to the reopening of The Grove all these months?"

Dorman looked at him quizzically. "Well, SPEAR…"

"SPEAR," Boyce hissed. "That was only a front, you moron. I had to have some justification for wanting to stop, or at least slow down, Ethan's grand scheme. Because as soon as he began to inventory that collection, it was only a matter of time before he realized some major pieces were missing. And sooner or later the fingers were going to point in our direction."

"*Your* direction," Myra pointed out.

"The hell with you," Boyce said. "And the hell with you, too, you pathetic excuse for a man," he said to Dorman. "I was doing pretty well in buying the artwork back from current owners. I've got nearly all of them now and I was going to find a way to insert them back into the collection. But you—you with your lousy bureaucratic maneuverings, didn't buy me any time at all."

"Now wait a minute."

"I don't have a minute. Not since you started going off the deep end, using Lester to undermine me." He shook his gnarled fist at Dorman. "I know all about your development schemes. Listen, I like trees as much as the next guy, but unlike my father, I don't give a rat's ass if The Grove opens or not, just as long as nothing comes back to taint the Wheeler name in the process. But you went too far, using Lester the way you did."

"I don't know what you're talking about," Dorman said indignantly. "Just how did I use Lester?"

"When your candy-ass roadblocks didn't do the trick, I didn't feel bad about a little civil disobedience. What's a little red paint, after all? But I drew the line at causing physical harm to anybody. But not you. You had to send poor, gullible Lester off to do your dirty work, and a good man ended up in the hospital."

Dorman felt his blood pressure start to skyrocket. The nerve of this old prick! "Hold it right there, Boyce," he spat out. "I told you I didn't order—"

"You damn well did order!" Boyce thundered. "And that wasn't the worst of it! Then you had to go and get him involved in that barn disaster. Poor guy didn't have a chance!" Boyce was heaving, and then his face became a mask of pain. Tears started running down his craggy face.

"You're the killer, Uncle. A cold-blooded killer!" Myra taunted.

"I am not!" he cried. "I'm—I'm—" All at once Boyce stopped, his eyes bugging out of his head. He began to gasp for air and clutched at the neck of his shirt. He reached out for something to hold on to and missed, falling to the ground. Alarmed, Dorman went to help him, but Myra held him back.

"Don't," she said.

Dorman looked up at his wife and saw the same cold ferocity he'd seen the night of his mugging. At that moment it became perfectly clear to him what she was capable of. He felt acid rising in his throat and it burned like hell. "Shouldn't we call 911 or something?"

Myra looked at him, never blinking. She slowly shook her head before turning to look down at Boyce. Dorman followed her gaze. The stricken old man couldn't talk, but his eyes spoke volumes. The old man turned his head to Dorman in supplication. Dorman looked up at Myra, who stared him down. Then she turned to Boyce one last time.

"Guess you took one too many pills, Uncle."

Dorman stared back down at Boyce, feeling as helpless as the old man sprawled on the gallery floor. *Holy hell. What have I done?*

In a few minutes it was over. Boyce lay unmoving, sightless eyes staring at the ceiling.

"We didn't exactly kill him, right?" Dorman said shakily. "I mean, he had the attack all on his own, didn't he?"

Myra didn't answer him directly. She merely said, "We need to find some gloves so we can move him without leaving fingerprints, and a sheet to wrap him in for the night."

In a trance, Dorman followed Myra's directions. They found some old rubber gloves and a faded top sheet. Donning the gloves, they half dragged, half carried Boyce's body out of the secret gallery and into the wine locker. Placing the sheet on the floor, they lobbed the corpse on to the sheet and rolled it up. Myra then closed the sliding wall rack and turned the temperature of the wine locker down as far as it would go.

"We need to move the car out of sight," she said.

Dorman felt an overwhelming urge to piss in his pants. He was trying to get himself under control and not doing a very good job of it. Myra, however, stood calmly looking at her uncle's body for some time before speaking. Finally she said, "It's time to end this once and for all."

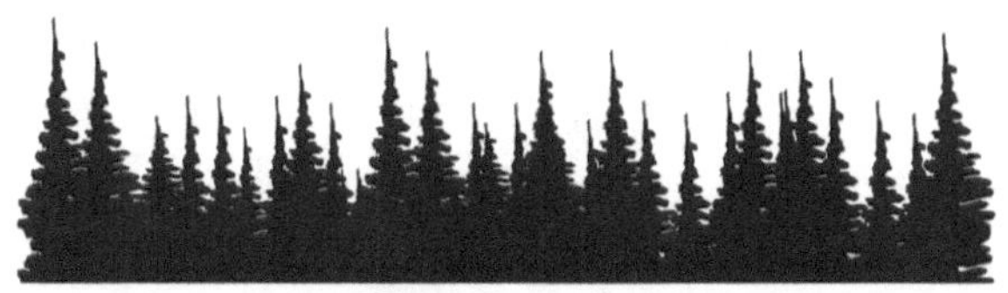

Chapter Thirty-Five

Never in his life did Brit think he'd be settling down to a night of domestic tranquility and actually enjoying it. But there it was.

"Hey, you mind if I take that last pork chop?" Jason reached over the kitchen farm table with his fork.

"Not so fast, son," Brit cautioned, blocking Jason's move. "I'll thumb-war you for it."

The two men were about to go at it when Jenna called a halt. "There's only one civilized way to deal with this: *I'll* take it." With that she quickly grabbed the chop and began to cut it.

"That's one of the many things I love about your sister," Brit said, grinning. "She's a woman who knows what she wants and goes for it." Jenna looked at him and beamed. They all laughed and continued eating the meal Brit had prepared in the Great House kitchen: broiled chops, instant mashed potatoes, applesauce cups, and a bagged salad. Wasn't fancy, but Brit figured it didn't hurt him in the points department. What woman wouldn't fall for a man who's willing to cook for her and invite her relative, no less?

Jenna sat back and sipped the Merlot she'd brought to the impromptu dinner party. She directed her question to Jason. "So how is Da doing…really?"

"Pretty good," Jason said, filling up his plate with more potatoes. "I've helped him get his notes organized and filed, and now that the financing's lined up, he's feeling a lot less stressed about the opening. I think that's, like, helping him keep it together physically. Far as I can tell there's only one thing he feels bad about."

"What's that?" Brit asked.

"The whole mess with Boyce Wheeler and the SPEAR group. Da's known that guy for a long time and I think he feels lousy they can't work things out."

Brit glanced at Jenna. "Yeah, well, Boyce isn't exactly known for his ability to compromise."

"So I've heard…but maybe the guy will lighten up once The Grove reopens."

Brit shook his head. "Doubtful."

"What I want to know," Jenna said, "is how you think he'll do once you leave for school at the end of August."

Jason put down his fork. "The truth is, that's been bugging me. He's doing okay now, but how much of that is because I'm there to back him up? Maybe I ought to postpone going away…you know, just until he's stronger."

Jenna reached over and put her hand on Jason's.

"That is really sweet, brother o' mine, but it's also completely out of the question. Neither your grandfather nor I will hear of it."

"So, what, you're going to put your life on hold some more?" Jason's eyes blazed. "Jenna, you may have pegged me for a flake, but I know exactly what you've sacrificed for me over the past four years, you and Da both. It won't kill me to put off college."

"For what, a year? Two? Look, there's no way of knowing how long we're going to have Da with us." Jenna's eyes were brimming. "But he's not going to appreciate you being on what he'll surely consider a 'death watch.' He wants you to live your life and so do I."

"And what about you?" Brit felt a bit awkward injecting himself into the family discussion, but he had to know the answer.

Jenna looked at him, her face a mixture of intense emotions he couldn't entirely read. "Me? Oh, well, Da knows I'll help him get The Grove exhibits up and running, whatever that takes. Once the pressure's off, I think he'll feel more in control. After that, I…I don't know." She looked at him intently. "I wish I did."

Brit nodded, his gut clenching. Was she up in the air about them? Or was she wondering about *his* feelings? That was the million dollar question.

Jason got up from the table. "That was a great meal, Brit. Thanks."

"Um, aren't you forgetting something?" Jenna prompted.

Jason sent her a puzzled expression. Then he got it. "Oh, yeah, you need help with the dishes?"

Brit shook his head and smiled at Jenna. "No, but thanks for the offer."

"Right, then. I'm outta here. See you guys tomorrow." At that moment the front doorbell chimed. "I'll send 'em back," Jason said.

A few moments passed and Jason called from the front of the house. "Uh, Brit? Tori Winston is here to see you."

Now what? Brit looked at Jenna, who said nothing, but raised her eyebrows. "I'll just be a minute," he said, thinking, I am *not* going to lose the ground I've gained with Jenna. A minute is all Tori's gonna get.

Tori was waiting alone in the foyer. Even though it was the end of the day, she still looked like she'd just stepped out of a fashion mag. But the expression on her face wasn't her usual self-confident, take-no-prisoners look.

"Hey, Tori," Brit asked. "Are you okay?"

"I…I was wondering if you've got a minute."

Brit glanced back toward the kitchen. "Yeah, sure. What's up?"

She hesitated, looked around, and took a deep breath. "Look, I wanted to let you know I won't be on the job site for a while. We're waiting for a lot of the custom furnishings to come in and I have some other business that needs my attention." She handed him a folder. "Here's a spreadsheet on what's due in. Sherrie knows what to do with it. She can call me with questions."

"Thanks." Brit flipped through the folder. *Tori could have dropped this off at the office. Something else is going on here.* "Is this really about other business, Tori?"

Tori looked up at him, sadness suffusing her face. "Yes…and no. I do have quite a few new clients, thanks to you and my exposure through this project, but…" She looked down at her turquoise leather boots and shook her head. "I went and did a really stupid thing, though." She finally met his eyes. "I fell for you."

Oh shit. Brit ran a hand through his hair. "Tori, I—"

She raised her palm. "No need. Really, I don't blame you at all. You were honest about your expectations. It just blindsided me and I just…I'm not used to not getting what I want, you know?"

The memory of falling for Jenna all those years ago, thinking she felt the same way, and then finding out she'd moved on—all those feelings came flooding back. "I do know," he said quietly. "It sucks."

Tori smiled grimly. "Yes it does. But what also sucks is what I did to you and everybody else associated with The Grove. Brit, I need to apologize. I am so sorry I opened my big mouth and bitched to my father. He had concerns and I magnified them instead of convincing him to stay with you. Because of my ego, this project almost tanked and I just want you to know I feel terrible about it."

Brit reached over and squeezed her shoulder. "You had nothing to do with the problems we've been having, Tori. Chances are your dad would have pulled the plug anyway—you just made it a little easier for him."

"You certainly are being nice about everything."

Brit couldn't help it; he glanced back toward the kitchen again. "We secured new financing, so it's all good."

Tori let out a sigh. "Somehow I don't think that's the only reason you're in such a good mood." She started to leave, but turned when she reached the door. "I hope Jenna realizes how lucky she is."

"I don't know about that, but I do know one thing."

"What's that?"

"The right guy is out there for you."

Tori let out a huff of laughter. "Right. You got a clone somewhere you're not telling me about?"

Brit smiled. "Seriously. You wait. It'll happen."

"I won't hold my breath," she said, and let herself out.

Brit took a moment before returning to Jenna. Finding The One made all the difference in the world. Keeping her was something else entirely.

Jenna stood at the kitchen sink, her hands immersed in warm, soapy water. There weren't that many dishes, so she decided to indulge herself by washing them by hand. She guessed she must be one of the few people left on earth who wasn't wild about dishwashers.

She felt it when Brit entered the room, but she didn't look up. Why had Tori stopped by? Could she really not take no for an answer? But a feeling of calm followed that thought, because Jenna knew deep inside that whatever transpired, Brit had in fact told Tori no.

She felt Brit's arms come around her waist. He nuzzled her neck. "You taste delicious," he said. "Better than a pork chop any day."

Jenna smiled and reached for a dishtowel. After drying her hands she turned in his arms and pulled him down for a lingering kiss. She loved this man. Plain and simple. She loved him. "I didn't just bring wine," she whispered.

"No?" he murmured, his hands reaching down and cupping her backside through her jeans before reaching up and fondling her breast.

"I also brought dessert…but I'm serving it in our room."

Brit didn't say a word. He merely took her hand and walked briskly toward the stairs.

It was dark now. He watched the Great House from the path, knowing that Brit and Jenna were in there, knowing he was probably on top of her by now. They'd probably gone at it hot and juicy down at the cove, and they'd no doubt had a lot of practice since then. It made him want to kill somebody. *Enjoy her while you can, asshole. Because it ain't gonna last much longer.*

He thought of the thirty-eight snub nose stashed in his duffel bag. "Untraceable," the dealer in the Tenderloin had said. He aimed a finger toward the house. "Pop. Pop," he whispered.

"Hey man, what are you doing out here?" Jason's voice jolted him out of his reverie. He dropped his hand.

"Nothin', dude, just hangin'."

"Me too. I had dinner with Jenna and Brit, but figured I'd better scram before they started drooling all over each other. They are tight, dude. I think maybe this is it for my sister. She definitely got a bite from the Love Bug."

"Yeah? Well isn't that kinda skanky? I mean, aren't you guys cousins or something?"

"I am. Jenna's not related, though, at least by blood. It's a long story."

"Well he's a cockhound anyway. I don't know what she sees in him."

"It is what it is. They go back a long way. Hey, I know you kind of dug her, but she's too old for you anyway."

"She's ancient, all right." He started walking back to the bunkhouse and Jason fell in step with him.

"Hey, there's an all-ages concert in Bellam's Cove. Starts in about an hour," Jason said. "Wanna go?"

"Maybe." His cell phone rang. The caller was unknown, but he decided to take it anyway.

"Yo."

The voice on the other line said, "It's Mr. D. We need to meet."

He looked over at Jason and covered the phone. "Man, I gotta take this. I'll catch you later." Jason gave him a funny look, shrugged, and walked away.

"What do you want, Pecker Head?"

"You can dispense with the name calling," Mr. D. said. "Can you meet me in the parking lot, where we first met, in twenty minutes? I have an interesting proposition for you, one I think you'll be pleased with."

"Twenty minutes," he said, and hung up. Maybe the prick took his advice and came up with a new plan to fuck up The Grove. *But how'd he get my number?* He hopped in his SUV and drove down the hill, taking care to park a couple of blocks away from the city hall parking lot. He walked back up the block and saw Dorman standing in the shadows, smoking.

"This better be good," he said as he approached the older man.

Dorman looked around the deserted lot as if expecting a police bust or something. "Oh it's good all right—good enough to keep you outta jail."

"What the fuck are you talking about?"

"I'm talking about Lester Small. They found some evidence—I don't know what—that points to somebody else being part of the explosion over at The Grove. And we both know that other person is you."

"You're full of shit."

"You don't want to believe me, fine. It'll all come out sooner or later. Maybe you aren't in the system, maybe you'll skate by...or maybe they'll find your cell phone number with his stuff."

"What? No fuckin' way, dude. Speaking of which, how'd you get my number?"

Dorman shrugged. He was trying to look cool but

he wasn't pulling it off. "Piece of cake, 'grunt'. Aren't too many city kids who work at The Grove. Once I got your name I had you checked out, down to your juvie record. I called your father's office and told him I was a teacher from Saylor and needed to reach you." The old fart snickered. "Your father said for me to tell you to call him sometime." Then Dorman got serious. "Fact is, I know a little something about you, and depending on how I feel, I can maybe push the investigation in another direction, like toward another construction worker, if it's worth my while."

"What is this, a shakedown? You'll have to do better than that."

Dorman shook his head. "No, kid, not a shakedown. Just a proposition that I think you might find interesting."

"I'm listening."

"We both want The Grove to fold, and the sooner the better. The only way we can do that at this point is to get Ethan Wolff out of the picture. So we need you to bring him over to Boyce Wheeler's place tomorrow so we can talk to the old man face to face. We'll even provide Wolff with an invitation so it'll look totally legit."

"What happens then—you gonna scrag the old man? Mr. D., I didn't think you had it in you!"

"Don't you worry about that. Your job is to get him there on time tomorrow morning. Think you can do that?"

"What the hell. You're on."

"Good." Dorman handed him a slip of paper. "Call me at Puerta del Mar as soon as you're en route. And don't bring anybody else with you."

"Whatever you say, Mr. D." He turned and began walking back to his car. *Let's get the party started.*

Chapter Thirty-Six

I t was a brilliant summer morning at The Grove. The fog had burned off early and the day promised to be picture-perfect. After the long and sensual night she'd spent with Brit, Jenna was feeling tired but very, *very* happy. They hadn't talked about a future together, but she'd sensed the time was coming soon. On her way to check on her grandfather, she stopped by the construction office to drop off Brit's bag lunch. She no longer felt insecure about being part of the family, or defensive about caring for Brit. It simply felt like the right thing to do.

Sherrie greeted her with a smile. She was on the phone, but held up a finger, signaling Jenna that she would be off in a minute. "You drink that tomato juice, you hear me? I want you strong as a bull by the time they let you out of there...Okay, baby. Gotta run. Love you."

Jenna grinned. "Don coulda had a V-8, huh? You knock him on the head?"

"He's had enough head knocking to last him awhile, I suspect."

"That's for sure. How's he doing?"

The sunshine in Sherrie's smile was blinding. "He's doing great. He's almost ready to come home for some good old-fashioned TLC."

"That's wonderful news. Tell him I said hello, will you?" Jenna turned to leave, but Sherrie stopped her.

"Wait a sec." She handed Jenna a large photo mailer. "This came in for your grandfather. You're going over to see him, right?"

"Yep." Jenna took the envelope and noticed the return address: Hayden Lake, Idaho. That's where the guy lived who was printing the negatives. *Omigod,* she thought, her insides turning to ice. *He found something.*

The walk to Da's place seemed to take forever. Jenna was torn between wanting to rip the damn thing open and trying to pretend it was no big deal. When she finally reached the cottage she noticed Dani's car parked out front. The front door was slightly ajar and she stuck her head in.

"It's me. Jenna. Am I intruding?"

"No. No. By all means come in, my dear." Ethan motioned to her from his favorite chair. "Dani stopped by to…" He looked at Dani, who seemed very tense as she sat on one end of the sofa. "…to tell me something. Isn't that right, my dear?"

Dani nodded and smiled tightly at Jenna. "I'm glad you're here."

Intrigued, Jenna took a seat, still clutching the envelope. She noticed that Dani had brought Mandy's notebooks, several of which were stacked on the coffee table.

"Dani has to leave us for a little while," Da said gently. "There's been a death in her family."

Jenna touched her friend's hand. "Oh, Dani. I'm so sorry to hear that! Not your mother?"

"No. My father." Her voice was calm and controlled, as if she were trying to keep her emotions from spilling out. "He was in a boating accident in Europe and I have to go back for the funeral." She was clearly uncomfortable talking about her family. Instead, she pointed to the envelope. "Are those the pictures you've been waiting for?"

"What? Oh, I almost forgot," Jenna said. "Here, Da. It's from your photographer friend." As she handed it over she glanced at Dani, who understood immediately what it signified.

"Would you like me to wait outside?" Dani asked.

"Of course not, Dani. You've been on the hunt for answers from the beginning. It's only fitting you should be here to see if indeed we've found some." Da smiled with a look of resignation, and for the first time Jenna noticed the lines of tension around his eyes and the stoic set of his jaw. It became clear how much stress her grandfather must be under, what with all the problems The Grove was having as well as sine matter of his strange family history. That, combined with his fragile health, must be weighing him down horribly. She fought against a well of tears; bad news was the last thing he needed to hear right now.

"Well," he began, putting on a game face. "We may

as well have at it." He opened the envelope and pulled out a handful of photographs, which he stared at for several moments without saying a word.

"May I?" Jenna asked, reaching for the photos in his hand. He silently turned them over to Jenna and she couldn't help but be shocked at what she saw. The pictures showed without a doubt that it was Lia. She was naked and her arms were tied over her head. It was obvious that she'd been drugged. A man was also in one of the photos, his slender body facing away from the camera. He was kneeling on the bed and he too was naked. No way was the man August Wolff.

"Oh, Da," she said, losing her battle against the tears. She handed the photos over to Dani, who looked at them with a cold, grim expression.

"Well, this certainly tells us why Peter Raines left suddenly after the earthquake," Da said.

"What incredible gall he had, to show his face again twenty years later," Jenna supplied. "Even if Lia didn't have this proof of what he'd done to her. And what made him leave again, especially knowing that Giselle was pregnant?"

"I have something else to tell you," Dani interrupted. "It may answer the question."

Jenna could sense her friend's intense discomfort. It radiated from her in waves. "Tell us," she urged quietly.

"The other day, Jenna, you mentioned to me that you'd determined from the commentaries that a special painting by Lia was missing."

Jenna nodded and held her breath. *Please don't*

mention the other missing artwork. He can only take so much.

Dani went on, her voice almost cold with suppressed emotion. "Well, you were only half right. In fact, *two* paintings by Amelia Starling Wolff are missing, and I think I know where they are." She took a deep breath. "They're hanging somewhere in my uncle's estate in Verona, Italy."

Jenna's eyes widened. This was completely out of left field. She glanced at her grandfather before addressing Dani. "What do you mean? What are they doing there?"

Dani herself appeared a bit shell shocked. She looked at Da as if to apologize.

"Go on," he said, encouraging her with his gentle voice.

"I don't blame you for being surprised. I felt the same way when I realized I had seen the lost painting Jenna was talking about." She wrung her hands and placed them on her lap with the fingers intertwined as if in prayer. "I grew up in…well, a very big house. I left Italy when I was fifteen, so it's been a long time, and I can't say exactly where I saw the painting you described. But I do remember seeing it one time, and another one that was clearly painted by the same person. The memory is hazy, but I do remember I saw them.

"My uncle is no art collector, so I suspect that my great-grandfather Luzio brought them home with him when he returned to Italy in 1926. It's the only logical explanation. Hopefully we'll find some indication somewhere that Lia gave them to him. Perhaps they had served their purpose and she was ready to move on. I don't know at this point. But how they got there isn't the important thing." She took another fortifying breath. "The important thing is what they depict."

"I remember," Jenna said. "Mandy's commentary described the painting as dark and foreboding, showing a woman who had possibly been ravaged."

"Yes. And the other one, the companion work…also depicts a woman in turmoil…who's pregnant."

It took a few moments for the meaning of Dani's words to sink in. Jenna sat there, stunned.

"What you're saying, Dani," Ethan stated in a calm, clear voice, "is that I could be the product of incest."

Dani nodded slowly. "When she painted the second work, it had to be going through her mind that Peter, and not Gus, was the father of her baby. And once she explained that to Peter so many years later, that's probably what caused him to leave Giselle, and you, so abruptly. I'm so sorry, Professor."

Jenna's mind had already begun working feverishly to make sense of all she'd just learned. "Wait a minute," she said. "Never did we find in our research any hint of a scandal concerning the birth of Lia's daughter. *Never.* Which means that everyone assumed Gus was the father. So maybe he *was* Giselle's father. They wouldn't have had any way to tell back then, but we can find out today, right? I mean…I mean, all we have to do is find someone in the Wolff family who isn't one of us." She looked at Da for guidance. "Isn't that right?"

Da looked at her, a sweet, forlorn smile on his face.

"Yes, it would be possible, if such a person were willing to be tested. But it's a rather unseemly request to make, wouldn't you say?"

Jenna didn't know what to make of her grandfather's reticence. Maybe Dani had been right about being careful what you wish for. Maybe the shame of it was too much to bear. But knowing where you really, truly came from was the most important thing, wasn't it? Or was it?

Dani took that moment to tell them she had to leave. Before she slipped out the door she gestured to the notebooks she'd left on the coffee table. "I've marked the passages that allude to the incident, or at least Mandy's conjectures about it. They're mainly in the red journal. Now I'm afraid I've got to get going. I've got a lot of details to attend to before I leave for Italy."

Jenna walked Dani to her car. "Is there anything I can do for you?" she asked.

"Thanks, but I think you've got your hands full here. I do hope the professor isn't too disturbed by what he's learned. On top of everything else, I hated to be the bearer of bad news."

Jenna put her hand on Dani's arm. "Better it should come from someone who cares about him. Dani, I am so sorry for your loss. You do what you need to do with your family, and don't worry about us back here. We'll muddle through until you get back." She hugged her friend, who hesitated before returning the gesture.

"Thank you," Dani said, her eyes glistening with

emotion. "I'll be heading out in a day or two and hopefully back within a week. And Jenna?"

"Yes?"

"Talk to the professor about it, but if you decide you want the paintings back, I will bring them back to you. I promise."

Jenna nodded and stepped back as Dani got in her car and drove off. Her heart ached for her friend, who was obviously dealing with a jumble of emotions surrounding her father's death. She went back inside to see her grandfather busy stacking file boxes in a corner of the parlor.

"Whoa, Da. Wait a minute. Should you be doing that?"

Da straightened and dusted off his hands. "I have to be doing something, Jenna. It's the way I process things. Besides, they aren't too heavy…and it's good for my muscles." He made a halfhearted joke of flexing his bicep.

"Speaking of muscles, where is my dear brother when you need him?"

"Brit's temporary foreman needed an extra pair of hands and I sent Jason to help out. That dear boy has already gotten my files down to just these dozen or so boxes. I am very happy about that."

Jenna looked at the stack. "What are you going to do with your papers now that you've sorted through them? Donate them to Stanford?"

Da handed Jenna a folder that was lying on the coffee table next to the journals.

"'Amelia Starling's Grove: How an Experiment in

Creative Living Shaped the Art and Design of the Twentieth Century,'" she read. "And the proposal's been accepted by a New York publisher? Wow! Da, you never cease to amaze me."

"Yes, well, I believe once The Grove opens, I'll have a bit more time to devote to it, which will be a definitive study, you know. It will become the standard against which all other histories of the period are judged."

Jenna thought about the collection's missing pieces and was glad neither she nor Dani had broken the news to him yet. She gestured to the boxes. "I have no doubt. It looks like you've got enough material to get you started, anyway."

"Most certainly. And I'm counting on you and Dani to help me out as well."

"We're working on it," Jenna assured him. "You'll have all the background information you could want on The Grove before we're through." She hesitated before adding, "But how are you doing with all this other stuff…*really*, Da?"

Jenna's grandfather took her hand and sat down next to her on the sofa. "To be perfectly honest, I don't know whether to be disgusted, or humiliated, or angry, or sad, or—well you see, it's such a maelstrom of emotion that I simply can't tell you what I'm feeling at the moment. One thing I do know, however: the way out of this mess is to move forward. Always forward. Whatever happens, we will tell the story of The Grove so that future artists and art lovers can appreciate the grand gift our ancestors gave them. It's our family's legacy, you know. And that means it's yours as well."

Jenna's throat tightened. She leaned over and embraced her grandfather. His body was frail, but he returned her hug with a surprising sense of strength and resolve. "I'm beginning to see that, Da. I can't wait to see it all unfold."

There was a knock at the cottage door and Jenna glanced through the door's decorative glass panel to see Parker standing outside.

"Come in," Ethan called out.

Parker entered the cottage and looked sheepishly at Jenna. "Uh, Good morning, Professor Wolff…Jenna."

Da smiled at him. "Good morning, young man. How may I help you?"

Parker continued to stand just inside the door looking shy and tentative.

She remembered their last encounter with his cryptic comments, and Declan's theory that Parker or Kyle may have been the one to break into her room. She no longer trusted this young man, no matter how polite he came across. "What do you want, Parker?" she asked coolly.

"Sherrie in the office gave me this message to give to you, Professor. It says that Boyce Wheeler would like to invite you to lunch today." Parker looked at his watch. "It says eleven thirty, so if we leave now I can have you there in time."

"May I see that?" Jenna asked. She read the note. It seemed legitimate, but strange, nonetheless. "Why didn't he just call?" she asked.

Parker shrugged. "I don't know. I think there's a number there. You can call him back."

Jenna looked directly at Parker. "I think I'll do that."

"What's the problem, Jenna?" Da looked concerned. "I think it's marvelous that Boyce wants to talk. Perhaps we can work this whole mess out between us."

"I know, Da. I'm still going to call. "She pulled out her cell phone and dialed the number on the note. A woman answered with the words "Wheeler residence."

"Hello, Mrs. Reynolds. This is Jenna Bergstrom calling. We met a few weeks ago. May I speak with Mr. Wheeler, please?"

The woman, who sounded as if she had laryngitis, informed Jenna that her employer was resting and looking forward to the lunch meeting with Dr. Wolff. Would the professor be coming?

Jenna glanced at Da, who was obviously anxious to mend fences with his neighbor.

"Uh, yes. He'll be there. Thank you…yes, goodbye." She watched Parker for any unusual response, but his face was blank.

"Okay, Da. You're on for lunch. Why don't I take you?"

"Um, excuse me, Jenna, but Jack Blaine, you know, he's the acting foreman guy, was in the office too and asked me to pick up some stuff from the hardware store in Bellam's Cove, so I said I'd drop Professor Wolff off and then head over to the store."

Jenna looked at him closely. "What sort of stuff?"

Parker pulled a piece of paper out of his front

pocket and read from it. "Eight feet of three-quarter inch PVC, some bonding cement, some—"

It sounded legitimate enough. Jenna put up her hand. "Okay." Parker nodded and put the list away.

Da was beaming. "Just give me a minute to get my sweater and cane." He headed toward his bedroom in the back of the cottage.

"Hey, sorry if I spooked you the other night," Parker said. "That's something Kyle would do, not me."

"What do you mean, something that Kyle would do?"

"Oh, he's like your shadow. He's got it for you. Bad. But you know I'd never hurt you, right?"

She looked him squarely in the eye. "I don't know, Parker. I'm not sure I know you very well at all."

Parker smiled, but his eyes were cold. "Maybe we can change that real soon."

Da came back out, waving off Jenna's attempts to help him. "Let's go, my boy," he said. "And Jenna?"

"Yes, Da?"

"Remember: forward. Always forward."

Chapter Thirty-Seven

Jenna watched them drive off, still feeling uneasy. *Stop being ridiculous. Maybe Da's right about him and Boyce being able to patch things up.*

She headed over to the museum building to continue tracing the missing art pieces per Dani's instructions. Ten minutes later, her computer screen still showed the same list of art brokers. Jenna realized her concentration was shot and decided to give it up for the time being.

What would Brit think about Da's visit to Puerta del Mar? She wondered if he'd be concerned, as she was, that Boyce might lose his temper again, and this time unleash it on her poor grandfather.

She smiled ruefully. Now she was thinking of Brit as more than just a friend, or even a lover. He was a confidant. A partner. That had to be a good thing.

Jenna could feel her anxiety level tick up. She tried calling Brit on his cell phone, but he didn't answer and she was too embarrassed to leave a message. Figuring

Sherrie would know how best to reach him, she headed back toward the construction trailer, so focused on thoughts of Da that she didn't hear the person come up behind her. Suddenly a beefy hand clapped her on the shoulder.

"Hey!" Jenna cried, whirling around.

"Ms. Bergstrom, it's just me!" Kyle said, alarm in his voice. "What's wrong?"

"Damn it, Kyle! Why'd you sneak up on me like that? You scared me half to death!"

"Sorry. I just wanted to ask you—"

"Look, if you're still worried about what happened at Saylor, I *told* you—"

Kyle stopped in his tracks, crossing his massive arms across his chest. His expression was hard. "You're like all the rest," he said. "I apologized for my behavior toward you. I tried to do what's right, and you said it was no big deal, but you lied. It obviously *is* a big deal, because you freak out every time I come near you. What do I have to do to earn your trust?"

Jenna took a moment to catch her breath. She looked up at Kyle and paused, considering the young man pleading his case. Something inside her, an instinct perhaps, told her to take a leap of faith that he was being sincere. "You know something? You're right. I made light of it, but you really did disturb me on the last day of school and yeah, maybe it's going to take a while before I can trust you completely. I guess that's a lesson you do need to learn." She straightened her shoulders and took a breath. "So I apologize for not doing the difficult thing and admitting that up front.

The fact is, your actions do have consequences above and beyond losing points on a behavior chart." She started walking again toward the trailer, recalled her last encounter with him, and stopped. "Kyle, you remember the other day when you met me in the museum building?"

"Sure, why?"

"You said the building was open. Was it? Really?"

Kyle hesitated, a sheepish look in his face. "Yeah it was, but only because Parker opened it. He knew I needed to clear the air with you and told me you were in there. I was going to wait until you came out, but he let me in with a key. Only he said not to tell you about it. So I'm sorry I only told you half the truth."

The pieces of the puzzle were starting to fall into place. Parker Bishop had a lot to answer for. "As long as we're being honest, something else has been bothering me. The night of the fire, you and Parker weren't where you were supposed to be, were you?"

Kyle froze, his eyebrows shooting up to his hairline. He licked his lips but said nothing.

"Come on, Kyle. Out with it."

Kyle hesitated a moment longer before letting out a deep breath. "We were smokin' a joint," he confessed. "Parker got some new shit and wanted me to try it out. I'm sorry. I told him it wasn't a good idea, but he said nobody would notice."

Jenna nodded. "I appreciate your being straight with me. And as long as we're clearing the air, I'll tell you my being skittish isn't all about you. I've been jumpy anyway with all the stuff that's been happening around here."

"That's what I wanted to ask you about," Kyle said, a hint of relief in his voice. "I found something… weird…and I wanted to know if I should tell Mr. Maguire."

Jenna went on alert. "What'd you find?"

The young man started chewing on a fingernail. "Just so you know, I don't normally mess around with another person's stuff, but I lost a certain USB cord and I thought maybe Parker would have an extra one since he's into gaming like I am. He wasn't around so I…um…checked in his duffel bag. I didn't find the cord, but I did find these." He handed two small cartridges to Jenna.

"These are bullets," she said, knowing she sounded stupid, but reeling from what he implied. "Are you saying Parker has a gun?"

"I didn't see a gun. Just those. I also found this." He handed her a copy of the photo of her that had shown up in her room.

Jenna's alarm bells started ringing loud and clear. Working to keep her breathing neutral, she put her hand on Kyle's arm. "Kyle, what do you know about Parker Bishop, really?"

He fidgeted, plainly uncomfortable, and finally answered. "I know he hates his parents' guts. I know he's had a hard on—sorry—for you for the past two years. And…and I know he knows the kind of people who could get him a gun if he needed one."

Jenna forced Kyle to meet her eyes. "Is he the kind

of person who would pay to have someone hurt someone else?"

Another hesitation. "Yes. But if he could, he'd do the hurting himself."

Jenna straightened, willing herself not to jump the gun. "Well, he dropped Ethan off at Puerta del Mar and is due back from Bellam's Cove in a bit, so I think perhaps we'll have a little talk when he returns."

"Shit, he's gonna know I ratted him out," Kyle said.

"Don't worry, we won't bring you into it," Jenna assured him. "Just…thank you for coming forward."

They'd reached the office, and she and Kyle waited for Sherrie to pause in her typing.

The office manager finished her task. "Yes, ma'am," she said.

"Sherrie, will you call me as soon as Parker's back from Bellam's Cove?"

"I didn't know he was off to Bellam's Cove."

"Yes, remember? He delivered the lunch invitation you got from Boyce Wheeler for Ethan this morning. Parker said he would drop Ethan off and then he was going to run some errands for Jack."

Sherrie looked at Jenna and shook her head. "Sorry, I didn't see any message like that. Maybe somebody else got it."

Jenna's pulse began to hammer. "No, Parker specifically said he got the message from you."

"Nope. I'm old, but I'm not senile, yet. I would have remembered. I haven't even seen Parker today, and Jack sent one of the other guys off to Bellam's Cove this morning for some pipe fittings."

Oh my god. Something is terribly wrong. Da! A wave of panic washed over her, but Jenna fought it back. "Do you know where Brit is?" she asked.

"He's out looking at a piece of property for a client who wants him to build an estate near here. I tried to call him earlier but he's probably out of cell phone range. I left a message, so he'll call as soon as he can."

"Sherrie, as soon as you reach him, tell Brit I'm going over to Boyce Wheeler's. Parker took Ethan there and Brit needs to get there right away. I mean *right away.*"

Sherrie looked up in alarm. "Why? What's going on?"

"Nothing good," Jenna said, and took off running toward the deer path.

Kyle started running with her. "You want me to go with you? Maybe I can help."

She stopped briefly. "No, I need you to stay here and show Sherrie what you found. Then tell her to call Detective Gabe de la Torre and tell him what's going on, okay? And Kyle, thank you, *thank* you for speaking up."

"Sure thing," he called after her.

As she ran towards the deer trail, a thousand possibilities screamed through her head, none of them good. Thinking she might need the element of surprise on her side, she silenced her cell phone. What would she find when she got to Puerta del Mar? She wished like hell she knew.

"What a putz you are, Mr. D." Parker and the professor were standing in what looked like the office of Wheeler, the guy who owned the estate. Wheeler wasn't around, but Dorman was pointing a pistol at them.

"Keep your hands where I can see them and keep your goddamned mouth shut." Dorman barked.

The professor stuck his hands in the air like it was some sort of spaghetti western. "What's this all about, Mr. Dorman?" he asked. "Where is Boyce?"

"Boyce is dead. No, don't look at me—I didn't do it. He had a stroke yesterday. We're just taking advantage of the situation, isn't that right, *Chief*?"

Parker noticed that Dorman was sweating. Good. He's probably wigged out by all this…but does he have the balls to pull the trigger? He caught the eye of old man Wolff and tilted his head slightly. Wolff seemed to understand because he started to slowly move in the opposite direction as Parker.

"Don't move," Dorman said nervously. "I'll shoot if I have to."

"Wasn't that your plan all along?" Parker asked. "You told me you had a plan."

"Plan? What are you talking about?" The professor turned to Parker. "What exactly is going on here?"

It was plain the old guy didn't get the drift. Parker sighed. He hated it when people were too stupid by half. "They lured you here to kill you, man, don't you get it? How else are they gonna keep The Grove from opening? It's pretty simple. They want to make it look like Boyce and you argued. Then he shot you and keeled over from the excitement. Am I right, Mr. D.?"

"Something like that. Except—" the fucker swiveled the gun and pointed it straight at him "—*you're* going to be the shooter who takes out one old man, causing the other one to stroke out."

"You double crossing me, Mr. D.? Is that nice?" He felt the weight of the thirty-eight stashed in the pocket of the baggy sweatshirt he always wore. Once these ass wipes were dealt with and the curtain came down on The Grove, all would be well. He could feel it.

The professor turned to Parker. "You brought me here knowing what this man's intentions were? How could you, my boy?"

The look of disappointment on the old man's face creeped Parker out. "Hey, they just suggested I get you over here so you could talk to Boyce Wheeler. They never said anything about popping you off. I put two and two together just now." Shit, why did he feel the need to explain himself to this guy?

"Shut up, you two," Dorman said. He was really looking stressed out. He kept glancing over his shoulder as if he expected someone to come in any minute.

"So, what," Parker smirked, "didn't you think you could trust little ol' me?"

Dorman snorted, waving an arm dismissively. "Anybody who trusts you is a fool. I told you we could pin Lester's death on you, and maybe that was a stretch, but it turns out you provide the perfect motive anyway."

"Oh yeah? What's that?"

"Here's the headline," Dorman said. "'Troubled Teen Murders Man He Thinks Stands in the Way of Perfect Love.'"

Parker could feel his anger starting to build. "What the fuck are you talking about?"

"You know what I'm talking about. Old man dies, Grove falls, Brit Maguire's finished, Jenna falls into your lap. Isn't that how you pictured it? Only now there's gonna be a little twist. You and the old man struggle over the gun. He dies. You die. The police find a mess and spend weeks sorting it all out. The 'doomed lovers' scenario seems like it fits the best." Dorman waved the pistol back and forth between the two men. "Move closer together—*now*. And don't think you're going to overpower me. I'm not alone."

"I'd say not, Mr. Dorman." Jenna walked calmly into the office, looking like a freakin' goddess, and stared Dorman right in the eye. "You can't hit all of us, so put the gun away before any of us gets hurt, won't you?"

Dorman's voice started to sound kind of screechy. "How'd you get in here?"

"Door's open, nobody's around, I walked in. But I'm wondering how you came to be in the position *you're* in?"

It was great. Dorman was really starting to breathe heavy, like he'd just climbed off that fat waitress or something.

"I heard you were reluctant to come back to The Grove," Dorman growled. "You should have followed your instincts; maybe you would have lived. As it stands, now there's a new storyline: lovers' quarrel results in four dead bodies."

"At the risk of sounding like a cliché, Mr. Dorman, you'll never get away with it." Jenna stood there, calm, cool, and sexy at the same time.

Damn, my woman has guts. Wait'll she sees what I'm about to do for her.

Dorman was getting more and more freaked out. "We'll see about that. Myra!" he called.

"I just saw Myra driving down the road," Jenna said. "Why are you pulling her into this?"

"You're lying!" Dorman turned to look out the window. As he did so Parker pulled out his thirty-eight and pointed it directly at Dorman. He heard a gasp from Jenna and something that sounded like "Don't do it, son," from the old professor.

"Um, Mr. D.?' Parker said softly.

Dorman whipped around.

"I told you before…if you ever tried anything with Jenna, you'd be road kill. But you didn't listen, did you?" And with that he shot Dorman twice in the chest.

"My God, Parker, what the hell have you done?" Jenna ran over to see if she could help Dorman, but Parker could tell it was lights out for good ol' Mr. D.

He watched his woman and the old man stare at him with shocked looks on their faces. They were beginning to annoy him. "You know, he didn't have it completely ass backward," he said, his tone curiously detached. "You and I really will have a better chance once The Grove bites the dust and that prick Maguire's no longer part of the picture. There's only one problem." He turned to look at the professor.

"Parker, look at me," Jenna said sternly. Her eyes were huge and she reached out to grab his arm.

He jumped back, swiveling the gun between Jenna and the old man like Dorman had done. "Careful, baby. I wouldn't want you to get hurt in the process here."

"Parker, please. You've got to listen."

Something inside him snapped and blood started rushing throughout his body. "No, *you've* got to listen!" He felt as if he could lift the earth with one hand, he was so strong. And she was his. She always had been. He had to make her understand once and for all how it was going to be. "You belong to me, don't you get it?" He jabbed himself forcefully in the chest to make his point. "It was me who fought Kyle because he disrespected you...me who followed you here to protect you. It was me who warned that cocksucker reporter off your tail, and it was *me* who warned you not to stay here and get hurt. All of that was me. Me!"

He paused to take a breath and felt the anger inside him start to bubble up and he didn't know if he could hold it in any longer. "Why didn't you see that?" he continued in a voice that sounded thin and shrill, even to him. "Why'd you have to go and spread your legs for that dickmeister Maguire? Don't you know how much that hurt me?" Parker could feel wetness on his cheeks. Were those tears?

"Baby, I didn't know," Jenna said softly. Her voice sounded different. He didn't know what to make of it.

"Well now you know," he sniffed.

"I'm very sorry I hurt you. How about we go back to The Grove. You know, talk it over, and…?"

He gestured to her grandfather. "I've got a better idea. I kill him and we go off together. Simple." He pointed the gun at the professor. "On your knees, old man." The professor did as he was told. He looked old and scared and weak.

"Baby, that's not such a good idea," Jenna said.

"Sure it is. He's the one that's keeping The Grove alive. Once he's gone you'll be free of it and we can be together."

"But that would make me sad," she reasoned in that same smooth voice that was really beginning to grate on him.

"Shit happens, baby. But you'll get over it. If it makes you squeamish, just don't look." He turned and aimed the gun at the old man's head, execution-style. Just as he pulled the trigger Jenna screamed and pushed her grandfather sharply to the side. The shot was off a bit, but the old man slumped over just the same.

Chapter Thirty-Eight

Heading down Highway Fifty-Seven back to The Grove, Brit considered the property he'd just seen. It was spectacular, with a large level building site and awesome views of both the West Marin Hills and Creation Bay. The client was a fan of Frank Lloyd Wright's work and insisted Brit was the only architect around who could infuse a modern, eco-friendly design with Wright's spirit of adventure and "oneness" with the environment. It seemed Vintage Maguire was going to have a lot going on in the next several months. Brit wondered if Jenna was going to be around to share it with him. He intended to ask her the next time they were alone together.

His cell phone buzzed and Brit noticed Sherrie had called. He was about to call her back when his phone rang again.

"Miss me that much, huh?" he answered with a grin.

"Brit, thank goodness. Jenna says you've got to get over to Puerta del Mar right away. Apparently Parker took the professor there, and Jenna didn't feel right about it. Turns out Ethan was tricked, so she's gone over there by way of the deer path. And Brit? Kyle found two cartridges in Parker's duffel bag. There's a good chance he's got a gun."

Brit felt his entire body turn to ice. "Jesus, Sherrie. Did you call Gabe? What about Boyce? Can he hold him until we get there?"

"Yes, I've called Gabe, and yes I tried calling the Wheelers, but there's no answer. No answer on Jenna's phone either. Gabe says he's heading out that way now."

"Yeah, by the time he makes it there from the station, who knows what might happen. Listen, I've just made the turn heading out to Boyce's estate. I'll let you know what I find."

Don't try to handle this one on your own, Jenna. Please. Please. Please.

Like a mantra, the words kept running through his head.

Jenna looked at Parker in shock.

"What? You didn't think I had the guts to do it? I've got more *huevos* than all of them put together!"

"You just shot my grandfather," she said incredulously. She knelt down and lifted her grandfather's head onto her lap. His eyes were closed and hers began to well with tears. "Come on, Da, this is no way to go out," she crooned. "You can do better than this."

"Come on, let's go," Parker said, rapping out a nervous beat on the side of his pants. He sounded hyped up, as if he were on speed.

Reluctantly she looked up, and what she saw filled her with cold, stark fear. Parker's eyes reflected an unnatural glitter; he looked unhinged. She sensed the pent-up animosity, the *evil* that might burst out again at any moment. She knew he'd crossed the line into uncharted mental and emotional territory, and that he wasn't turning back. She had to get away from him, but how could she leave her grandfather?

"Move it!" he ordered.

"Don't you see? I can't just leave him!" she cried.

"You want me to just finish the job? I can do that, you know," he bragged, brandishing his pistol. "Easy as pie."

"No!" Jenna cried. "No. Just…just give me a few minutes to say my goodbyes, and then I'll go with you, okay?" She gazed at him with what she hoped was a sincere expression.

Parker looked skeptical, but finally agreed. "Three minutes, tops. I'm going to raid the kitchen. I never realized killing works up an appetite! When I get back, we're outta here." He sauntered out of the room and Jenna looked down at her grandfather. After all they'd been through, to lose him this way was *obscene*. There was so much she wanted to tell him. So much she wanted to share.

"You'll always be my very own Da," she whispered, bending down and kissing him on his forehead. "You'll always be my family." The tears started to flow and she wondered with a sense of panic if they would ever stop, if she would ever be able to see clearly enough to get past her grief and stand up to Parker. She had to try for Da's sake, and Jason's, and Brit's…and her own. She would not let them down. She reached for the bottom of her shirt to wipe her eyes and when she looked down at her grandfather again she found that he was staring at her with wide determined eyes. She gasped and Da put a shaky, gnarled finger to his lips. He then took the same hand and bent his three middle fingers.

"What?" Jenna whispered. Omigod, she didn't know what he was saying. What was he *saying*?!

Ethan, his fingers still bent, slowly raised his arm to his ear. He struggled to bend his hand so that his little finger pointed to his mouth.

Jenna stared for a second before realizing what he wanted. "Phone?" she mouthed. He nodded, then waved his fingers as if to say, "Give the phone to me."

Jenna sniffed and nodded. She reached into her jacket pocket, pulled out her phone and switched it on. She was about to dial when she heard a drawer slam. She looked up to see Parker coming back down the hall. Quickly she shoved the phone underneath Da's body. He nodded slightly and closed his eyes again. Jenna laid his head back down and got up.

"He dead yet?" Parker asked without emotion.

Jenna took a deep breath and expelled it. "Almost," she lied. "Perhaps it's just as well."

"Now you're talking, baby. Come on, we're heading out to your favorite place."

"What place?"

"The cove. You know, where you did the nasty with Maguire? Hey, you saw me up on the trail that day. What'd you think, I couldn't figure it out?" In a much more deadly tone he added, "The thought of you and him doin' it made me so fucking angry. You know that, don't you?"

Jenna fought back the bile that was threatening to overwhelm her. She had to get this cretin away from Da so her grandfather could summon help, but she couldn't be too obvious about it.

"I'm sorry. I didn't know," she said, trying to sound contrite. "So, should we...do anything about what happened here?"

He looked around as if surveying his handiwork. Ethan was lying as still as death, and Dorman was bleeding out across the room. "I think our work's done here," he announced. "Let's go."

Parker grabbed Jenna's hand and led her back down the hall he'd disappeared to earlier. She stole one last glance at Da before leaving the room. He remained motionless and she hoped to God that he was still playing possum and not truly out of it.

"Look what I found," Parker said gleefully. He pointed to a box of kitchen matches and two half empty bottles of whiskey. "I've had a little practice with this. It's kinda fun." He took the bottles and began pouring them around the edges of the kitchen and out into the hall.

Horrified, Jenna grabbed his arm. "No! I mean, what are you doing, Parker? You're...um...you're going to send a signal before we have a chance to get away!"

Parker looked at her for a long moment and began to speak in a totally rational tone of voice, like the boy she thought she'd known.

"Jenna, do you really think I'm that stupid?" he asked. "I know there's no 'getting away.' I've known that since I was a kid. No, there's only me, and you, and the perfect expression of a perfect love. You were there for me, always. Like no one else. And now I'm here for you. I killed for you, you know." He gave her what appeared to be a look of sympathy before striking a match and setting the kitchen ablaze.

Chapter Thirty-Nine

Brit was still about twenty minutes away from Boyce's front door when his phone began to buzz. He noted the caller ID with relief. *Thank God it's you.* "Where are you, sweetheart?"

There was a faint breathing sound, then the words "Brit? Brit, my boy?"

Brit's heart sank. "Ethan, is that you? My God, where are you?"

"I'm at Boyce Wheeler's." Brit could hear Ethan coughing. "Oh, it's a horror scene here, Brit. Lots of smoke...blood..."

Oh Sweet Jesus, please don't let it be Jenna. Please God, don't let it be her. "Ethan?" Brit heard nothing but labored breathing on the line. "Ethan, can you hear me? Are you still with me?"

"Yes...yes, I'm still here," Ethan finally responded. "I had to crawl a bit, but I'm clear now. I'm all right. Boyce is gone...and Dorman. Brit, he shot Ralph

Dorman in cold blood…" Ethan's voice grew more faint. "Cold blood…"

"Who did this, Ethan? *Who*?"

"Parker. He had a little pistol, like the ones you see in the old gangster movies. He shot Dorman and then he…he shot me…"

Oh God. "Ethan. Talk to me. How bad is it?"

"Not…too bad. I'm still breathing, although it's getting difficult."

"I'll send an ambulance right away. Hang in there." Brit swallowed, afraid to ask the question, but knowing he would die if he didn't have the answer in the next five seconds. "What about Jenna? Is she there?"

"He took her. She was able to slip me her phone and that's what I needed to tell you. Parker took her. He said to her favorite spot…the cove."

Brit slammed on the brakes, realizing that it wasn't going to do him any good to go to Wheeler's when he needed to be at the cove. He pulled the fastest U-turn he'd ever executed on a winding road, coming within inches of the cliff's edge. But it didn't matter. The only thing that mattered was getting to Jenna. "Listen, Ethan. I want you to disconnect in a minute, but then I want you to keep your finger near the talk button. As soon as I hang up I'm going to call 911 to have them talk to you. They're going to want to keep you on the line until they get there, okay? Can you remember that?"

There was a brief, weak chuckle on the other end of the line. "I don't think I'd be up to multitasking right now, but I think I can manage that."

"Good. Now hang up and get ready to push that green button again as soon as it rings. And Ethan?" he added fiercely. "You've got too much to do to bail on us now, you hear?"

"That's what Jenna said. Now go find her. Good bye, my boy."

The click signaling the end of the call was ominous. Brit immediately called Gabe back and told him to send a fire truck and ambulance and get 911 back on the line with Ethan to keep him alert. Gabe did so and then called Brit back.

"What else did Ethan tell you?" Gabe asked.

"He said Parker murdered Ralph Dorman in cold blood. Said he used a small gun like they used in the old gangster movies."

"Yeah, Sherrie described the bullets. It's probably a thirty-eight snub nose. You can get 'em easily on the street. Look, you've got to let us handle this, Brit."

"Are you freaking *kidding* me, Gabe? If your guys had moved faster than a snail's pace this whole fucking mess might not have happened. But now he's got Jenna and he's taken her to the cove."

"Stay cool, Brit. I'm sending in a helicopter."

"I'm almost back to Fifty-Seven," Brit said, ignoring Gabe's suggestion. "I'll take the nearest fire road and cut across country to access the deer trail. I can get down there a hell of a lot faster than you can."

"Listen to me, Brit. This is a job for law—"

"Screw that! Not this time, Gabe. This time I handle it myself. I'm going to make a goddamned citizen's arrest if I have to, but I'm going to nail that prick if it's the last thing I do."

There was silence on the other end of the line. "I can't encourage you," Gabe said. "But I will tell you to be careful. Sounds like the kid's armed and dangerous."

"How many cartridges?"

"What do you mean?"

"That thirty eight you told me he's probably using. How many bullets does it hold?"

"Five rounds. But Brit, you can't rely on that. It may be a different weapon. He may have extra ammo on him."

"I gotta run," Brit said. "Wait!" was all he heard before he hung up the phone.

He concentrated on driving as fast as he could without killing himself in the process. He felt his jaw clench so tightly it hurt, and he could feel sweat beginning to form on the back of his neck. He couldn't remember ever feeling as scared as he did right now— not for himself, but for the woman he loved. If that monster did anything to Jenna…if he wasn't in time…

No. He brushed those thoughts aside. No more what ifs. Now it was time to *act*.

It shouldn't be such a beautiful day, Jenna thought perversely as Parker dragged her along the trail, down toward the cove that divided Puerta del Mar and The Grove. A slight breeze rustled the trees gently, taking the edge off the heat of the early afternoon. She could smell the rich scent of redwoods mixed with eucalyptus, bay laurel, and pine. The pungent blend merged with the smoke coming from the kitchen fire Parker had started. One could almost imagine a friendly campfire in the woods instead of the destructive force that Parker intended it to be. She heard a siren in the distance. Was Da able to call Brit in time?

Jenna noticed the soft loam of the forest floor beneath her shoes...the sharp thorn of a branch as it scratched her arm...the high twitter of a bird and its mate's answering call. Is this what happens when you face death? Do you experience your last minutes on earth in such sharp detail? She thought about Brit and wanted to weep. He would never know how she truly felt about him.

After a moment she shook herself mentally. Why was she acting as if she were already dead? As long as she was breathing, she had a chance to get herself out of this mess. All she had to do was figure out *how*.

They had almost reached the edge of the trees. Ahead lay the open beach of the cove. Once there, she knew there would be little chance to escape except by the sea. Jenna was a good swimmer, but even she had her doubts about being able to negotiate the waves well enough to secure her freedom.

"Come on, we're almost there," Parker rasped, keeping up a pace that could only be fueled by adrenalin.

Jenna fought the feeling of hysteria that arose with his words. Instead she managed, "What's the hurry?"

"You know they're coming after us. One way or another, before it's all over, you're going to be mine."

He can't be serious, she thought. Can he? She had to get through to him somehow. "Parker, you're a young man. You've still got time."

"Time? *Time?* Why do I need more time? To go to some friggin' school I can't wait to get out of? To get a lousy job and meet some girl who'll pork up as soon as she has a kid, just so I can go out behind her back like my dad does and nail whoever's willing? To grow old and bald and fat and find out my golf score's the only thing that gets it up anymore? No thanks. Time is not what I need more of."

Despite his erratic behavior, Jenna knew she had to try to reason with him, or at least stall him until someone could help her. She tugged on his arm forcefully enough to make him stop.

"Parker, I'm not going to make love with you," she said as calmly as she could.

He stopped, regarded her for a few seconds, and backhanded her across the face. "Yes you are," he said just as calmly.

Shocked, she tasted blood and felt the side of her face begin to throb. Ruthlessly tamping down her fear, she spoke evenly and without emotion. "Hurting me isn't going to make me love you," she explained. "Please. Tell me why you're doing this." Fighting the urge to recoil, she reached out and lightly touched his face. "Please," she repeated.

Parker seemed surprised by her tenderness. His eyes narrowed, as if he were trying to see what lay behind her action. Comprehension set in and he backed away, wagging his finger at her. "Oh, no. You're not going to trick me like you did before."

"What do you mean, 'like I did before'? What did I ever do to you, other than be your friend?"

Parker clenched his fists as he paced in front of her. "You led me on. You acted as if you were interested in me."

"I was interested in *everybody* my brother had become friends with, Parker. I wanted to know what kind of boys you all were."

"I'm a man, not a boy. And we talked for hours." He gestured to the shoreline. "You wanted to know about my love for the ocean. You *listened* to me. Don't you remember?!" He was beginning to sound manic.

Jenna tried to keep her voice as calm as possible. "Parker, I asked you about your love of surfing because I'd never surfed before and I couldn't imagine going out in such cold water. You said you wanted to be either a marine biologist or a surf bum, remember? I thought that was funny. But that's *all* I thought. Nothing more."

Parker began to pout; he brought to mind a petulant child. "You're wrong," he argued. "You fell in love with me. You just didn't know what love was."

Jenna sighed and took a chance on the truth. "I've only felt the way you described for one man in my entire life," she said. "And you know who that is." She immediately regretted her words, because Parker grabbed her arm, pressed himself against her and gave her a punishing kiss, grinding against her lips and forcing his tongue deep inside her mouth. She was about to gag when he finally let her go and began to rant. "You're through with that cockhound, do you understand? All he wanted was some pussy, and he's not going to get any more from you!"

Wincing at his words, Jenna tried to calm him down. "Okay, okay. You're right. You've made sure of that." She looked around for something, anything to distract him. The tide pools that formed one end of the cove caught her eye and an instant plan formed: she would catch him off guard and run like hell back up the trail.

"Come here. I want to show you something," she said in her most soothing voice.

Parker looked at her warily. "What?"

"Let me show you." She led him along the coarse, volcanic rocks that surrounded the pools, much like she and Brit had done after they'd made love on the beach. She kept up a quiet monologue, talking about the various sea creatures and wondering out loud how they managed to survive even though they'd missed the outgoing tide.

"They get left behind, but they cope," he said. "After a while, it's easy."

"Look down there," she said, pointing to an unusually deep pool. "The other day I saw a sea star there."

Parker took his eyes off Jenna in order to see where the creature clung to the side of the pool. In that instant she shoved him as hard as she could, using her strong right leg—the one she'd used to win many soccer games—to kick him in the groin.

"Fuck!" he yelped as he toppled off the rocks to the sand below. Jenna turned the other way and ran her heart out, leaping across the rocks and off the far end onto the sand. She headed straight for the path and had almost reached it when she heard the crack of a pistol shot hitting close to the tree by her head. Knowing that to stop meant certain death, she continued scrabbling back up into the forest, leaving the trail and heading for trees that would offer her the most protection. She found a large old-growth redwood and crouched down behind it, her heart hammering out of her chest. Should she stay and see if he passed her by, or else keep running and hope his shots continued to miss?

"That wasn't cool, Jenna," she heard Parker call from several yards behind her. "Come back now and I won't punish you too much…you might even enjoy it."

Jenna closed her eyes briefly. The urge to run was overwhelming, but instinct told her to stay put just a little while longer.

"Come out, come out, wherever you are," Parker sang, his voice sounding dangerously close.

Jenna was about to make a break for it when powerful hands caught her from behind, one arm under her breasts and the other covering her mouth. Her first instinct was to scream; her second was to cry with joy.

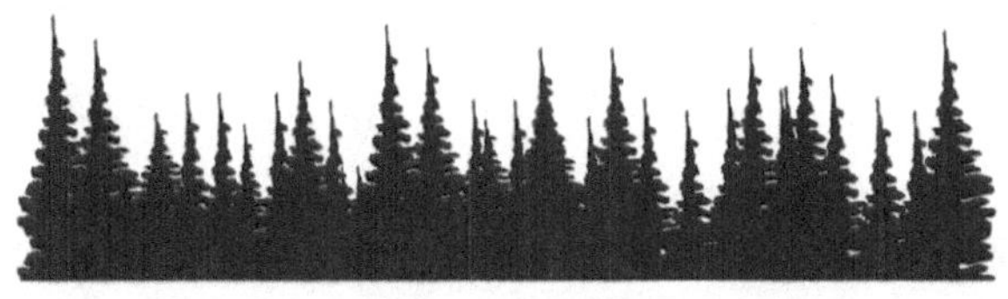

Chapter Forty

"Shhh," Brit whispered. The relief he felt at knowing Jenna was alive and in his arms was so strong he wanted to shout it to the heavens, but now was not the time. He squeezed Jenna slightly to make sure she understood it was him. She nodded slightly and he slowly released her. Together they silently crouched down again behind the tree. He noticed her swollen face and felt the desperate fear within him morph into rage, calculating and cold. He searched for calm and found it, knowing the time would come when this twisted kid would pay. "How many bullets?" he murmured in her ear.

Jenna looked at him in puzzlement. *What do you mean?* she mouthed. She held up one finger. *He shot at me once.*

Brit shook his head. "How many total?" he whispered. "Back at the house and here."

Jenna's eyes grew wide and she wet her lips. He could tell she was trying to remember. She was smart enough to realize it made a difference. After a moment she shook her head. "I don't know. Four, five...I can't remember."

Brit kept his voice as low as possible. "Did he reload?"

"Not that I saw, but he left the room at one point. I'm not *sure*," she hissed in a small, panicked voice.

Brit nodded. "I want you to take off in that direction," he whispered, pointing left and up the hill. "I'm going to draw him off."

"No!" Jenna cried in a harsh whisper of her own. "He'll shoot you!"

"No he won't, sweetheart," he murmured, cupping the back of her head. "I'm going to be okay, but you've got to do your part."

Jenna's eyes were huge as she locked gazes with Brit. He tried to tell her so many things in the look he gave her. Finally she nodded and took off in the direction he'd indicated. As soon as she was several yards away Brit stood up and started waving and shouting. "Parker! Parker Bishop!" A shot rang out and missed his face by mere inches, finding its way into the base of a young redwood instead. He took a deep breath and stepped out into an open gap between the trees.

"Parker," he said sharply.

Parker stopped and raised his gun. He had a clear shot, but hesitated. Apparently he thought better of it and lowered his arm slightly. Perhaps he wants to toy with his prey, Brit thought. *I know the feeling.*

"Well, well, well. If it isn't the cockmeister himself," Parker taunted. "Where's Jenna?"

"You've got to let Jenna go," Brit said evenly.

"Fuck you. What do you know about it?"

"I know about being in love. And it's not about holding someone against their will."

As Brit spoke, Parker became more and more agitated. His eyes darted back and forth as he scanned the trees. "Jenna!" he yelled. "Come back here or I'm going to blow this cocksucker's head off!"

Brit continued in a matter-of-fact voice. "They've got to come to you freely. You can't force it. You can't force *them*."

"You're full of shit, you know that? Jenna!"

A moment later Jenna came walking through the trees. "I'm here, Parker," she said, glancing at Brit. "You don't have to use the gun."

The little idiot! I don't need saving. Instead he said in a mocking tone, "Sure he does, Jenna. He needs to show you how brave and strong he is, don't you, Parker?"

"You shut up. You shut *up*!" Parker cried, waving his pistol back and forth.

"Brit, please," Jenna begged. "Please don't—"

"Don't what? Tell the truth? The truth about this little shit who thinks he can make you love him by force? Who thinks that gun makes him invincible? Who's so gutless he has to pay others to do his dirty work for him? You had that reporter cut up, didn't you? Didn't you, you little fuck."

"Yes! Hell yes, I did. He had no right sniffing around Jenna, and neither do you! But that's going to end. Right now. I'll show you invincible, you asshole." Parker pointed the pistol straight at Brit's heart.

"No! Please, Parker! No!"

"Do it," Brit growled. Do it *now*!"

"Aghhh!" Parker gripped the pistol with both hands and pulled the trigger.

Click.

Parker hardly had time to realize what had happened when Brit leapt on him, punching him in the gut.

Adrenalin kicked in for both of them as they pummeled each other. Brit was powerful, but Parker was surprisingly quick. Out of the corner of his eye, Brit saw Jenna picking up a hefty branch and begin to wield it like a club. He prayed she wouldn't do anything so stupid as to take a swing, hoping it was Parker and not Brit she was bashing. Unfortunately his wayward thoughts cost him; Parker took advantage of his distraction and kicked Brit in the ribs before running back toward the beach.

Winded, Brit nevertheless shot up and followed Parker, shouting, "Stay there!" to Jenna as he did so. She apparently ignored his command, again, because as he reached the edge of the sand, she came up right behind him.

"Parker, stop!" she called out, her voice sounding harsh over the crashing of the surf. Ignoring her plea, the young man raced straight for the water. "I'm a surfer, remember?" he yelled, and dove beneath the waves.

Brit and Jenna watched in shock as Parker continued swimming straight out to sea. They could see his head bobbing up and down for a long while, but then...nothing.

They heard the approaching rumble of rotor blades. "Gabe called a helicopter in," Brit said. "I'll let him know to start searching the water."

Jenna nodded, seemingly in a trance. After a few moments she dropped to her knees, still staring out to sea. Brit finished talking to Gabe and knelt down beside her.

"It's all over," he said quietly, putting his arm around her. "It's done."

Jenna turned and looked at Brit, tears streaming down her face. "He almost killed you," she said. "I almost lost you...*again.*"

Brit took her face between his large hands. Her eyes closed as if she were trying to keep the emotion from spilling onto the sand. "Jenna, sweetheart. It's okay. I knew what I was doing. Honest." He began to kiss the tears from her eyes and worked his way down to her mouth.

Suddenly she pulled back. "Da?" she asked.

"Doin' great. A flesh wound, Gabe says. They even saved the old house. All is well." He resumed kissing her and, much to his relief, she began to kiss him back.

Chapter Forty-One

Jenna couldn't help shivering as she looked around the hidden chamber at Puerta Del Mar the next afternoon. Between Parker and the horrific dealings that had taken place here, it was almost too much to take in. "This is amazing…and creepy. Hard to believe Boyce Wheeler's father stole all these pieces from The Grove collection and no one ever knew about it."

Gabe de la Torre had asked Jenna, Dani, and Brit to bring their records and identify the artwork his CSU technicians had discovered while taking prints at the crime scene. The upstairs still smelled of smoke and suffered from considerable water damage, but with care, the mansion could one day be restored to its former opulence.

"In a twisted way it makes sense," Brit said, checking out a bronze sculpture by Mason Tanner. "Wheeler's father knows the collection has gone to Ethan and not Giselle. Ethan's still in college, which means the artwork's probably going to remain in storage for a long time. He picks the top-selling pieces of the day, hoping they'll keep their value, and unloads them periodically whenever he needs an influx of cash. None of the pieces have ever been reported missing, so he's clear on that score." He turned to Dani. "All he has to do is remain one of those anonymous sellers you talked about, and by the time anything's discovered, he's dead and gone, so what does he care? He probably thought it was fair payment for the travesty of the Wolffs creating The Grove in the first place."

Dani consulted her notes. "You're looking at a hundred thousand dollars, at least, just for that piece alone."

Stealing and selling the artwork was one thing, but something didn't make sense. "I still don't get it. Why did Boyce buy them all back?" Jenna asked.

"Myra's become quite the chatterbox on that issue," Gabe said. "She claims Boyce was in the process of restoring these pieces to the collection before they were discovered missing. I guess he was worried an investigation might circle back to him and tarnish the family name. How he planned on returning them we'll never know, but apparently that was his real motivation for stalling the reopening of The Grove. SPEAR was just so much smoke and mirrors...pardon the pun."

"So, he did have a good heart, sort of," Jenna mused. "But if he was trying to right a wrong, why would he physically hurt others just to get his way?"

Gabe turned his head sideways to ponder an

abstract painting. "I'm not so sure we can lay the blame for Don's accident or the explosion at Boyce's feet."

"I'd like to know who was responsible, then." It was obvious Brit was still incensed by the attempted murder of his good friend and colleague.

"My money's on Myra," Gabe offered. "It turns out Dorman did have a credible alibi for that afternoon. He'd attended a client meeting in town that didn't entail using his car. So, logically it was either Lester, acting on Myra's orders and wearing gloves, or Myra herself. One suspect has paid the ultimate price, and the other will soon be doing time."

"What can they pin on her?" Brit asked.

"Attempted murder, if all the tumblers fall into place. Turns out she's a fanatic for keeping track of things, including all the antihistamines and antidepressants she'd been feeding Boyce over the past several months, medications that weren't his to begin with. With his already high blood pressure, those drugs could easily have caused him to stroke out. Since she gave the housekeeper the week off, that could work against her as well. Shows premeditation."

"So that must have been Myra on the phone. She did sound like she had a cold or something."

Brit shook his head. "That's beyond despicable. I hope they nail her."

"Don't set your expectations too high," Gabe cautioned. "She's cozying up to the D.A. Says she's got the dirt on quite a few city luminaries. Apparently Ralph Dorman wasn't the only one taking kickbacks from New Venture Properties. But she'll face elder abuse at a minimum. So in some fashion or another, justice will be served."

Dani had been quietly comparing the displayed artwork to her list of missing pieces. "It looks like we're only short three pieces, and I think I'll be able to track those easily enough, now that we know they won't get snapped up by the "mystery buyer.""

"Excuse me, Detective de la Torre?" A deputy sheriff had come halfway down the stairs. "Yeah, Benson. Down here."

"The lieutenant wants to speak to you. Something about a certain suspect who's willing to cut a deal?"

Gabe smiled at the group. "That would be Myra. Time to go. We're still processing these items, so we can't turn them over to you yet, but at least now you know where they are."

As they all walked to their respective cars, Jenna noticed Gabe stop in front of Dani and take her small shoulders in his strong hands. He leaned over and whispered something in her ear before enfolding her in an embrace. She hesitated for just a moment, then wrapped her dainty arms around his back and hugged him fiercely. He headed to his car and the look of longing Dani sent to his retreating back was so poignant it nearly brought Jenna to tears. What was keeping those two apart? Maybe the trip back home to her family in Italy would help her figure out her priorities, which Jenna hoped would include the man who so obviously desired her.

Brit and Jenna drove back to The Grove, stopping in Little Eden to pick up a pizza to share with Jason and Da for dinner. In an odd way Jenna felt deflated, as if she'd been riding atop a giant balloon filled with so much air it had finally burst. She didn't dare think about where she and Brit were headed. Instead her thoughts centered on the two men, besides the one she was sitting next to, who meant the most to her.

All summer long Jason had assumed the mantle of responsibility for Da, helping their grandfather while treating him with the utmost respect and kindness. He'd dealt with the betrayal of his friend Parker in a very mature way, as well as working through his friendship with Kyle, who had since returned to his family in the city.

And when she'd told him, along with Brit, about the possibility of incest in the family tree, he'd shown amazing sensitivity. All of it boded well for Jason's success as he entered the next phase of his life.

"You're awfully quiet," Brit remarked.

"I was just thinking about Jason, and about Da," she said. "One has his whole life ahead of him, the other is winding down. I think Jason's going to be fine, but what's going through Da's head knowing that the beginning of his life held such pain for those he loved?"

Brit reached over and took Jenna's hand as he drove. "Your grandfather is a remarkable man, and I know he's going to process what he's learned and deal with it the best way possible, whatever that way happens to be."

"I hope you're right." Jenna lapsed again into silence,

her thoughts circling back to Brit. Always to Brit. When he'd confronted Parker, he'd said he knew what it was like to be in love. Had he meant with her? Did he still feel that way? Since leaving the beach there had been no time for anything except answering questions from the authorities and collapsing into bed, only to rise and answer still more. In a surprising move, Brit had suggested they get ahead of the media and give an exclusive story to Declan, who had agreed to come out and interview them the next day. Knowing that Declan cared for her, was Brit testing her somehow? It was absurd, but could she blame him after what she'd done to him so long ago? She was determined to clear the air the next time they were alone.

They arrived at Da's cottage to find him sitting in his favorite chair, his arm in a sling. Jason was adjusting a pillow behind Da's back. Miraculously, Parker's shot had only nicked her grandfather, but his lung had collapsed when Jenna pushed him over so forcefully to avoid the bullet. She tried not to feel guilty about it, knowing there had been no choice. Today, however, the sober expression he wore seemed to have less to do with his injury and more to do with the unexpected guest sitting near him.

The man, probably in his late thirties, rose when they entered the room. He was tall and muscular, but leaner in build than Brit, with much darker coloring and a day-old beard stubble. He was dressed in jeans and a T-shirt, and had a self-sufficient air about him that made it easy to imagine him living in the wilds of Idaho. Jenna recognized the box of negatives at his feet.

His intense blue eyes claimed hers, holding them. She felt Brit reach for her hand and smiled inwardly at the testosterone on display.

"Ah, there you are," Da said. "I'd like you to meet Walker Banks, whom I have been trying to get down here for a visit for quite some time. He's the photographer who printed out my father's negatives for me. Walker, this is my cousin Britland Maguire and my granddaughter, Jenna Bergstrom."

Banks murmured greetings and shook their hands. He seemed decent enough, but Jenna still had reservations about him. After all, he'd been privy to a very dark, very salacious chapter in her family's history. Could they trust him? Would he try to exploit their family in some way, based on what he now knew? She decided to probe a bit to see what they were up against. She and Brit sat down on the sofa and, putting the pizza box on the coffee table, she stared right back at the stranger.

"Why are you here now, Mr. Banks?" she asked bluntly. "I'd think it would have been easier just to mail the box back as you did the photos."

Banks continued to look Jenna for several seconds, as if to show he knew she'd thrown down a gauntlet.

"Call me Walker," he said finally. "I've been meaning to get down to see Ethan for some time, and felt this was a good opportunity, since I wanted to return such private materials to him in person. Does that meet with your approval?"

Jenna could feel Brit bristling next to her and she squeezed his hand to reassure him. Because strangely,

Walker's answer *was* reassuring; at least he was perceptive enough to realize how sensitive the photos were to the family.

But her grandfather's next remarks put a completely new spin on the situation. "She's a Mama Bear, Walker, and a feisty one. I've noticed it runs in the family." He winked at Jenna before addressing her concern. "You might be interested to know that Walker is a descendant of August Wolff through the daughter of Gus's first marriage, just as you, Brit, are a descendant through Lia's son from *her* first marriage. So we are all related to one another in some fashion—by blood or not," he said, glancing at Jenna, "which pleases me greatly." He beamed at the others in the room, a fragile patriarch who by sheer tenacity had been able to cobble together the disparate—and distant—strands of a remarkable family.

Jenna couldn't help it; she grinned at Walker and shrugged, acknowledging her unwarranted jab at him. He grinned back.

Brit let go of Jenna's hand and leaned forward, his elbows on his knees. He looked from Da to Walker for a moment and then sat up straight, his hands on his thighs. "And unless I miss my guess, you're also our new silent partner."

Walker glanced at Da, who shook his head as if to say *It wasn't me.* "Guilty as charged," Walker said. "How'd you figure?"

"I remember Ethan said the new investor was really trustworthy. He compared him to family…and I guess he was right."

"I also said he prefers to remain in the background," Da admonished. He nodded to Walker. "So until you direct otherwise, dear boy, you can rest assured we'll keep the matter of your financial participation to ourselves."

"I'd appreciate it," Walker said. "I've just found, over the years, that when money leads the conversation, it's not always as straightforward as it ought to be."

"Damn right," Brit said. "So how long are you staying? I'd like to show you—"

"Oh!" The realization hit Jenna in a flash and she jumped up as if a spring had jabbed her. "You're a cousin!" she declared to Walker. "You're connected to August Wolff, but you aren't connected to Ethan or Jason!"

Brit looked at Jenna as if she'd gone round the bend. "Yeah, we've established that. So?"

"So Da, we talked about this. We talked about taking a DNA sample and seeing…and seeing…if—"

"I know, Jenna. Seeing if my father was in fact also my grandfather."

Walker remained silent, but Jenna could tell he was surprised by the possible consequence of the rape he'd documented. "It's a long, sad story," she explained as if he'd asked. "But the bottom line is that if your DNA lines up with Da's, then you two have got to have the same ancestor, and that would be August Wolff." She frowned. "Why didn't you tell me about Walker, Da?"

"I was respecting his privacy, my dear."

Jenna crossed over to hug her grandfather. "I can

tell he would do anything to help you." She looked at Walker. "Wouldn't you? Take a blood test, I mean?"

Walker directed his words to Da. "Of course I would, if that's what you want."

Da cocked his head as if mulling over the decision. "What I want…is to have some pizza."

Everyone laughed at the break in the tension.

"Now you're talkin'," Jason said. He retrieved some paper plates and napkins from the kitchen and began handing out pieces to everyone.

As the group proceeded to demolish the extra-large pepperoni-mushroom she'd brought, Jenna noticed that the pizza box was perched precariously on top of the notebooks Dani had left on the coffee table the day Ralph Dorman was murdered. "Watch it," she cautioned. "Those notebooks are priceless."

Jason took the box off the table and steadied it on his lap while he ate.

Jenna took a bite of her slice and dabbed her mouth with a napkin. She figured the group might like to hear some of the more interesting entries from Mandy's journals, so she motioned to the stack. "Walker, would you mind handing me the red notebook, please?" She watched, fascinated, as the man looked at the stack on the coffee table and froze.

"The red one," she repeated, thinking he may not have heard her.

Still the man hesitated, almost as if he thought the books would bite him. "I…don't know which one that is," he admitted.

Everyone in the room stared at him. What was the man's problem?

Jason was the first to break the stunned silence. "It's this one, dude." He put the pizza box down, leaned over and pulled the red journal out from the middle of the stack, giving Walker a puzzled look in the process. "Here you go, Sis."

Jenna dragged her eyes away from Walker Banks and looked at her grandfather. He was staring back at her, and it seemed as if the reality hit them both at the same time. Jenna's face lit up and was matched only by Ethan's ebullient smile.

"I'll be damned," he said.

Jenna burst out laughing at her grandfather's rare profanity and hugged Brit joyously.

Now it was Brit, Jason, and Walker's turn to look perplexed. "Will someone please tell me what's going on?" Brit asked.

"I'm sorry," Jenna said, wiping her eyes and not caring that the tears had begun to fall. "I'd like you to meet Professor Ethan Wolff, an art historian who happens to suffer from, of all things, the very ominous condition known as 'anomalous trichromacy.' And this gentleman," she added, pointing to Walker, "I believe suffers from the same thing."

"Anomalous Tricho-what?" Jason asked.

Walker grinned. "It means we're both color-blind," he said. "I'll be damned is right."

"Well hey, I knew that *Da* was," Jason said to Jenna, "but how did you—Oh. *Now* I get it."

"Well explain it to me, then," Brit said.

"Da can't see the difference between certain colors, like red and green, and other shades that are similar," Jenna explained.

"They all look the same to me," Da said.

Brit looked slightly affronted. "Why didn't you ever tell me that, Ethan?"

Da smiled. "Well, I've learned to compensate over the years and truthfully, I rarely think about it. But an art historian who can't distinguish colors? My reputation would suffer for it, I'm sure." He punctuated this last statement with a wink.

"Try photography," Walker groused, but he was smiling too.

"So Mr. Banks here couldn't tell which journal was red, which is why he hesitated." Jason looked pleased with himself. "And if I remember my bio chapter on genetics, the fact that you're both, like, color blind, means that the odds are way over the top that you, Da, are related to August Wolff, just like Walker is."

"Precisely, my boy," he agreed. "I'd say this calls for a celebratory toast."

Jason passed around paper cups and they made do with sparkling apple cider. Jenna couldn't keep from smiling. Her grandfather's face had become a study in radiance and she realized just how much the whole sordid business had weighed on him.

"To Lia Wolff, may your spirit no longer be heavy with the uncertainty you carried for so many years," Da said.

"…and to The Grove Center for American Art,"

Jenna added. "May it showcase the best and the brightest artists of the twenty-first century!"

"To The Grove!" everyone toasted.

After the last slice of pizza had been devoured, the impromptu party broke up. Brit offered Walker one of the renovated bungalows for the night, but the photographer declined, saying he'd already booked a room at the Havenwood Inn. They agreed to touch base the following afternoon so that Walker could learn more about the center he'd invested so heavily in.

Brit was the quiet one as they drove the short distance back to the Great House. Jenna couldn't stand it any longer. "We need to talk," she said.

Brit parked the car and turned to face her. "I know," he said wearily, "but not tonight, okay? Tonight I just want to…be."

Jenna swallowed past the lump in her throat. Now that the danger had passed, had he grown tired of their arrangement? "Oh. All right. Would you…." She could barely get the words out. "Would you like me to move my stuff out?"

His lips quirked and he reached for her hand. "Come with me," he said.

Brit had meant it about not talking. But his body communicated far more than words ever could have. He took her straight up to the master suite and simply…loved her. Thoroughly. Ravenously. Repeatedly. And she responded with equal force, crying out at the sheer beauty of the love they'd created. It was powerful. And it was right.

Afterward they came back to earth wrapped in each other's arms. She felt him drift into sleep and prayed that he would finally trust that her love for him was solid and steadfast and true.

Because it was.

Chapter Forty-Two

The next morning, Jenna woke up early and headed down to the kitchen to make Brit coffee and brew herself some tea. She felt that "morning after" kind of awkwardness, wondering what was in store for them. The night before had been so full of passion and promise that she wasn't sure what she'd do if Brit said it was time to move on. They couldn't put "the talk" off any longer, but how to begin?

"Hey," Brit said quietly, entering the room. He'd apparently just showered. His hair was damp and he smelled faintly of soap. He poured himself a cup and raised it in a mock toast. "Thanks," he said. After a pause he put down the cup. "About that talk."

Just then they heard a car door shut. "It's Declan," she said, and let out a breath. "Right on time."

They came out onto the front veranda just as Declan walked up the steps. He was wearing shades and dressed in a green polo shirt and tan slacks. His face was no longer swollen and the white bandage was gone. In its place was a four-inch jagged scar. Jenna walked over and gave him a hug. "I'm so glad to see you," she said, once again fighting feelings of guilt for the role she'd inadvertently played in his assault.

The three of them settled in the library of the Great House and spent two hours going over the parameters of the case. The story, replete with greed, murder, corruption, unrequited love, and other angles, definitely had what Declan had earlier referred to as "legs." That meant the coverage would last more than a day. He would report the facts and the follow up, and would return in a few days with a camera operator for some more in-depth interviews.

At the end of their session, Declan rose and gathered his notes. "Brit, I wonder if I might have a word privately with Jenna?"

"Of course," Brit said without inflection. He turned to Jenna. "I'll be in my office upstairs if you need anything." He shook hands with Declan and headed up the stairs.

"I don't know when we'll have a chance to say a proper good bye, so I thought I'd take the opportunity now," Declan said to her.

Jenna frowned. "What do you mean? You're coming back for the interviews, right?"

"We'll see. They may send another reporter for the on-air portion," he said.

"That's ridiculous! That's—"

"Reality. Actually, I wanted to tell you in person that I've decided to leave KTRN."

"What? Why?"

He pointed to his face. "No one has come out and said it, but in truth, television reporters with jagged scars on their faces aren't in high demand."

Jenna felt sick at his words because she knew he was probably right. On top of everything else, she was partly responsible for his career woes. "Oh, Declan," she said.

He sent her a tender look. "I didn't tell you to make you feel poorly, lass. I just wanted to let you know I'll be leaving the Bay Area by the end of the month."

Jenna put her hand on his arm. "What are you going to do?"

"I'm headin' back to Ireland for a bit. Got some family matters to attend to, and I'll use the time to figure out where I go next." He caught her eye. "I don't suppose you'd be wantin' to take a break, yourself? You did say you'd like to travel."

"I think you know the answer to that," she said kindly.

Declan nodded. "I figured you'd say that. He looks to be a good man, Jenna, if a might territorial. I'm just sorry it didn't work out between us."

"Yes, well," she said with a quirk of her lips, "I do love steak."

"Ah, lass." Declan moved in, took her face in his hands, and looked at her for a long moment. "I guess you know what I'd like to do right about now," he said ruefully.

She nodded.

"But it wouldn't make a difference, would it?"

She shook her head.

He sighed and very gently kissed her on the forehead. Then he stood back and gave her his trademark, heart-stopping smile, a smile the scar didn't diminish in the least. "All the best to you and that jammy up there," he said. "Promise me you'll stay in touch?"

"Only if you do the same." Jenna saw Declan to his car and watched as he drove down the hill and out of her life. He deserved a good woman; it just wasn't going to be her. Then she returned to the Great House, taking the stairs two at a time.

Unable to concentrate on much of anything, Brit stared out the dramatic picture windows of his expansive third-floor retreat. The midday sun was bright, bathing the sea in bold shades of green, turquoise, and blue. In the foreground, waves crested and tumbled decisively against the rocks, never tiring in their determination to wear down the rugged coastline. And over time, little by little, they had indeed changed the landscape.

In the same way, Jenna had come back into Brit's life and transformed him. Through a look, a smile, a tear, a sigh—day by day she had worn down the wall around his heart, the wall she herself had laid the cornerstone for so long ago. And now, once again, he faced the possibility of losing Jenna, not to Declan—he trusted her completely on that score—but to the idea of a life lived on her terms instead of everybody else's.

Yet somehow it was different...different in that he now grasped the reality of what it meant to truly love someone. Seven years ago he'd been like Parker Bishop: angry that the woman of his dreams didn't merge her life into his future plans. Today he realized the only thing that mattered was that the woman he loved follow *her* dream, whether it included him or not.

He looked at his king-sized bed and tried to imagine Jenna never being in it again. Never kissing her, tumbling her, losing himself in her. His mind rebelled and instead brought forth graphic images of Jenna stretched out upon the sheets, her blond hair flowing and her naked body glistening from their latest gymnastics. Just the memory made him hard. Whiskey would taste good right about now, he thought. Too bad it's barely noon.

"Hey," he heard from behind him. He glanced over his shoulder and saw Jenna, slightly breathless, her cheeks flushed, her hair a bit on the wild side. She looked like she'd been running. She looked…beautiful.

"Hey yourself. Let me guess. Did Declan try to lure you away?" He was only half joking. Jenna stepped up beside him. "As a matter of fact, after our story plays, he's leaving the station and he wanted to say goodbye." She smiled coyly. "Of course he did ask me if I wanted to go to Ireland with him." She glanced at him as if gauging his reaction.

Brit raised his eyebrows at her, trying to remain cool while his insides absorbed the punch to the gut. "Didn't you once say you wanted to do some traveling? You deserve it, you know. You put your life on hold for quite a while. Maybe it's time you—"

"Oh shut up," Jenna cried. "I'm not going anywhere."

West Marin was earthquake country, and Brit could swear he felt the earth shift beneath his feet. He leaned his back against the window and crossed his arms. "What did you say?"

"I said I'm not leaving. I'm staying right here."

"What? Why?" he asked.

Jenna leaned against the window next to Brit, as if they were two colleagues waiting for a bus. "Lots of reasons. For one thing, the investigation's not completely over yet and I might still have to answer some questions. Then there's The Grove museum exhibits; lots still to do there. Dani has family business and Da's not up to the task."

"Okay," he managed. "What else?"

"Well, there's the big book on The Grove that Da wants Dani and me to help him with. Knowing Da, that's going to be a real challenge."

Brit could only nod. If this was all she'd based her decision on…

"And I'm thinking, since I'm a multimedia artist anyway, I could try my hand at producing a PBS-style documentary on The Center and all its history."

"No doubt," he muttered.

"But you know what really clinched it?"

"Tell me, damn it."

Jenna crossed her arms in a defensive gesture just like his. "I decided I wasn't about to walk out on the man I love twice in one lifetime. That was just pushing my luck too damn much."

Speechless, Brit turned back to the window again. Now his insides were tumbling and crashing and jumping and leaping, mimicking the waves outside. He felt joy spread through him like the coldest beer on the hottest day of the year. He turned to Jenna and smiled. "Yeah?"

Jenna turned serious. "Yeah. But I'm taking a chance here. A big chance." She held up her right thumb and forefinger, two inches apart. "I am this far over the line of feeling like I belong, really belong, here. This far into believing it's okay for me to carry on the family tradition and still be me. It's going to take all I've got to not just get swallowed up by you. I don't want to lose *me* in *you*. Do you understand that? So I figure the only way to keep that from happening is to know—really know —that you love me as much as I love you."

When Brit reached for her, she held up a hand to ward him off. "I'm not talking about lust," she said. "I know you feel that for me, and would demonstrate it several times a day if I let you. No, I'm talking about the 'I'll be there when your butt grows bigger and your boobs begin to sag' kind of love." Her eyes started to glitter with tears. "Because that's what I feel for you and I don't think I could stand it if…if you didn't feel the same about me."

Jenna seemed embarrassed by what she'd just confessed. He thought of the times they'd made love and her complete vulnerability and openness to him. God, he loved this woman. This strong, incredible, loving woman. He took her hands in his and kissed them reverently.

"Jenna Bergstrom, I fell in love with you seven years ago and I never fell out—although God knows, I tried.

When you came back into my life I was scared to death because I didn't want to be so vulnerable again. But you easily broke down the walls I'd put up because I was meant to love you. And I do. I love you deeply, and I'll love you when your beautiful breasts begin to sag, and when your pert little butt starts to spread." He touched his forehead to hers. "I am so thankful you are staying with me," he whispered. "I want to build a life with you here. Whether we live at The Grove or some-place else, it doesn't matter, as long as we're together. I promise you'll never regret it."

"I'll hold you to it," she murmured, pulling his head down for a kiss that said *forever*.

Thank You

Thank you so much for reading *Sinner's Grove*. Readers like you are powerful, and you would be doing me a great favor by posting an objective review on Amazon, Goodreads, or other platforms based on the e-reader you use. In today's publishing world, those reviews are golden to authors like me.

Sharing your thoughts with others (including me!) on social media would be wonderful as well. You'll find me on **Twitter, Facebook, and Pinterest.** And don't forget to stop by my website (**abmichaels.com**) to learn more about my work. There you can join my Readers Group and receive a welcome gift along with monthly updates and special content.

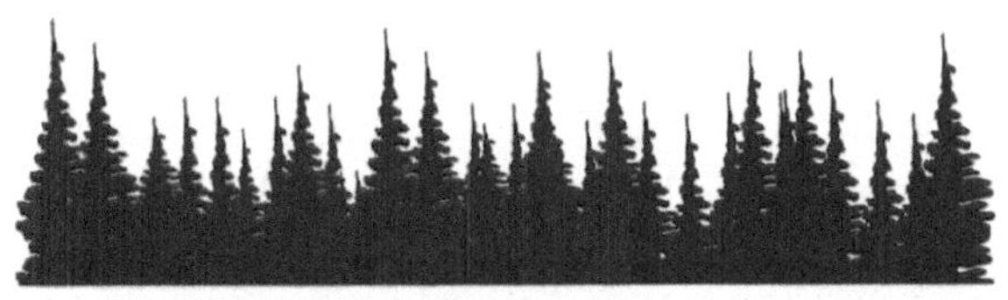

Other Titles By A.B. Michaels

The contemporary series, "Sinner's Grove Suspense" follows a number of descendants from "The Golden City" historical series as they work to re-open the famous artists' retreat north of San Francisco known as "The Grove." A brief excerpt from the second novel in the series, *The Lair*, follows, as well as introductions to book three, *The Jade Hunters*, and all five novels from "The Golden city" series.

Each novel is a stand-alone read.

THE LAIR

(Book Two of the "Sinner's Grove Suspense" series)

After her father dies in a boating incident, innkeeper Daniela Dunn must travel from Northern California's Sinner's Grove back to Verona, Italy and her childhood home, an estate called the Panther's Lair. It's a mansion full of frightful memories and deeply buried secrets, where appearances are deceiving and the price of honesty is death. As Dani is drawn further into her family's intrigues, she has an unlikely ally in handsome Marin County investigator Gabriele de la Torre. He says he's come along merely to support her, but his actions show he has an agenda all his own.

Gabe de la Torre needs to settle old family debts before starting fresh with the woman he feels could be The One. But once Dani finds out whom he's beholden to, all bets might be off. When a mystery woman reveals that Dani's father may have been murdered, the stakes rise dramatically and Gabe realizes they're now players in a dangerous game. Protecting Dani becomes his top priority, even as she strives to figure out whom she can trust: her relatives, Gabe, or even herself.

An excerpt from *The Lair*:

"Nothing like a wide awake drunk," Gabe muttered an hour later. They'd gotten back to La Tana and as usual Fausta had grudgingly let them in. "Hey, you can always give us a key," he'd joked, but his aunt had simply turned around and gone back to her room.

Once in their suite, Dani had been asleep on her feet, which were a little unsteady at best, so he'd pointed her in the direction of her bedroom and reluctantly bid her good night.

God she was beautiful. So elegant, so feminine, even though she didn't put on airs *at all.* He'd spent the entire evening fighting the impulse to touch her everywhere, even in places that demanded privacy at the very least. He'd known instinctively that she'd get along great with Marco and Gina, and she hadn't disappointed him. Man, she was driving him crazy. He heaved a sigh. Both tired and wired, he couldn't tell which was more to blame, the alcohol or the stress of keeping his desire in check.

He reflexively reached into the small refrigerator for a beer before he realized he was already half pickled, so he opted for water instead. Unscrewing the cap, he drank half the bottle while pulling his shirt out of his slacks. To keep his libido in check he decided to focus on something decidedly unsexy. Reaching for the jacket he'd tossed on the back of the sofa, he pulled out the report that Marco had given him earlier that evening.

"I think we're on to something," Marco had told him quietly. "We found a match."

He was just beginning to scan the document when the bedroom door opened and Dani appeared. Her hair was tousled and she walked a bit uncertainly, as if she were slogging through mud in high heels, even though she was barefoot. She wore an ivory-colored cover-up of some kind and she looked nervous. "I'm ready," she said.

He looked at her quizzically. "Ready for what, bella?"

"For us...you know." He didn't have a chance to reply before she tottered up to him and threw her slender arms around his neck, locking her lips with his.

After his initial shock, Gabe took a moment to enjoy the feel of Dani's curves against him. Jesus, after all that booze his body still reacted immediately, hardening in response to her softness. She felt so damn good—like falling into the most luxurious bed when you've been sleeping on the floor all your life. He smiled inwardly at her inexperienced but earnest attempt at seduction and cursed his inner cop—the prig who wouldn't let him take advantage of her while she was intoxicated. Reluctantly he took her by the upper arms and peeled her away from his body. "Uh, sweetheart, I don't think this is a good thing to be doing…"

"What?" she asked softly but defensively. "Don't I measure up to your other women friends? Don't I? Just a little?" She stepped back and before he could stop her she dropped the cover-up, revealing a perfect—and perfectly naked—female form encased in a 5 foot two inch frame. She was biting her full lower lip, practically screaming for his approval.

An image flashed before him of Dani pregnant. She was ripe and luscious—the epitome of Woman. Instead of cooling him off, the thought of her big with child —*his* child—only made him hotter and made what he had to do all the more difficult. He looked at her a long time, so long that he could see uncertainty, followed by embarrassment, overtake her. He reached down and picked up the wrap, putting it around her shoulders.

"I…I'm sorry," she mumbled. "I thought …" She turned to go, but Gabe took her shoulders and turned her back toward him.

"If you think for one second that I don't want to bury myself in you right now, you are sadly mistaken," he said roughly. "When you and I make love, I am going to be all over you. You are going to feel me everywhere and know when I've taken you higher than you've ever been before." He tore himself away and covered her back up. "And the next morning, you're going to remember everything I did to you and want me to do it all over again. Count on it. Now go to bed."

"But—"

"Please," he said firmly, turning her around and practically pushing her back into the bedroom. It took several minutes after her door shut for Gabe's upper brain to start functioning again. "Keep your eye on the prize," he repeated like a mantra. "Keep your eye on the prize." The prize, in this case, was a Dani who felt no regrets about whatever physical gymnastics they might partake in together. He'd waited this long for the timing to be right; he could wait a little longer, even though it was damn near going to kill him.

THE JADE HUNTERS
(Book Three of the "Sinner's Grove Suspense" series)

Award-winning jewelry designer Regina Firestone is proud to exhibit her famous grandmother's multi-million dollar "bauble" collection at the grand re-opening of The Grove Center for American Art. The fact that she's considering modeling the jewels in the nude like her grandmother did infuriates photographer Walker Banks, an owner of The Grove who's in charge of the exhibit. Their spat takes a back seat, however, when Reggie discovers that one of the most compelling pieces in the collection is not at all what it seems. Tracking down the truth will take the couple into the dark heart of a quest that's lasted more than a century – one in which destroying human lives—including Reggie's and Walker's—means nothing in the pursuit of a twisted sense of justice.

"The Golden City"
Historical Series

The "Golden City" series includes *The Art of Love, The Depth of Beauty, The Promise, The Price of Compassion* and *Josephine's Daughter.*

Each of these novels is also a stand-alone read.

THE ART OF LOVE
(Book One of "The Golden City" series)

At the end of the Gilded Age, the "Golden City" of San Francisco offers everything a man could want — except the answers August Wolff desperately needs to find.

After digging a fortune in gold from the frozen fields of the Klondike, Gus head south, hoping to start over and put the baffling disappearance of his wife and daughter behind him. The turn of the century brings him even more success, but the distractions of a city some call the new Sodom and Gomorrah can't fill the gaping hole in his life.

Amelia Starling is a wildly talented artist caught in the straightjacket of Old New York society. Making a heart-breaking decision, she moves to San Francisco to further her career, all while living with the pain of a sacrifice no woman should ever have to make.

Brought together by the city's flourishing art scene, Gus and Lia forge a rare connection. But the past, shrouded in mystery, prevents the two of them from moving forward as one. Unwilling to face society's scorn, Lia leaves the city and vows to begin again in Europe.

Gus can't bear to let her go, but unless he can set his ghosts to rest, he and Lia have no chance for happiness at all.

THE DEPTH OF BEAUTY
(Book Two of "The Golden City" series)

In San Francisco's Chinatown circa 1903, slavery, polygamy and rampant prostitution are thriving – just blocks away from the Golden City's elite.

Wealthy and well-connected, Will Firestone enters the mysterious enclave with an eye toward expanding his shipping business. What he finds there will astonish him. With the help of an exotic young widow and a gifted teenage orphan, he embarks on a journey of self-discovery, where lust, love and tragedy will change his life forever.

The Depth of Beauty was nominated for a RITA award in 2017 in the category of general fiction.

THE PROMISE
(Book Three of "The Golden City" series)

April 18, 1906. A massive earthquake has decimated much of San Francisco, leaving thousands without food, water or shelter. Patrolling the streets to help those in need, Army corporal Ben Tilson meets a young woman named Charlotte who touches his heart, making him think of a future with her in it. In the heat of the moment he makes a promise to her family that even he realizes will be almost impossible to keep.

Because on the heels of the earthquake, a much worse disaster looms: a fire that threatens to consume everything and everyone in its path.

It will take everything Ben's got to make it back to the woman he's fallen for—and even that may not be enough.

THE PRICE OF COMPASSION
(Book Four of "The Golden City" series)

April 18, 1906. San Francisco has just been shattered by a massive earthquake and is in the throes of an even more deadly fire. During the chaos, gifted surgeon Tom Justice makes a life-changing decision that wreaks havoc on his body, mind and spirit. Leaving the woman he loves, he embarks on a quest to regain his sanity and self-worth. Yet just when he finds some answers, he's arrested for murder—a crime he may very well be guilty of. The facts of the case are troubling; they'll have you asking the question: "Is he guilty?" Or even worse …"What would I have done?"

JOSEPHINE'S DAUGHTER

(Book Five of "The Golden City" series)

In the late nineteenth century, wealthy and head-strong Kit Firestone chafes under the strictures of The Golden City's high society, especially the interference of her charming but overbearing mother, Josephine. Kit's secret rebellion leads to potentially catastrophic results and keeps her from finding happiness.

When her brother nearly dies from a dangerous infection, Kit defied convention and becomes a working nurse. Through her troubled romance with a young doctor and a series of dramatic events, including a natural disaster and her mother's own critical illness, Kit begins to understand who her mother truly is and what their relationship is all about. She may not get the chance to appreciate their bond, however, because through no fault of her own, a madman has Kit in his crosshairs.

Set amidst the backdrop of the Gilded Age and beyond, Josephine's Daughter explores many of the social and medical issues facing women of that era—issues that resonate today. Independence, reproductive rights, birth control, childbirth and parenting are all put to the test in *Josephine's Daughter*.

About the Author

A native of California, A.B. Michaels holds masters' degrees in history (UCLA) and broadcasting (San Francisco State University). After working for many years as a promotional writer and editor, she decided it was time to focus on writing the kind of fiction she likes to read.

A.B. and her husband currently live in Boise, Idaho. On any given day you might see them on the golf course or bocce court, or walking their four-legged "sons" along the Boise River. More than likely, however, you'll find her hard at work on her next book.

https://abmichaels.com

www.ingramcontent.com/pod-product-compliance
Lightning Source LLC
Chambersburg PA
CBHW051205120726
47905CB00004B/987